The Lord's Bit

A novel by

M.A. Moone

Original Cover Art by Francis A. Bâby

Published in the United States by M. A. Moone

Printed by CreateSpace.Com--an Amazon.com Company

Available from Amazon.com, CreateSpace.com
and other retail outlets

To my husband, Tony, whose faith
and encouragement have never wavered.

Chapter One
Leona

Leona plugged in her percolator and picked up the scrap bucket sitting in her sink. The late morning sun was splashing a soft gold mantle on the highest peaks of the Cascade Mountain Range. A light frosting of ice dusted the new growth on the shrubs outside her kitchen window. According to the Central Oregon weatherman, it was currently 30 degrees. Frowning, she shook her head. *A body would never know by looking that it was almost the end of April!*

The evening before she had made apple sauce and a cake from the last of the winter-wrinkled apples in the root cellar. The peels and cores were about to make some chickens and a couple of old black-faced ewes very happy. Pansy, her little border collie, was already on the back porch, nose to the door waiting to go out.

Sometimes, Leona liked to hop her up by saying, "Ready to go, Pansy? Ready to go, girl?" just to see how she wagged her whole back end. But not this morning! This morning, Leona was fighting a feeling she despised. Helplessness! She tried to blame it on the fact that her arthritis was kicking up. Her knuckles ached from peeling too many apples and pain from her lower back was radiating down her right leg. The back pain didn't seem fair because

1

she'd taken the precaution of sitting on her kitchen step-stool instead of standing at the sink to do her peeling.

But in truth, it wasn't the pain causing her mood. It was that letter on the table. That was the truth. It was the same letter that had come twice before. It had come the first time when grief sat like a sharp black stone on her shoulders. She had just buried her husband. After many years of fighting it off, cancer had sapped the last of his life. That letter she had thrown away. *It's just too much, too much and too soon. A body can only handle so much* she'd told herself at the time.

But there had been a second letter as well. That one had gone straight into the burning barrel. But this third letter, propped between the napkin holder and the salt and pepper shakers, couldn't be ignored. That was the fact causing the knot in her stomach and the pain in her chest. The words in it made her want to just give in and start bawling, but she couldn't and she wouldn't. She wasn't a crying sort of a woman. Not anymore! Besides, the dog had her nose to the door waiting to be released into the frosty morning. She sighed deeply and squared her shoulders.

"I could blubber all I want and the facts wouldn't change. So why waste the time?" she mumbled to herself as she set the bucket on the dryer and shrugged into her heavy barn coat and old rubber muck boots. She pulled a stocking cap low over her ears and then smiled sadly at the dog.

The routine never varied. Leona would open the door and slowly reach for the hook that fastened the screen door shut. Pansy's eyes never left her hand. Once the latch had been flipped, a quick nudge from a shiny black nose, followed by a harder shoulder bump, swung the screen on its hinges. Then like quicksilver, Pansy flowed through the door and was gone with a single happy bark of thanks, leaving Leona to follow. She picked up the cane that hung on the coat rack and stepped out into the spring morning.

She negotiated the worn cement steps with care, using the cane for balance instead of the rickety stair rail that leaned outward, loosened by time and weather. Stopping at the bottom she breathed in the crisp air and looked around. The yard was overgrown now, but that she could ignore. She could ignore a lot of things but she sure wished now that she hadn't ignored those letters. You couldn't ignore the government. *No sirree! My father had it right...nothing is as certain as death and taxes.*

With grim determination she changed her focus to the glory of the mountains against the blue sky. She sighed, closed her eyes and knew with great certainty that she would always, always, be able to recall each detail, no matter where she was. If they took the farm for back taxes, and she couldn't see how they wouldn't, she would take this beauty with her as a memory. She hung her cane over her arm and fished woolen gloves from her pocket.

Pansy was completing her rounds, checking each detail of her domain. Her nose quivered at each new scent that told her of the night's visitors. Leona stopped to watch. She was such a pretty, alert thing. The way her white ruff and the cotton puff at the end of her tail stood out against her black coat reminded Leona of an old black and white photo. She continued to watch as Pansy trotted back from the rock chuck den out in the lava strewn field that bordered the south side of the property. Her husband's father had always called that worthless couple of acres "The Lord's Bit". And so it was.

She hadn't heard the dog's happy yipping so the chucks were evidently still safe in their den. Leona saw her lower her nose, casting for scent. There were often coyote, skunk and raccoon trails to discover. The varmints made an occasional hopeful night visit, just to check whether she'd remembered to latch the gate on the chicken coop. The pen around the hen house was still in good repair, but she worried that chicken wire alone couldn't always stop hungry coyotes. So, she was careful to lock the hens inside at night.

The sturdy house that held both the roost and the nests had been built many years ago by her husband, Peter. Over the years they had not lost a single hen to the marauders. Leona unlatched the door to the pen, carefully closing it behind her and then scattered all of the peelings on the ground. Most of the cores she saved back for the sheep. She could hear the hens clucking a welcome as she went inside the hen yard and pegged open the small door to their ramp.

They rushed out, strutting importantly down the ramp, beady eyes searching the ground. Leona had always had a fondness for chickens; there was something special about the way they called to each other when they discovered morsels of food. Invariably, they called the others to come and share. "Come, look what I've found," they seemed to say. "It's delicious. Do have some." They acted like they cared about each other. Even after all these years, she liked to observe their different personalities. She didn't name them though. No siree! They were a business. Later on, after they started really laying again, she would have a sign

4

out front on the road saying "Farm Fresh Eggs for Sale." If the hens didn't lay; off came their heads and into the pot they went. That's why she didn't name them; harder to whack off the head of something with a name. The breed she raised was called by the horrible name of Black Sex Linked, but they were the best sort of layer and good eating besides.

She put down the bucket and went into the hen house to refill the feeders with mash and cracked corn and noted the oyster shell pan was nearly empty. She always free-fed the calcium-rich nutrient to her hens. It helped to keep the shells of their eggs strong. Nowadays, they had fancy feeds with the shells right in them at the feed stores, but she preferred to let the hens decide how much they wanted. Besides, her way of feeding was cheaper. *I'm going to have to remember to get more this week,* she thought as she dumped the last of the shells from the bucket into the trough.

They weren't laying, other than the occasional egg, but shortly they would be because the days were getting longer. Soon enough she would hear their cackle of accomplishment on a regular basis. Like their call to food, it always made the world seem a little steadier on its axis when she heard it.

Her routine only took minutes; the last task being to sweep the floor and roosts free of any manure. Most of it dropped through the chicken wire under the roosts so that it could be collected for her flower and vegetable gardens from time to time. Thanks to Peter's foresight, he had excavated under the back end of the hen house, making it easy to remove the manure with the tractor's front scoop.

Leona replaced the broom in the corner of the coop, latched the door and picked up the bucket with the cores. She was frowning. Since she'd had to sell the tractor, she no longer had a way to easily collect the manure. She knew Will, the man who leased her hay fields, would come and help her, but she despised asking. The man did too much for her already.

Spring was far enough along that she was no longer feeding hay to the two sheep; there was now enough new green grass in their pasture to see them through. She walked down the path towards them and saw that Pansy was already there, sitting on her haunches watching Iris and Rose graze, her eyes adoring. Leona banged the side of her bucket with the cane. "Come on, girls. Don't make an old lady wait. Come get your treat."

The two ewes lifted their heads and immediately started her way, the older one limping on her right front leg, the younger of the two following her friend as she'd done since her eyes went bad. Pansy looked at Leona for permission to hurry them along. "Don't even think it," Leona said sternly, raising her voice to carry. "You know Iris can't be hurried these days."

She fed them their apple cores and then leaned over the fence and ran a thumb along Iris's Roman nose. "We just keep going like the 'energizer bunny,' don't we sweetheart?" Her voice was soft with threads of memory weaving themselves into a knot around her heart.

She raised her eyes to the rugged rim rock that defined the valley's edge. After Peter's Navy year, when they came home to the farm, chukar had been plentiful in them. The little Hungarian Partridges had been delicious eating. She and Peter had hunted them, she with her 20 gauge and he with his 12 gauge, until she was tied to the house by babies and chores. She hadn't tasted one in years.

She filled her eyes with the glory of the land and drank it in. *Dear God, there is not a reason I can think of that you'd take the time to help out a cranky, ornery old woman, but I do wish you'd come up with something to save this place. You know how long it's been in Peter's family. What if Neil comes home? What on earth am I to tell him?*

One of the Red-tailed Hawks that nested in a juniper tree on The Lord's Bit circled above looking for ground squirrels and eyeing her chickens. It gave a harsh, drawn out *"kreeee"* hunting cry. The cry and the distant hum of the traffic going by on Highway 97 were the only sounds she heard. The Lord, it seemed, was keeping his silence. She bowed her head feeling both foolish and helpless as she made her way back up the gentle slope on the foot path. *How can things feel the same and be so different,* she thought, thinking again of the letter.

This was the sort of stuff her husband had handled. The taxes, insurance and legal stuff he did! At her age, she couldn't just be expected to take it all up. She remembered how she'd slammed around the kitchen in such a temper at the unfairness of it all. *Broke Mother's brown batter bowl, for all the good that did me!*

Those damned medical bills...if only we'd known... She'd felt justified, almost righteous, tossing the second letter into the burning barrel then, with all the bills paid and the checkbook empty. But she knew she couldn't do it again. This letter was certified. The problem needed to be faced and a solution found.

Back in the kitchen, she pulled out a chair and sat at the small kitchen table. The oil cloth with dark green ivy twining over an ivory background was old and worn. She smoothed it flat with bony fingers, joints disfigured by the arthritis. *Old lady hands,* she thought, *all spotted, wrinkled and nearly worthless, just like I am.*

She pulled her "cheaters" from an apron pocket. Then she took the letter from its envelope and unfolded it, forcing herself to read its contents. She didn't know why she bothered. It didn't matter how many times she read it, those words weren't going to change. A delinquency notice was a delinquency notice. Three years of back taxes plus interest were owed to Deschutes County and must be paid. That was the bottom line. Only the amount was for over $8,000, which was more money than she had. She could add all the money in her checking account and her savings account together and come up short.

The money she had coming in was Peter's social security, the little she got from the hens and the money she made from leasing out her back forty acres. It barely paid for electricity and food, much less medical bills and insurance. She reminded herself that she wasn't one to cry. She never had been, but if it would relieve the pain in her chest, she'd like to give it a try. She refolded the letter and put it back in its place, then pulled her spectacles from her ears and put them back in her pocket.

Jack, her husband's best friend, would probably be by for his cup of coffee in a bit. She hadn't mentioned the letter to him yet. If he came, perhaps she would. He checked in on her at least once or twice a week. His boy, Will, was the one who leased the hay field. Maybe Will would have an idea. Jack could ask him for her. Lordy, how she hated airing her dirty linen! But, what choice did she have? Her own son, Neil, the one still alive, was somewhere in a witness protection program so she couldn't ask him. It had been 17 years since the telephone call that told them he had to go immediately…he wouldn't even be able to say good bye in person. That had been their last conversation. She and Peter were as patriotic as any American, but it sure didn't seem fair.

Sometimes she hated the things that came out of her mouth, knew they were wrong and mean spirited, but she couldn't seem to shut her yap. She rubbed her eyes with the heels of her palms and got to her feet, carefully pushing in the chair so she didn't trip over it. She was extra careful these days, always using her cane outside and the hand rail, when going up and down her stairs on the inside.

Thankfully, Peter had put in a bathroom when he remodeled their back porch, or mud room, as they called it these days. It was nice not to have to climb the stairs when she needed to go. *Besides, it wouldn't do for me to bust a hip. That's how old people end up in nursing homes. One careless step…and bam, into the home, flat on your back… eating that swill they call food and living forever with that deodorizer they use to cover up old people's smell.*

Leona pulled her musings to a halt, realizing once again she was igniting her own anger. She shook her head feeling ashamed of herself. *You take this mad stuff out to the weeds in the front flower bed and you'll get something done,* she chided herself. "At least it doesn't cost money to pull weeds," she said to Pansy.

She pulled the plug on the coffee pot. If Jack came,

she'd plug it back in. Otherwise, it was good for tomorrow morning as well. No sense wasting something useful.

Twenty minutes and two aspirin later, Leona knelt on a foam mat at the edge of a weedy flower bed by the front door. Already she could see peonies, snap dragons and daisies struggling for a spot among dandelions, speed well and the ever present cheat grass; three of the worst weeds known to gardeners. She tightened the string on her hat, pulled on her gloves and picked up her trowel. The weeds she tossed onto a piece of plastic after she pulled them. They would go directly into the burn barrel. *To heck with the county ban*, she thought. *If they want to arrest an old lady for burning a few weeds, they can. I could get three square meals a day, a bed, a roof over my head and not a danged thing to do but read and watch television. Medical would be paid for too.*

Leona jabbed her trowel into the earth with a vengeance. It was no longer sharp. She looked at it in disgust. Sharpening her garden tools was something Peter had done. She rocked back on her heels, ignoring the pain in her knees.

Pansy was lying on the grass, flat on her side, soaking the spring sun into her black coat. She was panting slightly in her sleep. Leona went back to weeding, her mind drifting from sharpened implements to chopped fire wood, the snow tires put on in November and taken off in May. Peter had changed the irrigation, kept the fences up, mowed the lawn, took care of the banking, did the taxes and a million other things over the years. *All those things Peter did…I suppose I took it for granted and never thanked him.*

Leona continued to weed steadily. She knew she should stop, that even now getting up would be difficult, but somehow it soothed her spirit to have her hands in the dirt and the sun on her back. She uncovered a large clump of Tom Thumb iris, dark purple velvet showing at the tips. The corners of her mouth turned up. She'd gotten them from Mollie Jessup, years ago. *That's what we did back then; we'd divide our perennials and give them to our friends and neighbors. We all had each other's chrysanthemums, iris and daisies.*

Her mind wandered a bit, and she thought how odd it was that people used the phrase "friends and neighbors." Weren't your neighbors your friends? Finally, she put down her trowel and looked around. Pansy had moved into the shade and she was feeling quite warm herself. She pulled off her gloves and flexed her fingers, looking at her swollen knuckles. The aspirin helped she decided, though not as much as the medicine. *It doesn't help as much as the Celebrex Dr. Brown had me get, but the price is right on aspirin.*

She got to her feet with just a little extra effort and was pleased that she could. *What a thing to have to worry about...getting stuck on the ground!*

Leona sighed and put her hands to her hips, stretching her back and looking around. Then she froze and a frown clamped down her face like she'd swallowed a bug.

"That car is back, Pansy," she hissed. "It's sitting over there again, just like before."

Their farm, now her farm, wasn't isolated. She could see barn roofs of several places across the road and her front yard was fenced with a good child and dog proof picket

11

fence. The gate was latched, but it wasn't locked. Leona had never felt the need for it once the boys were old enough to stay out of the county road that ran by the place. But, for some reason the car spooked her. It didn't make sense that it was there, parked under the ancient cottonwood tree, across the road from the rocky patch of ground.

When Peter had fenced the yard for the boys, he'd set the fence back enough that there was generous parking for visitors right in front, but this blue car sure wasn't a visitor. She didn't even know anyone with a car that fancy. It was long, low and expensive looking. She'd watched it from the living room the day before, pulling the lace curtain back just enough to take a peek, but had seen nothing. No one got out of, or into the car, as far as she knew. She wondered if the person in the car was taking a nap or was watching her. The second thought made the hair on the back of her neck stand up a little. If they were casing her place, probably by now they knew she was old and living alone.

She chucked her garden tools back into the carrier, started to haul the weeds along the front walk, and then simply left the pile where it was. She grabbed her cane and went inside as quickly as she could manage, calling Pansy to her heel.

Once in the house, she locked both the screen door and the heavy wooden front door. Only when she heard the dead bolt click into place did she draw a breath. She leaned her back against the door for a second, panting slightly, her heart thumping, before lurching forward, headed for the back door, fear riding her like a mad, wet cat.

When the back door was secure, she reached up and grabbed the varmint gun from the rack above the coat rack.

She looked at it and shook her head, wishing it were a shot gun, even as she reached into the cupboard for the .22 shells.

With the gun in the crook of her arm, she felt calmer. She stood, stroking the smoothness of the barrel, feeling her breathing steady. She started back towards the living room, but realized her way was blocked by Pansy. The dog stood rigidly in the doorway between the kitchen and living room. She was looking at Leona on high alert. Her ears were so pricked her forehead wrinkled and her head was cocked to one side, a sure sign she was trying desperately hard to make sense of things.

"It's okay good girl," she quavered. "I've got things under control here." She patted the gun. "That is a city boy's car out there, and they might know their hand guns, but they generally don't know one rifle from another. This'll scare him off should he try anything."

She cradled the gun and stooped forward to offer her hand. Pansy dropped her head and walked forward, her toenails clicking on the linoleum as she came. Leona could feel the tension flow out of the dog as she stroked her head and fondled her ears. "It's okay, Pansy. It's okay. I won't let anybody hurt us."

As she said it, she felt braver. She walked past the dog and through the kitchen, glancing at the letter as she went. *I really don't need a stalker, Lord. My plate is already full!*

In the living room, she stepped to the end of the old green mohair sofa and very slowly, pushed aside the lace curtain and peeked out. The car was gone. She dropped the curtain with a sigh just as the doorbell rang. For a second her heart stopped, but in the same instant, she was lifting the rifle

13

to her shoulder. Then sanity returned. It was Jack. Only Jack hit the button with the Morse code distress signal, three shorts, three longs and three shorts. It had irritated her for years, but not today. Quickly, she checked the safety and then leaned the rifle against the wall behind the curtain. Hurrying to the door, she flipped the dead bolt and flung it open. And there was Jack. He had never looked so good to her! She pushed the button on the screen door releasing the lock. The door was a new- fangled thing, made of both glass and screen, insulated too. Jack had found it for twenty dollars at a garage sale and he and his boy had hung it for her the previous summer.

Jack was looking through the glass at her, his eye brows lifted in surprise. "You locking things up these days, Leona?"

"You are a sight for sore eyes, old man," she said, not answering his question.

He looked even more surprised. "I am?"

He stepped into the room, removing his ball cap as he came. "What's up?"

She sighed. "It takes more to tell than just standing here can do. Come on into the kitchen and I'll plug the percolator back in."

Jack followed her into the kitchen, hooked his ball cap over the knob on the ladder-backed chair and sat at the table as he had done for the last 50 odd years. He was a small, wiry man and age had melted the flesh from his face so that he had a honed look. His gums had receded; making his teeth look long, almost feral, but his eyes softened the effect. Unlike most people whose eye color faded as they aged, at 76, Jack's lashes were still thick and his eyes a deep green, the irises rimmed in black. As a young man, his auburn hair had been thick and curly. Now, it was still thick and curly but as white as fresh snow.

Leona's back was to him as she removed the coffee basket from the percolator and plugged it in. She was uncharacteristically silent. Usually by now she was full bore into how the world was going to hell in a hand basket, the ineptness of doctors, the evils of government, the lack of respect shown by children and a host of other complaints, all of it, hard to listen to as a steady diet.

He saw the letter propped between the salt and pepper shakers and the napkin holder. He glanced at Leona's back, then peeked at the return address and frowned. He wondered if that certified letter from Deschutes County was what had gotten her tongue.

He sometimes asked himself why he came, but each time reminded himself of the promise he'd made to a dying friend. And too, he could still remember a different Leona, a softer person with a wicked sense of humor and generous nature. She was that person when Peter and he met her. Both men had been in their Navy uniforms, but it hadn't even registered that he was in the bar, once her eyes lit on his buddy. And she'd been a looker too, tall and slender with a feisty attitude and generous curves! Peter, who earlier in the very same evening, had waxed poetically about being foot lose and intending to stay that way, was engaged within the month and married as soon as he was discharged.

Leona reached in the cookie jar. "These are last week's, but they'll do. You liked them then, anyway..."

Her voice trailed away as she turned towards him, bringing the plate of snickerdoodles.

"I'm going to lose the farm, Jack," she said matter-of-factly as she handed him the plate. "And part of it is my own damned fault."

Jack looked at her, expressions of first shock, and then disbelief, fighting for space on his face. "Aw now," he finally said, "That can't be. It's paid for."

She shook her head. "Taxes aren't." She nodded to the letter. "It says I haven't paid the taxes since Peter died and I guess I haven't."

"But that's been three years, Leona!"

"You think I don't know that?" she said. There was no anger in her voice, only resignation.

"But his life insurance?"

"Medical bills. All gone for medical bills."

Jack ran his hands through his hair. "Jesus!" He couldn't seem to take it in. She'd never said a thing. Now, a lot of things were making sense. She was a pretty woman, kept herself up; looked better than women ten years younger. But she'd stopped going to the beauty parlor. Started doing her own hair…well, pulling it back in a bun. He shook his head as things fell into place. She'd stopped taking her arthritis medicine. She'd said she really didn't need it. Last winter she hadn't gone to Les Schwab's and gotten her snow tires put on, saying she was too old to be driving in the snow. She'd sold the farm truck and the tractor and lord knows what else after Peter died. Then their flock of registered ewes went, except for the two old gals she couldn't bear to part with, one lame and the other nearly blind.

He realized, suddenly, that he was lost in thought and staring at his hands. He raised his gaze. She was sitting opposite, her head bowed, too.

16

"How long you got before they start foreclosure?"

She picked up the letter and pulled it from the envelope, but quoted from memory instead of reading: "If taxes are three years delinquent, they send you a letter in July and then, after you've been notified, they put it in the paper. I'm not sure of the exact day, but my guess is once it's all done and legal, I'll have about three months to find over eight thousand dollars."

"In the paper? Jesus!" he said again, knowing how that would shame his old friend's wife. He looked at Leona with such compassion it was nearly her undoing. He looked away while she fought for composure, rising to her feet and going to pour coffee into thick, white ceramic mugs. By the time she returned to the table, she was marginally under control.

"The first letter came right after Peter's funeral, and the second one came right after I settled all the medical bills. I threw them both away," she said grimly. "If I hadn't let things slide so far, I might have been able to take out a second mortgage or something. But I probably can't now. Banks aren't lending and with this recession, nothing's selling."

Jack nodded sadly. He knew what she was saying to be true. "Sure doesn't seem right, Leona. Doesn't seem right at all! What will you do?"

"I don't know. I am sure sorry to trouble you with this, Jack. I know you have got your hands full what with Betty needing to be at The Homestead."

Jack waved her concern away. "That's a different deal and you know it Leona. She's happy there. She'd be happy anywhere. When Will goes to see her, she thinks he's me, and we never have looked a bit alike."

Leona nodded. "I know." She surprised herself and reached out and covered his hand. "Will told me. She doesn't know me either."

He looked at her hand thoughtfully, and then he looked at her. "You mind if I tell him about this? None of us had even an inkling you know."

"I know. I'm a pig-headed, proud woman, and that's a fact. I don't care if you tell Will. Maybe he can come up with a solution. I'm hoping you'll think on it, too."

Solemnly, he nodded and reached for a cookie, already thinking hard, thinking of the wiser heads he knew; men who knew of such things as foreclosures and back taxes. He would do what he could do to help his old friend.

"Then, I maybe got another problem."

Jack, cookie half way to his mouth, slowly put it back on his napkin. "Another problem? What in God's name is it?"

"Well, I'm not sure. But I might be being…cased."

"Cased? What in the hell do you mean by "cased?"

"Cased like somebody might be 'casing the joint'."

Jack leaned back in his chair, cookie forgotten. "Tell me about it," he said quietly, wondering if this could have to do with Neil.

"There's this fancy blue car that parks across the road and down a bit, under that big old cottonwood tree. You know, the one across from that rocky ground Peter's father always called 'The Lord's Bit'? I've seen it there three different times. Nobody gets out, at least nobody got out

18

while I was watching…and then as suddenly as it comes, it goes."

"How long does the car stay?"

"Not long. About 20 minutes or so, I'd say.

"Have you notified the sheriff's department?"

Leona snorted. "And what would I tell them that wouldn't make them think they are dealing with a nutcase? No laws are being broken."

"When you say, fancy car what do you mean?"

"Well, one of those low slung things like a Corvette, only rounder looking."

Jack nodded. "I think I saw it just down the road. It was a Nissan."

She shrugged. "If you say so."

He shook his head. "Don't get your knickers in a twist over this Leona. Like you say, the person isn't breaking any laws and really, when you think of it, a person that drives a car like that is probably a city boy with a lot of money."

Leona looked at him and gave a satisfied snort. "That's exactly what I said to Pansy when I got the varmint gun down… 'A city boy isn't going to know what I'm carrying.' I was wishing that it was a shotgun."

Jack looked at her in alarm. "Whaaa…wait a minute! Leona, don't be doing anything stupid. You don't even know if this is a real problem. The person may have been waiting for another person who didn't show. Folks have cell phones these days; they pull over to talk. They arrange calls at a pre-set time so they can conference call. It could be as simple as that."

Leona held up her hands. "Okay, okay. Maybe you're right. I know I'm a bit jumpy because of this foreclosure stuff. Now eat your cookies and drink your coffee. If those cookies are stale, feel free to dunk them."

Chapter Two
Chapman

Chapman Lewis filled his Nissan 350 Z with the sound of Jimmy Buffett belting out "Wasting Away in Margaritaville" to distract himself from his fatigue. He saw the Inn at the Rimrock sign ahead on his right and felt relief. *Almost there. Almost there,* he thought to himself as he pulled up to the front of his door. Getting out on rubbery legs, he pushed the locking mechanism on his key chain and retrieved the key card from his front jacket pocket.

Once inside the room, he shut the drapes that had been opened by the maid. Only a thin bit of light seeped in around the edges of the heavy insulated curtains. He removed his sunglasses and then made his way to his suitcase in the gloom. His kit of medical supplies was in a zippered pocket. From it, he removed a syringe and small bottle. He took both back to the window and in the faint light, managed to fill the syringe with the correct dosage. He carried it to the bed. He unbuttoned his shirt and quickly administered the needle into his abdominal muscles. Carefully, he put the empty syringe on the bed-side table and collapsed onto the bed. The vitamin B12 shots were giving him energy, and he was thankful for them, but they only seemed to last so long. He was sick to the soul of his daily fight with lethargy and fatigue.

It was only mid-afternoon, but he suspected he was mostly done for the day. He had been outdoors for several hours and even wearing the darkest sunglasses made, his eyes felt raw. Gently, he reached his fingers up and felt around his sockets, though he knew he shouldn't. His new eyelids were puffy. That wasn't good. With a groan he rolled over and forced himself to go drink a glass of water and wash his hands with anti-bacterial soap. It wasn't easy with just the small amount of ambient light slipping into the room from under the drapes, but nothing in the world could have induced him to turn on the lights.

He groped for his eye drops in the night stand by the bed and then again lay down on his back, carefully administering two drops in each eye. The relief was almost immediate. *"Keep hydrated Chappie; water, water and more water. Don't use these steroid based eye drops more often than you have to. Never ever touch your eyes without washing your hands with anti-bacterial soap. If you get even a little infection, you'll have to start using sterile gloves and that is a pain in the ass."*

The doctor's words had become his mantra. He tried to follow these new instructions to the letter, just as he had all the other instructions over the past two years; instructions about caring for his skin grafts, his diet, his depression, his compromised respiratory system and his damaged esophagus. Every day since the accident he had spent the majority of hours in it fighting to live. He had found it necessary to give up everything he had assumed was his right as a man, husband, father and friend. In his fight to survive he had shut down all emotions except survival. The new world that had taken the place of the old one was a

22

universe of doctors and surgery, of darkness, loss and relentless pain. The radiation blast that couldn't have happened, had fried his esophagus, seared the delicate alveoli in his lungs and turned his face into hamburger as the damaged skin died and sloughed off.

He toed off his loafers, removed his polo shirt and slacks, and with fastidious precision, hung them neatly over the end of the bed. Standing there in briefs and socks, he was barely more than a skeleton covered by red blotchy skin. His knees and elbows looked like gigantic misshapen balls separating lanky skin covered bone. Had the light been better, one could have seen his thighs and inner upper arms were a crisscross of scars from where they had taken the skin to graft on his face and neck. He drifted his right fingers over the inside of his left arm, feeling the pattern. There was no pain. Everything was healing…everything was healing except his heart, and he had no hope for that.

But all that was in the past, and he clamped his mind shut to keep from going there. He lay down on the bed, pulling the duvet over himself. He thought again about his physical appearance. He didn't yet have eye brows and wouldn't have the hair transplants until his new facial skin had totally healed. But he did have a semblance of a nose, reconstructed lips and new eyelids…and for that he gave thanks. He sighed. It was a lonely defeated sound as his body drifted towards sleep in a motel bed in a strange town where he didn't know a soul and probably not a soul would want to know him. Looking back was one long tunnel of pain, both physical and emotional. Looking ahead, he was aware that deep within him was the tiniest germ of hope, something that he could work towards. He had a plan…if he could get up the nerve and find the will to carry it out. *Tomorrow. I'll do it first thing tomorrow…* His muscles gave a jerk and then he was asleep.

When Chapman awoke several hours later, he lay quietly. It was his most vulnerable time, this time between sleep and waking. Only with tremendous discipline could he keep his mind from drifting back to what he had lost; what one rogue decision by some unidentified scientist had cost. He closed his eyes and visualized himself in a huge tunnel with a mighty lid sliding shut behind him, cutting off all memories, all ties. He would only look forward; an alien on a strange planet hoping to find his path…his peace and perhaps his health in a rocky field.

He rolled to his side and sat up, swinging his legs over the side of the bed and putting his head gently into his hands. He realized he was very hungry. He was always hungry these days. Luckily, what he could eat had expanded from prepared protein drinks and smoothies to things like oatmeal, eggs and just recently, pastas with sauce and even poached fish. Every day he was trying new things. His esophagus was healing. His doctor promised that one day he would be eating anything he wanted; as long as he remembered to chew it well before swallowing. Scar tissue now constricted his esophagus.

He got up and walked to the small refrigerator and pulled out a can of Ensure. He could not allow himself to dislike the overly sweet taste. That would have been counterproductive. He unscrewed the top and drained it with slow careful swallows. It would stave off his hunger until he decided what to do about dinner. He had dissected the ingredients and knew them by heart. All were good for his body; all things that allowed him to survive one more day. He would drink it if he had to hold his new nose to do so.

He could tell by the quality of light leaking in around the curtains that the day outside was waning. His eyes felt much better, and he turned on the overhead light and found it tolerable. He looked around the room. It wasn't a bad room. The bed was not so firm as to be uncomfortable. The sheets were good quality and didn't abrade his patchwork skin.

The down duvet was covered in soft white on white stripes, only the weave differed. The effect was subtle rather than stark. The furniture was sturdy and functional. It looked to have been made by some local craftsman. There was a desk for his computer, two chairs and a round table, plus a large wall piece that served as both armoire and entertainment center. Behind the door in the bathroom, were two fluffy polar fleece robes; one white and one black. The white was the smaller of the two, but it fit his frame better, so he wrapped it around himself and slipped into the matching fuzzy slippers. *It's a really nice touch. I'll have to remember to fill out the little form when I leave.* He looked in the mirror as he passed. Once he'd been somewhat vain, or rather, had taken his good looks for granted. Now his journey had been such that looking at the motley tufts of hair surrounding his bald crown and his skeletal, reptilian face didn't faze him. He was what he was and he could live comfortably with himself or not...his choice. These days it was more a matter of disguising himself so others were at ease talking to him, from the gas station attendant to the car hop or wait person. Sometimes, in a day those were the only beings with whom he exchanged words; his soft wool fedora pulled low, his cashmere neck scarf wrapped high and his ever present wrap-around dark glasses concealing most of his face. He carried on conversations the length of a tank fill, or a decision on what to order for dinner.

Instead of using his smart phone, he opened the desk drawer and retrieved the telephone book with far more yellow pages than white pages. He wondered what the sustaining jobs were in this part of Oregon. From the highway, it appeared to be mostly agricultural, which would account for the slim white section that listed the residents. He thumbed the book open to the yellow pages and scanned the restaurant section.

Tonight he wanted real food and his forefinger stopped at Anchors Away Café. He liked the alliteration in the name. He looked at the prefix...548...the number had been in service for a long time. He'd determined yesterday that all the older numbers, like for the courthouse, the fire station, the library and most of the schools all carried the same prefix. A nice filet of sole with mashed potatoes and maybe peas would be just right, he decided. He dialed the number.

"Anchors. How may I help you?"

"Hello, I'm new to town. May I ask if you take reservations?" Chapman was still sometimes surprised by the sound of his now gravelly voice."

"Sure. We can put your name down, but you don't need 'em on a Tuesday night."

"Well, that's fine then. Your name suggests you have seafood?"

"That's right. But of course we have steaks and stuff too."

"No, fish is fine. Thank you…by the way, I'm a burn victim so if you have an out-of-the-way table, that would suit me fine."

There was a pause at the other end of the line. Chapman had learned to alert people when he could. It was the shock and the pity that caused most people to behave awkwardly. If they had time to prepare, things went better.

"Why, yes, I'll be real happy to put you in a private spot. We have just the table. You ask for Millie when you come in."

"Thank you. I will. See you in a bit."

Chapman copied down the address of the café and shut the book. His 350Z had an extraordinary GPS system. As a gadget sort of a guy, even he was impressed. He'd find the place.

The shower was another nice touch. It was also a gadget lover's dream. Its spray went from needle sharp to a fine mist which was perfect for him. He had only been given permission to shower in the last month and he planned never to take them for granted again. *Only one of a thousand things* he thought as he stepped into the warm, gentle spray, *one of a thousand…or maybe more.*

The restaurant looked exactly as it should, he decided. Someone had a sense of humor. In addition to the name, Anchors Away Café, the big, stand-alone neon sign out front showed a cowboy, heels dug in and hauling back on a rope that was attached to what was obviously a ship's anchor. The building itself was unprepossessing, hidden behind mature pine trees that were fronted with flower beds. Whiskey barrels filled with sleeping daffodils flanked each side of the entry. The posts were wound with stout rope. He opened the door and noted that a sail boat somewhere was missing its wheel. One hung on the wall opposite, the only decoration. Behind the reservation desk was a large oil painting of a man at the helm of, not a sail boat but a fishing boat…a man wearing a cowboy hat and sporting a dark red handle bar mustache. His eyes were a lively green and his mouth showed the quirk of a devilish smile.

Chapman found himself grinning back at the man in the painting. He seemed to be saying, "Bring 'er on, life!" He heard quick footsteps and a very tall, skinny, red-headed woman came toward him from the dining room. She took one look at him, with his dark glasses, fedora and neck scarf and smiled. "Howdy, I'm Millie. Your table's waiting." There was kindness in her voice.

"Thank you, Millie. I appreciate it."

They walked through the dining room to the soft murmur of voices and clinking cutlery. Chapman had discovered that folks ate much earlier in rural areas than they did in cities. It made sense. Tied to the land like they were, there wasn't much to do outside after the sun went down.

Millie seated him in a softly lit, secluded booth and handed him a generous sized menu and a wine list. "Everything's good," she said.

He smiled and reached up to take off his hat. "For me, right now, the food has to be fairly soft and easy to eat…tasting good comes second to that."

Millie was staring at the tonsured look of his hair as he thought she might. He waited quietly, his smile in place, as she suddenly realized what she was doing. Her hand flew to her mouth and her face flamed redder than her hair, which, he decided, was really more magenta than red.

"I'll get your water," she choked out and fled.

Chapman gave a little sigh as she went. He searched inside himself for the words that would erase her embarrassment while he unwound his scarf and shrugged out of his windbreaker. He closed his eyes, looking for the kernel of truth that might help the situation. He found it was getting easier and easier as he practiced...this getting to the core of things. Millie seemed to be about his age or a little older, married from the ring on her finger; had seen a lot of life from the lines on her face...everyone had their own story, their own journey. He folded his scarf and waited.

He watched as she walked back towards him, carrying a basket of rolls and his water. Chin up, a smile was pasted to her face. "Here you go, sir... and, uh, sorry for staring like that. I know better."

"Millie," he said gently, "don't worry, I'm used to it. Don't think you are the first. Most people don't know this hairdo is one of the effects of a radiation burn. Most assume I belong to some monastery...you know, like Friar Tuck in Robin Hood."

She blushed, but it was a light rose highlighting her cheeks. "Yeah, I sort of wondered that myself."

She was looking at him more easily now and Chapman could see things were going to be okay between them. He picked up the menu. "I'll have a quick look and let you know."

She smiled. "Okey dokey. I'll be back in a bit."

He scanned the menu, looking with pleasure at all the things he could now order: clam chowder, seafood bisque, sautéed halibut with a citrus sauce, and pasta marinara to name a few. Then on the kids portion of the menu there was macaroni and cheese and spaghetti. No fillet of sole tonight, but the halibut, listed as one of the chef's specials, would do nicely. He shut the menu with a satisfied snap. He looked around the dining room. Only about 20 percent of the tables were occupied. It seemed that only one other waitress was working. Millie had been right about his not needing a reservation. He wondered if part of the light crowd was due to the poor economy.

Chapman ran his hand over his hair tufts and a new thought came to him. It was so simple that he was momentarily aghast not to have had it before.

Millie came back with her order pad. "I forgot to ask you if you wanted a cocktail."

He shook his head. "No, thank you, but I would like to order a cup of the clam chowder, the halibut special, some mashed potatoes, a side of asparagus…and a bit of advice."

Her pen stopped mid scribble and she looked at him in surprise. A grin broke out on her face. "Mister, if you knew how funny what you just said was…why when I tell them in the kitchen that you asked ME for advice you are going to hear everybody from the cook to the dishwasher laughing back there."

"Well, if you don't mind, let's call it an opinion then…everyone gets to have opinions, right?"

She finished writing his order and looked up at him. "That's right," she said with conviction in her voice. "Everyone is entitled to an opinion."

"It's about my appearance."

She suddenly looked less certain and he hurried on. "I've been so glad to be able to grow what hair I have that I didn't stop to think I might look a bit more... average to folks if I just shaved it all off."

Millie looked at him seriously and said. "Let me get your order in and I'll think about it."

"Thank you," he said simply.

Chapman felt a pooling of contentment that seemed to start in his chest and radiate to his entire being. All this felt so...normal. After so many months of self-imposed isolation in his fog of pain and despair...to reach the state of feeling normal was huge. To be able to sit in this funky dual décor restaurant with a ship's wheel on the wall and saddles draped over the room divider and talk with a skinny, magenta-haired, good- hearted waitress who had just taken his order for a real dinner...well it seemed just short of a miracle. He pulled the basket to him, pulled a crusty roll apart and removed a pinch from the soft center. He took a sip of water and put the bite into his mouth, savoring the yeasty flavor and chewing it thoroughly.

Millie came bearing his clam chowder. If he'd had more saliva, his mouth would have watered. The Ensure was just a distant, unpleasant memory to his taste buds.

"Okay, I'm still thinking. So enjoy your chowder and I'll be back." Without comment, she removed the plate of roll crusts and brushed crumbs from the table cloth before leaving. He had eaten them all.

Chapman paused before dipping his spoon into the thick soup. The odor was exquisite and his stomach was actually rumbling. He carried a small spoonful to his mouth and let the flavor spread before he started the careful process of mastication. He thought he should warn her that eating took him a very long time.

"Okay, here's the deal," she said as she set his plate and new rolls in front of him, whisking away the empty cup. "My OPINION is that shaving your head is the cool thing to do. Bunches of men are doing it these days and a lot of them are wearing suits. So it isn't just punks and bikers anymore. And maybe you should get a tattoo and an earring too."

Chapman gaped at her. "Ah…why would that be? I mean, the hair thing makes sense…but a tattoo…and an earring?" His voice trailed away.

She grinned. "Oh, no special reason, I've just always sorta liked guys with that look, ya know?"

"I'll have to think about it, Millie. This is an entirely unexpected thought. By the way, my name is Chapman."

"Well, Mr. Chapman. You do just that. Now, let me refill your water and I'll stop bothering you so you can eat."

"You're not bothering me, Millie. And Chapman is my first name. Lewis is my last name."

She pondered his name for a minute. "Okay, got it. Chapman Lewis." She smiled. "My last name is Anderson. My father-in-law used to own this place. That's a painting of him in the entry."

She walked away and Chapman tucked into his food, giving each delicious bite his full and careful attention. He could feel new energy as he ate. If he was up to it, he would power up his computer and work more on his project when he got back to the motel.

Chapter Three
Millie

Millie put her car keys in the bowl under the wall phone, dropped her oversized spring green, bling-studded purse on the kitchen counter, put her tips in the cookie jar and toed off her black Reeboks without unlacing them. It was just habit; her feet didn't hurt nearly as much as usual since it had been a slow night.

It was 11:30 pm and she had been up since 5:00 am and would repeat the same pattern tomorrow. She knew she should head straight to bed; knew she would have a dickens of a time getting herself up in the morning if she didn't…and yet, she wasn't one bit sleepy, not even a little.

She set three place settings on the table for breakfast and then got out her old Betty Boop cup and filled it with water. Two minutes in the old microwave and she was a tea bag away from a cup of chamomile tea.

As she did every night, she walked to the upstairs bedrooms and checked on the children. Listening to their steady breathing, tucking their blankets up around their shoulders and brushing a kiss to their cheek or forehead was a precious ritual. The feeling it gave her was one akin, she suspected, to how a religious person felt after praying. She sighed and went back into the kitchen, gathered her tea, turned off the light and went to sit on the couch.

Sitting there, in the darkness with her long legs folded and her toes tucked under a cushion for warmth, she thought about Chapman Lewis. *You think you got it bad...and sometimes you do...mostly from stupid decisions...but a guy like that was blind-sided. Nothing he did wrong caused him to get fried like an egg, and that's a fact. The fickle finger of fate got him, that's all.*

She thought how glad she was that he had called for a reservation; glad that she had answered the phone and put him in her section. She took a sip of tea and let it warm her throat. *If she hadn't known he'd been burned...if he had just walked in...he would have scared the bee Jesus outta her or anyone else in the place. Man! No eyebrows, a little skinny sliver of a shiny thing for a nose and skin that would have embarrassed a snake...looked like he could have been in a horror show without going through makeup.*

She sighed, remembering how she stared at him; how kind he had been, letting her recover herself. She had found it especially hard to watch those claw-like hands pulling the rolls apart. It took her awhile to realize he couldn't eat the crusty part, just the insides. She gave a sniff and dabbed the corner of her eyes with her sleeve. *Don't never take nothing for granted! That's the lesson here. That poor tortured man needs all the respect and kindness in the world!*

The tears were slipping silently down Millie's cheeks, but she didn't wipe them away. She took a big swallow of the tea. Already it was cooling. Her thoughts turned to her past; how she'd come to Redmond on the bus with her two babies and not a friend in the world knowing where she was. She set the cup on the coffee table and tipped her head back, closing her eyes, remembering the pain of

34

those days. Scenes of battered women's shelters, social services, and the ad she saw in the paper for a day waitress were vivid in her mind. She sighed remembering the old man, a rancher turned sailor, turned commercial fisherman, turned cook who gave her a chance. He hired her, retired his wife off her bad legs to look after two pre-school kids...her kids. Jack had taught her the ropes of Anchors Away himself. Talk about kindness! He'd even helped her fill out the forms for HUD housing so she could move out of the shelter. Then, after several months, just before she was due to go off shift, a man walked in. She didn't see him. Her back was turned to the room. A voice behind her had said, "I've come to meet the mother of those kids Mom is taking care of."

Now she smiled, her eyes still closed. She remembered she'd almost dropped the salt shaker she was filling. She'd whirled around, her heart jerking in alarm, and said, "Oh my God! Don't tell me they've done something wrong. Are they in trouble?"

Those had been her Betty Boop days. Her hair was curly, dyed coal black and very short. She had jet black eyeliner and a color of lipstick called "Pout Pretty Pink"...but not one curve in sight. A coat rack didn't have curves...well, she had boobs, but she pretty much looked like a boy from those on down. He'd just stood there with a little crooked smile on his freckled face, his cowboy hat tipped back on his head, looking at her as though he liked what he saw. "Nope." He'd said. "Not in trouble that I know of." He put out his hand. "My name's Will and you must be Millie the Mom."

She stood and looked at him; sturdy as a tree, chipped tooth, a shock of thick brown hair, blue eyes just a little too close together that anyone would ever call him handsome. "Well, I guess I've been called worse than that," she had said dryly, extending her hand, knowing even then that he was a person to trust.

"Thanks to your kids, my mom is making cookies again, and I sure do appreciate that. She said she's on a whole new educational path. Watches Sesame Street trying to get caught up with what Jake and Jenny are learning."

He shook his head in mock sorrow. "I believe soap opera has lost its biggest fan. That was what she said she was going to watch when she got retired."

"Well, if Betty is your mama, that makes Jack your dad, so I suppose you know how they saved my bacon."

He came around the counter and started doing dinner set ups for her like he'd been doing them all his life: napkin folded into a triangle, knife, fork, spoon, wrap and fold back. "Actually, Millie the Mom, I'd say, the saving was mutual. You needed a job and Mom needed off her feet. This job was killing her varicose veins."

He grinned. "Besides, my dad is a business man. You work for him, pay Mom for babysitting and the money stays in the family, right?"

Millie snorted. "Yeah, right! Betty doesn't charge me half of what anybody else would. Most days I can pay her out of my tips."

She stopped filling shakers for a second and watched how smoothly his hands moved. "Been doing this for a while, haven't you?"

"Long enough…mostly when I was a lot younger. But, just 'cause I'm good at it doesn't mean I like it. That's why you haven't seen me around here. I developed an allergy to the place as a kid."

His hands were a working man's hands, rough and calloused, freckled and browned by the sun. He was wearing a chambray shirt old enough that the elbows were nearly gone. His jeans had a patched hole on the thigh and his lace-ups might have seen a coat of grease only once or twice in their life…but never shoe polish. There was a whiff of the outdoors about him, and she would have bet he worked on the land in some capacity.

"So, why are you doing it for me then?" She couldn't keep a touch of belligerence out of her voice.

"Good question." He paused. "I guess, because I've come to ask a favor."

It seemed he'd begun spring plowing in the fields behind his parent's house. Jake, her five year old, was crazy about anything mechanical, and though he never said a thing, he stood at the back yard fence watching the tractor turn the rows until Betty came out and brought him in. Will had come to ask Millie if he could give the boy a ride, maybe take him up and down while he turned a couple of rows.

"There's no danger or anything. I'd hold him in my lap. Let him pretend to steer a little."

While he talked, Millie could feel her hands get clammy, her breathing turn shallow. She fought back feelings she didn't want to have, didn't want to pass on to her children. Memories stuffed into a little black cubby hole in her mind threatened to spill out. She couldn't let one man's despicable behavior turn her against all men. If she did, the creep of an ex-husband won the game, and she wasn't going to allow that to happen--not if she could help it. She wiped her hands on her apron and began to measure coffee into filters. She realized Will was waiting for an answer and forced a deep breath before looking at him. She noticed then that they were the same height and that they could look straight into each other's eyes. His looked merely patient and a little puzzled. She wondered what he saw in hers. "I'll tell you what. I'll talk to Jake tonight, and I'll let your mom know my decision when I drop them off tomorrow."

On the couch, Millie opened her eyes and lifted her head. It was all so clear, like it was yesterday and yet; this year they would be celebrating 11 years of marriage. She picked up her cup. The tea was stone cold and suddenly, she couldn't wait to get to bed and snuggle up against Will's broad back.

In the bathroom, she took off her make-up and took the scrunchie out of her hair. Then she looked at her face and thought again of Chapman Lewis. *The things we take for granted,* she thought to herself. She dropped her clothes into the clothes hamper and took her nightgown down from the hook on the door. She couldn't wake Will. It wouldn't be fair; he worked too hard…and not only was it spring planting time, she knew he had taken an hour or more out of it to go see his mom. But, if she could wake him, she would tell him how much she loved him and her life…just the way it was.

She slipped under the quilt and spooned her body up against his broad back with her arm over his waist. Stealthily she pushed his legs a little forward, pushing on his knees, moving them until she could slip her cold feet onto the warm spot. It didn't even interrupt his light snore. She smiled to herself. "I made over a hundred dollars in tips tonight," she whispered softly to his back.

The next morning she was pulled from deep and dreamless sleep by Will nuzzling her neck. "Coffee's on the night stand and the kids and I are making pancakes, so take your time," he said softly somewhere below her left ear.

"Mmmufff," she said without opening her eyes. Thankfully, Will had learned that coffee was the best alarm clock. Tickling didn't work. Cajoling didn't work. A real alarm clock had a fifty-fifty chance of being thrown across the room. But the thought of a perfectly good cup of steaming hot coffee going to waste couldn't be ignored. She slid herself up in the bed, eyes still closed; feeling like a cotton ball was lodged in her brain.

Ten minutes later, wrapped in her fluffy pink robe, a Christmas present from her family, she entered the kitchen. The cheerful banter around the table immediately subdued itself and three pairs of eyes watched as she sleepwalked towards the coffee pot. She poured more coffee into Betty Boop, set the cup on the counter and turned around with her eyes closed. She leaned back, supporting herself. Slowly, she lifted her hands to her eyes and pantomimed prying them open. Then she mock yawned and stretched. It was a morning ritual that she had done since the old days when Jake and Jenny were still home and now did for their younger two, the ones she'd had with Will. Her final act was the lifting of a finger to each side of her mouth and pressing the corners up into a smile. "Morning dumplins', thanks for letting me sleep in," she said and turned to pick up her cup.

"Hey Mom." Matthew said, cheerful, scrubbed and ready to tackle the day. Abby, on the other hand, supported her head in one hand and shoveled a mouthful of pancake in with the other. Like her mother, morning wasn't her favorite time of day. She looked up at Millie. "You have bed head," she said solemnly.

Millie chuckled and ran a hand through her hair. "How's that? Better?" She asked.

Abby nodded just once and went back to her pancakes. Millie and Will exchanged glances as she came to sit at the table, the coffee slowly making her feel among the present. He shook his head slightly as if to say "Apples sure don't fall far from trees." It was something they said to each other often in a joking way but each time Millie felt a prickle of fear. *Just don't let her be the hair brain I was. Let her be more like her father, all right Lord?*

She yawned for real, covering her mouth with her hand. "There's tip money in the cookie jar if you guys want to buy hot lunch today. I had a real good night last night."

Will looked up. "Busy?" he asked.

"Nope. Not really. I had one guy who was a really big tipper though." She watched the kids putting their plates in the dishwasher and washing the syrup off their hands at the sink, debating whether to talk in front of them. Then she nodded to herself. *There's a real world out there that they need to know about.*

"He had been badly burned and was very shy about his looks. I think he was lonely though. And you know me; I can't seem to keep my mouth shut."

Will leaned back in his chair. He was smiling fondly at her. "So, he gave you a good tip, huh?"

"Yeah, he did. Twenty dollars. It made me feel a little sad, you know…a party of one and he didn't even order a cocktail. How hard is that? I think it was because I treated him…normal, you know?"

Will nodded. "Well, if you see him again, tell him your children thank him because they get to eat a hot lunch instead of a peanut butter and jelly sandwich today."

He turned and looked at Abby and Matthew unabashedly eavesdropping. "Get your change and get movin' kids. Bus'll be here in 10 minutes."

"Go brush your teeth and don't forget your homework," Millie added as she generally did.

She turned to Will and touched his hand gently. "I was thinking last night how much I love our life. I guess that burned man caused me to take stock.

"How'd he get burned?"

"He said something about gamma rays."

"Gamma rays? He's talking nuclear then. The Hanford Nuclear Plant, maybe?"

"I guess. It was some sort of an accident. He didn't talk about it much. I got the feeling he wasn't supposed to. He only said something because my big mouth asked him if it was gasoline that burned him."

"What's he doing in Redmond?"

"Well, I don't know that for sure either, maybe to recuperate. He's so thin he makes me look fat. His little nose would remind you of Michael Jackson's, only it's even smaller; it's just a skinny nub of a thing. Wait. He did say he was looking for land. So I guess that means he is either an investor or wants to stay here."

Will nodded. "If he's an investor with deep pockets, doesn't matter what he looks like. He can cherry pick the whole damned county."

He kicked back his chair and bent over his wife, rubbing his cheek against hers. "You're a good woman, Millie the Mom."

Millie reached up and put her arms around his neck and he pulled her up to hold her close. She slanted her head and kissed him deeply. The kiss lasted. His hand ran up and down her back, the polar fleece soft under his callused hands until, with a sigh they ended it and stood, foreheads touching. Will pulled back with a grin on his face. "I got this little tune strumming through my head. It's "*Millie or the tractor, Millie or the tractor,*" he whispered.

She laughed and slapped him on the shoulder. "It's spring planting time. The tractor wins."

He took her hand and brought it to his lips. "Not how I'd have it," he said simply and turned to get his coat and hat from the pegs by the back door.

Millie followed him. "Where are you going to be today?"

"Well, I've got to finish plowing the south field and then, if there's time, I'm going to go and do the fertilizing over at Leona's. What's up for you?

"I'm going to go over to your dad's and spiff things up a bit, change the bed and run a load of wash for starters. Then I'm going to grocery shop, pick up the kids after school and take them to see your mom.

Pain flit across Will's face. "Like I say, Mrs.

Anderson, you are a fine woman."

Oh, pshaw! You say that so I'll throw a casserole together for tonight, Millie said to lighten the mood. Get outta here. It's burning daylight and I want to go kiss my babies good bye!"

Millie walked to the foot of the stairs intending to hurry Matt and Abby along, but they were on their way down, Abby struggling into her backpack and Matt zipping his coat. "Right on time!" she said happily as she gathered them into a three-way hug at the bottom of the stairs. "Teeth brushed?"

She felt their nods against her rib cage. "Wonderful! Study hard," she said as she walked them to the door.

Chapter Four
Jack

Jack took his head out from under his pillow. Any light in his bedroom still caused him to hop right out of bed. He didn't have to get right out of bed any more. *No sirrie! No more getting myself up at 5:00 am and dragging my sorry ass out to do chores or down to the restaurant. Nope, I don't hafta and I ain't gonna.*

It was one of the reasons he didn't want to ranch and one reason why he'd sold the fool restaurant. A pillow over his head solved the problem and he could sleep in. He looked at the clock. Eight o'clock; a civilized time to get up! His bladder was urging him to hurry.

He threw back the covers, put on his mules and headed for the bathroom. Lately, he'd taken to wearing a sweat suit to bed, and it suited him just fine; seemed like he was cold all the time these days.

On the stool, he wished for the days when urination was done standing with a satisfactory, manly stream. *Now, I try that, it just dribbles down my damned leg. Seems like God could have invented a body where the parts wear out all at once.*

That thought made him think of his wife. Today was Millie's day to go and see her. His days were Monday and Thursday. Tomorrow, he'd stop at Anchors Away and pick her up a muffin or a piece of pie before going to the nursing home. He rubbed his eyes with the palms of his hands. It sure didn't seem fair for a body to lose their mind so young; only 69. Unless the doctors came up with something new, she'd have to live the last days of her life here in flesh, but mostly gone somewhere else in spirit.

Then he thought of Leona and frowned. He'd meant to call Will last night and ask him if anything could be done. This was the United States of America! Surely no one would put an old lady out on the street. *Now how'd I forget that? It was on my mind the whole damned day. It was that television show, "24"; worse than any soap opera ever invented. Damned thing is a man's soap opera and that's a fact; hooks you and reels you in like you're a big-mouthed bass after a plug.*

Finally, Jack heard his sporadic tinkle stop. He sat there, remembering. He had great sympathy for Leona even though she drove him half-crazy with all her bitching. He suspected it was a cover up; part bitterness and part loneliness. He'd never seen her cry, not even when Peter finally died. He'd cried…feeling such relief on behalf of his old friend.

Leona's life had been extra hard through no fault of her own and that was a fact. He shook his head. He, on the other hand, had no complaints to speak of. He got to see his son, Will, almost any time he wanted. Leona had lost one son to a damned motorcycle accident and didn't even know if her other son was alive…might not ever know. He and Betty had four of the greatest, smartest grandkids ever born; Leona had none. Of course, no matter what Betty said, he was the one who found their mother for his picky son to marry. *No*, he corrected himself, *it wasn't that Will was picky, that was just what he claimed. Really, he just had to get over the grieving.*

Betty had always credited their oldest grandson, Jake, for getting his mom and Will together, and Jack agreed that it was Jake's love of tractors that had helped mend Will's heart so he could fall in love again. He smiled to himself thinking of the miles the little tyke had ridden on Will's lap.

Then if Jake got credit, little sister Jenny with her big brown eyes was flirting with Will before she could do much more than toddle. She'd smile, throw up her arms and head for him hollering, "Up. Pweese. Up." She had the whole Anderson family all wrapped around her little finger in a snap. What a bright little thing she had been! *Hell, she still is for that matter.*

He shook his head, his sweat pants around his knees, lost in memories. Now, those two were both in college over in the valley. He sure missed them.

"Well old man, are you going to sit here all day?" he grumped to himself as he levered to his feet. "It isn't like you don't have things to do." He wondered if Will was already on the tractor and guessed he'd go call and find out. He looked at the clock. Eight fifteen! It had taken him a quarter of an hour to take a simple whiz! It was enough to put a fellow in a bad mood.

After Jack shaved, brushed his teeth and had run a hand through his curly hair, he walked down the hallway to the kitchen. This was another thing they had that Leona didn't: a small, one story, easy to care for house that they'd bought so Will and Millie could live at the ranch. *If I start forgetting all I got to be grateful for, I'm going to end up just*

46

like Leona and all the other crabby old people I know; every one of them sure they know how to run the world.

Millie answered the phone on the second ring. "Hey Dad! How ya doing?"

"Fit as a fiddle. How're things around there?"

"Normal as normal. The bus just took the kids and Will left for the field. Betty Boop and I are sitting here finishing a nice quiet cup of coffee."

Jack grinned at the picture of Millie and her ever-present cup of coffee in her Betty Boop mug. "Your husband remember to take his cell phone with him?"

"Um…no, he didn't. I see it here on the counter. You need him?"

"Not an emergency. I'll maybe drive over later. You going to see Mom today?"

"Sure as it's Wednesday. I'm taking the kids too. Sometimes she still smiles when she sees them, you know."

Her voice sounded tired. He worried that she worked too hard, but they had kids to put through college and every penny counted. "How are things at the Anchor?"

"Things are just falling apart. You'd better go right down and straighten everyone out; get things back in ship shape."

Jack chuckled. The only reason he went to the restaurant any more was when he didn't want to get his own dinner or to snag something to take to Betty. "Hell, between you and the college boy with the fancy degree in restaurant management, I expect to just sit back and let the dough roll in. Hey, you tell Will to call me if you see him. If not, I'll be over."

"Okay. Remember, I'm coming over to do your washing later this morning. Strip the bed for me, will you?"

"Now, Millie. You don't need to be doing that. I took care of myself before Mom and I married, you know."

He heard her chuckle. "No you didn't, Dad. Uncle Sam did. I want to do it, I don't have to do it, you know. I was just thinking last night…about all I have to be grateful for, thanks to you."

"Well," he said gruffly, we're on the same page this morning. I was thinking the same thing a minute ago. Life isn't so bad, is it?

"No it sure isn't…and Dad…we love you!"

"Bye, you sweet thing," Jack said as he hung up. God, he loved this good girl. She was the only one who understood his Anchors Away Café sign right off the bat. One day out of the blue, just after she'd started working for him she'd asked: "So how old were you when you knew you didn't want to be a rancher like your dad?"

He looked at her, amazed. "Now, what in the heck made you say that?"

"Your sign," she said. "I figure the rope symbolizes the pull of two different worlds."

He'd looked at her in amazement. "Yeah, that's right. Ever since I was pretty young, I couldn't see a thing but the sea. My mother even made me a little sailor outfit, and as soon as I could I enlisted in the Navy. That's where I learned to cook and swear. Then, after the Navy, and after I married Betty, we took a swing at fishing commercially."

She had smiled, showing those big dimples. "Figured it was something like that," she'd said with satisfaction.

Jack hung up the telephone, turned on the morning news to get the weather, but only half listened as he went about fixing his breakfast; his mind still on Millie. He could still remember how she looked when she answered the help wanted ad he'd put in the Redmond Observer. She was all hot pink lipstick and black curly hair…acting confident while her hands were hidden behind her back with her fingers crossed. He'd seen it because she was standing in front of the mirror behind the counter. As they talked, he saw how the fingers twisted and the worry clouded her big blue eyes. Then there were the two tykes sitting quietly in a booth, eyes big as saucers, just waiting and watching their mother. *Thank God she had experience; I'd probably have hired her anyway.*

Betty had come out from the kitchen then, and Jack had introduced them. She had been the real Betty back then, buxom with a snap in her pretty brown eyes: no resemblance to that shell of a woman hunched in a chair, looking at birds in a bird feeder at the nursing home all day. Her first question to Millie had been, "Those your children?"

"Yes, Jake's five and Jenny is almost three, but I can get day care help through social services."

Betty had snorted then, and Jack knew just what she was about to say. He had heard her opinion about kids growing up in daycare a hundred times. She opened her mouth, but he cut her off at the pass. He had a good feeling about this tall, skinny drink of water and out of the blue he had an epiphany.

"Not now, Mama. Don't scare her off before I get her hired 'cause when I do, I got a proposition to talk over with you."

Betty had snorted again, lifted an eyebrow, smiled at the children and walked on by, carrying a freshly made cherry pie. He had watched her go, moving her bulk deftly, placing the pie in the pie stand, straightening things, wiping the counter, her uniform tight over her bottom and her support hose bagging a little around her ankles. It was past time for her to be off her feet all day. She didn't complain but he knew her varicose veins gave her pain and were getting worse every day.

He turned back to Millie. He had a big smile on his face, feeling exactly like the cat that ate the canary. "Might as well show up tomorrow and we'll give you a trial run. Can you be here by 7:00 for the breakfast crowd?"

And that had been that. That night in bed he'd told Betty of his idea. No more working in the restaurant for her. Instead, she'd be at home keeping track of Jake and Jenny. She squawked like a wet hen, but he knew he had her. "Ask yourself this, Mama, would you rather those two little ones be in some sort of state sponsored daycare or here where you can take care of them like you did Will?" At that she'd agreed to at least meet and get to know the children... if Millie went along with the plan.

The sun was coming in the kitchen window and making bright patterns on the old oak table. Jack had deftly fried up two eggs and put them on a piece of whole-wheat toast while lost in old memories. *They're as good as that sun for warming old bones, those memories.*

He turned off the kitchen radio and took his breakfast into the living room and put it on the television tray in front of his La-Z-Boy. He sat down and hit the clicker. He had his favorite news channels, all conservative. In the old days you couldn't get the news this late in the day. Now it could be gotten 24/7. He wasn't sure that was a good thing. But now, he wasn't interested in the news, he'd already gotten the weather and farm report on the radio and knew Jenny and Matt, over in the Willamette Valley, were getting rained on. What he was hooked on was the cooking channel. He ate and watched Rachael Rae tell about marrying herbs with a muddler. "Ah, bull pucky, Rachael Rae, you're just making extra work for folks. Tell 'em not to put 'em into the pot until the last 10 minutes if they want flavor. That's what you should tell them." He shook his head with happy disgust as he shoveled egg into his mouth. It was one of his favorite things these days, giving advice to chefs on the boob tube.

He used the last corner of toast to wipe up his drippings and popped it into his mouth as he looked about the room. Over the years, Betty had crocheted doilies for the end tables and antimacassars for the arms and backs of the chairs. Never mind that men didn't use pomade anymore and that their new chairs and couches…well a dozen years ago new…had come with extra material specifically made for protecting the arms. He could picture her, needle flashing in and out while they watched Jeopardy or some such thing. It seemed like her hands were never still. Now they were. Now hand her knitting needles or a crochet hook and she'd look at them in the strangest way. He'd taken her a ball of blue angora yarn and her knitting needles once. He wouldn't do it again. It made him too sad. She'd petted that ball of yarn like it was a kitten and he'd wanted to leave it with her but the caretaker had said no. He could bring her a stuffed animal maybe, but the yarn and needles she'd said, could be a problem.

Jack took his dishes to the sink and ignoring the dishwasher, washed them, dried them and put them tidily away. As always, he left the kitchen pin neat. He made sure the light was off. It was time to get moving. Millie would soon be coming and he had to strip the bed. Leona was again on his mind. Maybe he could even ask Millie what she thought. Somebody was sure to have an idea.

Chapter Five
Will

Will finished loading bags of fertilizer into his pickup and looked around. Their two Australian Shepherds had followed him from the yard and had been waiting patiently by the Ranger. Now, they wagged bobbed tails and gave short encouraging woofs, waiting for permission to jump up with the sacks. He grinned and raised a hand to acknowledge them, but refused to be hurried. Tuffy and Digger liked the kids and Millie just fine, but Will was their boy if a truck ride was involved. It was a mystery how they knew that this was their lucky day.

He noticed the new leaves and beginning buds on the fruit trees, the greening of the lawn and the fact that the raspberry canes would soon need to be staked. Then there was the garden plot that needed to be tilled. Millie would be after him to get the ground ready for planting before long. And somehow he would find the time to do Leona's plot as well. A light breeze made him glad for his coat. *Days don't get any better than this for a farmer,* he thought and started for the truck. Then he stopped and turned back to the house, remembering that he'd forgotten a lunch.

He walked back into the kitchen. "Guess if I take a lunch, I'll be a happier man come noon." He grinned his crooked grin. Millie looked up from her coffee. "Peanut butter sandwiches, right?"

"Yep. Made by Abigail this very morning. They'll be quite tasty."

"Hunger's a wonderful thing," said Millie dryly. She got up and pulled a battered Coleman thermos from on top of the refrigerator. "Might as well have coffee to go with it." She walked to the sink and turned on the hot water tap.

Will found a plastic shopping bag and dumped both kids' lunches into it. Besides the two sandwiches, there were two bananas and two juice boxes. He had a jug of water in the truck. That would do him.

"I keep meaning to tell you Mil...the schedule you set up for us going to see Mom has sure made things easier all the way around." He paused and watched her fill the thermos with hot water to warm it. "Thanks, Babe," he said simply.

She looked over her shoulder at him as she poured the water out. She knew his thank you wasn't about warming the thermos. "She's worth our time and more, Will. I have a long memory, especially when it comes to our children." Her blue eyes looked into his. "It's working for now, isn't it? Dad isn't looking so frazzled, and I think he really appreciates us all going together on Sunday. In fact, he said so." She laughed and shook her head. "Well, he didn't exactly say it, but it was what he meant." She paused. "Come to think of it, on the phone this morning, he actually said he was grateful for a lot of things, so I'm assuming that was one of them." She handed Will the thermos of coffee and gave him a hug. "Dang," she said, "Coffee's gone. I'm going to have to stop and get myself a latte on the way to Dad's."

He hugged her back as best he could with one hand full of sandwiches and the other full of thermos. "Ah, poor baby! Try to stand it. I'll see you tonight."

When they broke apart, Mille got the cell phone and slipped it into Will's coat pocket. "If you get a minute, call your dad. He wanted to talk to you about something."

"I'll do it. See you this afternoon," he said as he left.

Will checked to make certain his fence stretcher was still in the pickup's cargo box and headed towards the barn. He had noticed that the wires were loose on the fencing around the sheep's pasture over at Leona's. He wanted to get the fertilizing done on the pastureland he leased from her. If he made it over there after working his own fields, he'd tighten it up for her. No reason in the world he shouldn't have time to finish working the new field and make it to Leona's, he mused, except for the million and one unexpected things that could go wrong during the planting season.

As he bumped down the lane he reflected on his decision to start growing Kentucky blue grass for its seed. Except for Leona's orchard grass hay field, this year he'd planted all blue grass. It had been a hard decision to make, but his son, Jake, was thrilled. In fact, the notion had come from his son, who was learning some new and interesting things at his old alma mater, Oregon State.

Central Oregon grew a lot of hay, sometimes getting up to three cuttings a year, but the market was volatile. On the good years, it became glutted and the prices tumbled. On a bad year when the rain hit wrong and the hay was either ruined or fit only for cattle-- not horses with their sensitive digestive systems-- prices went to over four dollars for a hundred and twenty pound bale of decent hay. Jake had pointed out that blue grass seed growing was much less risky in the long run. Especially since the straw left behind when the seeds were harvested was becoming extremely marketable due to its decent protein and low sugar content.

He stopped and opened the gate that led from the corrals around the barn to the fields behind. The sun had melted the light frost that had been on the ground earlier and was starting to have actual heat in it. It was going to be a great day of mostly tractor work, a finishing of the plowing in one new field and harrowing in another. Then it would be on to Leona's, if he had daylight left.

He looked around as he opened the gate. As always, his eyes roved over every detail, mostly making a mental list of all that needed to be done. He looked carefully at his new young herd of Maury Grays, the cattle from Australia that were gaining in popularity with the organic meat growers. He'd bought them at auction the week before and would soon be turning them into the horse pasture, where they would graze all summer with the horses. In the fall, when he brought his other cattle in off his BLM allotment, he would turn them all in together to graze on the straw stubble.

The youngsters turned their heads to look at him as he drove through the gate. Despite their name, not all the calves were gray. Some were nearly white with black spots. Will grinned to himself. The breed had also been suggested by Jake. *The kid's a natural,* he thought, thinking of the gangly, blue-eyed sophomore who had his mother's dimples and curly brown hair…not that he had ever seen Millie's real hair color…but she had assured him that it was dark brown. He grinned to himself. Jake was away but his roots were home in the soil. It put the boy on the moon when Will took his advice.

His thoughts turned to Jenny as he pulled the gate shut and slipped the chain in place. *She won't be coming back to stay, just to visit,* he thought with a pang. Jenny was their gifted child. She had skipped a grade in school and was still bored until they had hired a tutor for her. She was just all around bright, but her special gift had turned out to be languages. Next year, she was all signed up for a work study program in Shanghai. Already, she spoke French, Spanish and a little German. Her goal was to be a translator. She wanted to go to the Middle East for her junior year. Farsi was on her list of languages to learn. Will frowned. She was still fearless. To her, the world was still the same friendly place it was when she was three and threw up her arms demanding, "Up, pwease."

It made a knot form in Will's stomach just thinking about it. He pushed back his cowboy hat and scratched his head then pulled it back down and hopped in the truck. *Worrying is a sorry waste of time. College is where she belongs. She's stretching her wings and is finally finding the cage big enough.*

He drove along the irrigation berm, turned in beside his old tractor and pulled his truck up under a large cottonwood tree where it would be in the shade.

He looked at his watch and pulled out his cell phone. His dad should be up and about by now. He was probably sitting in front of the television watching the cooking channel. He punched Jack's button. Instead of his dad, he got the voice message. At the beep he said, "Hey Dad. It's me. Millie said you wanted me to call. I'm plowing the new field today so I might not hear if you call me. Why don't you come on out if you have time. Things are looking good."

Will knew his dad would probably come. For one thing, there was nothing he liked more these days than leaning on the edge of the pickup bed beside his son, shooting the breeze. He'd want to talk details about the kids, about Abby's wanting a new 4-H horse and the fact that Matt had signed up to play on the summer baseball league again. Dad would also have to bring up his worries about Jenny. He couldn't quite get his mind around the fact that Will and Millie could let Jenny go traipsing around the world, even to the dangerous parts. As far as his dad was concerned there might even be terrorists on the airplane just itching to blow up Americans.

Then, there's the other reason Dad will likely come, Will thought to himself. He looked around. The patch of ground he was calling the "New Field", had once been part of the land claimed by a man named Hoot Riley. He had raised potatoes on it up until the 1930s. In fact, a partly fallen in dugout potato cellar had stood not far from where Will had parked the truck.

When his grandfather bought the place, the cellar was still partly full of potatoes. There was no sign of it now. No sign of the violence and pain that had happened on that spot either. No sign of the stench and horror that followed the finding of Grace, Will's first wife, by Deschutes County's K-9 dog. She had been shackled to a beam, and beaten to death.

The why of it remained one of many unsolved murders in Deschutes County, and it had nearly ruined Will's life. He stood, stroking his own dogs' heads, lost in thought, remembering all that Grace had and had not been.

He closed his eyes. One thing she was not…a farmer's wife. She was a good time girl and that had been fine with Will at first. He liked to party as much as the next guy…but after a couple of years he realized being a mother wasn't going to be part of her plan.

By that time, his dad had started terminating leases he'd had on the place so that Will could start living his dream of following in his granddad's footsteps and becoming a rancher and hay farmer.

While that was happening, he'd held down a full time job at Ranch Supply and a part time job as night bartender at Bronco Billy's Saloon and Steakhouse. Grace would come in after her job at Wells Fargo Bank had ended for the day to sit and visit with him at the bar. She would have several drinks, usually champagne cocktails, some bar snacks and then leave.

Sometimes she would bring other young women from the bank and they would sit at one of the booths and drink and flirt. Grace's flirting had made him uncomfortable but since some of the gals were single, Grace had presented it as 'teaching them the ropes'. Later, after her death, the police learned she had frequented several other bars in town after leaving Bronco Billy's. When he thought she left to go home, she instead went on to party elsewhere, sometimes, picking up a man. None of his friends had said a word.

The sheriff's office had made his life pure hell for a while, until all the sordid details came out…until the DNA from blood under her fingernails didn't match his. Still, neither did the deputies solve the crime, nor did they bring the dog to the ranch until his father had spotted one of

Grace's shoes by the very gate he'd just come through and called them.

Will had blamed himself for working too many hours, leaving Grace young and bored, to entertain herself. He had beaten himself up until he nearly lost his mind. In the end, it was his parents and ranching that had saved him. His mom and dad encouraged him to quit both bar tending and his job at Ranch Supply. He moved home and spent his days in the hardest physical labor he could find. There wasn't a fence with a loose or broken wire, a gate that sagged, a roof that needed a patch or a ditch that needed dredging by the time he was through. He knew the day he took the front end loader and razed both the shack and the potato cellar was the start of his real healing. For some reason, that work did more for his soul than either psychotherapy or Pastor Mike's counseling.

Both Jack and Betty had helped their only son as best they could, their faces tight, their eyes sorrowing. Will remembered his mom, a red hankie over her hair, throwing boards on the fire, fanning herself against the heat and the unaccustomed physical exercise, but never pausing in her work.

Will sighed and went to lower the tail gate for Tuffy and Digger. He made it a policy to let the dogs jump into the truck, but never out. The thing that seemed to give out on cow dogs most often were their hips, and he figured that long jump down from the truck was something to be avoided. He stoked their heads and then lifted them down. Then he took a moment to watch as they joyfully staged a mock battle, jumping and snapping at each other as they feinted left and right for a superior position, right over the smooth ground where once a potato cellar stood.

Will climbed aboard the old gray and red Ford tractor, choked it a time or two, turned the key and pressed the starter. It caught the first time. He smiled at the sound and felt the bad memories slip away. The tractor was the same one he had used to give an excited five year old his first ride in the field behind the house. It seemed like yesterday.

Chapter Six
Leona

In the old days, Leona and Peter had never let their dogs or cats in the house; it was hard enough cleaning up after the two boys. That had changed when Peter got sick. Pansy was such a comfort to him. Now that he was gone, it was equally comforting for Leona to have her sleeping on the braided rug at the foot of the bed.

Once, during the night, a bad dream woke her. She was running and running, but mud under her feet kept sucking her down. She didn't stop but knew her strength was going and when she quit lifting her legs, the thick black sludge would pull her in like quicksand. In desperation, she tried to sit up in bed, and then realized the bed clothes were twisted tightly around her, caught in her old flannel night gown like a Chinese puzzle. "Ha," she said in disgust, "Here's my sucking mud!" Pulling and tugging and grunting she finally got the sheets and blankets straightened around and her gown back down around her ankles. By the time she was done, she was panting from the exertion. She lay back down, wide awake. Pansy got up from her rug and came to stand with her head on the bed, asking, with a small whine, what was wrong.

Leona pulled an arm from under the covers and stroked her head gently. "Nothing's wrong, dear, just a bad dream. It'll just take me a bit to get sleepy again." But, she didn't get sleepy. Images of the sinister blue car and the unknown stalker began to prey on her mind. The dark got darker. Her imagination took flight. Before long she had convinced herself someone was looking for her son, Neil, but had found her instead. When they were certain she was indeed old and alone, they would stalk her and torture her for information as to his whereabouts. "But I don't know!" she said aloud, at first plaintive and then with conviction, "I wish I did, but I don't! He's in a witness protection program and they don't even tell mothers where their children are. Torture me all you want, but that's the truth!"

Pansy came back to her bedside and whined again. Leona gave a little moan and turned to cradle the dog's head in her hands. "Just promise me you'll bite the shit out of them if they come," she whispered, feeling foolish and yet comforted at the same time as she used the swear word that had, at one time, caused her to wash her boys' mouths out with soap.

The next morning, long after dawn came calling, Leona awakened and realized she had slept after all. She thumped her pillow, turned onto her back, and let her fingers trace the design on her counterpane, feeling the embroidered stitches and love knots, worked long ago when her fingers still allowed her to do fancy work. She considered the dream and her ruminations. They seemed foolish now that daylight spilled into the room chasing the last of the shadows from the corners.

She lifted her head and looked around the pleasant room with its dormer windows and sturdy dark oak furniture. Above the wainscoting, she had painted the walls a soft eggshell white and had hung the old Audubon water color in its dark walnut, ornate frame. The stylized bird had been in her family for three generations that she knew of, maybe more, and she loved it.

She and Peter had talked about wall to wall carpeting for years, but never got around to it. The original hardwood floors had been simply covered with rag rugs that Leona had learned to make from reading an article in Good Housekeeping Magazine. It was a comfortable room in the daylight, at least. She looked down at Pansy who was again sitting at her bedside, worrying.

"Your mistress is a goose, Pansy, a foolish old woman."

Pansy's tail beat a tattoo on the floor. Leona sighed and threw back the covers. As she sat up, she realized she was going to pay for yesterday's gardening. Her hands weren't as bad as they might have been, but her back and hips were making their displeasure known. She put a hand to her lower back and lumbered to her feet, her spirits low. "Why would I want to dream up more trouble for myself? That's what I'd like to know! Why would I do that, Pansy? I've got plenty of trouble without making it up! I've got to make myself call the county today. I have to get this mess I've made…unmade!"

Even as she said the words, she knew she didn't believe them. Likely, there was no way to undo the terrible mess she had made. She stood and kneaded the tops of her hips for a minute, then shuffled to her closet and took the clothes she'd worn the day before down from their hooks. They would do until she took her bath before going to town. Already, she was chilled and hurried into her clothes and an old wool cardigan, its pockets bulging with handkerchiefs for her drippy nose. There was a thermostat in the room, but she had it set at 60 degrees to save on heating costs.

She hastily straightened her bed and then said, "Come on girl, it's past time for me to let you out to do your business, isn't it? We've got stock to feed. Those hens don't get fed they won't lay eggs, will they?"

Over a quick breakfast of coffee, Cream of Wheat and toast, Leona came to a decision. She couldn't get the blue car and its unknown driver out of her mind. Maybe she was being foolish. In fact, she probably was, but there was no harm in being ready. If trouble came, she didn't want it said in the community that Leona Larsen was a helpless old woman. *I never have been and I never will be,* she thought defiantly.

She opened the cupboard over the sink, pushed the aspirin bottle aside and took down the Aleve. With food on her stomach she figured she could get away with taking three. She didn't like to do it, knew they were ultimately hard on the liver, but she had to if she was going to feel like getting anything done.

Before going out to let the hens out of the coop and get her newspaper, she peeked out the window to see if there was a blue car anywhere in sight. She saw nothing but a glorious day. She opened the living room drapes, looking out the south facing windows to see if Pansy was checking on the rock chuck den.

She didn't see Pansy, but she saw that the robins were back, once again nesting in the juniper tree just over the fence in the field. She thought she'd seen them as she weeded yesterday. "The Lord's Bit, indeed!" she muttered, looking at the lava strewn land across the fence. "They're just rocks to pay taxes on!"

She looked around her sun drenched living room. The lacy inner curtains let in just the right amount of light. She'd always liked the look and she liked it now. *It's been a real good house,* she thought as she turned and walked slowly to the front door, feeling every step. For a second, she was surprised to find it locked and fumbled a bit, trying to twist the knob. She started to open the door but stopped, grimaced and turned to go and get her cane from the back porch. *I can be foolish, but I'd better not be stupid,* she thought to herself as she reached for her cane. *Besides, I can use it as a weapon if I need to.* She practiced balancing while she brandished it in front of her like a sword and felt immediately better.

When she walked outside, Pansy came to greet her, tail wagging. She made her way carefully down her front steps and paused to admire the work she had done the day before. The packet of weeds still needed to be burned, and she was going to have to get a hose after the clumps of mud that had somehow ended up on her sidewalk. But, right now, her back wouldn't put up with it. Slowly, looking around, savoring every detail of the crisp, spring morning, she walked down the front walk to her paper box. She knew the subscription was a luxury, but knowing what was going on in Central Oregon and reading the obituaries was as important to her as breathing.

As she walked around the house towards the hen house, she laid the newspaper on the back steps. Today she had nothing special to offer any of her animals, and she wished she had. She wished she knew if the hens and sheep anticipated the special treats, or if every day was a new day with no recollection of what had gone on the day before.

She completed her chores for the hens, checked on the ewe's watering trough and then retraced her steps, noting that the Aleve was working. Her pain was lessening.

"Let's go get the guns out, Pansy. We've got to be ready if they come. And then I'll have another half cup of coffee and read the paper; see who kicked the bucket since yesterday."

She wished Jack would call…wished he would say he'd found a solution to her problem…tell her if she'd just go and talk to this person or that, they would be willing to cut her a deal or work out a payment schedule. But that wasn't how real life played out. She was going to have do it herself. Grovel before some stranger, that's what she was going to have to do.

Leona realized she was talking more and more to the little Border Collie and knew that she was lonesome. After Peter's death she had stopped attending their church; the sympathy people there gave threatened to undo her. She shook her head at herself. "Peter wouldn't put up with my behavior for a minute, Pansy. He would tell me to stop being so fool proud and get my butt back in our pew. 'It is one of the places you receive much more than you give', he'd say." Leona smiled at Pansy. "Then he'd say, 'the Lord is our partner, Leona, and we've got to hold up our end of the bargain'."

She climbed the stairs, thinking of her task. The first thing she would do is to clean the guns. Then, she'd load her shotgun and leave it behind the drape by the front door. She'd put Peter's 12 gauge under her bed. The .22 she'd leave in its rack by the back door. The rifle she'd leave in the gun safe. No telling how far the bullet from it would travel if she missed the sucker she was aiming at.

"Kick on that 12 gauge is liable to knock me back a bit if I don't remember to snug it to my shoulder and brace myself, Pansy...but all I got to do is shoot in the general direction," she said as she opened the door to the boys' room and took a deep breath.

Peter had encouraged her to turn the room into a proper guest room after they had left home, but she hadn't. The twin beds still had the plaid spreads that matched the curtains on the window. She gotten the set at Sears and they had lasted well. She had, however, donated most of their clothes.

The walls were covered with posters, mostly half naked blonde girls with names like Farrah, Bo, or Cheryl with a few professional football heroes thrown in for good measure. Those she recognized being a football fan herself. There was Joe Namath of the Jets with his number 12 jersey, Don Horn holding his helmet showing a bucking bronco and Johnny Unitas, in her opinion the best of them all and dead too young from a heart attack.

On the desk that Peter and the boys had built into the corner of the room sat a computer under the cloth cover she had made for it. *I'll bet they don't even make computers like that anymore,* she thought, remembering how the boys had been so crazy about it. Peter had learned to use it too, but she never had. Jack used one all the time, emailing things about politics, recipes he'd gotten off the cooking channel, jokes and such back and forth with people. Sometimes he printed out some of the jokes and brought them over to share. She pretended to think they were a silly waste of time, and she scolded him for the waste of paper, but she still had every single one in a file folder. She didn't know why.

She opened the closet door and turned on the light. Besides the few hanging clothes, the boy's shoes were all still there along with their CD collection, yearbooks, Neil's stamp collection, a bunch of sports equipment, ski gear and of course, the gun safe. Her three men had planned it all out and then built it in the odd little corner space that was no good for any other use.

Peter had taught both boys to be good with tools and guns. He'd taught them how to ski as well. It had been their one real family luxury, season's passes at Mount Bachelor. Leona squelched the pity party that threatened and reached into the pocket of Neil's letterman sweater for the key. She pushed aside the few clothes and revealed the steel door. *This isn't as hard to do as I thought it might be. There must be something to what they say about the passage of time. One thing, their smell is gone, totally gone. Just smells of moth crystals in here now.*

The lock turned smoothly under her hand, and it was quite easy to pull the two guns from their rack. She backed out, laid them on Neil's bed, relocked the safe, dropped the key back in its pocket, pulled the clothes back in place and turned out the light.

Leona stood looking at the shotguns and saw that Pansy was looking at them too. She hadn't seen them since she was a fairly young dog but seemed to remember something about them as her ears were pricked and her tail was wagging slowly as if she were dredging up memories.

"You remembering how Peter used to take you rock chuck and sage rat hunting, girl? You were sure easy to teach."

She sat on Giles' bed and held out her hand. Pansy came immediately to have her ears scratched. "You used to make Peter laugh right out loud the way you could catch those sage rats sometimes. And remember how you learned to fetch both of his slippers?" Her gnarled hand smoothed over the dog's head and ears. "But you liked the sheep best, didn't you girl? Peter always said you could have won a herding competition, and I believe he was right."

Her mind turned to how they had taught Pansy to carry a bag to Peter when he was out in the fields. She hadn't been much more than a pup. First they taught her the "Go find" command. "Go find Neil, Pansy...or go find Leona, Pansy." Soon she was able to find either of them and get a treat. The next game started by teaching her to carry the bag from one to the other and receiving a treat when she did. They had begun with short distances, but by the end of the training, Pansy would carry the bag loaded with a lunch, a needed tool or a note, all with great pride. *They're the smartest breed in the world, so I guess it was no big thing, but it sure made us all tickled with ourselves. It tickled her too.*

Leona stood up and collected the guns. All the ammunition and cleaning supplies were in the cupboard by the back door. She checked to make certain both shotguns were empty and then carried the 12 gauge into her bedroom. *No sense carrying the gun down when I can carry the bullets and cleaning swab up,* she thought.

Once the guns were in their places, cleaned, loaded and the safety locks on, Leona sat at the table with the paper, studiously ignoring the letter. She figured, looking at the clock, that 10:00 was the perfect time to call...and she would, just as soon as she finished seeing who'd kicked the bucket.

Chapter Seven
Chapman

Chapman lay on his back, his fingers laced behind his head. He had put in his eye drops and was engaged in a slow, steady cadenced breathing. His lung capacity was diminished and he had been told it always would be. He repeated his mantra, *I can live with that.* What he didn't know was how much capacity and quality of life he could regain. No one in the medical profession seemed to even want to speculate on that. But for now, he had a plan and today he would carry it out.

He drew the air in deeply through his nostrils, picturing it filling his lungs completely and then slowly let it out, compressing his stomach and diaphragm muscles as he did so. This was a morning routine he never skipped. He thought of it as pushups for his lungs. He would do it every day of his life. In return, God willing, he would never be on a ventilator again. *"Use those lungs, Chappie. Visualize healthy air sacks able to constrict and expand. Pull the air in and force the air out. Only time will tell how much capacity you can regain with dedicated work."*

At the time the doctor was giving Chapman the instructions, he had been using a breathing machine and every breath was painful enough to make his entire chest hurt; like breathing in sub-degree weather. Now, lying in the comfortable bed, he could do his forty breaths without any discomfort. Mostly, it felt good. When he was done, he felt more energized, as though he had pumped out all the carbon dioxide and had oxygenated his blood.

He finished the exercise and thought about his day, his life. Earning money was not an object. He had more money than he knew what to do with now. It was all in the hands of a financial advisor, his attorney and his accountant. He kept in touch with them through the internet, or his smart phone, but only when absolutely necessary. His sole focus was to regain his health, both mental and physical. Out of kindness, he had left his wife, Marcie and his son, Jock. She could remarry and build a new life with someone not shattered, broken and disfigured. His son would have a father who could be a regular guy, not someone wrapped up like a mummy and apt to disappear into black holes of depression. No kid deserved that and Jock was young enough, his wife was sweet and pretty enough, to have a real life; the storybook sort of life he had planned for them all.

He rolled to his side and grabbed his wallet. In it was an old picture of Marcie and Jock, his son only three. But it was his most treasured possession and when he looked at it, in an odd way, it gave him comfort.

His actual leaving had been sudden, though he had planned for it carefully. He finally allowed himself to recognize the havoc living with him was causing Marcie and Jock. The day before he left, he had stood at their bedroom door and overheard his wife talking to her mother in Indiana. She was sobbing, "I can't do it Mom. It's just too hard. Jock is having nightmares and wetting the bed. He creeps around like a beaten stray. Chappie isn't the Chappie you knew.

He's not the man I knew and I don't think he'll get better…on the outside, maybe, but not the inside."

He had left the following day.

Chapman closed his eyes, remembering. At that point in his life, he didn't think he would "get better" either. Of all his regrets, the grief he had caused his family topped the list. How could he have been so sick and so selfish as to put them through so much emotional pain? Back then, he had been like a wounded viper, lashing out in all directions, sticking fangs into anything or anybody within reach.

He looked at the picture again, carefully preserved behind plastic, and ran his thumb gently over the surface. *More than two years later and I can still barely take care of myself, Marcie. I did the right thing by you and Jock.*

By now, he was certain Marcie had recovered her own mental health and maybe had remarried. His lawyer and friend, Jason Wilson, could have updated him, but he didn't ask, didn't want to know. He had made that clear to Jason. All that was good in him fervently hoped his family was thriving. He prayed that his son was now his happy, inquisitive former self. He would be seven now; just the right age for starting little league and cub scouts.

Chapman suspected Marcie might be the only woman he would ever love. He knew, because the doctors had confirmed it, that Jock would be the only child he would ever father. He had also been apprised that he had a high risk of contracting some form of cancer.

He set aside the wallet and lay back on the bed, unable to keep his mind from drifting. He thought with mixed feelings about the time he had spent traveling.

After making certain that Marcie and Jock were taken care of financially and signing over the titles of their house and SUV, Chapman had loaded what he needed into his newly purchased Nissan sports car. He had written Marcie a carefully constructed letter full of details, including the name and phone number of Jason, who had been instructed to tell her the terms of the divorce. He put it on their kitchen table as he walked out the door. Then he left the state of Washington without looking back. He had been certain she would not have a single objection to his going. Certainly, she had signed the divorce papers without protest.

After he left the Tri-cities of Kennewick, Pasco and Richland, he headed east, driving further each day as his stamina allowed. At first, he traveled after the sun was low in the western sky. Then, as his eyes healed, with help from the Z's tinted windows and his very dark glasses, he could drive during the day. The journey became more interesting. He booked all his rooms and ordered any items he needed using the internet. During the first weeks, even driving more than 2-3 hours created a fatigue so great he would have to pull over, drink a can of Ensure and sleep with the seat reclined. His car became his universe; his computer his link to the world. He had thought he would drive to the East Coast, possibly Virginia, where he had been raised. But somewhere along the way he decided to visit all the Western National Parks instead. It seemed to him that hiking in the high, clear mountain air might help work on his lung capacity. He was hopeful that he could even recover some of his strength.

It had been a good plan, but it had failed, only partly due to the altitude. He'd made it as far east as Utah to visit Zion and Bryce, taken in by the cleanness of the air, the redness of the surreal rock formations and the blueness of the sky. Then he turned back and drove to the Southwest, his driving time lengthening to up to four hours without stops. He visited the Carlsbad Caverns and the Grand Canyon in Arizona, but the weather was getting hotter by then, the light bright and unrelenting. So, he headed north to Oregon. Crater Lake was a place Marcie had always wanted to visit. He had booked a room at the lodge and had sat for hours looking out at Wizard Island, the volcanic cone showing above the cobalt blue of the nearly bottomless lake. He imagined the holocaust of power and energy released when the mountain blew its top. *It must have been rather like a nuclear fission reaction,* he thought.

He realized then, that emptiness was threatening to pull him back into the black hole he had managed to claw himself out of. His current lack of stamina and energy had as much to do with his state of mind as his damaged body. *There has to be more to life for me than this. I guess I need a purpose. I am not suited to being an adventurer and wanderer. I am, by training, a nuclear engineer, but really, I could have been a fine electrical, structural or mechanical one. I need problems to solve, things to design and build. That's my nature.*

He sat on his bench by the lake, swathed as always, dark glasses and hat in place. The fact that folks mostly avoided him no longer troubled him very much. He was slowly learning techniques that reassured them and found the truth, somewhat glossed over in detail, worked the best. Humor he found, disarmed people and often he saw a spark of admiration in their eyes; at other times true compassion.

At Bryce Canyon National Park, he was resting on a rock bench at Sunset Point when he noticed a little boy watching him. Finally, with a glance toward his parents who were standing at the rail taking in the red rock spires, he walked over, plopped down beside Chapman and asked, "How come you don't got a nose?" He was only four or five and talked with a soft drawl. His horrified parents had turned from the view and rushed to intervene, but Chapman had raised a gloved hand to stop them.

"I don't?" Chapman carefully put his fingers to his little nose and pretended to be surprised. "You are sure right about that! Wonder where I left it this time? Could you tell me please, did I remember to put on my ears?"

The boy had stood in front of Chapman then, looking carefully under the rim of his fedora. "Um…yep. They're both there. How come your glasses are so black? Are you blind?"

"Actually, I'm not. I can see that you have not only remembered to put on your ears, but your nose is well. Your parents must be very proud of you."

The little guy had nodded seriously. "Actually, I just leave them on all the time. It's easier that way. You should try it."

Chapman could feel the corners of his reconstructed lips turn up. "Thank you, I believe I will give it some thought."

He had turned to the parents then. "What a great kid! Are you guys visiting from the South?" he'd asked in his movie star husky voice.

It turned out that they were from Georgia. They had a short pleasant conversation as strangers will do and then moved on, their boy anchored between them; each parent tightly gripping a hand.

Chapman sat and looked across the vista then, happy with the brief exchange. Jock would be just like that little boy, confident, curious and certain everyone was a friend. He had done the right thing in leaving. He was still certain of it. He would remember Bryce Canyon more for that insight than all of the spell-casting spires called hoodoos, the superb vistas, the craggy rimmed canyons and the meadows covered by early spring wildflowers.

Chapman suddenly felt close to being swamped by sadness. This time, with single minded determination, he was able to visualize the giant lid shutting off all that lay in his past. He sat up and swung his legs over the side of the bed. *I remember when I was too weak to even do this. One day, I'll have enough muscle tone to hop out of bed, but for now, this is good enough,* he thought. He tried to turn his mind towards what he had taken to calling his "project," but a question continued to nibble at him.

He reached to the end of the bed for his white robe. *When I left Crater Lake why did I come north instead going south to Yosemite? There are no National Parks in Central Oregon.* He realized with certainty that he was, at least for the present, done with wandering. Something had called to him as he drove the farm to market roads exploring the countryside, continually startled by the mountain vistas.

Then one day, soon after his arrival, he had pulled off the road under a big cottonwood tree to take a nap in its shade, his energy gone. When he woke and put his seat back up, he found he was looking out the window at a small farm.

His first impression had been that the place was tired and work worn. A faded sign proclaimed it was "The Larsens." Underneath, the name it said in smaller letters, "raising Suffolk and Romney Sheep." And below that, it said, "est. 1889." But it wasn't the farm or the simple, dormered two-story farm house that caught and held him. Instead, it was the field of rocks adjacent to it. *Now how can one piece of ground look so fertile and then right next to it, be a field not fit for anything?*

He studied the plot. It was fairly level, except for one area where the land dipped down and then rose to a small outcropping of solid looking rocks. He wondered how big the piece really was. It looked to be about two acres, but was long and narrow, so it was hard to judge. Right in the middle was an ancient Juniper tree. It was an absolute giant. Some of the gnarled limbs were dead, but it still looked immortal and impervious to time. There were five of the large trees in all, growing with determination on the lunar looking soil. One shared its shade with the farmhouse lawn. It had been used as a giant fence post; helping to hold up old-fashioned metal stock fencing, making the other, regular fence posts look puny and insubstantial. As he looked beyond the field, he saw and marveled again at the mountains anchoring the western sky. Washington's Cascade Mountain Range had its own dramatic, snow-capped mountains like Mount Adams, Mount Rainier and Mount Saint Helens, but they were widely spaced. These mountains were all visible at the same time and majestic didn't even begin to describe them.

His eyes went back to the rocks. He pulled out his Blackberry and called up his favorite search engine and asked for the definition of an acre. It was 43,560 square feet.

He whistled. If there were only one rock every square foot, that was a lot of rocks...but there were many, many more. He hit the calculator function and did some rapid calculations. *If there are two acres, there are way more than 500 thousand rocks in that field.* He smiled to himself. *See, I am an engineer! No one but an engineer would even want to know something like that!*

Chapman put away his Blackberry and started the Z. He thought about the hardy pioneers that had settled the area. He thought about the man in 1889 that had looked at that patch of ground and decided to let it be. Life would have been tough back then. He'd put his efforts where they belonged, improving what land was fertile and fencing it for his sheep. *He could have built a rock house or a barn with those rocks,* Chapman mused. Then he shook his head. Probably *it wasn't worth the time and effort, not to mention having the skill to do it.* He wondered how one learned to do rock work and decided to explore it on the internet once he got back in his room.

Over the next few days, Chapman explored the area. He drove east to Prineville and visited its historic Crook County Museum. He found out that the town had been quite a hell-hole in its day. The docent had been most helpful and seemed not at all put off by Chapman's theatrical look, with his scarf, upturned collar and soft fedora. It helped that in the dim light Chapman was able to trade his black glasses for a pair with amber lenses.

"You should drive up into the Ochoco Mountains if you have the time. It's real pretty and you get the feel for what the old time lumbering and ranching was about," he'd said and handed Chapman a map.

"Thank you for your help and the information, sir. I believe I will take your advice."

"Look for the wild horses, or maybe you'll see a herd of antelope or elk around Big Summit Prairie."

So, Chapman stopped at Burger King for a large chocolate shake to mix with his protein powder and did just that. He didn't spot any herds, other than grazing cattle, but he'd had a nap on top of a deserted picnic table in the shade of huge, copper-barked Ponderosa Pine trees and then drove on to the crest of the mountains, visiting the rest stop there.

On his way back to the motel, he'd detoured to take a look at the field of rocks. Why it intrigued him, he wasn't sure. A Red-tailed Hawk lifted out of the juniper near the center of the acreage. Chapman watched it catch the thermals and hunt first over the rocky ground before heading west towards what looked to be a canyon. It was so peaceful that he again took a short nap.

The next day, he retraced his path, traveling on Highway 97. He stopped at the Oregon High Desert Museum, south of the city of Bend. He'd spent several hours, and would have stayed longer, if his stamina had allowed. It was a wonderful interpretive center and he learned a lot about the history, geology, flora and fauna of the area. He watched an interesting program on river otters and had two bowls of tomato and basil soup in a corner of their cafeteria. Signs everywhere pleaded with people not to feed the Golden-mantled ground squirrels and chipmunks. It was obvious that the signs were not heeded. The charming little beggars were everywhere looking for handouts.

The day before, he'd gone to Lake Billy Chinook; one of the largest reservoirs in Central Oregon. There was a brisk spring breeze blowing caplets of foam on the dark canyon waters. Still, die hard fishermen and women sat hunkered over fishing poles on bobbing boats, hoping for the best. He stopped at the Cove Palisades marina and looked at photographs of the "lunkers" caught by some of those who persevered. He saw kokanee, bass and trout all held straight out towards the cameras by grinning people, obviously hoping to make them look even bigger than they were.

He noted an old newspaper article touting that it was legal to keep one bull trout over 24 inches even though it was an endangered species.

Chapman knew little about fish or fishing except how he liked them prepared. His stomach rumbled. He paid for a fudgesicle from the porch freezer of the little store and ate it in a sunny spot protected from the breeze.

Again, on the way back to his comfortable room, he found himself detouring to the rocky field. This time he had brought a pad of paper. He parked under the same cottonwood tree and took pictures with his Blackberry. He then did a pencil sketch of the area. He included the juniper trees, the fencing and the mountains in the back ground. It took him longer than he had expected, but he was pleased with the results and had converted them, using auto cad when he returned to his room.

Now, Chapman turned on his laptop and reviewed yesterday's drawings. They weren't bad. Good enough to use if he got to move forward with the project forming in his mind. He ate a banana and a yogurt then headed for the shower.

In the shower, he finally admitted to himself that as much as he had enjoyed learning the area, he felt the most alive and engaged with life when he was sitting in the Z and imagining the possibilities of a lava strewn field.

He shut off the shower and reached for his towel. *Today's the day. Today I'm going to walk right up to the farmhouse door, introduce myself and ask whoever lives there if I can buy their rocky field.*

With the help of his computer, he was going to design and build a stone wall…and if there were rocks left over, who knew what next. He was going to move rocks, one at a time until he couldn't move another. Then he would rest. His muscles would get stronger, his stamina greater. It seemed quite logical to him. But first, he would eat a real breakfast and get a haircut.

Chapter Eight
Millie

Millie stood in the shower and let the warm water course over her shoulders, her head buried in the spray. There were benefits from working the dinner shift, and this was one of them…an extra-long shower with plenty of hot water and nobody home to interrupt her. Methodically, she washed her hair and shaved her legs, thinking about her day.

She'd made a list while eating breakfast, and stopped when the length got discouraging. Jack's birthday was coming up on Monday but they were having the party after church on Sunday so Jake and Jenny would be able to be there. As the start of his long birthday celebration, the kids were driving home from college and dropping by his house to both surprise him and pick him up in time to go for pizza. Then, Will and the little kids would join them there and they would all go to the Friday night basketball game. She smiled to herself. *What wouldn't I give to be a mouse in the bushes, watching him open the door to his grand children? He is going to be proud as punch walking into the gymnasium with them.* Unfortunately, she would be working.

Shopping for a birthday present was high on her list. Right now, she hadn't a clue as to what to get Jack. His wants were so simple. When she'd asked him, he'd smiled sadly and said, "Sweetheart, the things I want, money can't buy. Just having you all together and Leona's applesauce cake is all I need." She knew he'd been talking mostly about Betty when he'd said money couldn't buy what he wanted. She also knew when he said, 'having you all together' didn't mean he suspected about Jenny and Jake; he just meant his family in general.

Grumpy Leona Larsen, Millie realized, had to be counted as part of the family. There was never a question as to her being invited. She had seemed delighted to be asked and had volunteered to bring her famous applesauce cake.

Grumpy Leona was what Abby and Matt secretly called her. She shook her head. *We shouldn't let them do it. It may be true, but it's disrespectful as heck and unkind besides.* She gave a little sigh and toweled herself off, mentally adding to her list of things to do: Talk to kids about kindness.

Millie pulled into the driveway of the little, one story house Betty and Jack had bought and moved into when it became clear that what was between Will and her was serious, with an engagement ring to prove it. She sat for a moment and looked at it, remembering, sipping on her latte.

Back then, they were just finishing dinner, when Jack announced he and Betty planned to move into town, "so you kids can have the place to yourselves," was how he'd put it. She and Will had looked at each other slack-jawed and then began to protest. Betty had raised her voice at that point. "Kids, you aren't talking us out of this, so don't try. You think I'm not glad to be giving up this big house. You think I don't deserve a brand new house where I'm not tryin' to erase other people's dirt for forty years?" She sounded half mad and very determined.

Jack had looked at her in shock, his mouth open. "Why, Mother..." he had started, but she had rounded on him. "Don't you 'why Mother' me, Jack Anderson. I'm not saying a thing about your folks or your mother's housekeeping. I'm just saying I want that house we looked at last week! It is the right size. It's in the right location. It's one story; no more stairs for these old legs. No more walking clear out to the implement shed when I want to go somewhere in the car..."

Betty was ticking the points off like she was firing rounds out of an automatic rifle. Her face was getting redder with each point. Finally, she threw her hands in the air, slapped them down on the dining room table so hard the dishes jumped and shouted, "Besides, I really, really like it Jack! I really, really like it!" Then she'd burst into tears which caused five-year old Jake and three-year old Jennifer to start wailing along with her, certain someone had done something dreadful to their beloved "Nana."

It was immediate bedlam. Millie had turned to comfort the baby in her high chair and Will had pulled Jake onto his lap. Jack had gotten up from his end of the table and rushed to Betty. He reached down, pulled her up from her chair and put his arms around her. "Now, Mother, now, Mother," he kept saying, one hand awkwardly patting her on the back, "shush, now. We are upsetting the children. You can have your house. Of course you can have your house."

Millie looked at the little, natural wood, custom home that had caused the furor. To her, it didn't look that special, though, when she thought about it, it did have its good points. It had a nice sized lot and the garage attached with a door right into the laundry room off the kitchen. It was also close to shopping, the elementary school and not too far from Anchors Away. She shrugged her shoulders, acknowledging that life worked its mysterious wonders, sometimes almost in spite of people. But the best thing about it was that Betty loved it from the beginning and never stopped. Until her mind had gone, she loved being there for the kids when they came home from school, making them cookies and listening about their day. *And what a blessing it was to have her!*

As Millie unfastened her seatbelt, grabbed her new, bling-loaded, fifty-percent off, chartreuse shoulder bag and stepped from the van, she noticed a small metal bowl of dry cat food and another of water beside the front steps and raised an eyebrow. She rapped on the door and then opened it, calling, "Yoo-hoo! I'm finally here Dad."

Jack, as per usual for this time of day, was on his computer in the spare room. He and his other retired friends spent hours sending each other emails. The most popular topics were: government bashing, nostalgia pieces, World War II clips, off-color jokes and silly poems about getting old. Jack also played computer games though he guiltily minimized them on his screen when someone came into the room. "In here," he called, "just finishing my emails."

"Okey dokey. I see your sheets and towels on the washer. Thanks for stripping the bed."

Millie started the load and then walked into what Jack had taken to calling his "office." "Hey, Dad, before I start running the vacuum, what's that cat food doing by the door? Got a new pet?"

Jack swiveled on his chair and gave a sheepish grin. "Naw. A feral cat found that vent screen I've been meaning to replace. She made the opening large enough to squeeze through and had her kittens in the crawl space."

Millie grinned. "A feral cat, huh?"

"Well, I don't know for certain if she's feral, but she won't let me get closer than ten feet, that I do know."

Millie thought for a minute. "Do you know where they are, under the house, I mean."

Jack ran his fingers through his snowy curls. "As of last night I do. When I went to bed, the mama must have come home from hunting because all of the sudden I could hear high pitched mewing. I believe she's got her nest somewhere under my bed."

There was a twinkle in his eye as he talked. It was good to see. "Well then," said Millie, "looks like you've got a challenge on your hands."

Jack swiveled his chair around, showing Millie his back. "Not me. Those kittens get a little older and I'm going to the Humane Society for cat traps and I know just where the pet carrier is. It's in the rafters of the implement shed over at your place."

Millie smiled at the back of his head. *Yeah, right, you old softie! I'll bet a month's wages you'll have the whole group tamed and be peddling them around the neighborhood instead.*

"Well then," Millie said again. "I guess we're going to find out if mama cat will tolerate the sound of a vacuum running over her head."

She saw Jack's shoulders hunch a little as if wincing, but he only said mildly, "Yep, I guess we will," and continued his hunt and peck typing.

Millie spent the next hour dusting, running the vacuum, putting fresh sheets on the bed and cleaning the bathroom. She'd save mopping for the next time. The kitchen was Jack's domain and it she left strictly alone.

As usual, they finished up her visit with a companionable cup of coffee. They had that in common; a love of the bitter brew. Jack even ground his own beans. They sat at the kitchen table and caught each other up on life's doings. Generally, it was Millie catching Jack up, but today was different.

Millie said, "Will came back to the house after you called and I gave him the cell phone. Did he call you yet?"

There was a worried look on Jack's face as he shook his head. "Nope. Not unless he tried when I was in the shower. I'll give him a call after you leave."

Millie's forehead wrinkled. *I can read these Anderson men like books! Something is really bothering him.* Gently she asked, "In the meantime, anything I can help with?"

Jack looked at her, seeming torn and finally sighed. "I guess Leona wouldn't care if you know about her trouble. She's such a private and proud woman…she wouldn't like people to know…but you're family and maybe you or Will can think of something."

"Leona? Oh dear! Hasn't that poor woman already had enough trouble in her life?"

Jack shook his head. "That is sure the damned truth. But now she's about to lose her place for unpaid taxes."

"She didn't pay her property taxes? Why?" Millie asked incredulously.

"She didn't have the money to pay them. I guess Peter's medical bills wiped them out financially. But did she file for bankruptcy and salvage something? Nope. Not her. She's too damned proud!"

Coffee forgotten, he poured out his sadness. "When she told me, pieces started fitting together like a jigsaw puzzle. She stopped having her hair done, just grew it out and put it in a bun. She stopped showing off her quilt-making and canning at the fair. She dropped all those women's clubs she and Betty used to go to. She did a whole bunch of things that I thought were because she was grieving Peter or just getting too old...truth was, she was broke; living on a little social security, her egg money and the money Will pays her to lease her hay fields."

He looked up at Millie and his eyes were bright with tears. "I noticed she's been using her coffee grounds twice. The coffee tastes like shit sometimes, and it has been on the tip of my tongue to tell her not to be so damned cheap..." His voice trailed off and he put palms to his eyes and sighed before continuing.

"I was doing some research about it on the internet this morning. Do you know that 60 percent of all bankruptcies in the United States are due to medical bills? Think of it. Sixty percent! It's a damned disgrace in a country this rich!" He looked at Millie sadly. "All this time she's never said a word. Peter's been gone for over three years and she never said a thing."

Millie sat thinking of the bitter, proud, tough old woman and knew without a doubt that Jack was right. "How much? How much does she owe?"

"She said it was over $8,000.00 if you include the interest."

"Dear Lord above!"

Jack looked at her. "It breaks my heart," he said simply. "She hasn't paid them since Peter died and she's only got about three months before they start foreclosure proceedings. The banks sure as hell aren't lending with the mess they are in, so it's not likely she'll get a loan."

"Only three months? That just doesn't seem right at all! I can't believe the county would do such a thing with so little warning!" Millie's blue eyes snapped sparks.

Jack shook his head, remembering. "Naw. They did send her letters, but Peter was dying when the first one came and she just tossed it." He shook his head. "I can understand it a little. You remember how she was. Then, when the second one came she was at wit's end, broke and still worn out from taking care of him. She just couldn't deal with it." He sat, head bowed for a minute. "If you'll remember, by the time hospice was called, she was in real bad shape." He gave a little shrug. "This last letter she got was certified. She knew then she couldn't ignore it any longer. Hell, that stubborn, ornery old woman hasn't even been down to talk to them yet! I'd like to wring her scrawny neck sometimes!"

Millie gasped. She had seldom seen her easygoing father-in-law so distressed. She covered his hand and found he was trembling. "Thank God Peter isn't here to witness this," he said sadly.

"Listen," Millie said, "get in your Explorer and go talk to Will. Do it right now. He's plowing in the new field at the old homestead. Then, maybe you should call Leona and offer to go to the courthouse with her. Or maybe Will could go. Somebody needs to go with her."

Jack nodded, appreciating her common sense. He pushed his coffee mug back and looked at her for a long moment, thinking. Then he nodded again and stood up. "Thank you, sweetheart. I believe I will go see my son."

She smiled up at him. "She's lucky to have you for a friend, Dad."

Carefully, he pushed in his chair and Millie watched as he headed to the coat closet for his old Levi jacket and ball cap. *That is one of the dearest men on this earth. Aren't I lucky that his son takes after him?*

Millie lingered at the table, thinking. Her father-in-law had always been the sort of man to pitch in and help whether it was family or friends. He was a soft touch for any fund raisers in the community, especially if it had to do with kids. *It's going to break his heart if something can't be done to save Leona's place.*

She looked around the kitchen that still carried many of Betty's touches. The tea towels had crocheted borders, a cross stitched sampler hung over the kitchen table. It said, 'No matter where I serve my guests, they always like my kitchen best.' Leona had one in her kitchen too. They had made them for each other as Christmas gifts one year. Millie smiled remembering how the two women enjoyed each other's company. *He'd probably give Leona the money, if she'd take it...but the thing is...he really has to save it for Mom's care. It's got to be tearing him apart.*

92

Millie thought of her kids; the first two and the second two, all doing their homework around this very table. Matt and Abby still did on the days they came here. Her heart felt over-burdened; Leona's plight all stirred in with family memories. *Poor Leona! All this time she's been suffering, and we thought it was just missing Peter and getting old. It's a good lesson to all of us not to make assumptions.*

She heard the dryer buzzer and got up to wash the mugs out before heading to the laundry room to do the folding. The day seemed, suddenly, endlessly long.

As she walked out the back door to leave, she saw the tiger stripped backside of a cat jet around the corner of the house. "Well, hello Mama," she called in a friendly way. Setting her purse down on the step, she walked across the lawn, following the cat. "Here kitty, kitty" she crooned as she went around the corner. Then she stopped in her tracks. The cat was sitting, facing her, near a shrub. They studied each other for a moment. Millie backed up a few steps and squatted down. "See, I'm not trying to catch you." She made her voice melodic. "Aren't you the pretty thing? I like your white bib and paws. I hear you've got babies under the house. Aren't you clever? You be nice to Jack and see what happens. He's a real push over for babies, you know," she crooned.

The cat's ears were pricked and her tail was wrapped around her legs. Jack had said ten feet was how close she'd let him get and Millie could imagine him doing the exact thing she was doing, holding a one-sided conversation with a spooky cat.

93

"I'm not going to come closer. I just want to look at you." Millie liked how the cat had positioned herself to disappear into the shrubs at the least sign of danger and yet was brave and curious enough to stay and look at Millie. She thought how Abby, her animal lover, would enjoy this new development.

She gave a little sigh and rose slowly to her feet. "I've got places to go and things to do, kitty. See you later." She turned and walked away, looking back once before she turned the corner to retrieve her purse. The cat sat like a statue, her white chest shining against the gray of her coat. "Good bye, Mama. Take care of those babies," she called.

As she turned the key of their old minivan, she smiled knowing exactly what to give Jack for his birthday.

Chapter Nine
Jack

In the twenty minute drive to the ranch, Jack's mind jumped and skittered over things plaguing him. He cursed himself soundly for not remembering to call Will about Leona the evening before, even though he knew one more day wouldn't make any difference...except to Leona. Briefly he grew maudlin over how a person's memory could play tricks on them. Thinking of memory caused him to think of his wife's dementia. It had just been little things at first, misplacing her car keys, forgetting words, drifting off in the middle of sentences. Then the little things got bigger. Being unable to find the car keys, then finding them in the freezer, was one example that stuck in his mind; because it was then that he first started to really wonder.

He could ignore it no longer when she had gotten lost driving home from town. He and Millie had both been working at Anchor's Away. The kids had been dropped off by the school bus and had been waiting on the steps when young Jimmy Brown, who had been in Will's class at school, led her home and then came to the restaurant to tell him. When they asked, "Where were you, Nana?" According to Jimmy, she'd said that she didn't quite know.

Jack shook his head, trying unsuccessfully to shake away the painful memories. What puzzled him, troubled him deeply, was that the signs had been in plain view. Why hadn't he put the pieces together until he got slapped, like a pie in the face, with the evidence? Pounding the steering wheel with his fist he shouted, "Shit! You jackass! You worthless piece of crap!" Waves of frustration and anger washed over him. He knew life wasn't fair. *Of course it isn't. A fella needs spikes like the loggers wear to stay atop and not get crushed,* he thought.

He hoped last night's forgetting didn't mean that his mind was going the way of his wife's. He shook his head. *Sometimes a man has to swear to get the load off his chest.* He'd learned fluent swearing in the Navy and found it a good release, though he had his boundaries. He never swore around women and children these days, other than a few dams and hells…and he never took the Lord's name in vain. He considered swearing one of his vices, but was unwilling to give it up. The cigarettes and hard drinking were gone, but he'd kept the swearing.

He drove down the gravel lane that led to the ranch house where he'd grown up and where Millie and Will now lived. As he drove past it, he remembered the pet carrier in the implement shed rafters. He promised himself that on the way back from seeing Will, he would stop there and get the thing down.

At the gate by the barn he stopped long enough to look at Will's new Murray-Grey calves. The calves looked back at him. He thought their short, broad faces and the dark skin around their eyes and muzzle gave them an intelligent look. *They look like an Aberdeen Angus with a paint job to me.* Jack thought, as he got out and opened the gate.

He was partial to the Angus breed since they came originally from Scotland, the land of his ancestors. Jake had told him this new breed had originated in Australia; the first being a cross between an Angus and a Shorthorn. It seemed that a rancher had kept some heifers instead of shipping them, simply because his wife had liked their grey color. Little did he know he was starting a new breed of cattle.

Jack grinned to himself as he eased through the gate and got out to secure it. *That Jake! He knows more obscure facts about ranching and farming than the law allows!* He looked to the right at the field behind the house. He remembered Will on the tractor, the little guy on his lap for hours. *Where in the hell did the time go?* He asked himself as he gunned his Explorer down the dike road leaving a windrow of dust behind him.

He could see Will in the distance, working the field. There was a rubble pile burning, and Jack knew that the last vestiges of the old homestead had been unearthed and were being obliterated forever. *It's past time to close the book on that sad chapter of our life. It will be a good thing to cover that spot with a field of grass.*

He honked his horn to get Will's attention as he pulled in beside the truck to wait until his son had finished the row and turned back towards him. Will looked up and raised a hand.

His honk brought the dogs, Tuffy and Digger, barreling up out of the irrigation ditch. They made a bee line towards him. Jack got out and prepared to handle the muddy, wet greeting he knew was coming.

When they were about twenty feet from him he held out both palms and said sternly, "Tuffy, Digger, down!"

Both dogs checked their momentum and dropped on their bellies as though they'd been shot, though Jack noticed that ol' Tuff had managed to inch along forward a good two feet. He ignored it and said, "Good dogs!" Then he pointed to the back of the pickup and said, "Truck!"

With happy yips the dogs flew past him into the pickup bed. From there, Jack could receive his greeting and give both dogs their due.

When the dogs felt the greeting had been given and received properly, they calmed themselves and flopped on their sides in the truck bed, happy to rest in the shade of the tree.

Jack stood with his arms resting on the back of the old farm truck, watching his son and thinking about what he wanted to say. Half of him was ready to throw up his hands and let the law have its way with Leona. If what he read on the internet was right, it wasn't going to be pretty. The other half of him was ready to fight. *Probably my Scottish side. Those clansmen didn't let people waltz in and take their lands without one helluva fight.* He decided his fighting side was the stronger of the two.

Will had turned at the far end of the field and was making his slow, steady way back, his furrows straight as strings. Jack felt his spirit calm itself in the spring day with the steady chuff of the tractor in the distance and the chirping of birds in the cottonwood tree over his head. His son had a level head. He too had known the old Leona, the woman whom he called Auntie, the woman who made him cookies every year for his birthday, the wife of the man who had given him a lamb to raise on a bottle; later taking the championship ribbon at the Deschutes County Fair. If anyone could put a steady hand on this rudder, it would be Will.

Will turned his tractor and plow until they were again facing north and then got off. He walked up onto the ditch road and trotted towards his dad. "Hey, Dad, I called, but you didn't answer," he shouted as he closed the distance.

Jack remembered when he could do just what Will was doing, jog a quarter mile and arrive not even puffing. Now, he creaked for a good thirty minutes after getting out of bed in the morning, reminding himself of the tin man in the Wizard of Oz. *A drop of oil in these old joints might be just the thing* he thought, still leaning on his forearms over the side of the pickup, hands folded, smiling at the son who looked nothing like him. He was in fact, a carbon copy of Betty's dad...like Betty too, with his thick brown hair and summer blue eyes.

Will went to the cab, rooted around in his cargo box and brought out a jug of water and the thermos of coffee Millie had given him. "There's some left...probably lukewarm, but strong and black."

Jack took it with a nod of thanks. "Nothing wrong with coffee that's gone a little cold," he said, "nothing at all."

Will took a long drink of water, recapped the bottle, leaned his forearms on the pickup bed in the time honored male fashion and said, "What's up?"

Jack took his time pouring the coffee into the thermos lid. "It's your Auntie Leona," he said. "She's got herself in an unholy pickle and I don't know what, if anything can be done. She's about to lose her place."

Like Millie, Will was stunned. "What? That can't be right. What did she say?"

Jack sighed. "I saw the foreclosure letter, Will. At least, I saw the last one she got. The other ones, she evidently threw away. Now she's got three months and then, according to what I read and what it said on the internet, there'll be a sheriff's sale."

"A sheriff's sale? You mean everything auctioned off like you see in those Oklahoma Dust Bowl movies?"

Horror was written all over Will's face. "I thought they owned that place. It's been in their family since before the turn of the 19th century hasn't it? Their sign says 1889."

"Yep. They do own the property but even if you own a place, you got to pay the taxes, son."

"Why in the heck didn't Leona pay the taxes then?"

"All the money they had went for Peter's medical bills. I guess she's been just barely getting by; no money to pay over eight thousand dollars in taxes."

"Eight thousand dollars? How did they get to be eight thousand dollars?"

Jack sighed and spoke slowly, like to a child. "She was so worn out from taking care of Peter that she just threw the letters away when they came."

Will dropped his head between his hands and groaned. "Can't she file for bankruptcy or something? Maybe she could do one of those reverse mortgages…"

Jack beamed and clapped his son on the back. "That's the ticket, son. Those are the kinds of ideas we're looking for."

Will looked up, his face sad. "It doesn't seem right, Dad. She's had more sorrows already than one person can bear. I can sorta understand why she did what she did…it must have seemed like sweeping dirt under the rug…out of sight, out of mind."

Jack nodded. "Peter's been gone over three years. She's been keeping her poverty to her chest and trying to grieve his loss all at the same time. She's a stubborn, proud woman and that's a fact."

Will lifted his cowboy hat and scratched his head. "Last night Millie had a customer come in. She said he was in some sort of an accident. I'm guessing probably at the Hanford Nuclear Plant. He evidently looked like a fried scarecrow, almost afraid to show his face because he'd been so badly burned. She said he was a real nice guy too. Sure makes you stop and think. His predicament…and Leona's too…comes along to remind you your own life isn't so bad."

Jack reached out and put a hand on his son's shoulder. "Millie and I were talking about that thing this morning on the phone. Maybe that fellow was what got her thinking. We got it good son. Not like Leona, all alone except for a couple of banged up sheep and Pansy."

Jack paused to think, and a grim look came over his face. "I really don't think Leona's nerves are so steady any more either. She's claiming someone is "casing" her. Said she was getting the guns out so she could defend herself."

Will looked at his father. "Casing her? You mean like a stalker? Got her guns out? Jesus, Dad! If she thinks she's got trouble now, just let her take a shot at someone and she'll lose more than her farm. You don't really think she'd do that do you?"

"Yes," said Jack. "I believe she would…shoot first and ask questions later…if she got herself all wound up. She says the guy has been sitting across the road from her house in a fancy blue car for several days now. Stays for about 20 minutes or so, never gets out and then leaves."

Will looked keenly at Jack. "You know, it could be perfectly innocent...but on the other hand...Neil comes to mind. There's a lot there we don't know. What do you think about me calling Teddy and asking him to have a patrol car drive by her house every now and then?"

Teddy worked for the Deschutes County Sheriff's office. He was also a "wantabe" cowboy and was generally available to help when Will had cow work to do.

Jack said, "Well, it's something. I'll tell her you are doing it. Might ease her mind a bit. She doesn't want to call them because of sounding like a crazy old lady."

"Yeah, that and asking for help just aren't strong suits for Aunt Leona."

"True, son."

They stood, leaning on the pickup; each lost in their own thoughts until Jack slapped his son on the back and said, "Thanks, Will. You got a good head on those shoulders. I'll go on over there now that I got some ideas to hand her."

Will smiled at him. "I'll keep thinking on it. Plowing is good for thinking." A strange look crossed his face, and his father knew where his mind had gone.

"It does my heart a damned sight of good to see the last evidence of Hoot's place being burned to a crisp, and I'll feel even better when there's blue grass growing in its place." Jack said with feeling.

Will looked at him, nodding his agreement. "What is it you say, Dad? If it doesn't kill you, it makes your stronger?"

Jack nodded. "Yep."

"Well, then I'm stronger, aren't I?"

Jack let out a bark of laughter. "Yes, indeed. I believe you are." He tossed his half-drunk coffee into the dirt and screwed the lid back on the thermos, handing it to his son. "See you later and thanks for the help. Millie thinks I ought to go see the folks at the county with her, so I'll offer that too."

"Let me know how it goes. I'll probably be over there later today fertilizing, but I probably won't see her, and if I do, I won't say anything unless she brings it up," Will said as his dad walked to his SUV.

"Sounds right," Jack said over his shoulder. "Bye, son."

Chapter Ten
Will

Will watched his father drive off. He remembered when they'd both been about the same height. He wondered when his father had begun to shrink and how he had not noticed.

Looking at his watch, he saw what his stomach was already telling him. He poured coffee into the lid of the thermos and reached in the cab for sandwiches. While he ate, he thought of Leona's sons, Giles and Neil. The three of them had been babies together; had grown up together. Buying a package of cigarettes from the machine in the lobby at Anchors Away for two quarters, they'd had their first smoke together.

Will sighed and looked unseeing into the distance. *Goddamn it, Neil, we should have been raising our kids together! Where in the hell are you? Your mom is going through a whole bunch of shit and you probably don't even know about it!*

He sighed. He still missed Giles, but not like he missed Neil. Giles had been two years older and obsessed with only one thing…airplanes. He had spent his high school years working after school to earn enough money for flying lessons at Robert's Field and earned his pilot's license during his junior year. He never missed an R.O.T.C. meeting during high school and had joined the Navy following graduation; following family tradition. There he learned to fly fighter jets. Three years later he'd died in a stupid motorcycle crash while off-duty in Iraq. *I guess he was doing what he loved over there, flying F-14s. There must have been some consolation for his parents and Neil in that. Serving his country...they can be proud of that...but it doesn't seem right that neither son made it home.*

No one was surprised when Giles had joined the military, but when Neil turned down an athletic scholarship to Oregon State, applied for and accepted a commission with the Naval Academy in Annapolis, everyone was shocked. Neil was a natural athlete, graceful as a cat on the field. Some said he was the best quarterback the high school ever had. The announcers called him "Joe Cool" because he was so steady and fearless in the pocket. As halfback, it was Will's job to keep him from getting creamed before he passed the ball. He did his job well enough that Oregon State had offered them both scholarships. When Neil told Will he had made a different decision, Will was crushed.

"I have a hankering to see the world, buddy boy, don't take it personally. When I get done, I'll come home and we'll raise our kids together, just like our folks did us."

Only he hadn't come home much and when he did, things had changed. There was a look in Neil's eye and a distance between them that he couldn't bridge.

The Larsens went to Annapolis when Neil graduated and Peter came home proud to tears when he talked of the ceremony. Leona didn't say much. He had overheard his mom telling his dad that she was taking it real hard, having both boys in the military and so far away.

Will finally took pity on the dogs who had been patiently watching each bit of the peanut butter and jelly sandwich disappear into his mouth, strands of drool hanging like cellophane tinsel from the sides of their muzzles. He flipped them the last of his crusts and poured an inch of luke-warm coffee to wash down the sandwiches and then started on the bananas.

When Giles died, the Air Force had shipped his body home. Will had come home from OSU to attend the service. Neil had been there in his Academy uniform, hiding his distress behind aviator sunglasses. They'd lifted a few brews together and Will remembered he'd cried and Neil hadn't. It was the last time they had spent any time together. Neil said little about what he was being trained for; it was something to do with Navy intelligence.

Will made a grimace, tossed the thermos in the cab of the pickup, lifted the dogs out, and headed back to his plowing. *We've all got a story, only some get second chances and some don't. Some of us get to live happily ever after, at least for a while.* He forced thoughts of Leona Larson's sons out of his mind.

Back on the seat of the tractor, he adjusted the cushion, stomped down on the clutch and pushed the starter. It started like the champ it was. Over the years, he'd been good about maintaining it, knowing when it cranked over for the last time; he would lose something special...both to him and to Jake.

He retrieved his iPod from his pocket and put in his ear buds. Then he goosed the tractor into first gear, smoothly released the clutch and accelerated slowly, his mind on his work and his kids.

They were good kids, all of them. He had not one complaint, other than it was hard when the first two left. He'd told Millie, "We never should have let Jenny graduate early; them both leaving at once is about to kill me."

"They aren't going to Mars, sweetie, they're just going over the hill. They'll come back when they can." "Over the hill" was how they described the trek over the Cascade Mountain Range and down the other side to the city of Corvallis, home of Oregon State University.

He thought again how different Neil's and Giles' personalities had been, and realized his own four were each their own person too. His youngest two came to mind and he smiled to himself while Willie Nelson crooned 'Georgia on my Mind' into his ear buds and the heavy plow carved furrows through the earth.

Unlike Jenny and Jake, who seemed to know exactly how they wanted to spend their lives almost from the get-go, not so with the last two. Matt, his youngest, reminded him a little of Neil when he was young. He liked whatever he was doing at the moment. Millie called him "my little experience junkie." If it was baseball season, like it was now, he was entirely devoted to his team. During the summer, he was up for anything, including little league. He had a lot of accomplishments under his belt for one so young. He could out fish the whole family and often did. At age nine he was a better roper than any of the other kids around and was the only one who showed any interest in learning to cook. His grandfather had been delighted. Last year, Jack was babysitting for them when Matt was sick and couldn't go to school. Will had dropped in to see them during the day and they were both watching the cooking channel; Matt lying on the couch and Jack in his recliner, both totally engrossed.

Leona Larson thought Matt 'hung the moon' because he had asked her for her famous snickerdoodle recipe. She told the story after church when they'd all come back to her house to have a quick visit with Peter. Will thought back. All four of the kids were outside running off energy. Matt had been only five at the time, his hair still a mop of almost black curls.

"My snickerdoodle recipe?" she'd asked him. "Why on earth do you want that?"

She said he'd looked at her out of Jack's green eyes and said, "So I can make Grandpa Jack cookies. He said he likes your cookies best but you won't give him the recipe."

"Well I won't," she'd said, "but I will give it to you. It's our secret though. I don't just give it out to any Tom, Dick or Harry."

Little Matt had looked up at her and said, "That's okay Aunt Leona; I don't even know anybody by those names."

Leona had laughed so hard she had to wipe her eyes with the hem of her apron when she told them the story. Even Peter, lying wan in his living room bed was smiling. "You've got a gem there," he'd whispered. "I've never met such a cheerful person in my life!"

He is too, Will thought. *He and Jenny both have that capacity to see the good in everyone and trust them, but Abby is a different kettle of fish. Talk about being her own person! She came out of the womb fully formed; an adult in a pint-sized body...passing straight from infancy to adulthood in the blink of an eye.*

She was late to talk, almost three...but when she started, it was in full sentences that included please and thank you. She had been in her "big girl chair," the youth-sized chair that had once been his, for the first time. As always, she sat silently taking it all in, while Matt and Jenny talked about their high school activities. Then, without warning, she evidently decided she really liked the mac and cheese. Will had been watching her polish it off and saw her look at Millie, grunt and then point at the baking dish. But Millie and Jenny were teasing Jake about another new girlfriend so they weren't paying any attention. Then, before Will could intervene, her clear, little voice said, "Mommy, I'd like more, please." Just like that. "Mommy, I'd like more, please."

They'd all gawked at her. Millie had looked at her in disbelief and then asked, "Abby, honey, did you just ask for more of something?"

"Yes, please. Mac and cheese."

"Coming right up," Millie said without missing a beat and put another spoonful in her little dish. Abby had looked at it, gave a little sigh, looked up at her mother and said. "Thanks a lot," and proceeded to dig in.

Jake looked at her, his face puzzled and said, "Abby, I didn't know you could talk."

Jenny had said, "Yes, please. Mac and cheese! She starts to talk and the second sentence out of her mouth is poetry! And I thought I was the language whiz."

Will downshifted to make his turn and realized he was grinning like a fool. How Abby started talking had become a family story. She still was crazy about mac and cheese; both kids were. His dad had put it on the menu at Anchors Away because of that.

He frowned. Strong willed and full of surprises were words that described his youngest daughter. She was sometimes too willful and right now her will centered on her 4-H projects. This was the first year she was old enough to even join and she wasn't about to settle on a single project. Oh no! She wanted to take a horse, a calf, and a lamb to the fair. In fact, if she had her way, she'd get a chick from Leona and take it too. If he and Millie could find some quiet time together, they had to figure out a way to reel back her enthusiasm. That was the hard thing these days, finding time together. He thought back to the morning and how good his wife had felt under his hands and grinned. "Damn!" he muttered. "I'm not sure when we do find some private time, that I want to spend it talking."

But they had to talk. Abby had been dropping not so subtle hints that the ranch horses just wouldn't do for a 4-H project. "Dad, you know perfectly well that we're supposed to be learning to train our own horses. Rowdy and Dandy already know everything and Bill is too old."

She actually had a point and Will knew it. 4-H was about the learning. It had been the same when he was a kid. Sure, some parents bought their kids blooded stock that had been professionally trained, but they were mostly business people who just didn't get it, wanting ribbons and glory for their kids even if it wasn't deserved. Not his kids. No way. Jenny hadn't been interested in the animals much, although she had taken to sewing with a passion. But Jake had raised his own beef and his own sheep. One year he'd even bought a piglet to raise.

So, he decided he and Millie needed to talk. It seemed like they somehow had to find the money for another horse…and Abby was going to have to find a way to make some money to do her part. *I can put her to work weeding the garden. That would take some of the load from Millie. Now, there's an idea worth keeping. And we could tell her a new horse means she has to devote her entire time to it, just one project, not three or four.*

His mind moved on to other things. He wondered how his dad was getting along with Leona. Maybe he'd go online himself and see what he could find out about foreclosures. He could also, he realized suddenly, kill two birds with one stone and ask Teddy about the process when he called him about Leona's stalker…or whatever the person was. He decided to call his friend that evening.

Chapter Eleven
Leona

Leona had finished the paper, had read Dear Abby, the letters to the editor and the obituaries twice. The minute hand crept past 10:00 and on towards 10:30 and then kept going. Still, she smoothed the letter on the oil cloth, memorizing the telephone number, reading the words and calling herself all sorts of a fool. *Old age is making a coward of me and that's all there is to it! I can stare a hole in this thing and it's not going to make any difference at all! I've got to call.*

Tears too deeply buried to fall only blurred her vision. She tried to summon her protective anger and failed. With a deep sigh, she got to her feet and walked to the kitchen wall phone. She remembered a saying of Peter's. *"It's better to be bit by a snake you can see than one you can't."*

As she reached towards the receiver, the phone's ring broke the silence and nearly stopped her heart. She looked at it numbly and listened to its persistent demand to be answered. Finally, she picked it up and cradled it to her ear. "Hello." Her voice quavered dreadfully. "Larsen's residence."

"Is that you Leona?" Jack's familiar voice nearly made her knees buckle. "You sound kinda puny. That stalker isn't back, is he?"

Leona could hear the anxiety building in Jack's voice. She cleared her throat and said, making herself sound half angry, "Jack, you old fool, of course it's me. No one is bothering me a bit. I just haven't done much talking today."

"Ah well, that's good then. Listen, have you made your appointment with the tax people at the county yet?"

"As a matter of fact, I was just walking to the phone to do it when you called."

"Well Millie thought you might like a little company when you went. What do you say to me tagging along with you?"

Leona pulled the long curly cord towards the table and slumped heavily in a chair, holding the receiver in a death grip, staring at it until she heard Jack's voice saying, "You there, Leona?"

"Yes, yes, I'm here Jack," she quavered. I am just trying to think why you'd want to do such a thing. But, before you change your mind, I'm saying yes, real quick."

Well that's good then. Call me when you get the appointment and we'll go. Right now I got Martha Stewart coming on the boob tube to teach me how to cook."

Leona said simply, "I sure do thank you, Jack. I can't tell you how I've been dreading to make that call. Knowing you are going to be there with me…well, it makes it a whole lot easier. Maybe after, we can stop and see Betty. It's been awhile since I've been."

"Well we'll just have to see what time they give you for coming in. Could work out fine if you're feeling like it after talking to them. Bye now."

Leona hung up the phone and rubbed the heels of her palms into her eyes. *I called him an old fool and he was just calling to offer help. I have become someone even I don't like.* She sighed and picked up the phone and dialed, knowing the number by heart.

"Good morning, Deschutes County Courthouse," a woman's no-nonsense, professional voice said, "How may I direct your call?"

"Well," Leona said, "I didn't pay my property taxes. Got no way to pay my taxes that I can come up with, so I guess you'd better direct me to somebody that I can talk to about it."

There was a pause on the other end of the line. "I see. Have you gotten a letter from Deschutes County?"

Leona fought down irritation. She wanted to say, "Of course I got a letter, you dumb bunny. You don't think I'm calling to entertain myself do you?" But she bit her tongue. "Yes, I got a letter. I got more than one. I didn't have the money then and I don't have it now. I've got to come in and talk to someone and find out if anything can be done or if you are just going to come and throw an old woman out onto the road."

"I see. May I please have your name?"

"Leona Larsen. I'm Peter Larsen's widow. Land's been in the family since 1889. The farm is off of Coon's Market Road."

There was a moment of silence and then the woman said, "One moment please."

Lenora heard the soft buzz of being put on hold and after a long moment another woman's voice said, "Hello, Mrs. Larsen. I'm Cecilia Woodruff, and I'm the person you'll ask to see when you come in about your taxes. "Would tomorrow afternoon at 3:00 PM work for you?"

"Cecilia Woodruff. Yes," Leona said, shortly. "I'll be there. A friend is driving me over." As an afterthought she added, "Thank you."

"Oh, and by the way, Mrs. Larsen, in case you haven't been to the courthouse recently, be prepared for the new security regulations. A guard will check your purse and possibly your body for unsuitable objects."

It was on the tip of Leona's tongue to make a smart remark about little old ladies packing heat, but she remembered she really wasn't so dumb that she wanted to irritate the people at the courthouse. She had too much to lose. "And exactly what is it I need to bring with me when I come?" She asked as pleasantly as she could.

"Well, this first meeting is just preliminary. You will be assigned a case number and a date to appear in front of a judge. You just need to bring the letter."

It was all Leona could do to keep from groaning. "Thank you. I will. Good bye," she managed to say.

"Good bye, Mrs. Larsen. I trust your friend knows to come to the new courthouse and not the old one?"

"Well of course he does!" Leona said with as much conviction as she could muster. Thank you again. Good bye, Mrs. Woodruff."

She held the buzzing receiver in her hands. *Well, at least that's done.*

Only wish I'd done it before. She got to her feet. Suddenly, the wall to the phone seemed a long way to walk. She felt distinctly weak. *I'd better eat something. Here it is, almost 2:00. I can't believe I forgot that.* She knew she would have to wait until after the hour to call Jack. It wasn't fair to interrupt his time with Martha, Rachel Rae or some other cooking guru. She hung up the phone and set about making herself a tuna sandwich and even added a few sweet pickles she'd canned during the fall.

As she ate, she thought about where Peter kept the deed and the rest of the paperwork on the property. She wished, belatedly, that she had been more involved with the business side of the ranch or at least had tried to figure it out when Peter was still able to help her. He'd even suggested it to her a time or two. But she'd said, "Now, Peter, I don't want to spend the last of our time together doing stuff like that." But now she wished she had made herself. But she hadn't. *Ah well, if wishes were horses a beggar could ride,* she thought to herself as she took her plate to the sink, looked at the clock and reached for the phone.

"Jack. Leona here. I made the appointment. It's for 3:00 o'clock tomorrow. Can you make it?"

"Howdy, Leona. Of course I can make it. Where's the meeting?"

"In Bend...at the new courthouse. You know where that is?"

"Sure I do. It's right near where the old one was. I can find it with my eyes closed."

"Well, that'll be fine then. I sure can't thank you enough."

"And Leona, I'm driving. Could be you aren't going to like what you hear and won't be in fit shape to drive," Jack said bluntly. "I'll pick you up around 2:00."

Leona sucked in her breath and closed her eyes. She felt relief flood through her. It had been a long time since she'd driven her old Buick much of anywhere and the thought of driving the 20 odd miles to Bend had been a worry on her mind. She chuckled. "Jack, you want to fight with me you got to pick a different battle. I'm more than happy to let you drive and navigate. You are a blessing to me Jack Larsen and that's a fact."

"Well," said Jack. "Well then that's settled. See you at 2:00."

"I'll be waiting." Leona paused, not quite ready to let the connection go. "You learn anything from that high-nosed wonder woman on TV today?"

"Well, I did in fact, Leona. I did in fact. They got this little gadget now that will take the peel off a lemon or a lime real slick. I just might have a hankering to get one and make us a lemon meringue pie at our next get together. I always did hate zesting anything."

Leona nodded her head in agreement. "It's such a fiddly thing to have to do. I don't even believe I could make these old hands do it anymore."

"Well, I'm going online to MarthaStewart.com and see what I can come up with."

"You do that Jack. I can already taste that pie. They got lemons eight for a dollar at Food 4 Less, but they aren't very big. Maybe we can stop on our way to see Betty and have a look."

"We'll just have to wait and see how you are feeling about things by then, Leona. Could be this isn't going to be as bad as you think."

Leona sighed. "No, Jack. I think you got it right the first time. I think it's likely to be real bad news. But you know, I've been worrying and fretting about this place for so long that after I got the call made, I felt a sort of relief."

"Well, I'm proud of you for setting that appointment. I have told both Millie and Will what's happened. We're all just as sorry as we can be. It's just a damned shame. That's all I got to say." He paused, hoping she didn't jump down his throat when he told her he'd shared her concerns about a stalker. "I sure hope you don't mind, but I told Will about your stalker, too. He's wondering if you'd like Tommy Lee have somebody run past your place every now and then...and he's thinking on some other ideas too."

"Not that I think it will do a lick of good, Jack, but I guess it's fine for Tommy to drive by. Won't hurt. I guess I got a right to use some of our tax dollars just as much as the next one."

After Leona hung up the phone, she felt restless. She'd told Jack the truth. Making the call had somehow relieved her mind. She felt energized and knew just the chore to keep her busy...she'd dust the old pecan dining set and rub it down with furniture wax. She didn't use the dining room any more, but still, she couldn't walk into the room without seeing her family and friends around that big table with all three leaves in. Maybe she'd even do the coffee table in the living room. One thing for sure, the high desert air did dry out the furniture.

Leona finished the dining room set lost in the smell of lemon, bee's wax and memories. It seemed that not only her husband but both of her sons were there with her. Their faces were crystal clear at the different stages and ages, from when the boys were toddlers, right up to their high school graduation parties. When nostalgia verged to sorrow she just rubbed the paste in harder, ignoring the pain in her hands. *I guess a mother's love is forever. It's my lot to miss them till my last breath. You just got to accept what the Lord has handed you and do the best you can.* She sighed and stood for a moment, looking into space. "Hard though. Real hard," she said aloud.

Her energy was lasting so she did the ornate buffet loaded with snowy, old fashioned damask table cloths, matching napkins with crocheted hems and the set of silverware they had gotten when she and Peter were married. Then she moved on into the living room, going first to pull the drapes so she would have better light. She paused to look out the front window and froze. The car was back! As she looked, she saw the car door open and a man emerge. She narrowed her eyes. It was a distance, but she could see he was in some sort of disguise. His hat was pulled low and dark glasses hid his face. An unholy rage filled her. Her polish cloth fell from her hand. "No!" She shouted. "No! Damn you! Leave me alone! Neil's long gone and I don't know where."

She lurched to where her shotgun leaned behind the edge of the drape and snatched it up. Vaguely she was aware that Pansy was barking, but she didn't pause. She tucked the rifle into the crook of her arm, flipped the locks and stepped outside, letting both doors slam in Pansy's frantic face. The stalker had crossed the road and was headed for her front gate. She grabbed the rail and crabbed down the front steps and raised the gun.

"You get out of here!" she shouted. "You just get out of here and leave me alone!" She took a step, snugged the butt of the gun to her shoulder, and released the safety just as her right heel slid on a patch of mud left from her day of weeding. She went down like a rock. The shotgun blast was the last thing she heard.

Chapter Twelve
Chapman

Chapman was no more than half way across the road when the screen on the farm house door burst open and a shouting old lady brandishing what he first thought was a cane in her left hand, came lurching down the steps. He only thought that for the nanoseconds it took her to reach the front walk and begin to snug, what he realized was a rifle, to her shoulder. Both his muscles and his brain froze. But before he could do more than throw up his hands, he saw the woman suddenly crash over backwards as though someone had pulled the rug out from under her. The gun discharged into the air with a boom followed by a gut wrenching thud he could hear from where he stood as she hit the ground.

He began to run. As he sprinted across the rest of the road, an old Ford pickup came gunning towards him. The driver cranked the wheel and slammed on brakes so hard that whatever he was towing was whipped towards Chapman, missing him by inches. But he didn't stop. He heard yelling and dogs barking as he hit the latch on the gate and rushed on through into the yard.

It was immediately clear to him that the woman was either unconscious or dead. She lay as she had fallen, sprawled flat on her back, unmoving. She was on the side walk, her head, fortunately seemed to have missed the corner of the step. However, he could see blood pooling slowly on the corroded cement beneath it.

Ignoring the searing pain in his lungs, he tugged off his gloves and reached for the carotid artery, searching for a pulse with shaking hands. Behind him he could hear shouting and cursing. He felt clumsy… time warp slow, as he tugged his iPhone from his pocket. Black spots swam before his eyes. The man was there now, kneeling beside the woman, swearing softly. Then he whispered, "Jesus, Aunt Leona!" and he too reached for her carotid artery.

"She's…alive," Chapman croaked past shards of glass in his throat.

The man looked at him then, and Chapman held out the phone, his whole arm trembling with the effort it took. "Call," he wheezed. "9-1-1…Call!"

The man grabbed the phone and Chapman's hands dropped to his knees as he rocked back and forth, like an asthma patient, fighting for air. The black dots continued to swirl and burst into golden halos. His inhaler was in the car. He would just have to wait this one out. He could hear the man giving directions to the dispatcher. "You'd better tell the EMTs to come prepared to treat two people, one is unconscious from a fall and the other with severe respiratory problems."

Chapman held up one hand in a stop motion and shook his head. Already the spots were diminishing and the pain receding. His mind was starting to work. He wondered who the man was. He'd called the woman Aunt Leona. A nephew then? Somewhere, in the house he guessed, a dog was barking frantically and from the sounds of it, throwing herself against the front door. More dogs were barking from the back of the man's truck.

Slowly, he raised his head and pulled his knees out from under him; sitting cross- legged on the ground. The man was looking at him, one hand tugging at the shock of brown hair that fell over his forehead, his cowboy hat pushed back. He looked like a quiz show contestant working on a puzzle. Finally, he nodded, satisfied about something and Chapman felt himself surprised. He knew what he looked like with his hat pulled low, his scarf pulled up and his dark glasses hiding most of his face, his claw-like hands exposed…a burglar or worse.

"Anything I can do to help?" The man asked softly, his tone friendly.

Chapman shook his head and held up one finger asking for another minute. The man seemed to understand. He nodded again and stood up. "That crazy dog is going to be throwing herself out the front room window next," he said. "I'd better let her out." He turned then and stepped on the gun. "What the fuck!" He looked at Chapman, his brows raised in question.

"Shot…fell." Chapman rasped out.

"Shot? Shot at you?"

"Not…sure."

Suddenly, the man turned and strode up the front walk calling, "I'm coming Pansy. Hold your shirt on, girl."

As he opened the screen door he said over his shoulder, "if you can, move away from Leona a bit so Pansy doesn't think you are the one that hurt her…it would be good."

Chapman nodded and turned so that he could crawl away to sit with his back against a small tree.

The dog came through the screen door like a black bullet. Her energy carried her down the walk, past where Leona lay, claws scrabbling on the cement walk and then back to the inert body where a sound, more moan than whine, rose in her throat as she assessed the situation and tried to make sense of it.

Immediately she went to Leona's head and smelled her breath. Then as Chapman watched, she lifted her head and looked directly at the man who'd let her out. It was plain to Chapman that she was asking him what had happened.

The man walked down the steps, smoothed down the old lady's blouse and then put a gentle hand on the dog's head. "I think she's going to be okay, old girl." His voice was gentle. "Help is on the way. She just hurt herself. That's all. Remember, she's a tough old bird."

The dog looked from his face back to her mistress, gave another moan and lay down, her chin on the woman's chest, perhaps reassuring herself with the slight rise and fall of breath or the feel of her heart beating.

After a minute, the man walked over to Chapman saying, "We don't dare move her. No way to tell what is or isn't broken. I can't see anything other than that blood under her head."

He paused. "I think she slipped on a patch of mud. There's mud on the sidewalk from where she's been weeding her flowers and there's mud on her left heel. We'll leave it to the experts to figure out. We're lucky it's a mild day. Could be snowing as well as not."

He leaned over held out his hand. "My name is Will Anderson, and if you are who I think you are, my wife, Millie, knows you."

Being able to lean back against the tree had helped Chapman's breathing. It was still ragged but the air was no longer whistling in and out. He registered with wonder that it would be the first time he had shaken anyone's hand since the accident. After a slight hesitation, his bony hand came up to clasp the beefy one. "Chapman...Lewis." Then he asked, "Anchors...Away?

Will dropped down on his haunches, facing Chapman and said simply, "Yep."

"Lucky...man."

"Yep."

In the distance they could hear the faint wail of a siren. Pansy, now crouched as close to Leona as she could get, lifted her head and matched the wail. Will didn't even try to shush her Chapman noticed and was glad.

Chapman could see Will studying him. "She shot at you, didn't she?"

Chapman shrugged. "I don't know...maybe at a hawk?" He lifted an arm and pointed to where the Red-tail sometimes perched in the old juniper tree.

Will thought for a moment. "Naw. She thought you were stalking her. I can see it all now. When Leona riles herself up...she's...not rational...but I like the hawk story. If that's what you want to tell the EMT's, that would be okay with me."

Chapman's jaw dropped. "A stalker? She thought I was a stalker?" His shoulders dropped. "It's the way I dress...scares people."

"Maybe." Will said. "She told my dad you came all the time."

Chapman could hear the curiosity in his voice. There was no anger or suspicion, just pure curiosity. He sighed. "I was coming today...wanted to ask her...to sell me that field..." He lifted his arm and bent his elbow, thumb out, pointing in the direction of the vacant field behind him.

The ambulance had turned onto Coon's Market Road and would be there in seconds. Will gave a bark of laughter and got to his feet.

"We can talk about it later," he said, nodding. "Now, I'd better go move my rig out of the ambulance's way." He lightly touched Chapman's shoulder. "You stay right where you are. I like it better when you can breathe. Besides, I need you to save your breath so you can tell me more about wanting to buy that crappy piece of land."

Chapman did as he was told. He couldn't have moved if he had wanted to. He heard the sound of more swearing and then the sound of a diesel roaring to life, mingled with the siren's wail. He closed his eyes and dropped his head. After the EMTs had helped the woman on the ground, he would have to ask Will to bring him a can of Ensure from his car.

Like a well-oiled machine, the aid car stopped with its back bumper near the gate and two people ejected themselves from the vehicle. In seconds, there was a folded gurney lying on the sidewalk and a woman with a stethoscope was listening for a heartbeat, feeling for pulse, lifting an eyelid to check pupils, gently feeling Leona's scalp, neck, torso, securing her neck with a C-collar, assessing and reporting her findings in a staccato voice to the man with a small handheld computer. Pansy stood back a little, watching and listening. Chapman recognized the drill. All the data would be at the emergency room and in the doctor's hands before they even arrived. She was in good hands. He heard the words, "probable severe concussion" and closed his eyes. *What if she had fallen and hit the corner of that step? Will said she thought I was stalking her. I could have been the cause of her death.*

Then Will was there. "Listen," he said, "Would a shot of oxygen help you?" Chapman opened his eyes. "No, but if you could go to my car and open the cooler behind the driver's seat…there's a can of Ensure…" Before he had finished, Will was striding away calling, "Be right back. Hang tight."

Chapman watched the EMT's slip a scoop stretcher around the still unconscious woman, carefully tightening the straps before doing a coordinated lift onto the backboard on the gurney. With practiced moves, they secured her neck and head with wedges and straps. Then, popping the legs of the gurney, causing it to rise, they wheeled her down the walk, Pansy close at their heels.

"No doggie, you'll have to stay," the man said.

Will snagged her collar as he came through the gate, Ensure in hand. "It's okay, Pansy. Good girl. It's okay." His voice was soothing and Pansy didn't struggle. "My friend says he doesn't need oxygen, just this. So you guys are good to go." He held the gate open with his hip, dog in one hand, Ensure in the other.

The two looked over to where Chapman sat, nodded and wheeled the gurney through.

Will closed the gate and turned the dog loose. She

remained like a statue beside him, watching intently while the EMTs loaded her mistress and shut the rear doors. Even when Will popped the top on the Ensure can and brought it to Chapman before returning to talk with the EMTs, she moved not a muscle.

It was all Chapman could do to lift his hand and take the can, tip it up and let it slide down his throat. He knew he would have to sit for a bit, his pants soaked from the damp grass, his bony spine feeling every nuance of the bark at his back, the day cooling around him. But, he noted, his breathing was back to normal and the pain was all but gone. The woman, whose name was Leona, seemed to be in good hands. The man named Will, who was Millie's husband, seemed to have the rest under control. So it really didn't matter how long he sat. He heard the emergency vehicle start and the siren come on. He watched while Pansy raised her head and howled mournfully towards the empty sky. He wondered what she was thinking. Chapman could see Will talking on his cell phone as he walked back and dropped down beside him.

"No, Dad. There's no sense rushing over there right now. I signed the papers and now I'm going to go in and see if I can find her purse. I suppose that's where her insurance and Medicare cards are, anyway. Do you have any idea where she keeps it?

"That's okay, Dad. Don't worry. I'll find it. Too bad Pansy can't talk." Will was silent, humor showed in his blue eyes. "He's swearing a blue streak." he mouthed at Chapman and then nodded his head.

"Dad, listen for a minute." He looked at his watch. "I'm not going to tell Millie yet. No sense bothering her at work. Let's not tell her until we know Aunt Leona's prognosis. If it would make you feel better, come on over with the kids and you take her purse to the hospital. I'll wait here. Maybe Mr. Lewis will wait too."

Will paused, listening. "That's fine Dad. Yep, I'll keep the kids. Don't drive too fast."

Will listened again. "Fine," he said. "I'll look there first. Bye Dad." He snapped his cell phone shut and looked at Chapman.

"You are about to meet the rest of Millie's family, except for my mom who lives in a rest home and two kids who are in college. Can you handle it?"

Chapman waved his hand. "I can. I'm happy to sit for a while longer. Go." Will nodded and strode towards the house, leaning down to scoop up the shotgun as he went. "Crazy old woman," Chapman heard him mutter as he snapped on the safety and cradled the gun under his arm.

When the screen door shut, Chapman closed his eyes and was instantly asleep. He slept through Jack's arrival with Abby and Matt. He slept through the 20-minute search of the house for the missing purse. He awoke only to the gentle hand that shook his shoulder. He blinked. The sun was dipping behind the mountains. The air was decidedly cool. A ring of concerned faces, including Pansy's, surrounded him.

"Time to wake up now, Chapman. Time to go." Will said softly.

Chapman smiled, instantly concerned that his ghoulish looks not frighten the children. "Ah, your family," he said.

"Yep, this is my dad, Jack, and my younger set of kids, Abby and Matt. Say hello to Mr. Lewis, kids. He's the reason you got to have hot lunch today."

"Hey, Mr. Lewis," said Abby, speaking for them both. "Thanks a lot. It was hamburgers and tater tots."

The connection wasn't immediately clear to Chapman, but he smiled at them and said, "You are most welcome."

Will's father leaned forward and stuck out his hand, "Jack Anderson," he said. "Will's been telling us what happened here. That old woman is going to give us all heart failure before she's done." He suddenly stopped himself. "Anyway, I'm pleased to meet you." And for the second time in two years, Chapman held out his claw of a hand and had it taken into a gentle handshake.

Without a word, both men walked behind Chapman. Each put a hand under his armpit and easily lifted him to his feet. Will said, "thanks to Abby and Matt we finally found the purse...in her breadbox. Dad's going to take it to the hospital now. I'm going to unhook the fertilizer spreader from the truck while the kids pen up the chickens. Then we'll follow you to where ever you want to go."

Just like that, Chapman thought. No questions, just the need seen and acted upon. "Thank you," he said simply. "I'm staying at Inn on the Rimrock. I'm probably fine, but when I run out of energy like this, it takes a can of Ensure and an hour or so of sleep before I really recover." He smiled at them, feeling a million years old and cold to the core. "I'll be in my car."

As he turned to go, he noticed that Jack had slipped a hand under his elbow. Somehow, Chapman was unsurprised. "I've never been escorted by a fellow carrying a purse before," he said in his gravelly voice.

Jack chuckled, but then said glumly, "Well, it isn't every day one of my oldest friends tries to shoot my sweet Millie's newest friend, either. This seems to be a day of firsts."

They slowly made their way towards the Z. Chapman thought to say, "I overheard Will say he wasn't going to mention this to Millie. Is she at work?"

"Yep, and we all thought we'd mosey on over to Anchors after we get some things done. Kinda surprise her, you know? How about joining us?"

Chapman opened the door of his car and sank inside. Right now a hot shower was all he wanted, but he nodded. "When you are ready to go, just call the Inn and ask for me. I'll meet you there." He paused and looked up. "Foods good there, you know."

For the second time, Jack chuckled. "Dad burned right I know! And it will be especially good tonight because that college educated chef running the place will know I'm there." He gave the roof of the car a little thump. "Will and the kids won't be long. I'm off to the hospital. You take care."

With that he turned and walked briskly to the dusty maroon Explorer parked by the mailbox. Before he opened the door, he turned and brandished the purse. Chapman gave the Z's melodic horn a friendly toot. Fatigued and cold as he was, something important was happening this day and he recognized it. He closed his eyes and leaned back his seat to rest and wait for Will.

Chapter Thirteen
Millie

Millie was in hyper-drive, her term for what happened when the early crowd all came in at once. It was not unusual; people often came in waves, the first rush mostly senior citizens looking forward to the early bird specials. Today there were two; one beef and one fish.

She knew it was bedlam in the kitchen. The last time she threw a glance at her young boss, Trenton, he'd wrapped a red bandana around his head as a sweat band and had two sauté pans going, one in each hand, barking orders at his equally sweat soaked assistant.

The phone rang as Millie headed for the kitchen with yet another 'beef tenderloin medallions with a red pepper aioli sauce' order to put in. "Anchors Away, How may I help you?"

Millie, this is Dad. You busy?"

"The early crowd came in a flock, Dad. What's up? Everything okay?"

It was unusual for Jack to call the restaurant and Millie's 'mom alert' went off in a flash.

"Everything's just fine, but we all decided to come in and have dinner after we get chores done. Save the big booth for us if you can. Be 'bout an hour I expect. Thanks honey. I won't keep you."

Millie found herself listening to the dial tone. She looked at the phone, shook her head, hung it up and quickly wrote Anderson in her reservation book. Then she grabbed a reserved sign and put it in her apron pocket before hurrying towards the kitchen, her mind back on the job at hand. She looked over where Carla, the other waitress, was delivering another two orders of salmon filet in a tarragon cream sauce, with wild rice and sautéed spring vegetables, the other early bird special. All Carla's tables looked content. She hustled to make certain hers were as well.

When the crowd thinned, her father-in-law's cryptic call started to worry her. *Who was "we"? Were some of his old cronies throwing him an early birthday party? It wouldn't be Will and the kids.* She'd fixed a tuna casserole and had it in the fridge all ready for them. *But why did Dad's voice sound like that? And what was that background noise? Was he down at the fire hall?* She decided to call home and double check on things just for peace of mind.

There was no answer. She pictured the phone in the kitchen ringing to an empty house and looked at her watch. After 6:00. They should have been there getting ready to eat. *Maybe they are coming here, but why?* She decided to try Will's cell. He picked right up. "Hi honey," he said cheerfully, "we're just a couple of miles out. Got our table ready?"

Millie leaned against the reservation table, holding the receiver in both hands, and laughed weakly. "Good grief, William, your dad about scared me to death with that mysterious phone call. What happened, you decide you couldn't stand one more casserole?"

There was a pause. "Never!" Will said firmly. "We've all had a big day and decided to come down and tell you about it."

"Well, that's a relief. See you in a bit."

"Oh, and Mil, put on another set-up besides the four of us."

With that Will disconnected and Millie was left listening to a dial tone for the second time in a little over an hour. "Those Anderson men," she muttered as she got five settings of tableware and belatedly pulled the 'reserved' sign out of her apron pocket and plunked it in the middle of the table of the big corner booth.

She made brisk work of setting the table, wondering who the extra place was for and decided it was Leona. Jack must have decided that she needed cheering up. She had probably finally made her appointment with the county. *Wonder how he talked her into it?*

She seated a party of four in Carla's section, started around the tables with a fresh pot of coffee when she heard the bell over the front door jingle. She looked up and watched her children elbow their way through the door and power walk towards her. "Uh-oh! I got trouble," she said to the couple she was serving, "They let the demons loose."

Something was definitely up. Millie held up her hand like a traffic cop. "Whoa, youngsters. What's up?"

"We can't tell you, Mom," Matt said, sliding under her hand and wrapping his arms around her waist while Millie lifted the coffee pot high. "Grandpa said we had to wait. We only get to tell you once, 'cause you're working."

"That's right, I am. Say hello to Mr. and Mrs. Barnard and then scoot on back to your table." She reached out and gave Abby's shoulder a squeeze. "It's the corner booth. I'll be over soon as I can."

Dutifully, they both said, "Hi, Mr. and Mrs. Barnard," in sing-song voices and then Abby immediately added, "Mom, we have a guest, but we can't tell you who."

Millie laughed. "Well, aren't you both tryin' to torture me tonight? Hope I can stand it."

"You've got to Mom, Dad and Grandpa gave us orders not to tell," Matt said seriously.

Millie made a shooing motion with her left hand. "Scoot" she said and turned back to her table. The older couple was grinning up at her. She shook her head in mock disgust. "Kids!" she said, mournfully as she poured their coffee.

"Your son is the spitting image of Jack with black curls," said Mabel Bernard. "He even talks a little like him."

Millie nodded. "You should hear the two of them watch the cooking channel together. It's a crack up," she said over her shoulder as she moved to the next table where Carla was taking dinner orders. She had her smile ready, but her mind going at warp speed.

"Say Carla, would you mind taking over tables four and five so I can spend a little extra time serving my family?" she asked as they walked away.

"Sure thing, Mil. I'll whistle if it gets to be too much."

"'Preciate it." She winked. "I'll put my big tippers at those tables, okay?"

Carla nodded. "'Preciate it."

Millie turned and nearly dropped to coffee pot when she saw her husband, her father-in-law...and Chapman Lewis making their way to the booth where the children, like squirming puppies, waited. Jack was stopping to talk to people along the way but the two other men went on to the booth and slid in. *Chapman Lewis?*

She put the coffee pot back on its element and automatically walked to the reservation desk for menus. *Well, the kids did say it was a surprise...and weren't they just about right?"*

The five at the table were looking up at her, expectant grins on their face. Even Chapman's thin lips were curved upward. "Well, I can hardly wait to hear how this all came to be," she said drolly as she handed the menus around. "Hello, Chapman, by the way."

"Hello, Millie," he said in his gravelly voice, "Nice to see you again."

She noted that Will and Jack had book-ended the children and was grateful at least for that. "Nice to see you too, Chapman. Now, you gonna tell me how you happened to meet practically all my family in one day?"

Chapman just smiled as Jack took over the conversation. "It's a good news, bad news story, Millie. You got to know this first: Leona's in the hospital with a bad concussion but she's going to be okay."

"Good grief! Leona? What in the world happened? When you said you were bringing a guest, I figured it would be her." Millie's words came out in a jumble, a good match for her mind.

Then everyone started talking at once and the words flowed over Millie, only bits and pieces sticking.

136

"You see, I stopped at Mrs. Larsen's to ask her if she would sell me that vacant field to the south of her house."

"I came over the hill and thought he was the stalker and tried to stop him with the truck."

"But Mrs. Larsen thought I was a stalker, too, and she had her shotgun, but she fell…"

"Chapman was calling 911 by the time I got there…Leona was unconscious."

"The emergency room doctor says she has a concussion for sure, but they are going to run a couple more tests in the morning. Right now, she's resting comfortably. I just left her."

"We have Pansy at our house."

"Dad says we can earn money by doing Aunt Leona's chores…"

Millie held up her hands in surrender. "Whoa! Now, just whoa. You dudes do realize you've all been talking at once, don't you?" She looked around at the five upturned faces. Now, just stop and let me see if I got it straight. She looked at Chapman, ignoring the rest. "Leona tried to shoot you because she thought you were a stalker…but all you were doing was coming to make her an offer on the vacant field…" Her eyes widened. "You mean that worthless pile of rocks beside her house? Is that the field you are talking about?"

It was hard to read Chapman's expression behind the dark glasses, but he nodded.

"Okay. Okay. I got that. So, she comes out, and instead of shooting you, she falls down and knocks herself out. But, Will is coming along with his fertilizer wagon and when he tops the hill he sees you, thinks you are the stalker too, and tries to run you over?"

Chapman gave another nod and Millie held up her hands before anyone could speak. "No more. I gotta digest just this much. I'll go get your waters. Anybody want something stronger? I sure do."

Without waiting for an answer, she turned on her heel and walked away, shaking her head as she went. *Poor Leona has got herself in a fix this time. Chapman didn't say it, but she was aiming to either scare him off or shoot him with that gun. That woman needs some serious help. I can't blame that poor man if he presses charges.* She looked around at her diners. Everyone seemed to be happily eating. The Bernards would soon be ready for their check, but she had just refilled their coffee so they wouldn't mind a little wait. She grabbed a tray, loaded it with five waters, two baskets of rolls, a small bowl filled with pats of butter, and hurried back.

"Okay, I got the first part, as whacko as it sounds," Millie said as she deftly passed around the water and bread. "What comes next?" This time she was looking at her husband.

"Well, after we got Leona off to the hospital, Dad came and left the kids with me. Then he went to the hospital with Leona's purse…after we found it in the bread box."

"Leona's purse?"

Jack took over. "We figured it would have her Medicare and Supplemental Insurance cards in it. The hospital would need those. Only Leona doesn't seem to have any insurance."

Millie stopped him with a look. "Not important right now, Dad. Tell me more about what the doctors said."

"Well, she's got a real bad concussion is what they said, but they didn't rule out other damage, so we don't know. It took her a long time to regain consciousness. I can tell you that 'bout scared me to death."

Millie let out a big sigh. "That poor, ornery old woman! I swear even though she makes some of it herself, she's had more trouble than anyone else I know. Hard not to feel sorry for her." She looked at Chapman evenly. "You pressin' charges against her?"

Chapman looked aghast. "Good heavens, no! I don't even know that she was shooting at me. There's often a Red-tailed Hawk in the juniper trees of the rocky field and I hear she has chickens."

Millie and Will locked eyes in perfect understanding.

"Well, that's good then. Why'd you want to buy that field? It's not good for a thing that I can think of."

"It's a long story, but the short version is that I wanted to use it for physical therapy. I want to use the rocks to make a wall around it."

"Hmmm." Millie said. "Okay, that's enough for this session. You guys decided yet?"

"Mac and cheese please," Abby and Matt said in unison.

"Make that three, please," said Chapman, "a double order for me. And look Millie." He lifted his fedora to show Millie his shaved head.

"Oh, my word," she gasped. "Why, Chapman, that looks real good."

"Thanks for the suggestion. No earring or tattoo though. Not yet, anyway."

139

She looked at her children looking at Chapman, not in a bad way, just in an interested way. She felt weepy all of the sudden.

"So," she said, sounding gruff instead. "What about you two? Sounds like you've had quite a day. I don't know what you had for lunch, Dad. But I do know Will's only working on a couple of PB&Js."

Jack said, "If I can still get it and it's not over-done, I'll have the salmon. If not that, then the tenderloin medallions with red pepper aioli will be fine. Gotta see if that boy knows his stuff."

Will said, "Steak, the biggest one you got."

Millie scribbled furiously. "Got it. I'm bringing a salad bowl and soups. You got privileges," she said and smiled at all of them. "Think of some more things to tell me when I come back. This is nearly entertaining if it weren't for poor Leona...and Abby and Matt, no more bread until after you get your dinners."

Her family didn't often drink, but after she ran the Visa for the Bernards she put in her family's dinner order and went to the bar for a bottle of red wine. Trenton had over-ruled the salmon in favor of the medallions. "Give them a bottle of the 14 Hands Merlot on the house. Tell Jack it's payment for his honest critique of my newest recipe."

More customers were coming in. She put them in Carla's section and went to get the soup and salads, adding the bottle of wine and three glasses to the tray.

"Looks like the next wave is starting, so I might not to get to hear much more of this story, but I got to ask...Chapman, have you given up on the idea of making that rock wall since Leona tried to take a shot at you?"

Chapman looked up and deliberately removed his glasses so Millie could read his expression. She thought he actually looked a little pale, but his voice was steady. "Millie, I'm having the time of my life, if you want to know the truth. If Mrs. Larsen won't let me lease or sell me her land, I'll find other."

"Well," said Millie, "If she doesn't, it's because that concussion knocked all the common sense out of her," she said meaningfully, looking at Jack and Will before turning on her heel and leaving them to their food.

Chapter Fourteen
Jack

Jack woke late, feeling groggy and somehow out of sorts. The events of the day before brought him fully awake. The possibilities of all that could have gone seriously wrong pinned him to the sheets. He lay like a corpse, looking up at the ceiling. What if Leona hadn't missed? What if Will had actually hit Chapman? Not with the truck, Will wouldn't have done that...but what if the fertilizer wagon had clipped that skeleton of a man as it fish-tailed? *Could have broken every bone in his body and would have undone all that reconstruction work he'd suffered through or maybe even killed him.* He closed his eyes and sent a prayer of gratitude that none of those things had happened.

Finally, Jack threw back the covers and headed for the bathroom. Something was nagging at him. He had to do something or take care of something, but he couldn't quite place what it was. He sat on the stool and thought about Leona. *Now hasn't that old woman landed herself in a mess? I suppose I'd better get through the shower and get down to the hospital, see if they've had to put a straightjacket on her yet.* He felt as sour as a green lemon.

He pulled up his sweatpants and shuffled for the kitchen. *I'm not doing a damned thing until I have my coffee, Leona or no Leona.* The feeling that he was forgetting

142

something important continued to trouble him. He ran his fingers through his wiry curls and rubbed his eyes, thinking hard, but drawing a blank. He set his kettle on to boil, poured beans into his electric grinder and kept his thumb in place on the button until the sound of the grinding beans hit just the right pitch. Generally, just the odor of the coarsely ground beans was enough to start him whistling, but not today. He went on making his coffee with twin frown lines puckering his forehead. *What in the hell is it that I am forgetting?* A stab of fear lodged deep in his gut. *Lord, please don't let my mind go bad like Betty's. Maybe if I stop trying so hard to remember...* His mind flipped to Chapman. He shook his head. He'd learned a bit of the story from Will over the phone, but it was still a shock to see him in person. Jack shook his head again. *Thank God I told Will about Leona's so-called stalker. Thank God I did! But, what if Will had hit him with that fertilizer wagon? It would have been my fault for believing that trash Leona was saying about a stalker and spreading it on to Will in the first place.*

Jack found himself gripping the edge of the counter with steel fingers. "I'd like to wring her scrawny, damned neck!" he muttered to his Melitta carafe, his mood changing from out of sorts to sour and on to just plain foul by the time he had water dripping over the ground beans.

Then he let out a huge breath, understanding at last that it was plain old-fashioned anger fueling his Scottish temper. It was Leona! He was so damned sick of her and what she'd become! He turned his back and leaned against the counter. He felt a hundred years old. He closed his eyes, thinking hard, trying to relax away the fist in his gut. *What I'm NOT going to do is go rushing down to that hospital. I'll just call and ask the floor nurse for an update. I'm just her friend, or trying to be. I'm not her husband!*

He looked at the kitchen clock. He really had slept late. It was past 8:30. *They probably haven't even given her the CT scan yet. If they have, the doc probably doesn't have the thing read yet. Besides, I go see her feeling like this, I'm liable to give that old bag a piece of my mind, and I don't have it to spare.*

He turned to pour a cup of coffee and paused to look at the sunlight haloing the trees. It was going to be another perfect day for farming. Only Will had broken one of the release levers on the fertilizer wagon when he'd jammed his truck brakes and sent the old thing jack-knifing. Poor Will! He'd be wasting part of the day in the shop.

Jack shook his head. It was time to get his mind on something else. Deliberately, he hitched up his sweat pants, picked up his coffee and went in his living room to watch the last of the local news. Then he'd have his breakfast and do his emails, same as usual. Besides, today was his day to go to the Homestead and visit Betty. *No good getting myself in a lather and then going to see her. No good at all.* Suddenly, he remembered what was nagging him. "Son-of-a-bitch!" he shouted into the quiet air of his living room. The appointment! He was to have taken Leona for her appointment with Deschutes County about her taxes! Then afterwards they were going to go see Betty. He sat in his chair, unsettled, his coffee untasted. *Now how'd I forget that and what do I do about it? Wonder if I can cancel it for her?* He frowned. *A man should be able to have his coffee before making telephone calls. A man should at least be able to do that!*

144

He took his first sip of coffee and sighed. The knot in his stomach was back and wouldn't be soothed, even with special fair trade Arabica beans. "By God, I'm just plain pissed at her, and that's an honest fact!" he admitted to the empty living room and punched the clicker for the television viciously. He could remember exactly the last time he had felt this amount of gut-wrenching anger. It was when the doctor had finally given him the straight scoop on his wife's hopeless diagnosis. He had realized the futility of the anger then, and he realized it now.

He drank his coffee lost in memory. Back when Betty had been diagnosed, he'd finally had to schedule a session with Pastor Mike to get a handle on his anger. It had seemed so damned unfair. God! How they had planned for their golden years! Betty had saved cruise brochures from Triple A for years. Alaska, the Panama Canal, the Caribbean and Hawaii were all on the list. It might, he decided, be time to schedule a visit with Mike again…for a little one-on-one about Leona.

Maybe time to sic him on that old bat, too, he thought as he grabbed the clicker and turned off the television. *Shoulda done it a long time ago. Shoulda done it before Pastor Mike gave up trying to visit her but was still asking about her. No, I should have jammed her hat on her sorry head and hustled her skinny butt to church. That's what I should have done. That's what Peter would have wanted.* He stood up, grabbed his cup and headed for the kitchen phone.

Jack hung up the phone after talking to Leona's floor nurse, his face black. He had been told that unless Leona signed a paper waiving confidentiality other than saying the patient was resting comfortably; staff wasn't allowed to share information. She did say he could come and visit as Leona was no longer stuck in a loop of asking what happened to her. He shook his head in disgust and grabbed the phone book again, this time to look up the number for the Deschutes County Courthouse.

At least the woman in the tax assessor's office was very pleasant and understanding when Jack told her why Leona had to cancel her appointment. After he hung up, he stared long and hard at the telephone and then, with a sigh, turned to churches in the yellow pages. *Betty probably knew that damned number by heart before her mind went,* he thought.

Billie Jo Mullins, the church secretary, answered on the second ring.

"Hello, Billie Jo. This is Jack Anderson. I'm looking for a little time with Pastor Mike sometime today or tomorrow."

"Well, hi there, Jack. I've got his book right here. How's Betty doing?

"She's about the same, Billie Jo. She still seems to know the grandkids a little bit, but with the rest of us, it's a day to day thing."

"I keep meaning to stop by and see her. I will one of these days. I just let other things get in the way and I know," she paused, embarrassment coloring her voice, "that's a lousy excuse."

"Ah, Billie Jo, that's real kind of you, but I don't know that it matters so much anymore. She doesn't seem unhappy now that her medications are working right. I don't believe time has meaning for her..." Jack's voice trailed off. *How many times have I said that?*

"Well, I will go Jack. I'll feel better about myself if I do. Now Pastor Mike has a slot at 3:00 tomorrow afternoon. Is that soon enough?"

Jack said. "That's just fine, thanks. By the way, Billie Jo, Leona Larsen's in the hospital. She fell and gave herself a concussion. Took her a long time to regain consciousness. So I guess they think it's pretty severe."

"Leona Larsen! Good grief! I haven't thought of her for a while. Pastor Mike felt real bad when she stopped coming to church after Peter died. She wouldn't even let him come and visit her at the farm. But, I'll be sure to tell him." She paused. "Bless her heart. What are the doctors saying?"

"It only happened yesterday afternoon so the results of whatever they are doing to her probably aren't even in yet. Besides, they won't tell me much unless I'm family, or I've got a paper with her signature saying she's waived confidentiality. When did they get so snooty about all of that in this town?"

Billie Jo chuckled and Jack remembered why he liked her so much. She always seemed so comfortable in her own skin. "Now, Jack, none of that! It makes you sound old and cranky. This is the 21st century so get on or get left behind."

Jack found himself chuckling back. Billie Jo was even older than he was and he felt like a scolded school boy. "Okay, ma'am, I'll be good. Thanks for your help."

"If I don't see you when you come tomorrow, I'll see you Sunday," she said meaningfully.

"Shoot, you'll see all of us, except Jenny and Jake. I guess you know they're both in Corvallis," he said proudly.

"We're celebrating my birthday by coming to church and then going to see Betty."

"Well, of course I know they're at OSU, Jack! How're they doing?"

"Real fine, real fine, the both of them."

"Well, happy birthday to you. What a wonderful way to celebrate!"

When Jack got off the phone, he felt marginally better and began to make himself oatmeal and toast. As he worked, he thought about his day. First thing he would do is stop by Anchors Away and pick up a piece of pie for Betty. Maybe he'd get a slice for Will and take it to him. He'd also take the time to critique Trenton's tenderloin medallions. It had gotten busy last night, and he hadn't had a chance to let him know that the red pepper aioli sauce with the spiced up almonds had been really tasty. *Seems like that kid has too much talent to stay in Central Oregon for long. Like our Jenny's languages I guess. She's got too much to offer a little puddle like this. But I sure don't see how her parents can let her go traipsing off to places like the Middle East. I've got to put a bug in God's ear about that one.*

As he shoveled in his oatmeal, Jack's mind wandered through his other worries. Like the fact that Will and Millie worked so hard and seemed tired all the time. Like Leona's debts...and what he was going to say to Pastor Mike. How could he explain his anger? Then there was his memory... seemed like it was getting worse.

The yowl of a cat interrupted his musings. *And like what in the holy hell am I supposed to do with a mama cat and a bunch of babies?* His granddaughter had made it clear that taking the lot to the pound was probably the worst idea he had ever had. He sighed, got up and carried his nearly empty oatmeal bowl to the door, opening it slowly. Sure enough, the yowl had been for him. There she sat, looking meaningfully at the empty cat food bowl.

"Well, hello Mama. You come up short on the mouse hunting last night? Or didn't you even go? Is that why I didn't hear those kittens mewing under my bed? Or have you moved them?" He kept his patter smooth as he stepped through the door and walked down the steps. Still, it was too much for her. She jumped to her feet and scooted under a bush. Jack put down his oatmeal bowl with its remaining bit cereal and milk at the edge of his sidewalk, not far from the bush and went back into the house. He poured himself another shot of coffee and grabbed a cup of cat food out of the bag next to the door.

The sun had warmed the steps and he wanted to sit and see if he could coax the cat to eat in front of him. *That would be a good thing to be able to show my Abby girl...and I can talk to Betty about it, too.*

After Jack poured the cat food into the metal bowl he had been using for that purpose, he retreated to the top step and began to sip his coffee. Sure enough, in a very short time, the cat reappeared, sat, looked at him long and hard and then got up and strolled casually to the oatmeal bowl, her tail jerking as she walked. He smiled to himself as she daintily began to lap at the milk, stopping every few seconds to check him out.

"That's okay, Mama. I'm just sitting here drinking my coffee and enjoying the sun. You want more than that bit of milk; you're going to have to come closer, aren't you?" His patter rolled off his tongue. She was such a pretty thing and her eyes were about the same green color as his and Matt's.

When she'd finished the milk, she sat and curled her tail around her front legs, a sure sign she'd stay unless he did something to spook her. "You'd better come on over here and try out that cat food I bought for you. You don't eat, you can't take care of your kittens," he crooned to her as he drank his coffee, finally feeling the knot in his stomach dissolve. The cat watched his every move.

With his cup empty, he stood to get on with his day. She again bolted under the bush as he suspected she would. He walked down the steps to get the oatmeal bowl, and then went inside to do his emails and take his shower.

Jack pulled into the parking lot of The Homestead at 11:30, hoping to encourage Betty to eat her lunch before feeding her the pie. The least he would be able to do is get her outside in her wheelchair. He buzzed in the code and opened the front door. As usual at this time of day, the lobby was nearly deserted with most of the residents in the dining room. Jack waved to the young man behind the front desk and headed straight for his wife's room. She might not listen, might not understand, but he had a whole lot to tell her.

Betty was sitting outside the door to her room, tied into her wheelchair with a soft sheet, listing slightly to one side. As usual, staff were getting the other residents ready to go to lunch. He heard a voice murmuring in the next room down the hall and poked his head in the door. "Howdy, ladies. I'm going to pick up Betty's lunch tray and take her out on the patio if that's okay with you."

Two women were helping another resident into her slippers and robe. Both were youngish, incredibly obese but had round, kind faces. They looked like sisters. "Sure, Jack," one of them said. "That would be fine. It's the perfect day for it."

He walked to the front of the wheelchair and leaned down to look into Betty's face. He knew better than to touch her right away. It sometimes frightened her. "Hello, Betty." He said tenderly. "Want to have your lunch on the patio this fine day?"

His wife of 45 years lifted her head slowly. Drool had escaped from the corner of her mouth. Confusion showed in her eyes. "Hello," she said pleasantly, without recognition. She sat up straighter and scanned his face again and again. He waited patiently. "Hello, Betty," he said again. "I brought you some cherry pie from Anchors Away. We're going to go get your lunch and then take you to the patio."

Jack watched her fingers tighten on the arms of the wheelchair. She looked even more confused. "Should I walk?" she finally asked.

Jack's back had begun to protest his bent over stance, but he persisted. "No. I don't think so. Let's go get your lunch." He set the small pie box in her lap and made certain her feet were on the foot rest and then grabbed the handles of the chair. *It's funny,* he thought as he pushed his wife. *I'm a stranger to her, but she's a stranger to me, too.* He looked at the shrunken, listing woman in front of him, her thick hair, no longer honey blonde from a bottle but a lank dishwater grey.

They had had a good time together, he decided as he wheeled Betty back to her room. The little patio off the dining room had been deserted, as it generally was. Sun had given warmth to several of the corner tables. He had been

151

able to get Betty to drink her cranberry juice, eat all of her Jell-O and most of whatever the entrée was; something with carrots, peas, hamburger and rice. She had also eaten the pie. "Cherry pie from Anchors Away, Betty. Remember all those pies you used to make?" Jack rambled on in a soft voice, rather like he'd done with the cat; just patter to help the time go by. But for an instant, he thought he'd made contact. She fixed her eyes on his. "Yes," she said, but nothing more and soon her eyes lost focus. He'd told her about Leona, about Chapman, about Abby insisting he keep the cat and kittens until homes could be found. She sat without agitation through it all. And as the sun left the patio, he was telling her about going to see Pastor Mike and, after that, maybe Leona. But by then she was asleep.

Chapter Fifteen
Will

Thanks to Chapman, it had taken Will less than two hours to replace the bent and cracked release mechanism on the fertilizer spreader. The man knew nothing about farm equipment but, puny as he was, he seemed to know his way around a computer and an acetylene torch. Now he was back at his motel room resting and Will, with his fertilizer spreader fixed, was just about to leave Leona's shop for the field. *Lucky for me she didn't sell Peter's welding set along with his truck and tractor,* he thought. *This could have taken most of the day.*

Chapman had come driving up just as Will was on his way to feed the hens. From the way he moved, Will thought he might be hurting a little from yesterday's exertions. But he said nothing and Chapman had accompanied him while he went to take care of the hens and water the sheep. He watched carefully as Will opened the door and filled the feeders. He'd listened carefully when Will explained the purpose of the oyster shells and showed him that the bag was nearly empty. Will checked the automatic waterer and did a quick sweep while Chapman continued to watch closely. After asking a question here and there, Chapman surprised Will right down to his socks.

"You know, Will, I could take this over for you, if you'd like. It seems pretty simple. You certainly are a lot busier than I am."

Will had thought a moment, lifting his cowboy hat and resettling it on his head. "What are you, Chapman, an angel in disguise?" He thought of all the chores to be gotten through. "That would be great...if you're sure you don't mind."

"I'm sure I don't mind. Now, show me the sheep."

Will opened the hoppers and dumped in four sacks of fertilizer pellets. He climbed on the tractor and slowly headed down Leona's pot-holed lane towards the leased pasture. *I've got to bring the grader blade over here and fix this before the ground gets too hard,* he thought.

One thing kept sticking in Will's mind. *How did Chapman know I needed help?* It was a little uncanny how he had showed up just after Will had driven over on his old Ford tractor. *I sure don't remember telling him...*and then Will remembered he'd been talking to his dad on his cell phone. Perhaps he'd overheard. *That guy sure doesn't miss much.*

He and Chapman had talked little when they were doing the repair. Either Chapman was on his computer figuring out how to do a part template while Will was straightening the part in Peter's old vice, or Chapman was under the hood showing Will how to run a bead that wouldn't interfere with the gears releasing. He'd found that on the computer too. Will took over and finished the job when Chapman told him simply that he was going to have to leave. Will could see for himself that what little color the

154

man had was gone, his skin almost transparent. He'd walked Chapman to his car, opened the door, reached into a cooler and handed his new friend an Ensure. "Just like yesterday," he had smiled and said, unscrewing the top.

"Thanks," Chapman had said, taking the small bottle in his thin fingers. He sank into the smooth tan leather seat and took a careful sip. He took another and looked up at Will's worried face. "Believe it or not, every day is a little better," he said. "I just have to finish this, rest here a bit and go on back to my room for a real nap. It's almost done. Go on, get it finished. You've got a field to fertilize."

So Will had left him and finished welding the new part in place. When he looked up, the car was gone.

As Will pulled into the field and jumped down to engage the lever mechanism so the fertilizer could churn out the bottom of the hoppers, he thought how easily he and Chapman had worked together. *Like Jake and I used to do. Get on the same wave length somehow and get the job done.*

Will could almost visualize the sort of man Chapman had been. He would have been a man's man and good with his hands. *Hell, for all I know, he might have been handsome.* One thing for sure, Millie had said he didn't talk about his past and that was just fine with Will.

"He's not going to tell us a thing, Will. I'd give him a little opening to talk about himself that first night and he would look right at me with those poor snake eyes, slitty behind those amber glasses, smile a sweet smile with those lip slivers…and before I knew it we were talking on a whole other subject. He's not talkin'! Period. The end. And you know, had it been us, we might not want to even think, much less talk about it."

It had been breakfast table conversation. Will grinned to himself and shifted the tractor into second gear. They'd sure surprised her last night. He'd give money to have a snap shot, *no, better a video like on YouTube, of the expression on her face when we all walked in.* He whistled through his teeth as the wagon started kicking out the fertilizer. *Smooth as silk. Mr. Lewis and I did a pretty good job fixing the old beast.*

He remembered what Chapman had said at Anchors Away. "I'm having the time of my life," he'd said. *The time of his life? He gets shot at, almost run into, has to run and torture those poor scared lungs, then sit and shiver on the damp ground. He uses up every bit of his energy and that's what he calls having the time of his life?* Will stepped on his clutch and down-shifted at the corner. He looked over his shoulder at the spray of pellets. *Well, hell. I'm having the time of my life spreading the equivalent of shit, so maybe we're both crazy and just don't know it.* He shifted up to second and started the return trip, so interested in his own thoughts that he didn't think about the iPod full of music in his shirt pocket.

At Anchors Away, Chapman had asked Will and Jack if they knew of other rocky properties in case Leona didn't want him messing on her land. The question had sent his dad sputtering. "I can't believe you still want to have anything to do with that crazy old woman! You bet there are other properties, all kinds of properties, right in this county and they're just full of rocks."

Chapman had picked up his wine glass. Millie had put in a small amount and he had not yet tasted it. There was a funny look on his face as he swirled the lovely ruby liquid in the bowl of the glass. "Well," he said, "here's the thing…" He looked around the table, including Abby and Matt in his gaze. "Sometimes, when I look in the mirror, I scare myself…and I'm not an elderly widow lady, living alone…"

Will found he was holding his breath as Chapman raised his glass. "Besides, something about that particular parcel speaks to me." He finally took a small sip and lowered the glass. "But, it never hurts to have a back-up plan." He said the last in a low whispery voice and Will could see he was again reaching the end of his stamina.

His dad had nodded then. "Well, you can count on us Andersons to help you look for other parcels should it come to that. But Leona sure does need the money. For old time's sake, I have to hope you two can work it out before August."

They'd left the restaurant soon after. Jack had insisted on paying and Chapman had let him, choosing not to play king of the mountain. Will admired him for that. *In fact, there's a lot to admire about the man.* He thought about the upcoming birthday party and wondered if they should invite him. *He's met the rest of us, might as well meet Jenny and Jake. No need for him to go to church and to see Mom…unless he wanted to.*

As he looked behind him, the spreader was working fine and nearly half the field was done. Over his head small puffy clouds sailed towards the west. A breeze had come up. He was glad he had on his jean jacket. *When I'm done with this field, I'll give Millie a call and ask her what she thinks about the party deal.* He patted his pocket and realized he'd

157

once again forgotten his cell phone. He frowned. He'd forgotten it as many times as he had remembered it, but today, it gave him a sense of unease. *I'm going to get one of those cases that can hook on my belt and just leave it there. That way when I put on my pants, I'll remember it. I'm putting people out, Dad included, to have to come and find me should they want to talk about something.*

Will started thinking about his dad's voice when he talked about Leona at the restaurant. Will had the sense of something more than disgust at her behavior in his tone. Though he tried to control it in front of the kids, it was pretty clear to Will that his infrequent but famous temper was smoldering like banked coals.

As the tractor chugged along, Will's unease mounted, remembering his dad's quick, early morning call. *He seemed pretty frustrated, both with her, the hospital's policies and with himself. I hope he doesn't do anything he'll regret.*

Suddenly, he shifted up into third gear and began barreling down the field, the spreader bumping and bucking behind the tractor, still faithfully spewing fertilizer despite the speed. Will held the flat wheel with both hands and hoped everything would hold together and that there weren't any hidden holes or ditches.

He finished the field in record time, jumped off and reset the spreading mechanism to neutral, jumped back on the tractor and sped up the lane, ignoring the back jolting bumps as he headed for Leona's house. He knew Leona had a list of numbers by her kitchen phone and that her house key was in its hiding hole by the back porch. *Thank you Lord for old ladies who don't have speed dial and who think cell phones give you cancer* he thought. *Otherwise, I'd be up a creek without a paddle because I don't remember anyone's numbers any more.*

He stopped the tractor in the lane, opened Leona's yard gate and trotted towards her back door. He grabbed the hidden key and let himself into the mudroom.

The house felt very empty as he walked into the kitchen, no Leona and no Pansy to greet him. His eyes scanned the list as his hand picked up the receiver. His Dad's numbers were there, both the cell and the landline. He stabbed in the numbers for the house. When the answering machine came on he hung up and dialed the cell phone. When his dad answered, Will sagged against the kitchen counter with relief. "Why, howdy, son. I was just thinking about you. Got a piece of cherry pie in the Explorer and was wondering if I had time to bring it to you before my appointment with Pastor Mike."

Will closed his eyes and shook his head at his own foolishness. His dad was obviously fine. He looked at his watch. 2:00 o'clock. His stomach growled. He'd not only forgotten his phone, but his lunch. The only thing he had remembered was his iPod. *Now that has to say something about my character, doesn't it?* He thought sourly to himself.

"Listen, Dad. I'm just finishing up here at Leona's and am heading home for lunch. That pie sounds real good, but I'm going to need a little more than that. Want to meet me there?"

"Sure. In fact, I'll stop and pick you up a Subway sandwich. Want the usual?

"Hey, that would be great. Yep, the usual. Thanks a lot. How's Mom?"

"Well, it wasn't a bad day at all. She ate real good and my conversation was so interesting that I put her straight to sleep, after." Jack chuckled at himself. "See you at home."

Will hung up the phone and got a glass from the cupboard. He realized his mouth was cotton dry. He drank two glasses full of water standing at Leona's sink, looking out at the field the Larsen's had called "The Lord's Bit" ever since he could remember. Now, he was starting to think of it as Chapman's field. *I sure hope they can work things out. It would be a solution to Aunt Leona's immediate problems with Deschutes County and if Chapman wants to stack rocks to get well...these are great rocks to stack.*

Jack was waiting for Will, sitting on the wide front porch of the big, two-story ranch house with his feet on the rail. Besides the Italian sausage hoagie and pie, there were potato chips and a large coke for Will and a packet of cookies for Jack. "You know, Dad, if you weren't my father, and I weren't already married, I'd ask you to marry me."

Jack cackled. "Your mama always believed the way to a man's heart was through his stomach. And a 2:00 o'clock lunch can do wonders for a man's appetite. You gonna wash those hands?"

Will looked down, grinned at his still greasy mitts and headed for the door. "If I have to, but I'm so hungry I could eat a horse. Be right back."

He returned with his cell phone and a glass of milk for his dad. Neither man said much; Jack enjoying watching his hungry son tuck into his sandwich. Will wolfed down his spicy hoagie, silently wondering what had caused him to push the panic button like he had and vowing to be better prepared in the future. *Looking in my rear view mirror at it, the whole thing didn't make a lick of sense.*

As he ate the last of the cherry pie, Will said, "I heard you say you had a visit with Pastor Mike coming up. Anything wrong?"

"Ah, well. I got up in an awful foul mood and finally got it figured out that I'm madder than hops at Leona. So, I got the idea to go see if he could straighten out my thinking before my guilt kills me."

Will looked at his dad and shook his head in wonder. "You know dad, I could tell you were pretty riled last night, but here I am, nearly 40 years old, and you are still surprising me. Good for you!"

Jack smiled. "I'll tell you what. You know you've made the right decision when your gut unsnarls itself…besides, talking with Pastor Mike really helped after your mom got so bad."

Will nodded, remembering. "I should have gone too, I suppose."

His dad looked at him but only said, "Well, I'm on my way. Don't want to keep him waiting. Remember, the kids are coming here on the bus today. I think Millie will be here but I don't remember for sure. I got to go see Leona after I see Pastor Mike."

Will stood, gathering up their trash. "You get an update on her condition?"

Jack glared. "That's another thing that fried my butt. I got to get a special clearance with her signature before they'll tell me squat. When I called for my appointment, Billie Jo told me I was being old and cranky. Imagine that!" he said with a twinkle in his eye. He turned to go down the

161

steps, waving a hand over his shoulder. "Bye, son. Kiss that pretty wife of yours when she gets home."

"I sure will Dad. Thanks for the lunch. Remember, tomorrow is Friday so I'm on to go see Mom."

"I'm going to have to get one of those fancy blueberry things to keep track of this family, we're hit and miss and fly by night." Jack grumbled.

"It's a Blackberry, Dad. Blackberry."

Chapter Sixteen
Leona

Leona lazily floated towards consciousness to sounds she couldn't identify, odd sounds. A clamping of fear squeezed her heart until she was afraid to open her eyes. These were the sounds she couldn't identify; a rhythmic whooshing noise, the quiet murmur of voices, soft clinking sounds. It was all strange and frightening. Fuzzily, she wondered if she were in the middle of yet another bad dream. Something bumped her bed. Her mind jolted towards the light and then she felt the pain and moaned.

"Finally! She's almost with us," a gentle voice said. "Come on, Mrs. Larsen, open your eyes, dear."

She felt a warm hand cover her cold one. "You can do it. Come back to us." The hand gave hers a squeeze. "Are you in pain, Mrs. Larsen?"

Who is that calling my name? Leona tried to open her eyes. Black dots seemed to be in the way of seeing anything clearly. She felt the pain more acutely and moaned again.

"There! Her eye lids fluttered. She's almost with us."

The warm hand lifted from hers and stroked her hair. "Come on, Mrs. Larsen, open your eyes, dear. You've had an accident, but you are okay now. You're in the hospital. Open your eyes."

Slowly, consciousness returned. She tried blinking away the black dots. When she opened her eyes, the lighting was muted. She tried to turn her head and look for the person who was speaking but it hurt too much.

"It's okay, Mrs. Larsen. Don't try to turn your head. You gave yourself a good crack when you fell and the doctor had to clean some dirt out of the wound and patch you up. Wait, I'll move where you can see me."

The hand left her head. She heard the sound of a motor and the bed slowly elevated. She could vaguely see shapes at the foot of her bed through the receding black dots.

"Here we are, Mrs. Larsen. I'm Sandy and this is Julie. We're your nurses. Are you in pain?"

Leona considered. She licked her lips and made a smacking sound. Immediately, Sandy was there with a moistened swab which she expertly guided around the inside of Leona's mouth.

"Feels like cotton in there, doesn't it. This will help. And when you are really awake you can have some sips of water."

Leona couldn't seem to take it in. She did hurt…everywhere! Slowly her vision cleared. She licked her lips again and closed her eyes.

"Oh no, Mrs. Larsen, no you don't. Not back to sleep. Not yet. Stay with us. You need to tell us how you are feeling. Can you say something…tell us. Try, Mrs. Larsen."

She moved her mouth and whispered, "pain everywhere."

The nurse called Sandy nodded. "We can fix that for you. You are already on medication through your drip, but we can beef it up." She said something to the woman next to her who nodded and left.

Sandy returned her attention to Leona. "You've had an awful concussion so I'm sure your head aches. Do you hurt other places too?"

Leona tried to nod, but it felt as though her aching head were held in a vise. She licked her lips again, wondering how she was going to be able to form the words to tell this woman about the pain that radiated down her spine. But Sandy read her mind and was there with the moistening swab.

"You took a nasty fall and evidently hit your head real hard," she repeated. "But you'll be good as new in time."

Leona's eyes focused and reality came ferociously back. She remembered grabbing the shotgun, getting herself out the door and down the steps, lifting the gun towards the thug coming towards her…and nothing after that.

She moved her tongue around in her mouth. It felt rough and thick. "Is he dead?" she tried to ask.

Sandy smiled and patted her hand. "No, Mrs. Larsen, you aren't dead. You are just fully waking up after hitting your head. Now, here's Julie with your pill and some water. As soon as you take it, we'll let you go back to sleep for two or three hours. The doctor will be in to see you later this evening, so we'll have to wake you then, too."

Obediently, like a baby bird, Leona opened her mouth for the straw and the pill. She managed several long sips after the pill went down and the relief to her dry mouth and throat were immediate. Sandy then spread some sort of ointment on her cracked lips. "Here you go. Next time you wake up, you are going to feel much better, I promise."

As Leona sank away from the light her last conscious thought was, *I wonder where the cops are.* The black into which she tumbled matched the darkness in her heart.

When Leona next woke, someone was calling her name and patting her hand. "Time to wake up, Mrs. Larsen, you have a visitor."

Again, her mouth was so bone dry she couldn't even lick her lips. Tentatively, she tried to move her arms and legs. The pain was still there, but dulled and no more than she was used to. She moaned and opened her eyes. The nurse was there, leaning over her with the straw poised. "Let's wet your whistle so you can talk. You have a visitor. He's been worried about you." The nurse seemed to be peering closely into Leona's eyes as she spoke.

This time, Leona drained nearly half the cup though it made a dull pounding begin in her head again. She closed her eyes with a sigh. *You'd think they'd have sense enough not to give a thirsty person, one that's cracked their head, ice water,* she thought. "People shouldn't keep waking me up," she said frostily, though even to her ears it came out slurred. "How can a body get better if they don't get their sleep?" This time she sounded better.

She heard a soft masculine chuckle. Then the nurse said, "I'll leave her to you, Pastor. Try to keep her awake for a few minutes, if you can. We have to wake her every 2-3 hours with a grade three concussion like hers." She patted Leona's hand one more time and then left.

Leona heard a chair being scooted forward and felt a giant paw enfold her bony fingers. "Well, well, Leona, this has to seriously piss you off."

Leona's eyes snapped open. "What a way to talk!" She ignored the pain and turned her head.

"Careful, Leona, they've got you on a little donut thing to protect the sutures on the back of your head."

She ignored him. They looked at each other in the dim light. "Haven't seen you for a while, Pastor Mike." She said and felt the smarting of tears behind her eyes.

"We've all missed you," he said simply.

She snorted as best she could. "Right! Everybody misses that cranky old biddy, Leona Larsen, just about as much as they miss a case of piles!"

He grinned at her and said, "All sour and no sweet, that's how you see yourself, eh?"

"That's how I see my life! That IS my life and now, if I remember rightly, I've probably killed that stalker. You can't miss with a shotgun at that range! When do the cops come?"

There was a deep sigh and the scoot of chair legs. The pastor stood and leaned over her. His hazel eyes drilled hers. "You didn't kill anyone, Leona. You can rest easy on that. As far as anyone knows, you were shooting at a hawk that was after your hens."

Leona was quiet for a long time. Mike Carlsson put the straw to her lips. "Drink," he said. She drank.

"Well, I would guess he got away clean then."

"What do you mean?" The pastor asked in a deceptively mild tone.

"Well, if I didn't at least wing him, I would imagine he got away. He can come back any time…unless I scared him good."

She couldn't see the frown on the pastor's face. "Well…you didn't wing him, but you did scare him. However, he came to your rescue after you fell anyway." Pastor Mike sighed quietly to himself. Leona's eyes had fallen to half-mast. "I'll fill you in on more details later, I can see even this much talk has worn you out," he said.

It was a fact. All of the sudden it felt to Leona as though a drain had opened and all her sand had run out.

He sighed again and looked heavenward, as if asking for guidance or patience. "If you'd like, I'll say a little prayer before I leave."

Leona nodded and drifted off to the rumble of the Pastor's prayer of thanks for her survival, the skill and efficiency of the hospital staff and the kindness of friends. A picture of Jack came to her mind. *Wonder if Jack's been here* was her last thought.

When Leona next woke, it was to the irritatingly cheerful voice of someone announcing her dinner and the motorized bed being further cranked up.

"Time to wake up, Mrs. Larsen. We have a little dinner all ready for you."

She opened her eyes, blinking, trying to focus. "Take it away," she croaked.

"Oh, I don't think the doctor would like that. Look! Here's a chocolate milkshake for your throat. Let's start with that."

It was a girl, a teenager, Leona decided. She was holding a plastic glass with a bendable straw towards her. Her nails were long and painted pink. They looked professionally done. Her first thought was, *How do you suppose a youngster like that can afford a fancy manicure?* But she said nothing and put her lips around the straw, giving it a good pull. To her surprise the shake tasted good.

The girl gave a satisfied sigh. "There, that's better. You can't get your strength back unless you eat. Can you hold this for yourself now, Mrs. Larsen?"

"Course I can." Leona said sourly and sat forward to grab the cup from the candy striper's hand.

The sudden jerking movement caused her to gasp in pain. "My back. It's not my head. It's…my back!" She sucked air in through her clenched teeth as a spasm tore down her spine. Already the girl had hit the call button.

"Lean back and try to relax. Please, Mrs. Larsen. A nurse is coming."

Leona did as she was told, trying desperately to let the mattress support her entirely. It worked, but marginally. She looked at her tray. On it was a small plastic container holding three pills. "What are those pills?" She rasped out.

"Yours. But you are to eat first, the nurse said."

"Give me the damned things," she snapped.

Lying perfectly still, she allowed the girl, whose name tag said, "Clara" to help her take the pills, hoping desperately that one was for pain.

"I guess it's okay, because you are at least drinking your shake." Clara said, looking at Leona doubtfully.

A nurse, not Sandy or Julie, rushed in. "What's happened?"

169

The vice grip on her spine had loosened its hold, not from the pill Leona suspected, but because she was lying perfectly still. She didn't intend to test her theory.

"I think she had a back spasm." Clara said.

Leona nodded carefully.

"Are you still in pain?"

"I can handle it, long as I don't move." Leona said grimly.

"Hmm, so it's not your concussion. Well, the doctor is just down the hall and will be here in just a sec," she said briskly. "We'll let him decide what to do for you, because you ARE going to have to move, if only for the bed pan."

Leona's face soured like she smelled something a week dead. "I'm not using a bed pan," she snapped but she lay perfectly still while she said it.

The new nurse seemed not to have heard her. She looked at the tray. "How would you like to try some of the Jell-O or the mashed potatoes?" she asked pleasantly.

Leona looked at her realizing that the night shift must have come on. She was somewhere in her late 50's or early 60's and packing about 30 pounds she didn't need. Her hair was frosted and ratted into submission. *Probably been wearing it like that since high school,* Leona thought. "No, thank you, I do not care for more," she said with false pleasantry, enunciating each word distinctly.

Larry Brown, M.D., walked into the room just in time to hear the exchange. He lifted his eyebrows. "Hello, Leona. Sounds like you are feeling more like your old self," he said as he slipped a pen light out of his pocket and bent over her to closely examine her eyes. "Your pupils are looking better." He stepped back.

Leona stared daggers at him. "My old self could move without having muscle spasms. This self can't!" she finally said.

The doctor nodded at Clara. "Thanks for your help, Clara. Better get on with your deliveries."

Dr. Brown held a chart in his hands. "Why do I think you have stopped taking your Celebrex, Leona?"

"Because I can't afford Medicare part D. If I can't afford that, how can I afford a prescription that costs eighty bucks?

He looked at her oddly. "Is that really true, Leona?"

She started not to answer and thought better of it. "Yep. The county is going to auction off my place on the courthouse steps for back taxes. I am flat broke. Peter's illness took everything."

Dr. Brown sighed deeply. "I'm terribly sorry to hear it Leona, but I have to give you this news straight," he said. "The concussion is the lesser of your problems. It was severe. But, because you were unconscious for so long…much longer than normal…when you were admitted you were given a CT scan. It found bone spurs, big bone spurs, on L-5 and L-6. They must have really taken off after you stopped taking your medicine. When you fell, those spurs rubbed against some nerves. That's what is causing the pain and the back spasms. Ultimately, it is going to take about 6 months for the pain to go away. At that time, when the swelling is down, we'll get a surgeon to operate and scrape the vertebrae clean with a laser."

He talks like a man with a lot of patients to see before he gets to go home to dinner, Leona thought.

Larry Brown had been both their family doctor and the Anderson's family doctor for years. She said, "Listen, Larry…now I'm going to give it to you straight." She paused and looked him in the eye. "I don't have any money to pay for any of this other than what Medicare, part A will cover. So, just give me a shot or something so I don't get the spasms. I've been living with a bad back for a long time."

"But why aren't you on Medicaid then?"

She snorted. "I own the farm, except for back taxes and interest."

He shook his head sadly, recognizing the truth. "Okay. Okay. Let's deal with the here and now. I don't know if you realize it yet, but you are on a catheter. We were going to take it out, but now we won't. You are also on a drip. It's that needle taped to your arm. There's a cocktail of things in it to help the swelling in your brain go down and to reduce the pain in your head and back. We're going to increase it, and that should aid in healing the soft tissue torn by the bone spurs. Once we get you out of pain, then we'll deal with this other stuff. Right now, you're not to worry about it, doctor's orders!"

Leona knew her starch was gone. She felt flat as road kill. "Bring on the drugs, Doc…and go home to your wife," she whispered hoarsely. "You look tired."

He tried for a smile. "I will and I am. Good night, Leona. I'll see you in the morning."

After the doctor left, Leona closed her eyes, but sleep did not come. It had felt good to tell the doctor her exact circumstance and that surprised her. It felt as though she had been talking about someone else's troubles. *Must be the drugs,* she decided. She seemed to recall that Pastor Mike had been in. She thought hard trying to remember what he had said. It came to her that he said she had fallen and that the fall had caused her to miss the man she was shooting at. She felt her thoughts begin to ramble. *Wonder how Pastor Mike knew I was here? Jack or Will must have told him. Where IS Jack? Why hasn't he come? Maybe he was here when I was sleeping. Pansy...who is taking care of Pansy? I hope someone is checking on the sheep's water and feeding the hens...Did Pastor Mike say the stalker had come to my rescue? That can't be right.* It was her last thought before she again drifted off to sleep.

Chapter Seventeen
Chapman

Only the faint gray light of early dawn seeped around Chapman's window curtains when his eyes blinked dryly open. Automatically he rolled to his side and reached for his eye drops, momentarily amazed when he saw the arm holding the bottle was still encased in the blue cotton, oxford shirt he worn to dinner the night before.

He lay back, carefully administering two drops of the steroidal antibiotic, antibacterial, lubricant into each eye. He blinked rapidly as he recapped the bottle, set it on the night stand and rolled back onto his pillow with a deep sigh. His mouth felt gritty, and he remembered he hadn't even brushed his teeth, just went to bed. *You've fallen to a new low, Chapman Lewis!"* he scolded himself. But he knew he didn't really mean it. Instead, he somehow felt vaguely pleased.

It had been quite a day. He'd come home from Anchor's Away, used his eye drops, slipped off his loafers and crawled under his duvet and now it was morning. He didn't even remember dreaming. He doubted he'd even moved much. He started his breathing exercises, then rested his hand over his chest in the region of his lungs and rubbed slowly as he breathed. They hadn't let him down. He'd had enough air…just enough…to do what needed to be done. Gratitude washed over him.

Jason's long hoot of laughter came over the smart phone like a ring tone. "I'll see what can be done. Somebody in his office will get back to you."

"That would be perfect, Jason. Thank you very much."

"You are entirely welcome…hey, Chapman, surprise me like this more often."

"It might just happen, Jason. You never know. Have a good meeting downtown."

There was a pause on the other end instead of a disconnect tone, and Chapman suspected Jason was waiting for him to ask about his family.

"Take good care, Chapman," the attorney finally said. "And good luck."

Chapman was whistling when he went out the door to find some breakfast at Anchor's Away. Biscuits and gravy with eggs on top sounded just right. His stomach growled.

From Anchors Away, Chapman headed for The Big R. The big red ranch supply building was right on Highway 97 where Will said it would be. The parking lot was already filled with trucks, SUVs and cars like Subarus and Hondas with either snow or studded tires…all speaking to the harsh winters, he assumed.

Chapman had left off his fedora and scarf but a clerk barely gave him a second glance, directing him past the check stands to a side room where he found a helpful man with a ruddy complexion and cheerful smile to direct him to the oyster shells. "I've got hens myself," the man, whose red vest name tag said 'Vess', volunteered. "It's a good sound; that of a hen proud of laying an egg, isn't it?"

"Actually," Chapman said, "It's for the hens I'm taking care of. I haven't yet heard that sound. But now that you've mentioned it, I'll look forward to it."

The man nodded. "You can't help but recognize it as bragging, once you hear it...just like, once you hear them calling each other when they've found something to eat on the ground...well, it's just distinctive, that all I can say. Sometimes I cast a handful of grain in their chicken yard, just to give them something to do." He gestured to the bag. "Bring your rig around after you pay for this, and I'll load it for you."

As Chapman walked back towards the row of check stands he realized that both employees seemed to accept his appearance without undue pity or alarm. He smiled to himself. *John Q. Public, that's me.*

The elusive sense of well-being was back. On the way to the counter, he stopped in front of a rack of pet supplies. He thought of Pansy and by association, Tuffy and Digger. He picked up a twisted rope meant to be a toy for tug-of-war. Then he spotted an odd shaped oval made of tough rubber. 'For hours of enjoyment add peanut butter' the directions said. He shrugged to himself and picked up three. *Why not, I have to go to the grocery store today. I might as well get some peanut butter.*

On the way out of the store, Chapman took a quick look at wheel barrows, tape measures, chalk lines, shovels and promised himself he would be back.

As Chapman backed the blue Nissan beneath the sign that said 'Pick Up Here,' the man named Vess came out carrying the bag of oyster shells over his shoulder as if it were a down-filled pillow. *One day, after I move a few tons of rock, that is going to be me!* He depressed the button that popped the deck lid.

After Vess had deposited the crushed shells he came around to the car window and leaned down. "She's a beaut. I want one," he said, his eyes scanning the interior of the cockpit.

"Thank you, it's been a great car, but what I need is a truck," Chapman surprised himself by saying.

The man sighed. "Too bad," he said and gave the roof a light thump.

No, Chapman thought as he drove away. *Not too bad. This car has served its purpose. I might find the time to go kick a few tires today and then I might ask Will what he thinks.* He remembered both Will and Jack drove a Ford, but in the parking lot, he'd seen just about every make of truck known to the West.

Instead of parking under the cottonwood tree, Chapman parked in the generous parking space in front of Leona's house. He could have used the lane on the north side of the property that led to the barn, but for some reason he felt odd about it. He wrestled the bag of oyster shells to his shoulder, disgusted by the weakness of his muscles, and walked through the front gate stopping a moment to look at the spot where Leona had fallen. He could see the dabs of dried mud around the pile of dying plants on a piece of plastic. He could picture her on her knees weeding, tossing clumps at the plastic and missing with a few of them. He shook his head and walked along the side of the house, stopping again to look at the rocky field and then the distant mountains before heading down the slope towards the

181

henhouse. *It's really peaceful here. To think of losing it must be breaking her heart.*

The hens were in the yard when he got there, scratching and clucking in the sunshine. Will had been right. Being locked in at night wasn't essential. He carefully put down the oyster shells next to the henhouse door and leaned against the wall, feeling his breathing ease and his heart rate settle. He walked up the step, opened the door and looked in. Sun slanted through the one small window, turning the interior golden. Will had told him Leona kept things tidy and he was clearly right. The broom was standing in the corner behind three lidded buckets carefully labeled in black paint; one said "mash", one said "corn" and the third said, "oyster shells." He picked up the bag and headed inside. The bag was only 25 pounds and though he didn't heft it easily, it was definitely not beyond his strength. *I'll wager most of those smaller lava rocks in the field weigh no more than this.* His enthusiasm for his project ramped up a notch.

Inside the henhouse, Chapman paused and took in more details. The simple structure seemed efficiently designed. He saw what Will had called roosts were made of 2X4s, a comfortable place for the hens to sleep. He looked at the neat row of straw-filled nesting boxes and saw a hen. She looked at him with beady eyes, but didn't move as he lifted the lid on the bucket for the oyster shells, opened the bag and dumped it in. He put more mash and corn in the feeder, then swept the floor and roosts just as Will had instructed. He checked the hens' water and saw there was plenty left. It only took minutes to complete the chores and on a whim, remembering what Vess at Big R had said, took a small handful of the corn with him as he left the snug house.

The hens in the yard were talking softly to each other and scratching here and there in the dirt. He let himself in the gate, closed it carefully, and cast the grain in a wide arc. Immediately the hens scrambled after it, clucking happily as their heads bobbed, to snatch up each unexpected treat. He stood and watched as they carefully scanned the ground, tipping their heads to look with one round eye at a time, running to a new spot if another hen made a certain sound. He found himself grinning. *It's not like they don't have the same food in their trough inside. Wonder what makes this so special?*

Chapman jumped when his cell phone rang. So few people knew his number: his doctors, his lawyer and his accountant...and as of last night, Jack and Will.

"Chapman here."

"Good morning Chapman, it's Will. Where are you?"

"Hi Will. Actually, I'm standing in Leona's chicken yard watching the hens. What's up?"

"Well, since I guess we didn't manage to kill you off last night, Millie and I wondered if you'd like to come to Jack's birthday party on Sunday."

Chapman found himself with a lump in his throat the size of Rhode Island.

"I'd like that very much," he croaked, his husky voice even deeper. "Does Jack know or is it a surprise?"

He heard Will laugh. "So far, by some miracle, he hasn't a clue about the actual party. Jenny and Jake are driving over from college this afternoon and then are going, unannounced, to his house to pick him up for the high school basketball finals tonight. We're all hoping it doesn't give him a heart attack. I'd invite you to the game too...but those bleachers are so danged uncomfortable I didn't think I'd be doing you any favors. Anyway, Sunday is the big day. What he thinks we're doing is going to church and then going to see Mom. So come to the ranch about two o'clock. Millie's having Trenton down at Anchors do up a special recipe."

"Two o'clock would be fine. I'll get the address from Millie at dinner tonight…or will she be at the game?"

"Don't I wish! Don't we both wish! But Friday night's a big night at Anchors so there is no rest for the weary." Chapman could hear a note of resignation behind the joking voice.

"Anyway, we'll see you at the ranch and you can meet the rest of the family. Right now I'm on my way to see Mom. It's my day."

Chapman nodded into the phone. Will had mentioned their rotation schedule to visit his mom the previous night. "Good for you. I'm on my way to meet some sheep. Anything else you want me to do while I'm here?"

"Nope…other than the oyster shells. I'll be over there later today to get the irrigation system going on the field I fertilized. Be nice if it rained, but it's not in the forecast. By the way, the lame ewe is Iris and the blind one is Rose…just in case you want to know."

"Iris and Rose…and Pansy…Leona must like flowers."

Will laughed. "That she does. Her place used to be a showcase when Uncle Pete was still alive."

"Which reminds me, Will, how is Leona?"

"Well, we still don't know much. Dad sicced our pastor on her. Pastor Mike said she was pretty doped up with pain meds and barely awake. The back of her head is in a donut-hole pillow so she can lie on her back and not be on the gash she gave herself when she fell. Pastor Mike said she was as grumpy as ever. Said she thought she'd killed you and was about to be arrested."

"I hope he told her that she hadn't."

"He did. I half wished he'd let her stew a bit. Guess I'm a little mad at her, too."

"Too? Is someone else mad at Leona? I'm certainly not."

"Yeah, my dad."

Chapman digested the news. "Do you think she'd talk to me if I went to see her?"

"Geez, I'm not so sure...ask Millie. I know my dad isn't ready to go see her yet. He's afraid he'll lose it."

"Okay, I'll ask Millie tonight. Now I want to change the subject. After I go to the courthouse, I'm going to kick a few truck tires today. Got any suggestions?"

"Whoa! You sure did change the subject! I'm a man! Of course I've got suggestions. I've got opinions too. You looking at a particular make and model?"

"Not yet. This is a brand new idea. I'm just in the information gathering stage."

"Well I like to support Redmond, but Robberson Ford in Bend is a pretty good outfit. You could at least start there. It's not that far from the courthouse.

"Thank you, Will. That could work out fine. I've got an appointment in the assessor's office at 2:00. If I have a chance, I'll tell Millie what I found out tonight.

"Good enough," Will said. "Okay, I'm outta here. Got a date with a tractor. Don't take any wooden nickels."

Chapman disconnected and looked at the hens still scrounging for kernels of chicken feed. He wished there were toys for hens; something to occupy their minds. There really wasn't much for them to do. He noticed a five gallon bucket upturned in a corner of the pen and walked over and pushed it with his foot, wondering if it had a purpose. It was old and rusted and had been used for target practice judging from the holes. But it was still sturdy. Perhaps Leona sat on it and watched her hens. He noticed something in the dirt where he'd shifted the bucket and stooped to see what it was. *Grass! It's some sort of grass, trying to grow with just the light from the holes in the sides of the bucket.* He picked the bucket up to look and was immediately surrounded by squawking hens, fighting over the nearly translucent blades, running right over his loafers in their excitement. In seconds, the grass was gone. Chapman set the bucket down, shaking his head. *I'm right. They need something to occupy their minds.*

He let himself out of the pen and again carefully closed the gate. As he walked down the slope towards the sheep pasture, he heard the hen in the hen house behind him letting the world know she had successfully laid an egg. He smiled, glad he'd had the conversation with Vess at the Big R. *That cackle does sound proud. I wonder if I'm supposed to gather the egg?* He made a mental note to ask Millie as his attention turned towards the ewes. He could see them grazing contentedly on the new spring grass.

Standing with his arms on the top rail of the fence he watched, aware of a profound silence broken only by occasional bird song. The distant snowy mountains broke the skyline and made the sky above them look impossibly blue.

186

Elvis' rendition of "There Will be Peace in the Valley," came to him. The line, "There will be peace in the valley for me-e someday…throbbed though his mind. He straightened and went to fill the ewes' water even though it didn't really need it yet. He connected the hose to the faucet by the barn in order to do so. As he topped off the trough, he let the song's chorus run through his mind.

> *There will be peace in the valley for me*
> *some day. There will be peace in the*
> *valley for me, oh Lord I pray.*
> *There'll be no sorrow, no sadness,*
> *no trouble, trouble I see.*
> *There will be peace in the valley for me.*

He realized then how much he was counting on Leona Larsen to sell him her piece of ground. He knew for certain that he didn't want to lease it; he wanted to own it. Suddenly, he was in a hurry to visit the courthouse in Bend, but he methodically finished his chore, unhooked and coiled the hose before turning to tackle the gentle slope in front of him…one slow and steady step at a time. He knew he had maxed his endurance once again and needed a nap but was quietly satisfied with his small accomplishments.

Chapter Eighteen
Millie

Will hung up the wall phone and turned around, smiling as he leaned back against the counter. For once he and Millie had found some time to talk and he'd remembered to ask her about inviting Chapman to the party.

"He got a little choked up when I asked him to the party, Mil."

Millie looked up from frowning over a cook book and smiled. "Nice to give that man something happy to think about." She paused. "Do you think Leona will sell him that worthless chunk of land?"

Will shrugged. "Beats me. You know, at first, I think he would have been happy to have been able to lease it...but now, he's got something in his mind...I believe he's determined to own something. As of right now, he's still on the Leona deal and is going to talk to someone in the assessor's office today. He wants to find out if it can even be divided. Since Measure 49 was passed, folks who have owned their land without deed change before 1985 generally can, at least for certain things. But, getting it done is a whole bureaucratic nightmare. He's liable to give up on it before he even starts and I wouldn't blame him."

Millie thought for a minute. "If he does, Leona's right back where she started, isn't she?"

Will shrugged again. "Maybe worse. I've never seen Dad so pissed at her. She may have lost the best friend she has."

Millie shook her head sadly. "Let's not borrow trouble, Will. We've got enough stuff on our plate."

They looked at each other in silence until Millie sighed and said, "Honey, look and see how much sugar is in the canister, would you?"

"Sure," Will said, turning from his dark thoughts with effort. He twisted to look at the row of old-fashioned aluminum canisters at his back. He lifted the dented lid of the one labeled "sugar" and said, "It's about half full, why?"

"Well, Leona was going to bring the cake to Dad's party, but she sure can't now. She wouldn't ever give me her apple cake recipe. Dad's going to be pretty disappointed to be blowing candles out over something else." She smiled up at him. "But, I've found one cake in an old cookbook of your mom's that looks pretty good."

Will leaned back against the counter again and folded his arms over his chest looking at her. He was uncharacteristically still in his sweats. On the days he went to see his mother, it was easier to do the chores in them, come in, shower and go. Now, he thought of several things he could say to his wife, one being that a store bought cake would serve just as well. But, he knew her. Nothing was too good for her father-in-law, and so he stayed silent just drinking in the picture she made in her fuzzy pink robe, long hair down her back, listing ingredients she would need to buy. She felt his look and glanced up. "What?"

He looked meaningfully at his watch. "I'm about to take my shower," he said, his voice soft, his eye brows raised in question.

Her mouth made a sudden "o." Her eyes sparked and then shot to the Betty Boop wall clock.

Carefully she put down her pen, leaned back and stretched languorously, like a cat. When she dropped her arms, her robe fell open a bit. Will could see the soft swell of her breasts above the neckline of her nightie. "Well now, Mr. Anderson," she said, seeing where his eyes had fallen, "that's just too bad about your shower. I, myself, was getting ready to take MY shower this very minute." She jumped up and turned towards the hall to their bedroom, setting off at a fast walk, working the tie on her robe as she went. "You'll have to wait…unless you'd care to join me," she called over her shoulder.

He caught up to her in three strides and she laughed as his hands closed on the back of her robe. She shrieked as he pulled and the robe came free, leaving her standing in her old cotton nightgown. She stopped and turned towards him and he dropped the robe to capture her in his arms.

She raised her arms to his neck and pressed herself hard against him. "Oh, Will," she murmured as his lips slanted towards hers and his arms tightened around her, "It's been so long."

"That shower is just going to have to wait, Mil," he whispered as their lips connected.

Afterwards, after the lovely loving and the showering together, long after Will had gotten himself together and left to see his mother, Millie's bones still felt too soft and her mind too mushy to get on with her day. While the list of things to be accomplished before four o'clock glared at her from the kitchen table like a wicked stepmother, she sat over a final cup of coffee and her mind rambled.

Jake and Jenny were picking Jack up and going straight to Papa John's Pizza Parlor before the game. Will and the little kids would meet up with them there. Then all of them would go to the game. *At least I don't have to think about getting something* together for their *dinner tonight.* That was a good thing.

She was picking up Abby and Matt from school so they could get presents for their granddad's birthday while she did some last minute grocery shopping. That was good too; though it was going to be tight time-wise. Will was taking Pansy with him to Leona's this afternoon when he went to get the irrigation going. That's another good thing. They'd had to tie the poor dog to keep her from trying to go home. She was confused and mourning terribly. Even Matt and Abby couldn't cheer her up for long. *She needs to confirm for herself that Leona isn't there.*

Finally, Millie decided to put a pan of brownies in the oven with the cake. The one thing she could do, she decided, was get the cake and the brownies made. She had the ingredients, except for walnuts but she could substitute pecans, those she had in the freezer. She decided to ask Jenny and Matt to frost and decorate their grandpa's cake together. *It's going to feel so right to have all my babies under one roof again.*

She looked at the clock and shook her head. "We shouldn't have to steal time to make love," she said, shaking a wooden spoon at Betty Boop. She sighed and began pulling ingredients from her cupboard, the lovely glow fading as she worked.

While the cake and brownies baked, she put tip money into her pocket and went upstairs to check the kids' rooms. If their beds were made, their dirty clothes in the hamper and things generally neat, she slipped a dollar bill under each pillow. Sometimes it was a little gift instead. She had done it at random times over the years, so they never knew when she would make her inspection. As a result, the rooms were generally tidy without nagging.

On a whim, she went first to Jake's room and then to Jenny's, leaving a dollar under their pillows, too. *For old time's sake,* she thought as she smoothed Jenny's pillow.

She mopped the kitchen floor, started a load of wash and was vacuuming the living room when Will returned to change into his work clothes.

She stepped on the off button when she saw him in the doorway. "Hi Honey, how was she?"

He crossed the room and took her in his arms. She could see the sadness that clouded his blue eyes. "Was she bad today?"

Will leaned his forehead against hers and breathed in deeply. "She wasn't bad or good. She just wasn't there," he said softly into her ear. "But the smell of that place gets to me, you know?"

She did know. Visiting his mom took a toll on her husband on many levels, but it was easier for him to talk about the odors. She laughed softly, determined to lighten the mood. "So you're filling your nostrils with the scent of the shampoo you so recently washed out of my hair?"

"Yeah, the smell of you and whatever it is you are baking. Your buzzer is going off by the way."

"Oh, crap!" Millie said and ducked out of his arms to race to the kitchen.

She pulled the pans out of the oven. They were both a bit brown about the edges, but Will had definitely saved the day. "They'll do," she said. "You are my hero. Talk about perfect timing."

He grinned at her and lifted his eyebrows suggestively. "Timing is important, isn't it, Mil?

She laughed, catching his meaning. "Go get your clothes changed, Lover Boy, and I'll get some lunch made. If I know you, you're starving."

"Yes ma'am, I am. That was quite a lot of exercise," he said as he walked down the hall towards their bedroom, his mood restored.

Over tuna sandwiches and big glasses of milk they talked over the myriad of details that made up their life.

"I haven't forgotten your garden Mil. I'll get it done this next week. Or maybe Jake would like to do it," he said, brightening.

Millie nodded. "I'll bet you money on it. Have you had time to think more about getting a younger horse for Abby?"

"Yeah, we'll dig the money up somehow. I'm thinking she's going to have to work her little butt off to earn part of it, though. Think she's old enough to ride her bike over to Leona's? I thought I'd till her garden, too, and Missy Big Britches can keep it going for her."

"Well, I'd like to follow behind in the van to see how she does for a time or two, but I guess she could do it. You and the Larsen boys were back and forth all the time on your bikes, weren't you?"

"Yep. I believe we were about eight when our parents turned us loose. Course, there was a lot less traffic then."

Millie bit her lip and sighed. "She really is pretty responsible for her age...it's just hard when I start thinking of all that might happen."

Will nodded and changed the subject. "It's sure going to be good to have Jake and Jenny home, isn't it? Did you happen to mention Chapman to them?" Will asked her.

"Maybe, but, I'm not sure. Anyway, you can tell them tonight, can't you?"

Will nodded and grinned. "By that time, I won't have to. Matt and Abby will have them half talked to death by the time two o'clock rolls around on Sunday."

Millie stood up to gather the plates from the table but Will bracleted her slender wrist with his blunt fingers. She looked at him with a question in her eyes. "Millie the Mom, you deserve diamonds and furs," he said huskily.

She drew in a breath and looked down at him. She wondered if her heart was big enough to hold all the love she had for her man. "Will Anderson, I have exactly what I want and you know it!" She tried to make her voice sound sharp and Leona-like. It must have worked because he released her with a laugh and stood. "Well, that scared me. I'm out of here. Cell phone's in my pocket."

"Listen up kids," Millie said as she handed each child a banana and watched meaningfully until seatbelts were fastened. "We're on a mission here. It's highly classified and

194

not to be revealed to a certain grandfather under any circumstances. Got that?"

Matt, whose turn it was to ride shotgun, grinned. "Yes ma'am! Mission accepted. What is it?"

"Kids are in charge of birthday shopping…while Mother runs like a madwoman through the grocery store throwing all sorts of top secret stuff in her cart."

"Mom! You're getting carried away here," Abby said sternly from the back seat.

"No she's not, Abby. It's just a game!" Matt said, coming to Millie's defense. He turned as far as his seat belt would let him and glared at his sister.

"Well," Millie said, "It is and it isn't. As usual, we're short on time. So, we're going to Freddie's and while you two go pick out suitable cat toys for your Grandpa Jack's new cat family, I'll get started on my list in the grocery aisles."

"You mean you're going to give us the money and everything?" Abby's tone had turned to one of wonder. "We get to pick out anything we want?"

"Well, I'm giving each of you fifteen dollars and you have to stay within your budget, but yes, this is entirely up to you."

"Cat toys! Cool! I like this mission, General Mom," Matt said.

"What if we don't spend all the money, can we keep it?" Abby asked.

Millie glanced in the rearview mirror at her daughter, catching her eye. Already Abby looked sheepish.

"Well, now, Private, not even first class, what do you think?" Millie said drily.

"I think I'm going to spend all the money on cat toys and make Grandpa a card at home," Abby said in a quick, sweet reversal of attitude.

Millie said simply, "Good choice." But inside she was thinking, *lordy, I'm going to need track shoes to keep ahead of this one!"*

"You know Mom, if you want, me and Matt could wrap them and everything. We've got time before we go to the game," Abby said in her most agreeable voice.

This is not the time to correct your daughter's grammar, Millie intoned silently to herself. Aloud she said, "That would be great. Thanks, darlin'. Maybe you could hide them under your beds in case Grandpa drops by. As far as I know, this is one surprise we're pulling off. He thinks church and going to see your Nana is the extent of the celebration."

"Are Jenny and Jake getting Grandpa a present?" Matt asked.

"Well, not something to unwrap. They are spending the gas money to come home for his party and your grandfather will think that is a hunky dory present."

Millie glanced at her youngest son. There was a wrinkle between his eyebrows as he tried to digest the concept.

She wheeled the van into the Fred Meyer's parking lot, whipped into an empty space and shut off the engine. "Okay, troopers, this is it." She unhooked her seatbelt. "Purse please."

Abby picked the green bag up off the seat beside her and hefted it onto the console. Millie pulled out her wallet and gave each child their money biting her tongue so she wouldn't lecture them on keeping it safe, counting change and all the other things that came to her mind. "Keep your receipts, please," was all she said as they got out.

As they walked through the sliding doors she said, "We only have 40 minutes to both shop and drive home. Please meet me under the clock at 3:20 with mission accomplished.

"Aye, aye, General," said Matt, saluting and turning on his heel to run-walk after his sister.

Millie pulled into the Anchors Away staff parking area in a cloud of dust, a pink scrunchie held in her teeth. She didn't look at her watch. If she was late, she didn't want to know it. Besides, it was worth Trenton's grumpy look to spend a few minutes hugging her two older children. She frowned, knowing they'd had to skip their last class in order to make it over the mountain and home by three o'clock. But what a nice surprise to pull into the ranch yard and find their Jeep parked in its old bay next to the farm truck!

She walked into the Anchors kitchen and smiled a sunny smile at Trenton, belatedly remembering the scrunchie. She pulled it from her teeth and started pulling back her hair. "The kids are home," she said, noticing immediately that Trenton didn't look grumpy at all. As a matter of fact, he was beaming. Diego looked over from where he was chopping vegetables and gave her a shy, pleased smile as well.

"Hey, Millie," Trenton said, "come here and look."

On the prep counter sat a huge pan of something with golden brown cheese still bubbling at its edges. "It's for Jack's party. Tell him it is going to be one of the signature recipes for Anchor's Away. I'm going to call it Jack's Lasagna…that is, if he likes it."

Millie finished wrapping the scrunchie around her pony tail and leaned over the pan, breathing deeply. The fragrance was amazing. "Wow! This is perfect. Everyone at the party will be singing your praises, Trenton!" she said with feeling.

"Yeah, well I've got a box to carry it to your van. You got room in your fridge?"

"Don't worry, I can find room." She quirked a smile at him as she fished car keys out of her purse. "Would you or Diego put it on the floor of the front seat, please? That way it's done right. I don't want to mess around with a masterpiece."

"Right," Trenton said dryly, holding out the evening's list of specials in one hand and taking her keys in the other. "Chef's Special tonight is baked lamb shanks served over a bulgur wheat pilaf. The fish is Sole Veronique, by the way."

She tied her apron strings and grabbed the papers. "Yum to both! You've really got my mouth watering tonight, boss. By the way, before I forget…thank you from the bottom of my heart, Trenton. I really meant it when I said it was perfect." She smiled thinking of Chapman and the fact that this was one food he could eat.

And then she was gone, through the swinging doors to the dining room, calling back over her shoulder, "Remember this is basketball finals night, we're liable to be slammed early on with folks trying to eat and get to the game."

At five o'clock Chapman called for reservations. "It has been a busy day, Millie. Is it possible to get a table by 6:00? I'm as hungry as a horse."

Millie laughed. "That hungry, huh? See you in an hour."

"Thank you so much," he said as he rang off.

She tapped the phone with one long pink fingernail. Will had said to ask him, or tell him something…she shrugged. It would come to her. She put a "Reserved" sign in her pocket, with plans to put it on his booth after the current party seated there had gone.

When Chapman arrived, Millie noticed he wore different sunglasses. This pair was tinted an even lighter amber. She also noticed how easily he removed his fedora at the door and glanced around the restaurant. He looked at the reader board by the reservation counter while Millie collected his menu.

"Want the clam chowder and a basket of rolls to start?" she asked as she seated him at his booth.

"Perfect! Make it a bowl." He picked up the menu.

"Back in a jiffy," she said. But instead of leaving, she paused to add, "We're out of horse, but both specials have gotten raves tonight."

"I saw the fish. I suppose I could force myself to substitute that."

They smiled at each other. "You have an interesting day?" She asked.

"Very. I came home from Bend and had a two-hour nap, got up and spent an hour on my computer." He shook his head. "Bureaucracies are amazing!"

"Aren't they though," she said dryly as she hurried off.

Millie came back and set the soup in front of him. "So it's the sole Veronique instead of horse, right?"

Chapman nodded, "Sounds great."

"I'll get the order right in. The side vegetable is French green beans. They're real tender. Should do fine for you."

As she made the rounds of her other tables, Millie thought about Chapman's tone of voice when he'd made the remark about bureaucracies. *He must have been referring to his visit to the courthouse. But he didn't seem sad or discouraged* she decided. *It's more like he's been given a puzzle to solve.* She was more than a little curious. *Please God, let this whole thing work out for that grumpy old woman and for this man who has had so much trouble. They could both sure use a break.*

As she refreshed coffee cups, she took the time to glance over toward the corner where Chapman sat and could see him slowly and carefully chewing the chowder into a puree before swallowing. Already a pile of crusts lay on his bread plate.

She wondered what his voice had sounded like before the accident and if it was his throat or something else that made him eat so slowly, but knew she'd never ask. *And I have to remind the kids not to ask either. If it's something he's needing to put behind him, far be it from us to bring it back up.*

By the time Chapman had finished the last of the sole Veronique, most of the locals had left for the game. Millie put a new arrival in Carla's section so she could spend a little

200

time with Chapman. As she refilled his water she said, "If you don't mind, I can come back in a bit, maybe sit for a minute. I'd sure like to know what happened in Bend today. Seems like Leona has been on my mind a lot. I even called the hospital."

"I need to talk about Mrs. Larsen, too," he said. "And please tell your chef, this sole is absolutely the best I've ever eaten."

She smiled. "Trenton is his name. He's something, isn't he? He's just invented a new lasagna recipe. We're going to have it for Dad's party, so you'll get to try it." Her eyes widened. "Oh, shoot, that's what Will said to tell you. You need to know how to get to the ranch!" She pulled out her pen and scribbled their address on a blank receipt. As she tore it out and handed it to him she said, "Put that in your GPS, techno-man."

Chapman looked up at her and she could almost see his eyes through the amber tinted lenses. *I wish he felt comfortable enough to take them off like he did last night.* She thought. His thin lips were turned up in a genuine smile. "Thank you. It will be a piece of cake. And then he said, "I'm certainly looking forward to this," with such sincerity that Millie felt her throat close.

"Okay, let me go check on my other parties and I'll be back." She scooped up his empty plate. "Seems like some raspberry sherbet would put the finish on that fish dinner, don't you think?

This time, Chapman laughed, a rough rasping sound, but a laugh for sure. "Certainly! Why not? After all, I do have a pound or two to gain."

When Millie came back, she handed Chapman the dish of sherbet and slipped into the other side of the booth. "Okay, you first. What did you find out?"

Chapman looked at her solemnly. "A lot, I'd have to say; some bad, some not so bad. Some of it money can fix. I've already contacted a lawyer for that. But here's the truth, Millie: I was out taking care of Leona's chickens and sheep this morning, and I could feel that desolate looking, rocky piece of worthless ground calling to me. I know I said I was willing to look at other pieces of property, and logically, I am…but, and this is going to sound corny…my mind knows that a different acreage would serve the purpose…but my heart doesn't." He stumbled over the last words.

They sat looking at each other across the table. Millie could feel tears welling in the corner of her eyes, but she didn't care. Something about this man tugged her heartstrings and that was a fact. "Will said something like that to me this morning. It all depends on Leona, doesn't it?" She managed to say.

Chapman nodded. "Absolutely! But even if she would agree to sell me that field, which is what I want, the process, according to my attorney, is brutal. It might be a year before the Land Conservation and Development Commission gets around to even getting it on the docket."

Millie nodded. "Will said something like that this morning too. Things are sure a mess in this county."

Chapman nodded. "They're complicated, that's for certain. The attorney I talked to said for me to get on the internet and read about Oregon's Measure 37 and Measure 49 before I even wasted my money coming to see him. He thought it might scare me away from even trying.

"Did it?"

"No. But, like I said, it's even more complicated because the property hasn't produced significant income for a number of years. But, I've really got to determine if Leona will consider even talking with me before I go further…and I want to know if you think I should go see her."

Millie frowned. "Well, here's the thing. I called the hospital just before I left home today and found out that Leona has a back injury in addition to the concussion. The nurse couldn't tell me much because of the patient privacy stuff, but she did say Leona was refusing an operation." She nibbled on her lower lip. "I think Leona's liable to be in there for a while. I also think she's not being very nice to the staff. I'm thinking that besides being in pain, she's scared to death about what's going to happen to her."

Millie stood and collected Chapman's empty sherbet dish before continuing. "After I hung up, I tried to call Dad to tell him about Leona's back. But I couldn't get him. Then I called Pastor Mike and actually got to talk to him. He said he would go see her tomorrow and have her sign a paper so he could talk to the nurses and maybe her doctor to find out more."

Millie found her words just tumbling out. She knew she had to get moving. Chapman seemed to be taking it all in and listening quietly. She drew a breath.

"Here's another thing that's on my mind. Before I met Will, I'd had a real bad experience and ended up on welfare, so I know something about how the system works. Leona surely would qualify for financial aid. I just know it. But she's very proud, you know? She doesn't like people knowing her business…so how can you help someone like that?"

Without pausing for his answer she continued, "I know without even asking them what Will and Dad would say."

"What would that be, Millie?" He asked quietly.

"They'd say you can't."

"But, you have a different idea?"

"Yes, I do. It's a little sneaky, and it has to do with you."

"With me?"

He sounded horrified. She smiled. "Now don't get a knot in your knickers, Chapman. I mean sneaky in a good way. A way that might get you 'The Lord's Bit'…that's what Peter Larsen always called that worthless chunk of land, in case you hadn't heard…and will get Leona out from under some of her debt…maybe have that operation. It's called reverse psychology. So, I'm saying, yes, you should go see her. Now, I gotta get moving before I get fired, but I'll be back."

Chapter Nineteen
Jack

Jack went to bed still grumpy, slept poorly and got up even grumpier, and his day headed downhill from there. It seemed everything was going out of its way to irritate him. His urine was a mere dribble, he felt a crick in his back and the spring on his toaster seemed to be wearing out, and he couldn't remember when he was supposed to go and see Pastor Mike. *Now, why in the hell didn't I write that down?*

On top of that, the news depressed him; Uncle Sam was out of control and that was all there was to it! He found himself shouting at the television, giving it various bits of wisdom including: "Throw the bastards out!" and "Too big to fail? Throw the book at those crooks!"

Even his coffee tasted bitter. He made a face as he sipped it. "I'd swear to God that Leona made this!" he mumbled sourly to himself as he tossed it out and went to put some dry food in the cat's dish.

He walked carefully down his front steps and mindful of his back, stooped slowly with knees bent, to put the food in the metal bowl on the ground. He hadn't even gotten himself upright when he heard her soft questioning meow. She was sitting erectly at the foot of the shrub, just beyond the front sidewalk, both white mittens perfectly together. He pushed the bowl towards her with his foot and walked back up a step, leaning his back against the sturdy handrail. He watched her assess him with unblinking eyes and moved one step higher, giving her more space. Finally, she uncurled herself at the speed of molasses, stretched, and after one last careful look at him, walked towards the food dish.

She allowed him to stand and talk soft nonsense to her as she ate. Afterwards, when the bowl was entirely empty, she moved a little ways off and shared his sunshine to groom herself. He could tell she was the fastidious sort from the way she went at it.

"That old bat Leona Larson used to be like you when she was young," he announced to the cat in a voice tinged with sorrow. He rubbed a gnarled hand over his wiry curls. "Damn it to hell, anyway! This whole thing is as upside down as a pineapple cake!"

He thought of calling his son, but remembered it was Friday and Will was probably either getting ready to go to The Homestead, or already there visiting his mother. *Besides, this is a problem you've got to solve for yourself...or with the help of Pastor Mike. Don't be putting it on your kids.*

He closed his eyes and turned his head so it faced east. The rising spring sun had real warmth in it. Still, he felt lower than a snake's belly.

"Besides all I got on my mind," he said, opening his eyes and directing his gaze towards the cat. "I got a birthday comin' up. Nobody's talking to me, but I suspect a party of some sort, and I sure don't feel a bit like celebrating." He sighed and turned to mount the steps and open the screen door. "Just as well if we skipped it entirely, there isn't a damned thing to celebrate about getting older," he groused. "Not one damned thing I can think of!"

"Ah, hell!" he said in disgust, "I got no business talking to the cat or the television anyway!" As he went in and shut the front door, a new thought depressed him even further. *Now, how in the hell am I supposed to sit through the ball game tonight with this back acting up?"* He reached a hand behind him and rubbed the spot, knowing he wouldn't miss seeing his beloved Panthers wax the Bend Lava Bears even if he had to be carried there on a stretcher. He headed for his bedroom and the tube of Ben Gay.

In the bedroom, Jack looked long and hard at his unmade bed. '*Maybe what you need to do is take a couple of aspirin and crawl back in,*' a small voice whispered seductively. The voice was so real, he blinked. Then he shook his head.

"Naw. That's just the devil talking. What you need to do is get yourself showered, dressed and to the chiropractor!" he said sternly to himself.

He walked back to the kitchen where his phone book had a neat list of frequently called numbers written in the back, all done in Betty's careful hand. *What I NEED to do is remember that I don't have all the answers and ask for help when I need it,* he thought as he stabbed at the buttons. *Even if it means getting down on my knees, like Pastor Mike is always preaching.*

Jack found the earliest he could get in to see the chiropractor was at one o'clock. He supposed he just have to put up with the pain until then. He dialed the church number. "Hello, Billie Jo," he said without preamble when the church

207

secretary answered the phone, "What time was my appointment with Pastor Mike supposed to have been?"

"Hello, Jack. The book says 3:00.

"I'll write it down next time. Thanks, Billie Jo."

"So, how's Leona doing by now?"

"I haven't the foggiest," he snapped.

The pregnant silence on the line confirmed what Jack already knew; he had been terribly rude. He was immediately ashamed of himself. "Hold on a minute, Billie Jo, don't hang up on me. I'd like to take that tone of voice back, if you'll let me."

The silence continued for several heartbeats and Jack imagined she was deciding whether or not to take him up on his offer.

"Well that was a first in all these years, you old coot. So I guess I'll pretend I didn't hear you." She tried to put some sass in her voice, but Jack could still hear the hurt and felt ashamed.

"Thank you, Billie Jo. To tell you the truth, Leona is one of the things I want to talk to the pastor about. I'm a pretty cranky...old coot, as you so correctly called me. See you about three o'clock then."

After his shower and doing the best he could to get some Ben Gay on his back, Jack called the florist and ordered a bouquet of spring flowers sent to the church office for Billie Jo. Then he eased himself back in his recliner and let his mind wander to Chapman, who had said at dinner that he was going to run to Bend if he could get an appointment at the courthouse. His eyes softened as he remembered. When Will had asked Chapman if he minded picking up oyster shells and going to take care of Leona's animals before he went, the guy had seemed tickled to have been asked.

He sighed knowing in his heart that one of the reasons he was so out of sorts was that he felt impotent. In truth, if the course of Betty's disease could be plotted and he knew how much money her care was going to take, he would be taking some of his saving out of the bank and paying off those damned back taxes...just to give them all breathing room to help her figure something out. But, he couldn't do it and he doubted if Leona would even let him. He reached for the clicker and turned the television to the cooking channel to pass the time until his appointment. He sighed knowing she was even less likely to take money from a stranger. *She'll never in a million years believe he wants to buy that worthless chunk of land, never in a million! I hardly believe it myself.*

By the time three o'clock rolled around, Jack was feeling physically better. The chiropractor had bent him like a pretzel, lectured him about losing flexibility and muscle mass, put an elastic girdle thing around his waist and skinny hips so he would be able to sit through the game and sent him on his way saying, "Go Panthers, eh, Jack?"

Not only that, Billie Jo had her flowers and they had done the trick. She'd said, "You shouldn't have..." about a dozen times before showing him into Pastor Mike's office.

Mike stood up when he walked in. "I just got a call from Millie, Jack. It seems she called the hospital and found out they're keeping Leona for a while. She's refusing to have a back operation of some kind and is in too much pain to be sent home."

Jack looked at him for a moment and sank heavily into the waiting chair. "Hit me with that again," he said. "I thought the only thing wrong was a concussion."

"Evidently not. Millie didn't know much. She called the nurse's station and got a hold of a nurse who was pretty fed up with Leona and got a little diarrhea of the mouth, probably out of frustration."

"Been there myself," Jack said dryly.

"Well, I dropped in on her yesterday evening but she was still pretty out of it...thought she'd killed that fellow. So, thank you for your call about that. I told Millie I'd go visit Leona and get those papers signed. Then we can find out what's really going on. Would you like to go with me? We can talk over what you wanted to see me about in the car." He looked at Jack with lowered lids and watched carefully.

Jack finally sighed. "I suppose so. I suppose I do. I just came from the chiropractor. It came to me, while he had the heat lamp on my back, that I don't do well when my head is telling me one thing and my heart is telling me another thing; makes my gut hurt and my back go out."

He looked at the pastor. "I'm too damned old for all this. It takes its toll...and I sure don't want to end up as cranky as that old woman, but that's the way I'm headed."

Jack got carefully to his feet. No pain. "Come on Mike, let's go see if we can't get her to sign those papers. Seems like the good Lord gives more and more for her to carry. I do have to say that."

Leona was asleep when they arrived at her room. They had seen the head nurse and she'd given them a clipboard and papers for Leona to sign. "Go ahead and wake her up. She'll be a little groggy for a while, but not too groggy to be unpleasant if our experience counts for anything." The nurse's lips were pinched tight.

Leona was lying flat on her back, her mouth open, breathing shallowly. Her waxen, work-worn hands looked out of place on the pristine white sheet folded back over a blue blanket. Pastor Mike stepped to the side of the bed and folded his huge paw gently over one hand. "Geez, her hands are like ice," he said softly to Jack.

Jack stood at the foot of the bed with the clipboard, more shaken than he'd like to admit.

"Leona," Pastor Mike said, elevating his voice, "time to wake up. You have visitors."

Jack watched her eyes flutter and then open. He watched as she recognized him, her eyes widening. "Oh, Jack," she whispered, "you did come." To his astonishment, tears began leaking from the corner of her eyes. "I thought maybe you'd given up on me."

He looked at the Pastor who was looking straight at him and cleared his throat. "Well, Leona, maybe I haven't, but I might…unless you start behaving yourself." His tone was harsh.

The two men had talked about playing 'good cop, bad cop' on the way over in the car. Jack had said, "I'm so blamed mad at her for trying to shoot Chapman Lewis I won't have a bit of trouble being the bad guy." And he didn't. He realized he'd spoken the truth. He looked at Pastor Mike and nodded.

Pastor Mike cleared his throat and said, "Now, Jack, can't you see Leona is in pain. How bad is it Leona?"

211

Leona's eyes shifted to him and brightened. "'Bout time you got here, Pastor," she said sharply.

"Now look, Leona, that's just what I'm talking about!" Jack said sternly, "That's not behaving yourself! Pastor Mike is a busy man. Yet he made time to come and see you twice. And the first thing you do is try to make him feel guilty. That just isn't right!" Jack was practically shouting by the time he had finished. He realized that his anger was real; he wasn't acting even a little!

"Then there's me. I cancelled your appointment with the county; I brought your purse to the hospital so you'd…"

" Jack," the pastor cut in smoothly, his voice gentle. "This isn't about you. It's about Leona and finding out about what's going on for her and what we can do to help while she's confined."

Leona snorted, now fully awake. "I'm not in any pain as long as I don't move more than a little finger. Dr. Brown said I had bone spurs in my back that irritated the nerves in my spine when I fell. He said I could fix it with an operation, but he left pretty quick when I told him I didn't have any money."

Jack felt his temper start doing a slow burn but Pastor Mike just said in a soothing voice, "Leona, I'm pretty sure that's not why he left and so are you." He kept his hand on hers. "That's your back. What about your head?"

"Guess they had to clean some dirt out of it and stitch it up. That's why I've got this little pillow thing…so the wound is protected."

"Well, that's a good thing then. It looks to me that you are being well taken care of. I'm sure sorry about your back." He paused, "Listen, Jack is holding a paper for you to sign your name to. It's a release of information form. If you sign it, we can talk to your doctor and see what he says about you...see how long you have to stay here and the other stuff."

He's as smooth as glass, Jack thought, admiration tamping down his temper and the disgust he felt.

"I'll sign anything to get out of here. The food isn't fit to eat, they wake you up at all hours and in the night you can't sleep for all the noise," Leona said and carefully raised her hand. "Gimme a pen."

"Jack walked the clipboard to the side of the bed, pulled the pen from the clasp and handed it to her, slanting the board so it was in the proper position. His jaw was clamped and his lips were white. Pastor Mike closed his hand gently around hers for support as she struggled to write her name.

Jack could see the effort it took her. When she was done, he took the clipboard away but didn't say a word. He was afraid what came out of his mouth would be worse than what a "bad cop" would say.

Her eyes slanted towards his. "Pansy. What's happened to Pansy?"

Jack walked back to the end of the bed to give himself a little time to get his voice under control.

"Will's got her. Everything is fine at your place for now."

His words were clipped, his voice tight, but Leona didn't seem to notice. Relief showed on her pale face. "Well, that's good then. I've sure been worrying myself about her." Jack looked steadily over her head and nodded.

"You know we're glad to do what we can." It was the best he could do. His throat was so tight and dry he couldn't have drawn spit.

"Now Leona, we don't want to overstay. If we can bring you anything, please tell us," Pastor Mike said.

"Mike Carlsson, what I need you can't bring to a hospital room," she said almost to herself. "What I need is a miracle. Can you bring me that?"

The pastor sighed. "No, I can't bring you that. But, I can say a prayer of petition and ask the Someone who can. Would you like that?"

Leona nodded and closed her eyes. Jack bowed his head and let the Pastor's words wash over and into him.

"Dear Lord, thank you for being with Leona when she fell. Thank you for sending two of your servants to help her in her time of need. We ask you now, Lord, to help heal her in heart, mind and body. Help her learn to turn her burdens over into your loving care until solutions can be found. Bless her, Lord, and bless your servant, Jack, who does your work so admirably. In Jesus' name we pray.

As Mike finished praying, Jack opened his eyes and found his pastor's eyes fixed kindly on him. He managed a weak smile. "Amen," he croaked.

Chapter Twenty
Will

Every spring, one of Will's least favorite jobs was setting the hand lines for field irrigation. It wasn't the hard work. He had a strong back. It wasn't the lifting or the setting of the long pipes either. Those things generally went fine, unless a cow or a horse had knocked something off-kilter. What he dreaded was all the things that had to work before water actually got to the field. First the parts had to mesh, then the water had to be turned on, then the pump had to be primed and started. Only when that worked, would the lines fill with enough pressure to force the giant sprinkler heads to start their ratcheting spray of water over the thirsty fields. But it never seemed to happen that way. Today it appeared as he shut the system down for the third time, that the winter had been particularly hard on gaskets. Pipe couplings leaked like sieves. He'd had to make a quick trip to the Big R for replacement parts. Still, as he finally watched the water spew, it hadn't seemed so bad. He was, in fact, whistling. He had been whistling for most of the day and every time he thought of his wife, he grinned without even realizing it.

There was great satisfaction in watching "The New Field" start its journey from seeded ground to Blue Grass, he decided. Any evidence of Hoot Riley's shack and potato cellar had been erased...*just like I got to keep doing with the ugly memories that are best forgotten...erase them.*

He had already finished starting the sprinklers over in Leona's field. Oddly, it seemed like Peter's old hand lines gave him less trouble than his newer ones. He glanced at his pickup where he knew three exhausted dogs were sleeping off a day of "doggie grab-ass."

On the day before, when he and Chapman had fixed the fertilizer wagon, he'd taken the dogs. He'd let Pansy check out the whole house, yard, chicken pen and the ewe's pasture. Afterwards, she had looked up at him with a deep question in her eyes, her forehead wrinkled with concern. "She not here, Pansy, but she'll be back before long," he said aloud. Her ears went down then and she glanced at Chapman first, then at Tuffy and Digger before looking back at him. She seemed to be thinking things over.

Chapman had his smart phone out taking pictures. "I've heard Border Collies are smart, but she seems amazing to me," he'd said.

Will had nodded and put his hand down as she sighed and walked forward wagging her tail, presenting herself to be petted. *Okay,* she seemed to be saying, *I get it. She's not here. You'll do for now.*

After he'd finished at the Larsen place and started on his own field, he noticed her mood had definitely changed. For the first time since Leona had been taken away, she seemed to relax a little. Her ears and tail were up and her eyes were bright. In fact, as soon as he lifted the three dogs out of the pickup bed, Pansy had his dogs in full play mode. She found something that looked like part of an old harness, and a game of keep-away ensued. It went on until Tuffy and

Digger gave it up and went for a swim in the irrigation ditch. It had been good to watch the joy with which she joined them.

Will looked at his watch. Jake and Jenny should be on their way over the mountain, and Millie should be picking up the kids from school. He checked the timer on the line one more time and pulled out his cell phone to call Chapman. He needed to remind him to bring the receipt for the oyster shells to the party on Sunday, and he had to admit to himself that he was damned curious what the tax people had to say.

"Chapman here."

"Hey Chapman. Am I interrupting something? This is Will," he added belatedly.

Will heard the husky chuckle. "Yes, as a matter of fact, I'm sitting at my computer learning more than I thought I ever wanted to know about your land-use laws. I thought the state of Washington was convoluted, but Oregon has to be worse…so I am delighted to be interrupted."

Will snorted. "They aren't MY land-use laws, Chapman. The government started interfering with land owners way back when Tom McCall was governor. The infamous Senate Bill 100 that created Oregon's Land Conservation and Development Commission was passed the year I was born."

There was a pause. "Tom McCall," Chapman finally said. "I haven't heard that name for a while. He also supported nuclear power. Oregon has The Trojan Nuclear Facility because of his support."

"Yeah, well, my dad and granddad generally liked him. So, he must have been one of the good guys. I suspect

217

what he envisioned was controlling big developers from chopping up agricultural land."

"Actually Will, that's what I've been reading about. I went to meet with a land-use lawyer after I finished at the courthouse, and he told me to go home and do my homework, understand what I was dealing with. Then, and only then, he said, if I wanted to pursue it, I should make another appointment and he would start taking my money."

"Whoa! He sounds like a straight-up guy. How'd you find out about him?"

"He's the friend of a friend who happens to be my attorney in Washington."

Will lifted his hat and scratched his head, wondering if he was being nosey, then decided he didn't care. The stakes were pretty high both for Chapman and Leona. "Well, are you learning anything?"

"Actually, I am. It's a mess. The whole tax thing is a mess too. I'm feeling choked by bureaucracy, and I'm not even involved in it yet."

Will heard the disgust in his voice. "I hear you. Good luck on it. Better you than me."

"Well, it's just an exercise anyway until we find out if Mrs. Larsen will even deal with the idea...or me."

"That's the wild card," said Will. There was no laughter in his voice. "Say, I wanted to remind you to bring the receipt for the oyster shells when you come to the party Sunday."

Chapman laughed. "I'm not going to do that, Will. I had a truly good time going there and doing those chores this morning. It feels like I should be paying you for letting me help a little. I'm hoping you'll let me do it every day."

Will smiled at the sincerity in his voice.

"Well, then I'll just let you fight that bill with Leona when the time is right…and that would be a great help if you are willing to keep feeding those hens and making sure things are okay with Iris and Rose. Thanks, Chapman. Talk to you later…oh wait. Did you have time to look at trucks."

"Not today. I think I was getting the cart before the horse anyway."

"Well, maybe we can go and kick tires together, that is, if you'd like…I know Dad would like to have his say, too. We could make it a guy thing."

"That sounds just right. Now I'm getting excited again. Just let me know when you two can find the time."

"Will do. See you Sunday, if not before. I'm heading in from the field right now and our oldest two should be pulling in shortly." Will laughed. "God, if we can pull this deal off with them picking up Dad…and him not having a heart attack on the spot, I'll be one happy man."

"You are quite a family," Chapman said simply. "Good bye, Will."

Will put his phone in his pocket and opened the truck door. *'You start dealing with the government you better get a big bottle of aspirin or a fifth of booze to help you get through it.' That's what I should have told Chapman!*

He looked at the tired dogs. They didn't even lift their heads as he got in the truck. He backed onto the berm and started up the lane. Behind him, he could hear the chut, chut sound of the sprinklers making their sweeps.

When he pulled into the ranch yard, Will could see Jenny and Jake's Jeep parked next to the old farm truck. He hit the accelerator and bounced his way to a dusty stop as close to the back yard fence as he could get. He hadn't expected them so soon and here he'd been wasting time chatting on the phone. He lifted the three dogs down and held Pansy by the collar until they were inside the yard. Then he let her loose and trotted towards the house. He was pretty sure she was done with going home so he didn't tie her.

He burst in the back door. Everyone was sitting around the kitchen table, including Millie, who was already in her uniform of a white blouse and black trousers. He glanced at the clock. *Past time for her to leave.* He looked at her face. It was radiant!

"Dad!" Abby screamed, "They're here! There here!" She bounded up from where she sat on Jenny's lap and flew to him. "They're going to let me and Matt go with them to surprise Grandpa. We can, can't we Dad?" She grabbed him around the waist and looked up into his face, imploringly.

Will laughed. "Whoa! Easy girl! Let me give these two strangers a hug first. Then we can talk." He felt his voice get husky as he said it. Both kids had work-study jobs at Oregon State. So, that, plus the fact that gas prices were on the moon meant that they seldom got home.

With Abby still attached like a burr, his warm gaze feasted on the tall young man who had helped him drive the tractor all those years ago and then passed to the young woman whose "up pweese!" had helped mend his broken heart.

"Well," he said, cleared his throat and started again. "Well, if you two aren't a sight for sore eyes."

"Dad!" was all Jenny said. As gracefully as a swan she had sailed across the space and had thrown her arms around his neck with Abby squashed between them. "We couldn't wait any longer. We knew sitting through our 3:00 class would be a waste of time, so we cut it."

Jake was standing now, waiting his turn. "It's no big deal. I'm all caught up with my reading, in that class anyway." He held out his hand and Will shook it, registering that his son shook hands like a man. *Where has the time gone?* He thought before he grabbed Jake into a bear hug.

"Dang, if you kids aren't a sight for sore eyes!" Will said again. Millie was standing now, gathering her big green purse in one hand, carefully dabbing her eyes with the other, her tissue damp and crumpled. He could tell it had been one happy reunion.

Millie walked over and gently peeled her daughters away from their father.

"Move away youngsters, I gotta kiss my man goodbye, then he's yours," she said as she slipped into his arms for a goodbye kiss. "I was hoping you'd get here so I could see this," she whispered. "I love you, gotta run." And then she headed towards the front door to a chorus of "Good bye Mom. See you when you get home."

"Seems to me you all had better be in bed when I get home. Big day tomorrow," she called over her shoulder as she went out the door.

Will turned to Jake and Jenny. "Well, let's sit around the table for a bit and you can catch me up like I know you did your mother." He poured himself a glass of milk, turned a chair backwards, straddled it and looked at his children re-seating themselves around him. "Talk," he said and reached for the pan of brownies sitting in the middle of the table.

"Dad," Abby said, "please, please, pretty please, can me and Matt go with Jake and Jenny? Mom said you were the final word."

He smiled and looked at his oldest two. "This was to be your birthday gift to Grandpa Jack. You want to share it with the peskies?"

Jenny and Jake looked at each other. "Abby has it all worked out," Jenny said with fond resignation.

"Yeah, Dad," Abby said, "me and Matt are letting them sign their names on the kitty toys we got for Grandpa's new cats. So, since we're sharing our presents to Grandpa, it's only fair they share theirs with us."

Will held up a hand. "Abigail!" he said warningly, "Button your lip." *What am I going to do with this child, Lord?* He closed his eyes and sighed. It was time to draw a serious halt to his youngest daughter's manipulation. He opened his eyes, his mouth firm. He said, "No! No, that is not how it is going to work. We're going to stick with the plan. This is Jake and Jenny's time with Grandpa Jack. You and Matt get to see him almost every day. The plan called for us to meet at Papa John's and that's what we'll do."

Abby sat back in her chair and folded her arms over her chest, her lower lip in full pout mode. "Well, we didn't get to see Grandpa today," she muttered.

Will ignored her and looked at Matt. "You got that, Scout?"

Matt grinned his sunny smile. "Mom said that is probably what you would say. She told Abby if she was along Jake and Jenny wouldn't get a word in edge-wise."

Will nodded, frowning at his daughter. "It's true, Abby, and you know it is. Now, here's what we can do. We

222

can follow them over in the truck and we can watch the reunion from the end of the driveway. Then we'll drive on and let them have their visit."

He looked at Jake and Jenny. "Now, that's settled. So, how's school going and how was the pass?"

Will stood in the shower letting the hot water do its work on his tired muscles, his youngest daughter on his mind. He and Millie needed to have a serious talk about her self-centeredness. She wasn't flighty, exactly...but her moods changed as fast as the flick of a switch. It was like she just wanted it all and assumed she could manipulate everything and everyone to get it. On the other hand, she wasn't lazy, or mean-spirited...she was generous to a fault...but sometimes she wanted praise without really working for it...and she wanted to be in the middle of everything and everyone's business. *What's that about?"*

He ran shampoo into his palm and soaped his thick, coarse hair. *So is getting her a young horse a bad thing, or a good thing? If she had to work hard to support it and if we made it clear that she was totally responsible for its care...maybe a good thing.* As Will stepped from the shower, he had a new thought. *Oh, I get it, Lord. This is our punishment, Millie's and mine, for thinking we were such good parents, isn't it?* He grinned wryly to himself and started toweling off. *I'd better get a move on or Abby will be shouting for me to hurry.*

As happy surprises go, Jenny and Jake knocking at his dad's door and seeing his father's reaction had been a doozy. Watching from the end of the driveway until Jack had

223

ushered both kids through his front door, Will could see their plan had been one hundred per cent successful. *And now if someone spills the beans before the party tomorrow, it really doesn't matter,* he thought, realizing that Abby and Matt would be with his dad all night at the basketball game.

"Well," he heard Matt say, from the back seat of the club cab, "I think Grandpa is pretty happy, don't you, Dad?"

"If all that hugging and back slapping is any indication, I'd say you are right." Will said, as he put the truck in gear. "Now, let's go get a table for them and get the pizza ordered, what do you say?"

Beside him, he heard Abby sigh. "I wish Mommy could have been here to see it."

"I reckon she wishes that very thing too, sweetheart…but we don't always get what we want," Will said pointedly.

"No, we don't," said Abby, "but some people fail to realize that."

Will was glad of the gathering dusk. He didn't know what to do with his face. Inside he was cracking up. *I've got to remember to tell Mil this one. How in the hell does she come up with this stuff? He wondered.*

"You know who else would like to be here?" Matt asked.

"Who?" asked Abby.

"Aunt Leona."

There was silence in the truck. *Leave it to Matt,* thought Will. Aloud he said, "You are sure right about that, son. She loves you kids a lot. Suppose we can find time to go see her before the kids head back over the mountain?"

"You'd better call first and see if she can have visitors," Abby warned.

Chapter Twenty-one
Leona

Again and again, as the day wore on, Leona's restless hands smoothed the soft hospital sheet and blue thermal blanket that covered her. She had spent a wakeful night despite the medication, and now she had too much on her mind to even try to sleep.

How she missed her own bed. How she missed waking up to the old Audubon water color in its ornate frame and Pansy on her braided rug. How she hated being bed bound, strapped to a machine and using a bed pan! But that wasn't what was bothering her most.

Her mind was clearer now, but she almost wished it weren't. Despite the disruptions caused when the nurses and candy stripers came in her room to minister to her needs, she felt dreadfully alone. *Where's Jack? Why hasn't he come to see me other than with Pastor Mike?* Her greatest fear was that despite what he had said about not quite giving up on her, he had. She remembered his tone of voice when she asked him if he had given up on her; it played again and again in her head. "Well Leona, maybe I haven't, but I might unless you start behaving yourself."

She remembered the words. "*Maybe I haven't...*"Did that mean he had been done with her for shooting that fellow, but let Pastor Mike talk him out of it? He might have been close to calling it quits and then made up his mind when she'd started complaining. It could be, she decided with clarity, he just couldn't put up with what she had become any longer.

She remembered his tone of voice. He hadn't sounded mad…or exasperated…no, he'd sounded disgusted. That's what Jack was, disgusted with her. Her hands continued sweeping the sheets as if soothing them. *You may have lost the very best friend you ever had, Leona Marie Larsen. One thing you know about Jack is when he's done, he's done.*

Fearful of moving, she sighed, closed her eyes, and tried futilely to sleep. But, her mind raced on.

Dr. Brown had been in the night before. He'd been satisfied with her progress. The head wound was healing nicely and her pupils were back to normal. The cortisone shot in her spine was doing its work, so he'd decreased the amount of medicine he'd prescribed and had ordered the drip and catheter bags removed. He'd explained again the simplicity of the operation that would remove the bone spurs from L-5 and L-6. "It's endoscopic surgery, done with a laser, Leona. The incision is less than an inch. You would be able to walk out of here, pain free. The cortisone shot is just a stop gap measure."

She just looked at him, her eyes blazing, until he'd looked away. Then she spit out, "Well you just tell me how I'm going to pay for it and I'll have it done straight away!"

She recalled her nasty tone of voice and was ashamed. He'd also asked her if she wanted to talk to someone about the difficulties she was facing. She hadn't been very nice then, either; practically handing him his head. Now, in a way, she wished she'd just said yes. But she hadn't. She'd been short with Pastor Mike too. She closed her eyes. *Probably that was the last straw for Jack right there.*

As the day wore on, Leona realized that since she'd been hospitalized, she had been taking her anger out on every human being who came in contact with her. In fact, if she was telling herself the truth, she'd gotten a perverse sense of satisfaction of seeing their eyes darken, their lips tighten and their cheeks bloom with color. "Like the man who has had a bad day at work and comes home to kick the dog," Peter would have said.

Look where all this has gotten you, Leona. You thought your life couldn't get worse, but it has. If Pastor Mike was right in what he said, was it yesterday? The man wasn't a stalker after all. Who was he then, this man who'd called 911? Nobody had bothered to tell her that!

Her thoughts continued to loop and twist back upon themselves, the same themes playing over and over. The nurse came and checked her temperature. When she pushed the buzzer, a nurse came with the bedpan and then helped her drink water from a straw. A different candy striper came to bring her lunch. She managed a pleasant thank you to each.

It isn't so hard, saying those two words. Too bad I learned them so late in the game. I would imagine Jack has told Will and Millie he's done with me. That's why they haven't come. Lord, wouldn't I love to see those two tykes. Will and Millie are doing such a good job with those two, too. Why haven't I told them that? Why haven't I told them how much I like Jenny and Jake? In all these years, have I ever told them that?

The day faltered forward. By afternoon she had vowed to herself that she would change her ways. She was 72 years old. She would probably lose the farm. She had nowhere to go. But maybe the state would have to take her in. Whatever happened, she would take it in stride…and she would apologize to Jack as soon as she could. It wasn't something she thought she could do on the phone.

In the afternoon, she was able to drift into a restless, dream-plagued sleep. When she awoke, it was twilight outside her window. Her hospital tray had been moved into the position for dinner but instead of a dinner tray, on it was a picture of…of… Pansy! She blinked and blinked again. "Pansy! Oh, Pansy!" she whispered. With both hands she reached up and carefully brought the 5X7 frame holding her dog to her chest. Someone had done her the greatest kindness in the world. She looked at the photo again. The dog was looking directly at the person who had taken the picture, eyes bright, ears alert. It was a beautiful picture. Leona looked closer. Pansy was sitting in front of the chicken coop. In the back ground she could see several of her hens.

"Well, it seems that someone is taking care of them," she said softly. She heard chair legs scoot and a man's gravelly voice said, "That would be me."

Leona was startled. She swept the room with her eyes and didn't see a soul. The voice, she didn't recognize.

"Who are you? Why aren't you where I can see you?" She realized as she said it, how crabby she sounded.

"The answer to your first question is, Chapman Lewis," the voice said. "And as for the second question, I put myself where you couldn't see me because I was afraid I might frighten you."

"Frighten me? Well, Mr. Chapman Lewis, I can assure you that I don't frighten easily. What's wrong, you got two heads?" Once again, Leona recognized she'd broken her new vow and hurried to add, "Well, whoever you are, I just can't thank you enough for this picture of my dog. She's very dear to me."

"You are welcome, and to put your mind to rest, Mrs. Larsen, I only have one head, but it has been pretty badly damaged, and so I am difficult for some people to look at. I would save you that experience by sitting here, out of sight, until I could explain that."

Leona lay quietly, digesting the words. For the life of her, she couldn't think of a thing, not one single thing that seemed right to say. Fortunately, Chapman Lewis filled the silence.

"Actually, I came here to thank you."

"Thank me? Why on earth would you want to thank me?" she asked, her voice colored with surprise.

"If it hadn't been for you, I never would have met the Anderson family, and, I wouldn't have had the opportunity to feed your chickens and water your ewes. Both are tasks I am enjoying more than you can imagine."

Leona could hear the sincerity in his raspy voice. He was an educated man. She could tell by the way he talked. "So how did this come about?" she asked. "How'd you get involved?"

"I'm the man you thought was the stalker. Will and I were the ones who called 911 after you'd fallen."

"What?" Leona said, horrified. "You mean to tell me that you are the man I tried to shoot?"

"Well, actually guess I am, if you say so…but I thought you were trying to chase the hawk away from your chickens. That's what Will and I told the EMTs, by the way."

Leona lay quietly, waves of emotions rolling over her. She wondered if she had ever been more ashamed of herself. Again, she couldn't think of a single thing to say. The silence lengthened. She sighed. "I am a miserable human being, Chapman Lewis. I haven't said a word of apology to a soul in more years than I can count…but if I could find the right words, I would apologize to you right now. I'd say I'm sorry, but that just seems too puny for what I did."

"No, Mrs. Larsen. It seems just right to me. I accept your apology. And I meant it when I said I came here to thank you. Because of you, the Andersons have taken me under their wing, and I found out how much, since my accident, I have deprived myself of feeling close to others."

Leona put the picture of Pansy back on her tray and smoothed a finger over the glass as if petting her. "You get in a car wreck?"

"Not a car wreck, a different sort of a wreck. A special kind of steam from a collision of gamma rays caused major damage to my face, lungs and throat," Chapman said in an even voice, giving no hint to the ensuing pain and trauma in his life.

"Well, drag yourself around here to where I can see you. One thing for sure, I can't run away."

She heard the sound of movement and Chapman stood by her bed, a stick of a man, swathed in scarf, hat and amber colored glasses. He removed his hat to reveal his shaved head with its blotchy skin. Then, very slowly, he removed his glasses. A lizard's eyes looked steadily into hers.

"Mother of God! What you said made it sound not very serious, but it was, wasn't it?"

"Yes, it was serious, I'm afraid. I'm lucky to be alive."

"Well, pull your chair around here. You aren't much to look at, that's for sure, but you do have a voice that could sell bibles to heathens. Is that because of the accident?"

Chapman nodded, "Yes, I must have sucked in a big breath when the explosion happened and it badly damaged both my trachea and esophagus. Leona's head rocked slowly in its doughnut. Even in the diffused hospital light she could see that he had undergone major reconstruction. After a pause she asked, "What were you doing hanging around my farm anyway?"

"Well, I was looking over that land with all the rocks to the south of your house. I was coming to ask who owned it, and if it was you, I was going to ask to buy it."

"What? Are you talking about that damned rocky field that runs off to the west?"

Chapman nodded. "But then I found out from the Andersons that you were the one who owned it and probably wouldn't be at all interested in selling."

Chapman sat down. Leona couldn't know that Millie had told Chapman what to say. She'd said, "I mean it Chapman, you do what I say. Just cross your fingers and if you do that, it makes a little fib okay." He didn't have his fingers crossed; still, he was most uncomfortable and hoped he was pulling it off okay.

"Why in the name of heaven would you want that worthless piece of land?"

"Well, that's the other thing they said, that if I told you, you probably wouldn't believe me."

Leona snorted. "Since when do the Andersons know what I will or won't believe…and what piece of land I will or won't sell? That's what I'd like to know!"

"It is rather far-fetched…so far-fetched that even they had trouble believing I was serious. So they thought you might not believe it either."

"You'd just better tell me then. We'll just see what I can and can't believe!"

Chapman cleared his throat. "Okay, here goes. He paused dramatically and then said, "You see, what I visualized doing was to move all those rocks laying around to make a stone fence or wall, if you will, around that long narrow field."

Leona was silent for a very long time. Then she shook her head back and forth very gently inside the doughnut shaped pillow. "No," she said, "probably not." You come to my house lookin' like you look, I wouldn't have given you the time of day, much less take you seriously about that miserable chunk of rocks."

Chapman got to his feet. "It's okay, Mrs. Larsen. Jack said there are plenty of other rocky pieces of ground in Central Oregon and I know that there are. But I have to tell you, I doubt there are many places as peaceful as yours."

Remembering Millie's advice, he backed away from the bed. "I've probably stayed too long. Goodbye. Thank you for visiting with me, and I'm glad you liked the picture."

Before Leona could get her wits about her to call him back, he was gone. If she could have, she would have jumped up and run after him. There were so many things she wanted to ask him...not about the property, but about her hens and the ewes, how Pansy was getting along at Will's, if Jack had said anything about her...it was only later that she thought about what the man had said. It sounded as if he were serious. He wanted to buy The Lord's Bit...make a rock wall...what kind of a fool notion was that? *Well, it isn't like I could sell it anyway, it belongs to Neil.* But even as she had the thought, the ramifications of what Chapman had said began to play in her mind.

"Those Andersons think they know me, do they? Well, maybe they do and maybe they don't." she said softly to herself. One thing for sure, she had things to think about now, besides going home.

Chapter Twenty-two
Chapman

It had dawned on Chapman that going to the party on Sunday empty-handed would not work for him. He called the ranch. Abby answered the phone.

"Hello, Abby. This is Chapman Lewis. I'm wondering about something to bring to your grandfather's birthday party."

"Oh, hi, Mr. Lewis. Do you mean food for the party or a present for Grandpa Jack?"

"Actually, Abby, I was wondering about both."

"Well, Jenny and Matt are decorating Grandpa's cake right now. Me and Matt got him presents for his mama cat and kittens. Jake and Jenny spent their money for gas to come home…that's their present to Grandpa even though you can't wrap it up."

Chapman tried mightily to interpret her words. "In other words, I'd better bring neither a birthday cake nor cat toys because those things are already covered. Also, I'd better not bring lasagna as I know you already have that."

"That is exactly correct. We've got bread and salad and candles and stuff too."

Chapman smiled at how she emphasized the word "stuff". "You do sound very well prepared. Thank you for enlightening me. Now, may I please speak to your mother for a moment?"

"Sure. See you tomorrow, Mr. Lewis."

Millie came on the phone. Chapman could hear happiness in her voice. "I heard most of this end," she said. "Handled your problem, did she?"

"I'm almost overwhelmed with her generosity of information," Chapman said dryly.

"Does that mean she about bowled you over?"

"Ah, pretty much. Right now it seems a little superfluous to simply ask what I might add to the party in the way of present or edibles."

"Well, aren't you the dearest thing, Chapman Lewis! As a matter of fact, if you could stop by a grocery store and pick up some vanilla ice cream, I would be ever so happy. I have no idea how it got left off my list."

"Certainly. I'd be glad to do that. Now, what about a present?"

Millie paused. "I'm stumped there. I had a heck of a time…wait. I can tell you this…chocolate and coffee are two of his favorite things."

"Besides raindrops on roses and whiskers on kittens, you mean?"

"Actually he likes bright copper kettles and warm woolen mittens about as much," Millie said without missing a beat.

"Well, I guess that gives me something to go on. Thank you, Millie. I won't keep you. I'll be there about 2:00."

"You aren't keeping me, Chapman. It's good to hear your sexy voice, and I wanted to tell you that everything

236

worked out great last night. Dad just couldn't get over the fact that Jake and Jenny had come home especially for him. Will said he was so happy it made him cuss a blue streak."

Chapman chuckled. "Once a Navy man, always a Navy man, I guess."

"Well, he's so darned perfect it makes him a little more human when I know he has at least one vice."

"It's a shame we can't clone him."

The line grew quiet. Chapman suspected they were both thinking about her husband. Finally, Millie said, "Uh-huh. But God came close with Will, didn't he?"

"It's a bit spooky how you and I read each other's minds, Millie."

"No it's not. We just sorta think alike on some things, Chapman. By the way, I'm going to get the brood together and go see Leona sometime later on, probably not until after dinner, but I just don't know with this gang. Jake and Jenny want to work in some time to see some of their friends, so who knows when we'll actually get there."

When Chapman ended the call on his iPhone after talking with Millie, he shut his eyes for a moment. *I'm feeling so normal. Dear God, how I have missed feeling normal.*

He realized that he had not told Millie about his visit with Leona. He'd even had the perfect opportunity when she'd mentioned she was going to get her "brood" together and go see her. Maybe it was because he hadn't done exactly what she had wanted him to do, but he didn't think so. It was just one of those things. The corners of his lips quirked. *The conversation moves fast when Millie's around. Let's just chalk it up to that.*

237

He reflected on his brief visit with Leona and remembered that he had indeed been very careful not to sound too interested, something Millie had said was important. It was the best he could do. And truth be told, even pretending that had been hard on him. He could barely admit to himself how much he wanted to own that small scrap of rocky land. *Don't start counting on it.. You'll set yourself up for a big fall if you do.*

Still, he was very glad he'd gone to see Leona. *She certainly liked the picture of Pansy.* It had been such a simple thing to do, take a picture using his phone and then upload it to the Walgreen's Drug Store just a couple of miles from where he was staying. They'd even had a stock of nice frames. It was easy to see what the picture meant to her, even before she'd expressed it.

Chapman had been sitting in his car in front of Leona's house while he talked to Millie. He had fed the chickens and checked on the sheep. The one with the limp had come right up to the fence and before he knew it, he was scratching her behind her ears and on the top of her head. He had wondered how many times Leona had done what he was doing now. Clearly the old ewe with her chin tucked and her eyes closed, enjoyed it as much as Chapman enjoyed doing it for her.

He sighed, finished the Ensure sitting on the console and tipped his seat back for his power nap. His final thought was that Leona really needed someone and he could possibly be that person. He felt a powerful stirring of hope.

When Chapman tipped his seat back up, a sense of calm purpose filled him. He knew, without a doubt in his being, that the stony ground Leona called "The Lord's Bit" was just a vehicle, a byproduct, so to speak. Things began to fall into place in his mind. He remembered wondering why he'd come to Central Oregon. He remembered his odd behavior, day after day exploring the area; how drawn he'd been to the field... his excitement over developing his plan...picking Anchors Away Café out of the phone book...and meeting Millie there.

Since his accident, though he had never been a religious sort, he realized being in control was an illusion to help people feel safe. The real control belonged to a higher power. When he was still in the hospital, he had memorized a prayer to that effect. It had been found in the wallet of the chaplain of the firefighters who responded at ground zero on September 11, 2002. The man lost his life that terrible day, but the prayer on that scrap of paper in his wallet had gone viral and lived on.

> *Lord, take me where You want me to go;*
> *Let me meet who You want me to meet;*
> *Tell me what You want me to say, and*
> *Keep me out of Your way.*

He thought again of the events leading up to this calm understanding and sense of purpose he was feeling. *It seems the chaplain's prayer was correct...it appears that my role right now is staying out of the way.*

He entered 'vanilla ice cream into the reminder "ap" on his iPhone for Sunday, started up the Z and listened to its sleek purr, knowing for certain that its days with him were numbered. He turned his thoughts to Jack's birthday present and to another visit with Leona, going to the grocery store…and buying a truck. He headed towards the Safeway he'd seen not far from the Big R on Highway 97.

Inspiration hit Chapman the minute he walked through the sliding doors with his basket and was greeted by the odor of Starbuck's coffee. He ordered a pound of fair trade, organic beans and had the barista tape a fifty dollar gift certificate to the sack. Then he ordered a hot chocolate with whipped cream for himself and sipped it as he pushed his grocery cart around the store.

He bought a jar of chunky peanut butter for the dogs' toys, microwave popcorn for the kids, 2 bottles of red wine for Millie and Will, two six-packs of Greek yogurt, and a carton of whole milk. He stopped for a long time in front of the Ensure, looking at it, wondering what might serve as an easy nutritional substitute. He finally shrugged, picked up a six-pack of strawberry and then headed for the produce section. There, he bought a bunch of bananas for himself and a florist's arrangement of dark purple iris arranged in a square glass vase for Leona. He even remembered to get a gift bag and a birthday card. The verse in the card seemed to suit Jack. It said:

"It's not a matter of the years a man has been around,
or the trail in life he chose to take…but the things he
does for everyone that make a man so great."

Throughout his shopping, the sense of calm purpose remained with him. He was wearing his glasses with the light amber lens. They gave the world a rosy tint that matched his mood. He decided to put the black ones in a drawer. His new eyelids were healing nicely, the redness and swelling nearly gone.

When Chapman got back to his room, he put Leona's flowers on top of the television, placed his fedora on the armoire, toed off his loafers and put his new supplies away. He was glad his room had been made up. He ate a banana and mixed milk, yogurt and protein powder in a glass. He was tired and ready for several hours of sleep but the feeling of utter exhaustion wasn't there. *Progress! That's progress. Other than that short nap at Leona's, I've been up and busy since 7:00 a.m.* He finished drinking his concoction and slipped under the duvet.

It was just turning towards dusk when Chapman walked into Leona's room with the flowers. She was watching television but hit the clicker as soon as she saw him.

"Well, I wondered if you'd be back to visit."

Chapman smiled. "Will said you liked flowers, so I got you some."

He set them on the wide sill in front of the window.

"Well for heaven sake, a body can't look at them from that distance. Haul them over to my tray and put them next to Pansy so I can have a good look."

Then she looked up at Chapman and said in an entirely different voice. "I forgot to say thank you." She paused and then said, "And I guess I forgot to say please." The last was said almost to herself.

They looked at each other. "You're welcome," he said simply as Leona reached out and pulled the vase forward, being careful of her movement.

"Iris are some of my favorites," she said softly. "They set off a bed of daffodils and tulips just right."

"Speaking of Iris," Chapman said, "she came right up to the fence and let me scratch her this morning."

Leona's eyes brightened and a genuine smile broke over her face. "That rascal! She knows a soft touch. I suspect she had you working on that little spot where the hair goes in a circle right behind her poll."

Chapman smiled down at her. "So that's what it's called. I've been calling it her top knot. I stand corrected."

Leona waved a hand. "Doesn't matter a bit. I feel real blessed to know you are looking after them. Will would do it, but that man has a heap on his plate as it is. Have you ever seen harder working folks?" Without pausing she said, "Get yourself a chair. You can stay for a little while, can't you?"

"Chapman turned to get a chair. "Actually, I can, if you're up to it. There are several things I need to know about animal husbandry."

"Of course I'm up to it! Millie and the kids were here earlier. I can't tell you the good it did me to see those kids. I've known them all, Jake and Jenny too, since they were real little, Jenny no more than a toddler; Matt and Abby, since they were bumps in Millie's belly."

Chapman turned the chair so he could sit facing Leona. "It does make one feel the world isn't such a bad place when you are around that family, doesn't it? They've invited me to Jack's birthday party tomorrow, which was awfully nice of them since they've known me less than a week."

Leona's hand flew to her mouth. "That's what I forgot to do. I forgot to tell Millie to get Jack's cake out of the freezer. I made it up when I cooked up the rest of my winter apples. That Jack is a fool for my apple cake."

Chapman thought fast. "Actually, I think Millie and the kids made a birthday cake. But, if you want, I can go and get it tomorrow when I go to your place to feed. At the party, I could give it to him as a present from you."

He watched emotions play over Leona's face. "I think he's real mad at me. You think that cake could serve as an olive branch?"

"I don't know," Chapman said honestly. "I do know unless you make the offer, we aren't going to know one way or the other."

If Leona noticed his use of the word 'we' she gave no sign. She looked at him thinking. "That's right," she said, "we won't. Let's do it. You go around to the back porch and on the ground is one of those builder's blocks with a hole in it. You can't miss it. The key is in a metal key holder right inside it."

That she had given him such personal information without blinking an eye told Chapman a world of things; the first being that she trusted him. He felt humbled by the honor. "I can do that. Is the cake in the kitchen?"

"Yes, just go on through the mud room." She laughed. "That's a fancy name for a back porch. You can't miss the refrigerator. The cake is in a dress box. You can't miss that, either."

He smiled at her. "Leave it to me. And I'll try to take some pictures on my phone so you can see the look on his face when he opens the box. That should tell you something more."

Leona nodded. "Yes. Yes, that would be awful nice of you, Chapman. It would mean a lot to me to have pictures of the party. I haven't missed one in nearly 50 years." Her eyes were suspiciously bright. "Now what do you want to know about the animals?"

Chapman smiled. "It's about the eggs. I meant to ask Millie or Will, but I forgot. I've been hearing hens cackle and the man at Big R said it meant they were laying eggs. Do I take them out of the nest?"

"Well, of course you take them out of the nest! I don't have a rooster so they can't hatch babies. I got a stack of empty egg cartons on a shelf in the mud room. You can find them easy enough. You put the carton in the refrigerator and every day you add eggs to it. Put the date on the carton when you start it."

"Okay, now, is there any trick to it? Will the hens just let me take them?"

"Some will and some won't. Since you don't know them and they don't know you, wear gloves. I got a pair in the pocket of my old barn jacket hanging on the coat pegs just inside the back door. If they are sitting on the nest, you got to reach under them and feel around."

Chapman ran a hand over his bald head and sighed. "Why do I think you are making this sound easier than it is going to be for a city slicker like me?"

Chapter Twenty-three
Millie

Millie knew immediately that her family had let her sleep in. She sighed and opened one eye. The pillow beside her was empty. She forced her other eye open, looked at the nightstand clock. Nine o'clock! Yep, her family had definitely let her sleep in. She stretched but didn't throw the covers off, remembering instead the conversation she'd finally found the courage to have with her two older children.

On Friday night, contrary to what she had advised, they had been waiting up for her when she came home from work. It had been just like old times with peppermint tea and chit-chat past 1:00 am. At first they talked of college life, their dreams and plans...but then talk had turned to the early years on the ranch and suddenly Millie knew she had just been given the opportunity to share information they deserved to have. Tired as she was, she opened the door to their past and walked them through it.

Now, she yawned, blinked, rubbed her eyes and wished mightily for coffee, but didn't rise. *It was past time to have that talk, way past time to bring up that poor lost soul who was their father.* She had told them the facts simply and without drama. She answered their questions, like she'd answered so many other questions, sitting around the scarred kitchen table

"He wasn't a bad man in a lot of ways, but something inside him was twisted and he wouldn't get the help he needed. I had to work and couldn't keep you babies safe. So I took you and ran away."

She looked at Jenny who was looking back at her, a tear standing at the corner of each velvet eye and took her hand. "You were barely talking and even you, with all those language skills stored in your brain, didn't have the words to express what he was doing to your little body. It was Jake who told me what he'd seen. He didn't understand it, but somehow, he knew it was very wrong."

Millie turned to her son, sitting like a stone, his face composed. She reached out her other hand and silently, without changing his expression, he took it. "Jake, you weren't even five years old, and yet you figured out that you needed to get your father to stop touching Jenny. Do you remember that?"

Jake nodded. "I remember, but it's more like a dream than a real thing."

Millie turned back to Jenny. "I will be forever grateful that we weren't rich enough that you two had separate bedrooms, because what Jake did was start hollering his little head off, like he was having a nightmare or something. Your father left the bedroom like his tail was on fire."

There was profound silence around the table, each thinking their own thoughts. "I really don't remember it," Jenny finally said. "Is that a good thing or a bad thing?"

Millie shook her head. "I don't know, really. What do you think?"

Jenny shrugged. "I don't hate guys or anything like that…and I knew Dad wasn't our biological father, but it feels like he is..."

"I wish he were." Jake said, flatly. "He's the best father a guy could have."

Millie looked at her two older children. "You have any more questions?" They shook their heads no, but even as Jenny was shaking her head, she was asking, "So, where is he now?"

Millie sighed. "You know, I don't know. I had a restraining order put out back then and DSHS helped me with expenses when I left Salem and came over here. That's when I got hired by your Grandpa Jack and met Will. You ever want to meet your father; I'll sure do what I can to make that happen. You've got that right. And you've got the right to ask me questions."

Millie remembered how Jenny and Jake had looked at each other. Jake had said, "You gave us his name, we can always look him up on the internet if we decide we want to know more. There can't be that many Preston Lloyd Staddelmeyers out there."

Millie knew she had to get a move on. Church was at 10:30. She stretched again, realizing that she was still bone tired. *My own fault. I get myself so wound up, drink more coffee to stay there…and then I don't go to bed at a decent hour. Last night was one thing, but Friday night I could have been in bed instead of playing Mexican Train with the kids.* She threw back the covers and sat up.

"Coffee! Coffee first, shower second, and I'll be a new woman." She said aloud as she reached for her robe.

The kitchen was deserted and the house suspiciously quiet but the coffee maker held half a pot. She reached for her Betty Boop mug and saw the note propped in front of it.

Mom,

Dad and Jake are working on your garden.
Grandpa Jack came and got Abby and
Matt…something about his cat.

He said he'd have them back by 10:00.
I've had my shower and am doing homework
in my room.

Everyone promises to be ready for church on time.

Love you.
Jen
p.s. Grandpa knows about his party.

Millie sighed. *Okay, so it isn't going to be a surprise birthday. No big deal. We didn't really think it was all that important anyway. Once Jenny and Jake showed up at his door on Friday, he must have suspected something was up anyway.* She arched an eyebrow and re-read the note and said aloud, a smile quirking her mouth. "Something about his cat…not the stray cat, but HIS cat. Well now, this is a most interesting development."

She could hear, when she really listened, the sound of the tractor. Jake had gotten a start on disking yesterday. Maybe he was harrowing today. She took a gulp of coffee and headed for the bathroom. *Fifty cents says we're going to be late for church, as usual.*

Millie felt like a new woman sitting at the table in a pale pink angora sweater and winter white slacks. Her hair was twisted into a knot at the top of her head and small chandelier earrings hung from her ears. She was looking at her list. As far as she could tell, if Chapman remembered the ice cream everything was tickety-boo for the party. Will and Jake were both taking their showers; her garden plot was ready to go. *The worst thing that could happen now is that Abby and Matt go to church without showers.* Not a bad "worst" thing she mused just as the front door swung open, and she heard feet pounding on the stairs.

Jack came into the kitchen. He was grinning from ear to ear. Millie looked up at him. "Well now birthday boy, don't you look fine?"

It was obvious from the crease marks that his shirt was new. It was a soft turquoise check that set off his white hair to a tee. She got up to give him a hug and pour him the last of the coffee.

"Thanks, Millie. You've got no idea how much I need this cup to settle my nerves."

Millie gave him the traditional eyebrow arch. "You want to tell me about it?"

Jack laughed a short bark. "Well, come to find out that mama cat didn't have her babies under my bedroom floor. She evidently moved them there. This morning when I went out to feed her, there they all were...the mama and three of the cutest kittens you've ever seen."

She smiled at him over her cup. "So, you just had to come and get the monsters so they could see what came to breakfast?"

"I did. I sure did. Those two kids were just as quiet as they could be. Sat their butts on the steps and watched without saying a word. Mama was a bit miffed that I had left without feeding her, but when I drove back in and rattled the bowl she came right away. I got the kids settled and pretty soon those kittens were playing and rolling around in the grass right in front of us."

Millie looked at the clock. "All that and you got them back here on time. Way to go, Grandpa!"

"Well, it helped that after she ate, she marched the little buggers off," he admitted sheepishly. "I got to tell you, Millie I think we've got a problem."

Millie sat back, enjoying the moment. "Nope, old man, you got that wrong. I don't have a problem...you've got a problem."

The fingers of Jack's left hand drummed on the old oak table while he took a gulp of coffee, holding the cup with his right hand. "That girl of yours has a will of iron. Must have got it from your side of the family."

Millie snorted. "Tell me about it."

His fingers drummed some more. "An old man hasn't got any use for cats. Not a mouse on the place that I know of. What'd she want to bring her kittens under my house for anyway?"

Millie decided to change the subject. "Who spilled the beans about your party?"

She watched the expressions flit across Jack's face. She knew he'd rather face a firing squad than rat out the guilty party. "Never mind," she said, reaching out and patting his hand. "Will and I didn't really figure we could keep it from you anyway. Anybody tell you we invited Chapman?"

He looked pleased. "No. No, they didn't tell me." He grinned. "Aw, you'll hear it anyway. My fault for coming so early and unannounced. Everybody's sitting around the table with their cereal when I walk in the back door, Abby jumps up and shouts, "It's Grandpa! Hide the cake! Hide the cake. He'll see it!"

Millie laughed. "Did you see it?"

"How could I with your children all fluffed out in front of it like banty hens protecting a brood?"

"Too bad. It's not Leona's, of course, but Matt and Jenny did a great job decorating it."

At the mention of Leona's name, Jack's expression turned glum. He looked at Millie. "I still haven't been to see her again. I can't seem to make myself go. I'm still all riled up inside over it even after I went with Pastor Mike and saw how puny and old she looked."

"I did." Millie said. "I took the kids and we went to see her when we were out running errands yesterday. She seemed really glad to see us, especially the kids."

"Well, I been talking with Betty about it; talked about it to her yesterday. I suppose, could she get her mind together, she'd tell me what Mike told me."

Millie straightened her back and put down her coffee cup mid-sip. "You want to share with me what those words would be?"

Jack looked down at the table. "You're doing God's job when you start passing judgment on other people. You think you're man enough to do that?"

"Ouch." Millie said.

Jack nodded. "Yeah, ouch. But, I've thought and thought about this. Leona did a wrong thing, a terrible thing really. If I don't hold her accountable, make her think about things, who will?"

Millie sighed and looked at him. It was on the tip of her tongue to say Leona needed to hold herself accountable and that judgment here on earth was left to the courts and afterwards, left to God. Instead she touched his hand and said, "Complicated, isn't it?"

"Damned right it is."

"Chapman isn't mad at her at all. He's just sad for her."

Jack glared at her. "Now, just how do you know that, Missie?"

"He told me when he was having dinner at the Anchor on Friday night."

As they hurried up the sidewalk to Zion Lutheran Church, Millie's eyes met Will's. She knew she couldn't get a word past the lump in her throat if she'd wanted to. Up ahead, Jenny had her hand tucked under one of Jack's elbows and Abby had her arm under the other. He was, she could see, absolutely in his element; the earlier sadness buried in the joy of the moment. *I guess God gave humans that ability; the one that lets us put things in little compartments to deal with later. It's a good thing we can do that,* she thought to herself. *Sure helps us keep going when we need to.*

Chapter Twenty-four
Jack

Jack took a sip of Millie's strong coffee, his elbows propped on the old-fashioned, redwood picnic table that was now serving its second generation of Andersens. Abby and Matt were sitting across from him, reading directions for a new-fangled dog toy called a Kong. Chapman had brought three of them. *I wonder what made him think to do that?* He'd even brought the peanut butter that was going to go inside each toy as soon as the kids figured out how to do it.

Jack smiled at the picture the two bent heads made, their sodas forgotten. The dogs, Tuffy and Digger, were sitting behind their bench, as close to Matt and Abby as possible, watching intently.

Pansy, on the other hand, was standing right beside him, her front feet on the bench. He knew he should scold her off, but he didn't seem to have the heart. Her ears were perked and her eyes were bright with anticipation. *Now how in the H-E-double-L do these dogs know the toys are for them?* He reached out and stroked the little Border Collie's back. "Just hold onto your horses, Missy. My grandchildren are very smart. They'll figure out how to do this in a jiffy."

Matt grinned up at him. "It's kinda funny, Grandpa. It's your birthday but the dogs are getting presents."

Abby said, "Matt, go ask Mom for a spoon or a knife. We gotta get the peanut butter inside."

Obligingly, Matt got up from the bench and ran for the back door. "No problem," he said cheerily over his shoulder.

Abby frowned. "Grandpa, do you got a pocket knife to break the tamper proof seal on this peanut butter?" She pushed the jar in his direction.

"It just so happens that I do, Abby, my girl. But it will take a kiss to get it from me."

Abby sighed and rolled her blue eyes, but when Jack leaned forward, she got up, put one knee on the table and lifted herself far enough to put both arms around his neck. She gave him, not only a kiss but a satisfying hug. Jack dug the knife from his pocket. "Well, for the price of that, you can use it twice."

She grinned, showing dimples. "Thanks, I'll remember that." She pulled the jar back towards her, opened a blade and slipped it under the seal just as Matt came clattering back, spoon in hand, with Chapman behind him. For once he had left his fedora and neck scarf behind.

"Happy birthday, Jack," he said, easing onto the bench beside him. "I was just introduced to Jake and Jenny. They seem to be wonderful young people."

Jake nodded. "Howdy, Chapman. Yes, they sure are that. Hey, thanks for coming to my shindig."

"I was more than pleased to be invited."

Chapman turned to Matt and Abby, smiled and said, "I see you have the rapt attention of the current dog population."

It was true. Pansy was now sitting on the bench, pressed against Jack. Digger and Tuffy, fast forgetting their manners, were standing one on each side of Abby and Matt, watching intently, noses going as peanut butter was spooned into the rubber well of each toy and the top screwed back on, making an egg shaped ball with a hole in each end.

Abby looked at Chapman. "You brought them. It's fair that you get to give them out."

Chapman smiled his thin-lipped smile and said easily. "Tell you what; I'll throw Pansy hers, while you two give Digger and Tuffy theirs. I think that will seem fairer to the dogs."

"All right," Abby agreed. "I'm going to say get ready, get set. The very nano-second I say go, we all throw them as far as we can in a different direction."

Jack noticed three things: Matt sent off a side arm bullet, like he was an outfielder throwing to home plate. Abby threw like a girl, cocking her elbow and tossing with her wrist. Chapman threw like a quarter-back aiming for a wide receiver, a long easy fluid movement that sent the Kong he'd been holding under Pansy's nose right to the edge of the back yard fence. *He's done that a few times before,* he thought to himself, and he wondered again about the man he might have been before the mysterious accident. Aloud he said, "Where's Will and Jake?

Chapman turned from where dogs and children were racing about in the late spring sunshine in a fast-paced game of keep-away. "He's on the phone. I'm in the market for a pickup, and Jake told us about a friend who bought a Dodge Ram 1500 on time and then lost his job and needed to sell it. They are calling him right now. I really came out to ask if

256

you wanted to go look at it with us and then got distracted by all this." His wave took in the children, dogs, blossoming fruit trees, the distant meadows and the rugged buttes that circled their little hollow.

"Hell yes I want to go. I forgot more about trucks than those boys ever knew."

Jack moved to get up from the bench. "We can't go yet," said Chapman restraining him by laying a hand over his forearm. Both of them were arrested by the sight. Jack sat back down, noticing the contrast. On the table, Jack's hand was blunt-fingered and thick-knuckled; his skin freckled and then freckled again with age spots. Chapman's fingers were long and slim, bone covered skin that was as pale and hairless as a baby's butt. With a jerk, Chapman removed his hand.

"My, my, ain't we a pair," said Jack softly. It was just the right thing to say.

Chapman nodded, sighed deeply and after a pause said, "We can't go until after your birthday feast. Both Millie and Jenny were equally clear about that."

The back door slammed. Will came out carrying three beers. He stopped at the top of the stairs and surveyed the yard. Matt and Abby were on their bellies, watching Tuffy and Digger working with their tongues to extract the peanut butter hidden inside each toy. He was whistling as he came down the steps.

"I don't know what made you think to get those things, Mr. Lewis, but you've made the mutts happy."

Jack knew he was referring not only to the dogs, but to his younger children. "Don't be calling my grandbabies mutts, they got Highland blood in their veins," he said cheerfully as he set aside his coffee and accepted a beer.

"Jake's still on the phone with Danny. They are thinking he could bring the truck by after dinner. I hope that's okay with you?" He looked at Chapman as he handed him a beer."

Chapman nodded and looked thoughtfully at the cold can in his hand. "It's been awhile since I've had one of these. Let's see how it goes." He lifted it to his lips and took a small swallow, warming it in his mouth before letting it slide down his throat. Jack found he was holding his breath, waiting for Chapman's response.

"Well, that went down just fine," he said, pleased. "Thank you, Will." Chapman raised his can. "Happy birthday one more time, Jack!" His voice sounded delighted. Jack and Will raised their cans. "Happy birthday, Dad," Will added.

"It's been a good day," said Jack watching Chapman's Adam's apple bob, "and it just keeps getting better and better."

Matt and Abby abandoned the dogs and joined them at the table. "Dad, can we set up the roping steer?"

Will nodded. "Ask your brother to help you when he gets off the phone."

"Roping steer?" said Chapman with a question in his voice.

"Aw, it's just a plastic steer's head that we stick into a bale of hay to practice with our lariats." said Matt.

"Matt's pretty good at it," said Jack. Will nodded in agreement.

"Could you teach me how to do it?" Chapman asked, looking straight at Matt.

Jack looked at Chapman and could see he was perfectly serious.

Matt nodded. "I think so. I could show you how to build your loop, make the throw and jerk your slack. Then you'd just have to practice."

Wanting in on the action Abby said, "Yeah, and if you don't know, I could teach you how to ride."

Well, thought Jack, as he and Will exchanged silent glances, *things keep getting not only better but more and more interesting around here.* He waited for Chapman's reply.

"A horse?"

"Of course a horse!"

Matt grinned and said, "There's Abby making rhymes again." No one laughed at the old family joke. All eyes were on Chapman.

"Ah, well, I don't know how to ride one, that is a given." He took another sip of beer, an unfathomable look on his face. He looked at Abby. "You're serious, aren't you?"

"Of course I am. We've got these old, really well-broke horses that would be perfect, wouldn't they Dad?"

Will nodded, "Bill worked for both of you. I don't see why he wouldn't work for Chapman should he decide he wants to learn."

"This is an amazing and generous offer, Abby," Chapman said. "I'll tell you what; let me think about it while Matt is teaching me how to throw a rope." He held out his hands, studied them, clenched them into fists, unclenched them and clenched them again lost in thought. Then he looked at them and laughed his low, raspy laugh. "It's so strange, it all seems in the realm of possibility. It must be the beer."

Matt asked seriously, "How many of cans have you had, Chapman?"

The other men burst out laughing, but Chapman looked Matt in the eye. "Only a couple of swallows. I want to be at my best when it comes to instruction time. I was joking when I said it must be the beer."

"Well, shoot," said Will, getting up from the table. "Let's get this show on the road. I guess I can haul a bale up here as good as Jake. Let me ask Millie if I can have 10 minutes to run down to the barn and grab a couple. Matt and Abby, go get the steer head out of the garage bay where the farm truck is parked. It'll carry easier if you each grab a horn."

After Will and the kids left, Jack nodded towards two lawn chairs sitting under an old lilac tree filled with deep purple blossoms. "My back and my bony butt are telling me to trade in this real estate for those chairs. Care to join me?"

Chapman stood, nodding. He scooped up the paper trash left from the packaging of the toys and deposited it in a trash can by the back steps. "I would indeed," he said.

They sat in companionable silence, surrounded by the old-fashioned fragrance of the lilacs and watching shadows creep over the hay fields in the distance. Suddenly, Jack asked, "You really thinking about riding a horse, Chapman?"

"Actually, I'd like your opinion. Right now, I don't have the strength or the stamina, but if my plan works out, and I become a human rock mover, those should improve. I fear what won't ever improve, besides my looks, is my lung function. I'll never be able to jog, play tennis or any of those things requiring accelerated breathing…but a horse…it came to me that a horse could be my lungs."

He turned to look at Jack. "Does that make sense to you? Can you see a problem with my thinking?"

Jack found his throat nearly closed with emotion. His thoughts had turned to Leona's land when Chapman had mentioned his rock moving plan. "You bet it makes sense, if you got the desire. Now we just gotta get that old woman to play ball on the rock pile."

Chapman sat forward, his bony elbows on his knees, both hands cradling his beer. "I've been to see her several times," he said softly.

It was Jack's turn to sit forward. "What's that you said? You been to visit Leona at the hospital?"

"Yes. If my energy holds up, I plan to go see her tonight as well."

"You mean she's talking to you?"

"Yes, we've had some good visits. I update her on her animals and that makes her happy."

"What's she saying about The Lord's Bit?"

"I haven't asked her."

"You haven't asked her?" Jack found himself nearly speechless, swamped by emotions; amazement, disbelief and finally guilt, were all vying for first place. He took a swallow of beer.

"No. Although I did apologize for making her think I was a stalker and told her why I'd come to see her."

Jack nearly strangled. For a moment he wondered if Chapman was putting him on. He took a deep breath.

261

"You...you apologized to her? She shoots at you...and YOU apologize to her? Explain that one to me, if you would be so kind." He couldn't keep the drip of sarcasm out of his voice. Chapman didn't seem to notice. He sat up and took another sip of beer.

"When I found myself coveting that particular piece of ground, I had to do some deep thinking. The purpose of the rock moving project is to give my life a little meaning. It's a vehicle that I believe will improve my health and entertain me at the same time. It is not really about owning The Lord's Bit, although I will admit that I am unbelievably drawn to that spot."

Chapman's voice wound down. He seemed lost in thought. He glanced up at Jack. "This is hard to put into words," he said.

"Well, you better keep trying, son. Right now, in the middle of an ocean without a compass, I am having a damned hard time getting over the fact that that old woman tried to take your life."

"I believe I can put myself in Mrs. Larsen's shoes, a little. I still remember very clearly when life held no hope," he said quietly, his lizard eyes behind amber sun glasses fastened on his beer can. "Since then I've gotten better at putting compassion for others ahead of my own issues. I look at her, and I see a woman in pain. I see a tough woman who has lost what is most dear to her, but struggles on. I see a woman who was scared to death but chose not to be a victim..."

The screen door opened and Jake stepped through, ending the conversation. "Danny's coming over about 4:00. Can you stay that long Chapman?"

Chapman looked at Jake and nodded. "Sure. I took a long nap before I came. I should be fine. Thanks for setting it up, Jake."

"Well it's a lot of truck, so it might not work for you. Don't feel obligated, okay?"

Chapman smiled. "I won't. Don't worry."

"Oh, and by the way, Mom said she meant it when she only gave Dad 10 minutes. You guys had better get your hands washed."

Chapter Twenty-five
Will

Will slipped under the covers and drew Millie into the circle of his arms. "That was some kinda party, Mil. It meant a lot to Dad. Hell, I think it meant a lot to all of us. I know it did me."

He kissed her tenderly on the lips. "Thanks, Babe."

She smiled sleepily. He could tell she was bone tired.

"You're welcome. It's been a lovely day, hasn't it?" she murmured." Already her eyes were at half-mast. She turned away from him onto her side with a sigh. He felt her cold feet sneaking into the warm spot under his calves.

Will turned and lay on his back with his hands crossed behind his head staring up at the moonlit ceiling of the bedroom. He felt entirely at peace; his usual worries seemed unimportant. Even the fact that Jenny and Jake had gotten a late start back over the mountain didn't bother him. He had a lot of confidence in their common sense and their driving skills.

He thought about the day as he waited for sleep. Pastor Mike's sermon had been friendship. *What was it he said? Something about how much was written about forgiving our enemies and how not very much was written about forgiving our friends.*

Will smiled to himself. He'd sneaked a peek at his dad out of the corner of his eye. He'd looked like a man with a bull's-eye on his forehead.

I'll bet Mom gets an earful tomorrow. His dad generally gave his mom the meat of Mike's sermon on Mondays when he went to visit. *Anyway, he's the one that's got to work out what's going on between Leona and him. Didn't make it any easier when Chapman handed him that cake she'd had him get from her freezer and then told him Leona said she'd made it for him from the last of her apples.*

That's another thing...Chapman's been to see Aunt Leona and I haven't. What does that say about me? She's going to think I'm pissed at her, too. With sudden clarity, Will realized he was not. *If Chapman can let it go like he has, be good if the rest of us could and then concentrate on Leona's real problems.*

Slowly, Will turned on his side. As he knew she would, Millie spooned into him, still sound asleep. He put out an arm and pulled her even more closely into his warmth and breathed in her scent, Chapman now on his mind.

He's something else...as skinny as a scarecrow, doesn't weigh enough to keep from blowing over in a good wind and yet... you add his heart into the mix, he's planted deep and strong. Wonder if he'll take Abby up on her offer to learn to ride. It would be good for the both of them. He caught on to the roping thing real quick, but it sure tired him out.

Millie's hair was tickling his nose. He reached up and smoothed it down as if he were petting a kitten. His eyes drifted shut, his breathing evened and slowed. His last thought was a sad one. *Likely, Chapman won't ever have this.*

Will rolled through the kitchen barely stopping to start the coffee maker before shrugging into his ratty old Carhartt barn coat and hustling out the back door.

A naturally early riser, he'd somehow slept in. It was a shade shy of six o'clock, barely enough time to take care of the stock, then get the kids up and fed before the bus came.

The dogs were waiting by the Ranger as he came out the back door pulling on a ball cap with ear flaps as he went. He lowered the tail gate and whistled them in. He gave them each an ear scratch and swore he could still smell peanut butter on their breaths as they greeted him with wagging tails and doggy grins.

"You guys about ready to do some cow work?" he asked. "If this weather keeps up, it's not too much longer until we move them higher on the mountain." He slammed the tailgate. "In the meantime, we'd better go look at the new babies."

He scanned the sky. Not a cloud in sight, other than the frosty clouds of breath made by panting dogs in the cold spring air. He frowned. These freezing nights and warm days were going to spike the sugar content in all of Central Oregon's hay. *Another good reason to switch to Bluegrass seeds and straw,* he thought to himself as he started the truck and threw it into gear.

The horses came snorting and crow hopping into the stock yard, frisky in the brisk air. The young Maury Greys came more cautiously. Will bucked a bale into the back of the truck with his knee. In the old days, he carried the bale

266

from the barn to the long wooden manger; now, he saved his back. He drove the truck along the fence, shoved it into neutral and hopped out, pulling his pocket knife from his Wranglers as he went. He had the strings cut and the hay spread along the feeder in minutes.

Driving with both hands on the way back to the house and concentrating on missing the potholes, he thought, *now why didn't I have Jake take a blade to this when he had the tractor out doing the garden?*

He burst through the back door, threw his coat and hat at the coat rack and headed for the stairs, taking them three at a time. Abby greeted him at the top.

"Dad, stop hurrying. I got Matt up 15 minutes ago. Help me part my hair." She was holding out a rat-tailed comb. Will grinned at her and took the comb.

"Good job, Skeezix. Turn around."

Obediently, Abby turned. "Why do you call me that, Dad?"

"I don't know why," said Will, concentrating to get the part straight and centered, knowing she'd be asking him to do it over if he didn't. "I guess because people used to call kids that when I was little…either that or Snickelfritz."

"You mean it's like a nickname?"

"Yep. Like a nickname."

"What do they mean?"

Will turned her around and handed her the comb. "I don't know. Ask your grandpa; he'll remember. Now, hop to it. I'm scrambling eggs."

Will turned to go and then stopped. Abby was standing where he left her, pulling bands from her wrist and making pony tails. "Hey, Abby."

"Yeah, Dad?"

"I forgot to say thanks for being so responsible."

"You're the one who got me the alarm clock, remember, Dad?" she said dismissively.

But I do believe she is pleased to hear it, if that blushing face means anything, thought Will as he hustled back down the stairs to make breakfast.

"Daddy, could I ask you something?" Abby asked as Will spooned eggs onto her plate.

Daddy? Not Dad? Uh-oh, here comes trouble, Will kept his face neutral. "Sure thing. What's up?"

"If Mr. Lewis decides to take riding lessons and wants to pay me, can I take the money?"

Matt stopped spreading jam on his toast and listened with both ears.

Whoa! Where's Millie when I need her? Will slid the egg pan back on the range and got down Millie's mug, thinking fast. "That's a real good question, Abby. Let me think about it while I take your mom's coffee to her. In the meantime, eat your eggs as fast as you can, but don't gobble."

He could tell his children had been having a serious discussion in his absence and he guessed it was about earning pay. "Looks like you two are figuring things out for yourselves. Drink your milk, Matt."

Abby sighed dramatically. "Matt says some of the things you do for other people are good deeds, but then HE'S not trying to earn money for a horse."

"I see your point," said Will. "I've been thinking about how you can earn money too. One of the things I thought of was keeping Mom's garden weed-free and watered. Then too, your mom and I were discussing letting you bike over to Aunt Leona's and doing the same for her garden, once we get it planted and school's out."

Matt thumped his empty milk glass down on the table, picked up his plate to carry it to the sink and said. "Well, I'm not going to charge Mr. Lewis for teaching him to build a loop and make a good throw. I had fun doing that. I'm only going to charge for things that aren't fun."

"Whoa!" Will said, holding up both hands like a traffic cop. "Let's remember one thing Abby said...if Mr. Lewis WANTS to pay her. That means he has to make the offer. If he does, then yes, Abby, after discussing the amount with your mother and me, you can accept if you still want to."

Millie walked into the kitchen. "Want to what?" she asked as she set down her mug and started opening her eye lids with her fingertips."

"I'll tell you later, Hon. I got us moving late this morning. Up the stairs, kids!"

"Thanks for taking your plates to the sink, darlings. Remember: teeth, coats, backpacks, homework, lunches...and a kiss for your mother," said Millie to their retreating backs.

"Thanks, Dad!" Abby shouted over her shoulder.

"You're welcome, Abby, but I mean it when I say no finagling on this!"

Millie turned from getting the kid's lunch sacks out of the fridge. She held them up. "Lasagna, apple cake and an orange. How's that for a balanced meal? Jenny fixed them before she left last night. There's one for you, too."

Will grinned. "Damn, that Trenton can cook, can't he?" Will shoveled in a mouthful of eggs. He knew better than to offer some to Millie.

"What a great Sunday! I think Dad liked every bit of it. But the best present was Jenny and Jake," Millie said.

Will nodded. Seeing the kids had been like a gift to them all. "Leona's cake sure touched him. I went to sleep thinking about that…and about Chapman."

Millie smiled at him, refilled his coffee cup and emptied the rest into her own. After she started a new pot, she pulled the Thermos from the top of the fridge and filled it with hot water. Pulling the pink robe more closely around her, she sat down. "Think he'll buy Danny's truck?"

"I don't know. Seems to me that he doesn't need that big V-8, but he was right to make Danny set a price on it. I would imagine the boy went right home and got his pencil out. Chapman handled that real well. But that's not what I was thinking about."

Will took a sip of coffee. "I was thinking I had a thing or two to learn from him; one thing being his attitude about Leona. It's like he doesn't even see that there's any forgiving needed." He furrowed his brow, looking at his empty plate. "I find it most interesting how he can sort of step back from a situation…or maybe rise above a situation and look at it from all sides."

Millie breathed in the steam from her coffee and then took a swallow. "He's a good man," she said simply.

"Dad told me Chapman's been to see Leona twice. I'm the only one in the family who hasn't been to see her and

270

I'm not liking that much about myself. It's something I plan to rectify today."

"Other than that, what are your plans?" asked Millie.

"Well, I got to go check the irrigation down at the new field and then move some hand lines over at Leona's. Then I'll come back here, hook up the trailer, load old Bill and go check on the new calves. I was going to check on how the springs are running, but I believe with this weather, they'll be doing fine. But still, I'm sorta hoping for some rain. Like to get that seed in the new field well started."

"How are you going to fit visiting Leona into that mix?"

"I figure Bill can wait in the trailer in the hospital parking lot while I run in and have my visit. How about you? How many balls you juggling today?"

"Same old, same old...plus tryin' to clean that friggin' lasagna pan I got soaking in the utility sink, planting my garden and staking the raspberries." She smiled. "And, unless I miss my guess, your dad's going to be calling me or coming by. That might take a bit."

He stood and picked up his plate, leaned over and kissed the top of her head. "You see how happy he was to get those cat toys? That was pretty brilliant, Millie the Mom."

"It wasn't a surprise party, but it was just about perfect, except for the fact that for the first time I remember, Leona wasn't with us."

They looked at each other, reminded of her plight. Millie said, "when you see her, be prepared. She looks pretty frail."

"What a sorry state of affairs," Will said, shaking his head. "I'll try to find out how long they are keeping her when I go in."

Abby and Matt thundered down the stairs, grabbed their coats off the coat rack by the back door and skidded into the kitchen. They grabbed their lunches from the counter and flung their arms around Millie for a quick hug and kiss.

Abby stopped before heading for the bus just long enough to ask, her eyes shining, "Dad, did you mean it when you said I could ride my bike over to Aunt Leona's."

Will nodded. "Yep. Your mom and I already talked about it."

"Cool!" "Way cool!" she said softly, almost to herself and then dashed out the front door after Matt.

"Well, sounds like you've had a busy morning." Millie's eyes were smiling over the rim of her mug.

"Yep." Will took his plate to the sink. "You're better at this kind of stuff. But I allowed as how Abby could accept money for teaching Chapman to ride, but only if he offered it."

Millie got up to pour coffee into the Thermos. He could see she was thinking. "So that's how the bike thing came up…a conversation about earning money."

"Yep. What I didn't say was that I got a line on a couple of geldings from Danny last night. They belong to his dad. I might go check them out, should I have the time."

Millie walked towards him as he was shrugging into his coat, plastic lunch bag and thermos in hand. "Can you stand having lasagna again for dinner tonight? Trenton made a ton of it. If not, I'll thaw a package of hamburger and some buns."

Will checked his pocket for gloves. "Lasagna's just fine." He took the thermos and bag from Millie's hands, set it on the table and wrapped his arms around her. "I need a good-bye kiss too" he said.

Will pulled into a double parking spot at the far corner of the lot at the hospital. The building was brand new, and he was looking forward to seeing what his tax dollars had paid for. He hopped out, looked at the three dogs, considering. Then he lowered the tail gate and motioned Pansy forward while telling Digger and Tuffy to stay put. As he lifted her into his arms, he said, "Come on, girl, it's not that I don't trust you not to run off looking for Leona, but just in case…"

He dumped her onto the seat of the cab, rolled down the window two inches and then shut the door in her face. "You guys stay put, you hear," he said as he closed the tail gate and went to check on Bill, who was standing quietly in the horse trailer, as he had so many times before. Will reached up and stroked his plain, honest face. "Hang tight, old fellow. This won't take long."

Will whistled softly when he walked into the bright, modern building. Everything in the lobby was tasteful, including the carpeting and the artwork. He was given Leona's room number at the reception desk and directed towards a bank of elevators. The elevators whisked him to the third floor in impressive silence. *Real nice to have this in a little town like Redmond,* he thought as he made his way to the door of room 322.

As Will walked through the door, he was surprised to see Chapman sitting in a chair pulled beside Leona's bed, one stork-like leg crossed over the other at the ankle. His laptop sat on the table top he'd made of his legs.

"Will Anderson, you are a sight for sore eyes, get on in here!"

"Howdy, Aunt Leona…Chapman." Will walked over to the wide counter under the window, took off his beat up old cowboy hat, set it beside him and leaned back. He grinned his chipped toothed grin as he looked Leona over. "I was expecting to see you looking real puny, but to me, you look pretty darned good. So how's the world treating you these days?"

Leona's bed had been cranked up. There was a snap in her faded blue eyes and a spot of color on her cheeks. "It's treating me better than it was yesterday. The doctor has been in and as soon as Chapman and I work out a few more details, and I can prove to these folks around here that I can walk on my own, I get to go home."

Will glanced at Chapman. His hat and amber glasses were on Leona's tray table. He looked utterly relaxed and comfortable, his fingers moving over the keys at a fast clip. "Hi, Will, that was a terrific party. Thanks again."

Will looked back at Leona. Contrary to what Millie had led him to expect, she looked better than she had in years.

"So, how are you doing on the walking part of things? Still in pain?"

"Some. But I'd rather be at home in a little pain than here, I'll tell you that!"

"Can't say as I blame you," Will said mildly. He moved to the bed and took her hand.

"Sorry I haven't been in to see you, Aunt Leona."

She patted his forearm. "Don't think a thing of it. I know how busy you are, Will. Thank you for taking Pansy in."

"She's down in the truck right now. I got Bill in the trailer. We're on our way to the butte to check on the new calves."

Chapman's fingers paused on the keys.

"Bill? You mean the horse I'm going to learn to ride?"

Will nodded. "Yep. If that's what you've decided."

"Well, I have. Mrs. Anderson thinks it's a good idea. I plan to give Abby a call."

"I told you to call me Leona". Anybody who takes care of my livestock has the right to my given name." She turned to Will. "Is Pansy doing okay for you?" He heard the longing in her voice.

"She is." A sudden thought came to him. "Just a minute, I'll be right back."

At the nurse's station, two women sat conferring over a chart. "Excuse me," said Will, giving his best "aw shucks" grin. "My name is Will Anderson. Is it possible I could take Aunt Leona for a stroll?

They looked up. "Leona Larsen?" they asked in unison.

"Yep. She says she's going to be able to go home when she can walk around on her own. I thought my friend, Chapman, and I could escort her around...maybe take a wheelchair with us in case she gets tired."

They looked at each other and back at Will. The older one said, "Are you Jack and Betty's boy?"

"Yes, ma'am, I am."

"Well, give me a minute and I'll come in and help you get her to her feet and show you how to support her. She needs to walk as much as she can."

Will walked back into the room grinning from ear to ear. "Chapman," he said. "How would you like to help me escort this lady down the hall?" He paused dramatically. "Then down the elevator, through the lobby and out the door. There's a little dog in the truck that would just love to have a visit."

Chapter Twenty-six
Leona

Leona blinked. "You asked a nurse and she said I could do that?" she asked, disbelief sharpening her voice.

"Not exactly," said Will.

Chapman looked up, closing the lid of his laptop. "Not exactly?" he echoed, turning the two words into a question.

"Aunt Leona always taught me that you don't let everybody know your business right off the bat. Didn't you, Auntie?" There was no mistaking the twinkle in Will's blue eyes.

"Why…yes, yes I did. Of course I did!" Leona said, understanding dawning. "Well, I reckon you aren't so thick as I thought Will Anderson! You asked me was I able? I'm able all right. I'm going to see Pansy if I have to crawl!"

She made a move to throw the blanket back but Will held up his hand. "Hold on a minute. We have to wait for the nurse. She said she'd come as soon as she can. I asked her to rustle up a wheelchair in case you got tired."

Obediently, she settled back and her glance slid to Chapman whose forehead was furrowed like he was trying to follow a foreign language. She lifted a finger and pointed to him. "Stick with us kid, and we'll have a real good time, just like that old song says. I do like Will's plan. Why'd you turn off the computer? You find out what we need to know?"

Chapman said, "I didn't shut it off, I just put it in hibernate mode so I wouldn't waste battery time while I was paying attention to what mischief you two are cooking up."

Leona waved a hand and said, "Smart man." Then she looked at Will. "Chapman and I were just doing some research, trying to figure out how much that worthless chunk of land Peter called 'The Lord's Bit' might be worth...ball park figure is all." She was pleased to see his jaw drop and figured she'd see if she couldn't drop it a little more.

"Earlier, we found out how much it was going to cost to have a person come and look in on me, help me out a little until I heal...but I can't come close to affording it. I can't afford any sort of care facility either."

She glanced at Chapman. His face gave nothing away. Will's face was one big question mark. "Soooo?" He finally asked.

"So Chapman found out that I can get a bed, pretty much like this one and a wheelchair pretty much like that one." She pointed to the one the nurse was wheeling through the door. "Hell, I can even get a walker and tall porta-potty thing should I need it...and Medicare pays for it all!" she crowed.

The nurse rolled the wheelchair towards the bed. Chapman stood up to pull his chair out of her way. "Hello, Leona. How nice for you to have people here to help you exercise."

"Hello, Sandy. I do indeed. Thanks for the chair, but I doubt I'll need it. I got my mind made up to get out of here."

"Well let me show them how we get you out of bed then." Sandy said pleasantly and then walked to the closet to retrieve a hospital issue robe. Over her shoulder she said, "You know, Leona, three days ago I couldn't wait to get rid of you. Now, I'm really going to miss you."

She returned and helped Leona swing her legs over the side of the bed, taking care that the hospital gown did not slide up or expose Leona's backside. "In fact," she said, deftly maneuvering the robe so Leona could slip her arms into the sleeves, "if I had a blue ribbon, I would give it to you for the most improved personality on the floor."

"Guess I finally remembered you catch more flies with honey than with vinegar," Leona said smiling at her and tying the robe shut at her waist.

Sandy turned and looked, first at Chapman and then at Will. "If you are going to be helping her, or know the person who is, tell them not to pull her. You just hold your arm out like this, brace yourself a little and let her use it like a lift bar. Watch."

Leona grabbed Sandy's forearm with both hands and gingerly levered herself upright."

"How you doing, Leona?" Sandy asked.

"Good. I'm doin' good. Stiff, but the pain, for right now, is real tolerable. It just feels like I've been gardening too long." She slipped her feet into the scuffs by her bed.

"Well, all right then. I'm going to walk you out into the hall. Then, one of these fine men can offer an elbow and the other can push your chair. Do as much as you comfortably can."

To the men, she said, "See how she's doing the work? All I am is her stable support, or her counterbalance."

Leona noticed that both men were watching as though their life depended on it; one with the eyes of a lizard, the other with his mother's bright baby blues…both with hearts of pure gold.

Chapman, deferring to Will, took the handles of the chair. Will stepped to her side and offered his arm. Slowly, she took her first steps down the hall with him. "I been up and walking around here last night," she said, looking up at Will. "I know where the elevators are."

"That's where we're headed, Auntie…one step at a time."

"Amazing what a shot of cortisone can do for a body."

"You know, it hasn't even been a full week," said Will conversationally.

"Seems longer." She felt the strength in Will's forearm and wondered, thinking of Chapman's bone thin body, if she should even tell Will their mad plan. He might think Chapman wasn't capable enough and if so, did she really want to hear it? She sighed. "You need to know, that Chapman is the one to take care of me. He's willing to come and sleep in the boys' room. My hospital bed will be in the dining room, if you could find the time to come and push the table aside."

Will kept his step in exact time with hers. For the longest time, he didn't say a word but, just when she was starting to feel anxious, he spoke.

"You are a surprise a minute, Aunt Leona. Did you two just cook this up?"

"Well, you know, he's been coming to see me every day. Brought me a fine picture of Pansy the first time. Hard not to like a man that does something that nice for an old lady…especially one who tried to blow him to kingdom come. So, it's not like I don't know him a little."

"I take it that's a yes."

She nodded her head. "He's been working at that computer for about an hour, trying to help me figure things out. When he realized how broke I really am, he, out of the blue, just offered."

They stopped at the bank of elevators and slowly, step-by-step, Leona turned to face the doors. They both looked at Chapman who was serenely pushing the wheelchair down the hall towards them. "That would be like him," Will said as he pushed the down button.

Once in the elevator, Will elaborated on his plan. "Okay, Aunt Leona, first off, how you doing?"

"Fine. Better'n I thought. Besides, if I tire, Chapman's got the chair. No changing your mind, Will Anderson."

"I'm not changing my mind, but you have to promise to do what I say. I want you to sit in the chair now."

"Why would I want to do that?" Leona asked sharply.

"Because, I think the staff is less likely to stop us if you are in the chair. We're just two men taking an old lady out in the sunshine. Got it?"

"Makes sense." She grinned at Chapman. "Chair please, my good man!" Chapman maneuvered the chair and Will offered his arm as a brace. She lowered herself gently just as the doors opened into the lobby.

With Chapman pushing, the three of them headed for the exit with Will continuing to lay down the law. "Now, Aunt Leona, Pansy is going to be real excited, you know that. So, you are going to stay put in this chair. I'm going to have a tight hold on her collar until we see how it goes."

Leona found she could not get a word past the tightness in her throat. To be out in the glorious sunshine felt like a miracle. Her eyes couldn't seem to drink in the budding trees, the neatly edged lawns and the dots of yellow daffodils here and there. A whiff of rock Daphne came to her on the breeze and she could hear bird song. All that in addition to the thought of seeing her dear dog made it hard to listen to Will's words. Her mind was singing joyful songs right along with the birds.

"Did you hear what I said, Aunt Leona?"

She managed a nod. Chapman was pushing her at a fair clip, but she said, "Crank this thing up, if you would Chapman. Time's a'wasting." Then, she heard the rasp come into his breathing. She looked up at Will who was walking beside them. He appeared to be listening to Chapman's breathing, too.

"Never mind what I said, Chapman. You are doing just fine. I got so excited, I forgot about your lungs."

"I'm getting a little—better.

Leona could see Will's old truck and stock trailer in front of them. As they drew closer, she could see a black and white dog with her nose stuffed against the two-inch space of open window. She tried to call out a welcome, but it was impossible; her throat was closed up tight.

Will picked up his pace and by the time the wheelchair came up to the truck, he'd opened the door a crack and was trying to get his hand through the collar of a dog who was whirling and yapping and turning herself inside out with joy and excitement.

Tuffy and Digger started to add their two cents to the happy barking, but Will silenced them with a sharp word. He finally simply gathered Pansy in his arms and carried her frantic wiggling body to the wheelchair, dropped to his knee and presented her head to Leona's waiting hands.

"Pansy, oh, Pansy! How I've missed you!" she croaked out, tears slipping unchecked down her cheeks. Her gnarled fingers buried themselves in Pansy's white ruff and she found her face covered with rough dog kisses that felt like heaven.

She heard Will say, "Careful of your back, Aunt Leona, don't go trying to bury your head in Pansy's fur."

He'd said it just in time. She wanted nothing more than to bury her head in her dog's fur and bawl like a baby; she was that happy.

"Course I won't," she said, directing her words to the dog. "Will I, Pansy? I'm going to be the most careful person you ever saw...so I can come home where I belong. Have you been being a good girl for Will?"

Oblivious to either man, she crooned on to the dog who was gradually relaxing enough that Will could loosen his hold and set her feet on the ground.

"You want her front feet in your lap, Aunt Leona?"

"Course I do. That way I don't have to lean forward, do I Pansy? I don't have to lean forward at all and I can pet my dear dog. Can't I? I can pet her and rub her ears all I want." Leona's patter flowed straight from her heart into Pansy's. Soon the little dog's frantic whines had ceased and she pressed against Leona's chest with her eyes shut, soaking in the sound of Leona's voice and touch.

It wasn't until Leona heard the sound of Will's stock trailer door open that she realized the men had left them alone. She could hear Will introducing Chapman to the old bay horse, Bill, telling him what a good cow horse he was, surefooted and steady. She remembered when Jack had brought the Quarter Horse colt home to Will as a gangly three-year old, a present to honor starting his ranching life.

Pansy's weight began to be uncomfortable on her thighs. Softly, with her hands giving a little push, she asked Pansy to get down. Still, her hands continued to stroke Pansy's head. "You be a good dog for Will. Do what he tells you. He's a real busy man and can use all the help he can get."

The dog's tail waved gently. She looked over her shoulder when she heard the trailer door slam shut, watching, her eyes on Will as they came back into view. Not for the first time she thought, *it's like she knew what I said, the way she's looking at him... like she's considering my words.* Pansy looked back at Leona and without urging, lowered her head to the robe covered lap with a sigh.

"I know sure as God made little green apples that I've put you behind schedule, Will. So you and Pansy go on now. Chapman can take me back up."

Will looked torn for a moment. He looked at Chapman and then back at Leona. "Sounds like a plan," he said.

Leona gathered Pansy's head in her hands. "You remember what I said," she whispered as Will's hand slipped through the dog's collar and drew her away. He leaned over and placed a kiss on Leona's cheek. "Bye, Auntie. See you soon."

"How's Betty doin', Will?"

"About the same. Today is Dad's day to go see her…but we all went to see her yesterday. I think it confused her more than anything else…"

Leona could hear the sad resignation in his voice.

"You are all doing the best you can, Will."

He opened the truck door and lifted Pansy in. As he shut it he said, "Yes, I suppose we are. You take care now."

With a final wave to both of them, he hopped in the truck and put it into gear. They watched until he turned a corner and was gone.

"Ready?" Chapman asked.

Leona nodded and said, "I sure wish I had remembered to thank him, Chapman. I guess my manners have gotten a little dusty."

Chapter Twenty-seven
Chapman

Chapman said little as he pushed Leona across the parking lot. He knew his energy was nearly depleted. After thinking it through, he asked, "Leona, would you mind if we stopped by my car?"

"Of course I don't mind. I'm in no hurry to go back to jail. You talking about that fancy blue car?"

"Yes. But since my traveling days are over, I'm going to sell it and get a pickup."

"Suits this country better."

"Yes, and I'll need it for my project."

Chapman rolled Leona up to the side of his car, set the brake on the wheelchair and with a touch to his key, unlocked the door. "Want one?" He asked as he reached into the cooler for an Ensure.

"Don't mind if I do. I've always wanted to taste one of those things seein' as how they serve them a lot in old folk's homes. Didn't know if they'd make me puke or not."

He leaned against the Z and watched Leona. Her eyes looked speculative as she took in the lines of the car.

"I think I'm going to charge you double for The Lord's Bit. Man that can afford a car like this has got to be loaded."

Chapman, in the middle of his first sip, nearly had to spit it out. He looked down at her. There was a satisfied smirk on her face and her eyes were twinkling. He laughed and she joined in.

She looked at him appraisingly. "You get that truck, trade that fedora in for a cowboy hat. It'll suit you better."

"First, let's see if I can ride a horse. If I can, you can help me pick one out, how's that?

"Before you take a lesson, start sitting backwards on a chair. You've got to stretch those groin muscles out if you want to ride comfortable," she said with seeming authority. "None of Will's saddles suit your skinny butt, there's some down in the barn. You'd have to oil them up, but they both have padded seats."

She lifted the bottle of strawberry Ensure to her lips, took a tentative sip and made a face. "In the old days, the folks thought the worse medicine tasted the better it was for them. The men who sold snake oil used to add things to their brew just to make it taste terrible." She took a swallow. "I reckon this is something like that."

"Something similar to that," Chapman said mildly. "But it kept me going through some difficult times, so I decided to drink it even if I had to hold my nose. It has to be cold though; warm, it's really atrocious."

They finished their drinks in companionable silence and then Chapman pushed her slowly towards the entrance.

"If there's anything else you want me to do at the farm, just let me know."

"I'm hoping tomorrow's the day they spring me from this joint. But, I've been thinking…wondering if you thought you could drive a Buick. Seems like you're the one likely to end up taking me home and I don't think I could manage the low seats in your fancy car. I might get myself in, but how would anyone get me out?"

"A point well taken," Chapman conceded. "Yes, I believe driving a Buick is well within my skill set."

Leona waved a hand. "The tires are a little bald, but she'll run fine. The keys are in my purse; don't let me forget to give them to you."

Chapman grinned down at the top of her head as they whooshed through the doors into the foyer.

"Yes, ma'am. I'll check your car out when I go feed tomorrow, how's that? Then, I'll just wait for your call."

He noticed Leona looking him over as he pushed the elevator button. "What now?" he asked. "Millie thinks I need an earring. Do you concur?"

"No. No I don't think that at all. I'm looking at how gray your skin is. You gettin' sick from drinking that stuff?"

"No, this is what happens when it is time for me to take a nap. I just run out of energy. The Ensure helped a little; it brought my blood sugar back up. But it takes sleep and sometimes a Vitamin B shot to revive me entirely." He rolled her onto the elevator and as the doors closed, punched the floor button. He then walked around in front of her and held out his arm as the nurse had showed them. "Let's see if we can do this."

He saw the doubt in Leona's eyes. "Listen," he said, "If we can get you vertical, you can use the wheelchair to assist your balance. I'm going to walk beside you to your room, get you settled and then go have a shot and a nice nap in my car. Please don't worry. I have my whole health management down to a science now."

288

With only a slight hesitation, she reached out and grasped his bony forearm. "We can do this," she said with a conviction she perhaps didn't feel. "And I'm not going to charge you double after all."

Chapman smiled down at her and braced himself. "Thank you," he said, and then…"Yes, I'm certain we can." He watched as she pulled herself upright with a slow and steady pull. "Excellent!" he said as he turned the wheelchair until she could grab the handles and walk from the elevator. "First class!"

After his nap, Chapman drove to Leona's farm. If she was indeed being released tomorrow, he wanted to be ready.

He found the key in its place by the back door and walked in for the second time that day. The first time it had been to put four more eggs in the refrigerator.

He walked to the stairs leading to the bedrooms and counted. *Eighteen steps. Let's see how I do.* He grasped the wooden rail and began to climb, slowly and steadily. He was incredibly pleased when he didn't have to rest. He stood a minute at the top, letting his breathing settle and trying to remember exactly what Leona had said about the layout of the rooms. The boys' room, he knew was to the right. Hers was the door on his left. The bathroom was straight ahead.

As he made his way to his new quarters, he admired the walnut wainscoting and the pillow tick wallpaper. He wondered if Leona had picked it out.

When he opened the door, it hit him immediately, how hard it must have been for Leona to accept that someone else would inhabit the room her boys had grown up in. It was not so different than his own boyhood room, though his posters had been of race cars, not football players. In place of the single bed in his room, this room held two beds. In place of wall to wall carpeting, this room had hardwood floors and an old-fashioned rag rug.

He looked at the old computer on a hand-built desk, smiled to himself and went to lift the cover. *I knew it!* The computer was one of the original Apple microcomputers. It was first known as the Macintosh. After that it was the 'Mac'. He touched the logo, lost in memories and then let the cover drop.

Really, he was here to see if the mattress and sheets would suit both the bones and skin of his still healing body. He lifted one plaid spread. The sheets were old, soft cotton and would do nicely. The mattress, however, was very firm. He frowned. *It seems as though I had better purchase one of those memory foam mattress toppers before tomorrow night. I'll ask Millie at dinner if she knows where I might purchase such an item.*

He opened the closet door, saw the lettermen's sweaters and realized again the depth of Leona's loss. He sat back down on the bed, trying to imagine what it would feel like to be inside her skin. *She's lost it all if she loses this place. Here, at least, she has solid reminders of happier days, happier memories.*

He pulled out his phone, checked the time and with an idea that led to sudden conviction, called Jack.

When the old man answered, Chapman could hear a television talk show in the background.

"Hello, Jack, this is Chapman Lewis."

"Just a minute, I got Martha Stewart blathering in my ear. Let me find the mute...okay. Howdy, Chapman. Say, I was going to call you to say thanks again for the coffee and the gift certificate. I had me a latte this morning; took one to Millie too."

"You are entirely welcome, Jack. I was really pleased to be invited your party."

Chapman heard Jack chuckle. "If a man's got to turn 77, that's the way to do it. My grandkids coming over the mountain, well, that would have been enough right there."

"You have a wonderful family, Jack."

"Yes. Yes, I sure do. They work too damned hard, Millie and Will do." He paused. "Don't know as it hurts them I guess…what can I do for you Chapman?"

"I was wondering if I could buy you dinner tonight at Anchor's Away. I have some things I'd like to run by you."

"Well, that's a fine idea. I never did get by to tell Trenton I'd be proud for him to name that lasagna after me. I can do that tonight. I can buy my own dinner though."

"Why don't I roll by and pick you up about 6:30?" Chapman said, ignoring his last comment.

"Pick me up? You mean to squire me in that fancy blue sports car?"

"I do indeed."

"Hot diggity dog! I'll be ready and waiting."

"I'll call right now for a reservation."

Chapman was smiling when he hung up, remembering Leona's comment about not being able to get out of his car once she got in. Evidently Jack had no such qualms.

On the way back to the stairs he stopped and looked in the bathroom. It was spotless, but sparse. There was a claw-footed tub under a dormer window, a vanity with an old fashioned oval mirror and a basic white porcelain toilet. He remembered the shower in the mudroom by the back door and nodded to himself. *I guess that makes sense on a farm. Leona would have liked her men to be clean before coming into the house and getting her floors and furniture dirty.*

He realized, if everything worked out, that he too would be coming through the back door sweaty and dirty. *And, there's not a reason in the world it won't work out, unless Leona changes her mind, and I can't think that she will.* He was whistling softly under his breath as he walked down the stairs.

True to his word, when Chapman pulled into the driveway, Jack was sitting on the steps by the garage, a cell phone held to his ear, He noticed a cat had been sitting at Jack's feet. She scooted around the corner at the sound of his car.

Jack waved and got to his feet. "Just talking to my granddaughter about the kittens," he said as Chapman put down his window.

"I seem to have cut short your conversation. Sorry, Jack."

"No problem, no problem at all." Jack walked to the passenger's side of the Z and paused a moment, seemingly stumped by the lack of a horizontal door handle. Chapman could see the light dawn as he reached down and slipped his hand into the vertical opening that held the door release.

"That's pretty damned fancy the way the Japs set the handle right into the door, vertical like that." He beamed at Chapman as he eased himself down into the seat and swung both his legs in like he'd done it a million times before.

They smiled at each other as Jack found and fastened his seatbelt. "It's good to see you, Jack," Chapman said.

"Good to see you too. Thanks for the invite." He looked around the cockpit of the car, noticing the sleek details. "This is some jalopy, Chapman. You ever turn it loose on some deserted highway?"

Chapman backed slowly out of the driveway. "More than I should have, probably."

"Well, crank this thing up and let's go see what Trenton has thought up for tonight's specials."

Chapman grinned and said, "Those are the exact words Leona said when she wanted me to push her wheelchair faster."

He noticed what his own parents would have called a "pregnant silence" from the seat next to him. "Oh she did, did she?" Jack finally said. "Now why would she want YOU to push her faster?"

He didn't say, 'someone in your condition', but Chapman knew he was thinking it. The tone of Jack's voice said he was once again prepared to be instantly irritated by his old friend once again. Chapman decided to ignore his tone.

"Will and I were taking her across the hospital parking lot to see Pansy, who was in Will's pickup, and she, of course, was very much looking forward to it."

The silence this time was even longer. Chapman stopped for a red light and glanced over at Jack, who was looking straight ahead, his face a study of conflicting emotions. Chapman decided curiosity must have held the trump because Jack rubbed a hand along his jaw, sighed and said grumpily, "You going to tell me how you and Will managed to make that happen? Last time I went to see her; she was "hooked up" if you get my meaning. Hell, she couldn't move!"

Chapman made a left onto Highway 97 and said. "Well, that is no longer true. She's off the drip, the catheter and the bed pan. In fact, if she can prove herself able to walk around the entire third floor on someone's arm, the doctor says she can go home. Evidently, the cortisone shot has really helped for now, and her head wound is healing nicely."

He merged into the right lane and put on his blinker for Anchor's Away and heard Jack snort. "This is Monday. There ain't supposed to be this many cars in the parking lot on a Monday."

Chapman noticed his voice still sounded grumpy and suspected it had nothing to do with Trenton's expanded clientele. "Well, at least they left us good places to park...and as always, I'm starving the minute I see the sign." He decided Jack might need some time to sort things out in his mind and concentrated on parking the Nissan where it wasn't likely to get its doors dinged.

In silence, the two men walked to the restaurant. Chapman opened the door and Jack walked in like he owned the place...*which I guess he actually does,* Chapman realized.

Jack waved at Millie who was pouring coffee and looking harried. She pointed to Chapman's usual booth. Jack nodded, picked up two menus from the counter and turned to Chapman, "She may be the best employee I ever had, but that girl works too damned hard." Then he said, "I know, I know, I keep saying that, but it's allowed...I'm old. Come on, let's seat ourselves." He waved and nodded to people as he went, but he didn't slow down.

Chapman nodded to Millie, glanced at the specials board and trailed behind him. *So far, so good,* he thought as he slid into his booth and removed his fedora before accepting the menu from Jack. *So far so good!*

Jack didn't even make a pretense of opening his menu. "So even if she's better, I know what it is to have a bad back. She isn't going to be able to take care of herself. I don't imagine she can bend down or turn very much without irritating her spine. How in the hell is she supposed to be going home without somebody to take care of her?

Chapman looked at him. "That somebody would be me." he said.

"You?"

Chapman nodded.

"You?"

Chapman nodded once again. "Yes."

"Jesus, Mary, Mother of Joseph, as my Catholic grandmother used to say; now I have heard it all!"

"It takes some time to think about doesn't it?" There was a note of sympathy in Chapman's voice."

Jack scrubbed a hand through his wiry curls. "That it does, Laddie. That it does."

Chapman smiled. "I presume that came from your grandmother as well."

"Yes, the one on my Scottish side. Now, here comes Millie. She know about this?"

"I don't know. Will knows...so she might. He was on his way from seeing Leona to check on his calf crop. He had the dogs and Bill with him. Chapman shrugged, "How good is cell phone reception on Gray Butte?"

Chapter Twenty-eight
Millie

The two men were deep in discussion when Millie brought water and rolls to the table, the menus still closed under their hands. When they saw her, conversation ceased. She raised an eyebrow.

"Howdy, boys. Something you want to tell Mama?"

"Howdy, Millie. You talked to Will lately?" Her father-in-law asked in a tone she couldn't quite identify.

"Nope. Closest I got was waving good bye to him as he went past with the horse trailer, taking Bill back to the pasture. You got something to tell me, you'd better spit it out, 'cause, in case you hadn't noticed, the early bird crowd came in a big flock tonight."

Chapman said hurriedly, "There isn't anything amiss, Millie. All the news is good news, at least I think it is." She saw him glance at Jack with a question in his eyes.

"It is. Of course it is. I just can't get my mind around it." Jack sputtered.

"Look at your menus, gentlemen, but don't look at the specials. The last plate possible left the kitchen 15 minutes ago. You think how to get your mind around whatever GOOD NEWS you have to tell me, Dad, and I'll be back as soon as I can to hear it."

297

Millie hurried away, shaking her head. She saw the Tomkin family signaling for their check, put on her smile and headed towards them. "What? Are you telling me you didn't save room for desert?" she said as she pulled out her receipt book. "You know it comes with the specials."

"Not tonight dear," Nellie Tompkin said. "We have to pick up some groceries and get home in time to watch Antiques Road Show."

"Well, all righty then. Here's your damage. See you at the counter."

She realized, from her many years waiting tables, that like a real flock of birds, when one customer flew, the others generally followed. She grabbed a coffee pot and started making the rounds of her section, handing out receipts, clearing dishes, asking about dessert, pouring a last cup of coffee and in between, manning the till.

A quick look at her father-in-law and Chapman showed them still deep in conversation. Chapman was sipping water and slowly eating the inside of a roll. Jack was talking with his hands, a look on his face that Millie couldn't quite place. *He's sure a puzzle tonight,* she thought.

Carla, as usual, was being her efficient self, helping clear some of Millie's tables as well as her own. Still, it was a good ten minutes before she got herself back to the corner booth and when she went, she took another basket of rolls and two cups of Trenton's newest soup, a concoction he called Red Lentil Soup with Lemon. "Sorry about that," she said as she set the soup and rolls in front of them. Carla and I needed roller skates tonight."

"What you need is a bus boy!" Jack said, sharply. "Where'd all these people come from?"

298

Millie shrugged; wanting to do nothing more than sit down with them and rest her tired feet and sore back. "I don't know. My bus boy's in the kitchen trying to get caught up on the dishes. Try the soup. If you like it, I'll tell Trenton. He could use some good news. That guy's soaked through three handkerchiefs tonight trying to keep the sweat out of his eyes."

Jack took a quick sip and then closed his eyes. Millie could tell he was intent on figuring out the seasonings. She looked at Chapman. "So, do I die of curiosity or is someone at this table going to tell me what's going on?"

He smiled and said without preamble, "Leona might be released from the hospital tomorrow and I'm going to move into Neil and Giles' room to help her out for a while."

"Well, butter my butt and call me a biscuit! That's some news!" She took a quick look behind her and saw yet more customers waiting to pay their bill and three more customers coming through the door. "Be right back. Get your minds made up what you want." She said as she hurried away.

Once folks had paid their bills and were on their way out the door, she seated the new people in Carla's section and made a beeline back to the table. "Scoot over," she said to Jack. I want details, and I want to hear them while I'm sitting so I don't fall over."

Jack said, "This whole thing is Chapman's deal and if it weren't Chapman telling the story, I'd be calling him a liar and that's the truth."

"Well then, Chapman, tell me."

"I told you the essence Millie and that is, the doctor is probably going to release Leona from the hospital sometime tomorrow. However, when she and I researched home health care for her, it became clear that she couldn't afford it…so I volunteered to stay and help and she accepted."

"Wow! Just like that! You offered and she accepted, meek as a lamb." Millie couldn't quite keep the doubt from creeping into her voice.

"Well, of course it was only after she became convinced by the research that I was doing on my laptop regarding the amount home health agencies charged. Their rates made it abundantly clear that using their services was beyond her means."

Millie turned to Jack. "I can see why you just said what you just said. This concept of Leona being reasonable takes some getting used to." She stood up, rubbing the small of her back. "Worked in my garden," she said in way of explanation. "Got my lettuce, beets and carrots planted. What about the soup, Dad?"

Jack smiled. "You tell him he got the turmeric just right and putting in the brown rice was pure genius. I expect he's too busy for me to go back and tell him how much I liked his lasagna?"

"Right now, that's for sure. I'll let you know about later." She pulled out her receipt book. "What have you decided?"

"Actually," said Chapman, "I'd like a whole bowl of that soup and since I can't have the special, any fish he still has is fine with me. If not fish, then an order of mac and cheese will do."

"Got it. Okay, now you, Dad."

"Aw, I've got myself so riled up, just bring me a hamburger and fries."

"You want a coke to go with?"

"Sure. That would be good."

"Millie," Chapman said, "Perhaps, a glass of your house wine, something white to go with the fish, while we're waiting?" He was smiling at Jack. "Would you join me?"

Jack brightened. "Dad-burned right…only, Mil, put a shot of bourbon in that Coke…Chapman's driving."

Millie put their order up and told Trenton his soup was such a hit that Chapman had polished off a cup and had ordered a bowl. "He says to give him any fish you have left…but mac and cheese would do him fine."

"My kind of customer," Trenton said without looking up, deftly plating a side of brandied baby carrots next to a huge porterhouse steak smothered in mushrooms.

"Remember he can't have anything rough. So, no bones, okay?"

"I remember, mother hen, now get the cluck out of here."

"Ha, ha!" Millie retorted and went to put their order in at the bar. She noticed customers there too were thinning out. "Hey, Jolene, Dad's here and wants a bourbon and coke and our friend Chapman wants a glass of the house white…" She furrowed her brow. "Make it a sauvignon blanc. He might end up drinking it with mac and cheese."

"Comin' right up, darlin'." Jolene sighed. "This ought not to be allowed on a Monday night. Folks should be home watching football." She tightened her blonde ponytail and gestured down the bar where dishes, glasses and bottles of every description lined the counter top. Clearly, she too was missing the bus boy.

While she waited for her order, Mille grabbed a tub from behind the bar and started clearing. She'd gotten a good start when Jolene set her order on the bar. "You are a peach, girlfriend. Now, scoot...and give Jack a birthday hug for me."

"Will do." Millie said over her shoulder as she hurried towards the secluded booth, checking for waiting customers as she went. Already, a dozen questions were humming through her mind.

"So," she said, as she placed their drinks in front of them. "Does this sort of remind you of last week, when you all came to dinner and everything that came out of your mouths was a surprise?"

Chapman picked up his wine glass and looked at Jack and nodded. "To more surprises," he said.

Jack too, picked up his glass. He was shaking his head as though he was baffled. He looked up at Millie. "Chapman was asking if I would want to help him tomorrow. Leona wants to come home in her Buick, but he says the tags have expired and the tires are bald. He wants me to follow him in case there's trouble."

"Due to her back, she doesn't think she can get out of the Z," Chapman added.

Millie nodded. "Makes sense to me...but why don't you just use the Explorer? Seems like it's the right height...or you can swap me and use the van."

Jack took a sip of his bourbon and coke. "Well, we talked about using my Explorer, but Leona has sorta worked this whole deal out in her head and Chapman feels, because she's had so many things going south on her, it would be best if she felt she was the ramrod of this deal."

"H-m-m! Well, sounds like you guys have figured things out. Let me know if I can help in some way. Usually they discharge in the morning after the doctor makes his rounds."

"I've already called Norco to have them deliver a bed, a wheelchair and a few other things Dr. Brown signed off on. They said they'd deliver between 10:00 and noon. If that is the time they want to release her, could you be at the house to accept delivery while Jack and I get her?" Chapman asked.

Millie smiled. "You bet," she said, mentally reworking her day. "Anyway, I wanted to go over and see what kind of job Jake did tilling her garden plot. I've got some extra seeds to donate."

Jack said, "I'm thinking I'll stop by and pick up Pansy. Having her running the yard when we drive up will make it a real happy home coming for Leona."

"That sounds real nice, Dad."

As Millie left them with their drinks and went back to her other tables, she realized the look she currently was seeing on her father-in-law's face was relief, plain and simple. Now that she recognized it, she could hear it in his voice, too. *He'd gotten himself into a real pickle and now, thanks to Chapman and Pastor Mike…and maybe the peace offering of the apple cake…he's seeing a way of getting himself out of it. The Lord does work in mysterious ways.*

Millie greeted the tourists standing waiting at the door with a genuine smile. "Howdy. Welcome to Anchors. You've come to the right place. Even though the Chef's early bird specials are gone, everything else on the menu is delicious."

Slowly the restaurant returned to its normal Monday night sparseness. Millie had picked up Jack's and Chapman's orders. "What's the fish?" She asked peering at a slim piece of white fish covered in a delicate cream sauce lying on a bed of polenta with more of the baby carrots on the side.

"Sole. It's from my emergency stash. Tell Chapman it was frozen. It should be good though," Trenton said, already turning from the window.

Later, as Jack and Chapman lingered over ice cream, Chapman with herbal tea and Jack with coffee, Millie asked Carla to take over and went to sit. "So Chapman, what's in this for you?" she asked.

He put down his spoon. "What do you mean?"

"I'm thinking this isn't at all what you were planning on doing. Last I knew, you had a project in mind to regain your health by moving rocks."

"Oh," said Chapman. "Well, there's that too. This is a win/win deal, Millie. Leona is willing to parcel off The Lord's Bit...legally if she can, but it is going to take more time and more money than she has...so we agreed that I would, in the meantime, lease it. That way, she has the money up front to pay her back taxes."

Millie looked at the man across from her. It seemed she couldn't remember what she thought when she first saw him. What she saw now was so colored by her admiration and respect for him that he looked almost normal.

Fleetingly, she wondered how that could be. She looked at Jack. He was looking at Chapman with surprise and she could sense he'd found the last piece of his puzzle.

"You'd do that? You'd do that for the woman who tried to gun you down?" There was wonder in Jack's voice.

"Like I say, Jack, it's a win/win situation for both of us. I've got the money and she's got the rocks. Besides that, to tell you the truth, I'm truly sick of motel rooms, no matter how nice they are…which reminds me, Millie, where would I go to get one of those memory foam mattress toppers for a twin bed?"

Millie rose to her feet. "Lots of places, Fred Meyers being the closest," she said. "Tell you what, to make this a win/win/win situation, I have some shopping to do there tomorrow. I'll pick one up for you and a few groceries besides…sorta a house warming deal to get you two started."

"That would be very kind of you, Millie. Thank you." Chapman said. The gratitude was easy to hear in his simple words. "Oh, and Millie, when you bring the check, please hand it directly to me."

Millie glanced at Jack's face and then back to Chapman. "Yes, sir!" she said, enjoying the bemused look on her father-in-law's face.

Chapter Twenty-nine
Jack

When Jack woke, the light quality told him it was early. He put his pillow over his head and closed his eyes. After a moment or two, he realized he was fully awake with no desire to stay in bed. *Well now, ain't this interesting? Don't tell me I'm becoming an early riser.* He stretched, feeling his spine give a satisfactory little pop. Outside, he could hear a riot of bird song. He lay thinking first of his dismal visit to his wife. He'd talked her ear off about how Chapman had put some sort of charm on Leona. She was now evidently as mild as a milk cow. Betty hadn't lifted her head. *She didn't even make eye contact. Not even once. Any more she's not happy, she's not sad, she's not...anything.*

He sighed and scrubbed sleep out of his eyes, thinking instead how he'd used his birthday gift certificate after the visit. He'd gotten both himself and Millie lattes before he went out to thank her for the party. That thought led to Chapman's invitation to dinner at Anchors. *That boy was a surprise a minute last night. But a reasonable Leona is something I got to see for myself.*

He threw back the covers and slipped into his mules. With hands kneading his lower back, he headed for the bathroom. *Seats in that fancy sports car were pretty comfortable. Back's not sore a bit. Nice to know I still got the strength to lever myself in and out of that thing.*

With that thought, he lowered himself to the stool and started thinking of Leona. *Those two are going to make quite a pair should this whole thing work out like I'm praying it does. I got to remember to call Pastor Mike and give him the good news. I got to tell him I finally got it figured out...the Lord had a plan going and I somehow got confused about who it was in charge of it.*

Jack pulled up his sweatpants and headed for the kitchen thinking of his new coffee beans, when the phone rang.

"Jack, this is Chapman. You aren't going to believe this, but the hospital already called me. Dr. Brown has just finished making his rounds and has released Leona."

"Good God, man! It ain't even 8:00 o'clock."

"You're telling me! I was still sound asleep. I barely heard my phone."

Jack found himself slightly mollified by that news. "Yeah, well I ain't long out of the sack myself; and nothing's going to happen here until I have my cup of coffee."

He thought furiously. "Listen Chapman, do what you need to do to get yourself ready, and come on over here. I'm going to call the hospital and ask to talk to Leona in person. I'll explain the situation to her. I'll say we'll be there as soon as we can."

"But, she doesn't even know you're coming, Jack."

"Well, I know that! Course I know that! I figure me calling will give her a chance to get used to the idea that we're both working on springing her."

Chapman was thinking it over. Jack could tell by the silence. It didn't take him long. "That is a splendid idea, Jack. And you say you haven't even had your coffee?"

"Yeah, and you and me are going to have our showers, and I'm making you oatmeal for breakfast before we go to that hospital. That's what I'm going to tell her when I call; I'm going to lay the law down to her about that. But, before I even do that, I'm going to make some coffee with those new beans you gave me; put a right start on my good mood."

Jack heard Chapman choke back his raspy little laugh and smiled to himself. "But listen here, Chapman, don't call Millie. Will always lets her sleep in as long as he can. She put in a long, hard night last night."

"I know she did, Jack. Actually, there's really no need to call her this early. We just eventually need to let her know she doesn't need to be there for the Norco delivery. They won't change their schedule at this point. Her plan will stay the same. We're the ones who have to hustle."

"Okay," Jack said, "I'll see you over here. My advice for you is not to rush yourself. We got some kind of day ahead of us."

"Good advice…and, Jack, I am really grateful to you for lending your support. I believe, from what she said, it is going to mean a great deal to Leona, too."

"Yeah, well we'll see. I got to meet this wonder woman you been talking about. See you pretty soon."

Jack hung up the phone, tapped the receiver thoughtfully with his forefinger. Instead of looking up the number for the hospital, he said, "Well you can just hold your horses 'til I have my coffee, old woman."

He flipped on his radio and measured beans into his coffee grinder. With one ear he listened for the weather report; with the other ear he listened for the grinder to reach the perfect pitch. *I don't figure this coffee can taste as good as those beans smell,* he thought as he waited for the water in his kettle to reach a boil. The first sip proved him wrong.

He drank half of his cup and then reached for the phone book. It took a bit to get connected to Leona's room, but when he did she came right on the line.

"Hello."

"Leona? This is Jack. I hear you get to go home today."

There was a pause and Leona's voice came back on, quavery now. "Jack? Jack is that you?"

"Yep. It's me," Jack said briskly, his throat tight as a tick. "Now listen here, Leona, Chapman just called me. We weren't expecting you to get sprung so early. We've still got to have our showers, and I got to feed that boy some breakfast before we come and get you. You know he's so snake skinny he can't go without eating."

Again there was a pause that grew longer. "Are you still there, Leona?" he finally asked.

"Jack," she said, "Jack, are you saying you're coming to get me out of here?" He could hear gladness in her voice.

"Well, of course I am. We both are. I'm just saying I got to feed that boy first. We'll be there quick as we can after that."

"Well, I'm sitting here in my wheelchair waiting for you, Jack Anderson."

"That's good then. Get your paperwork done."

He heard her snort. "I'd have signed my life away to get shut of this place, but I didn't have to. Bye, Jack."

"Bye, Leona. See you soon."

Well now, maybe this is all going to turn out all right. Just maybe it is. He set the table for two, got down his can of oatmeal and set a sauce pan by the stove. As he headed for the shower, coffee cup in hand, he was whistling.

By the time Chapman arrived, Jack was sitting on the front steps watching while the mama cat ate greedily. The minute she heard the car pull into the driveway, she looked at Jack, jerked her tail angrily and once again whisked herself around the corner.

Jack waved a hand in Chapman's direction and pointed for him to park his car on the far side of the driveway. Then he got up and walked to meet him. "I figure we'll leave your car here and take the Explorer to go get the Buick. I was figuring on stopping at Will's to pick up Pansy so she'll be in the yard for Leona's homecoming. But Millie can bring her when she comes," he said.

Chapman got out of his car, holding a small bunch of bananas in his hands. "I'd better take a minute to check on the hens and sheep while we're there."

Jack nodded. "Sounds right. Well, come on in. I thought while I'm fixing us a bowl of oatmeal and some toast, you can call Millie and Will and catch them up on the plan."

"Glad to," Chapman said, handing Jack the bananas.

Remembering Chapman's throat, Jack cooked the steel cut oatmeal longer than he might have. He took one of Chapman's bananas and sliced it into the hot cereal.

When Chapman finished talking to Will, Jack asked, "You like some cinnamon on your oatmeal?"

"I certainly would. I'm so hungry these days, everything tastes wonderful. I had biscuits and gravy at Anchors yesterday. I can't tell you how grateful I am to be eating real food again."

Jack grunted. "Both the biscuits and gravy are family recipes from my wife."

He could feel Chapman's eyes on him as he bent his head to dish up the cereal. *Wonder what in God's green apples made me volunteer that little bit of information,* he thought. *No way I want to start talking about Betty.*

"Jack, I know I cannot begin to imagine the fortitude it takes to see a loved one through an illness like this," Chapman said quietly.

Jack's head snapped up and his green eyes flashed. "Yes, yes you can. I believe if anyone can understand, Chapman, it would be you."

Chapman nodded and said simply. "Perhaps there is something to what you say. And I will say, I believe your family, all of you, demonstrate the steadfastness of love."

They ate in companionable silence after that, each thinking their own thoughts. Jack could see Chapman was deep inside his own head.

When only Chapman's toast crusts remained, Jack got to his feet and put his dishes in the sink. Chapman followed suit. "I'll do these later," Jack said. "Now it's time to rock and roll."

For the first time he could remember, he walked from his kitchen leaving dirty dishes in the sink. And yet, he felt a rightness of the soul that he hadn't felt for days.

When the doors of the third floor elevator opened, Jack and Chapman could see Leona sitting in a wheelchair at the nurse's station, watching for them. There were things on her lap and a large white sack by her chair. Jack couldn't remember the last time he had seen such a smile on her face.

"Howdy, Leona," he called, probably louder than he should have, but not as loud as he could have.

A nurse stood and came from behind the counter as they walked down the hall. "So, you two are taking Leona home. She's been waiting for a while now."

Jack caught the censure in the nurse's voice and said, "I reckon it took us a little longer than we figured," he said apologetically.

"It doesn't matter a bit, Sandy," Leona interrupted. "Jack told me they had things to do first. And they're sure here now, aren't they?" There was a healthy spot of color on each cheek.

By God, she's sticking up for us; that's what she's doing. He reached out and lightly squeezed her shoulder. "We sure are," he said.

Chapman reached for the bag on the floor. "Will this be going with us Leona?" The way he eyed it, Jack got the sense that he knew exactly what it contained.

"I suppose so. They tell me Medicare paid for it for me. And you know the rule: Waste not, want not. There's everything you can imagine but a bedpan in there--all of it pink," she said mildly.

Jack's eyebrows shot up. *I'll be damned! Where's the ranting and raving about government waste?* He noticed that she held a vase of iris in the crook of her elbow and on her lap, on top of her purse, face up, was a picture of Pansy."

312

"He leaned over her shoulder for a better look. "Why Leona, that's a fine picture of Pansy. Where'd you get it?"

"Chapman." she said. "The flowers, too. You think I'd let him move in with me without flowers first?"

Jack saw that they were smiling at each other. Then Leona said, "Sandy, honey, crank this thing up. Time is a'wastin'."

"Yes, ma'am," Sandy said and grabbed the handles, grinning.

"We're truly sorry for having kept you waiting so long, Leona," Chapman said as the doors slid shut. "But your Buick is right outside the front door. We are still a bit earlier than we planned. Norco won't deliver your items before 10:00, perhaps as late as noon. You might end up sitting on a kitchen chair for a while."

"Well, that's fine then. I can do that. A body couldn't ask for more. And it seems like the weather is holding, isn't it?"

"It is," said Jack as the doors opened, "but not for much longer. We've finally got a big system making it down from the north." He fell in beside the nurse as she pushed through the lobby at a good clip. Chapman trailed behind carrying the white garbage bag.

Jack grinned to himself. *Good thing it isn't me pushing that chair, I'd be trotting as fast as these old legs could carry me by now. And if I'm feeling like this, what must Leona be feeling?*

Sandy took the things from Leona's arms and stepped away from the wheelchair once it was at the curb by the waiting Buick. Chapman was the one to maneuver the chair into place, set the brake and open the car door. He smiled and said, "Ready?"

"You bet I am," Leona said. She reached out for the forearm he held horizontally in front of her.

Jack found he was holding his breath, but she seemed to stand with relative ease. He noticed that Chapman allowed her the time to get herself turned and ready to sit on the car seat. Only then did he once again offer his forearm. *He said he was going to leave her in charge of this and by God, he's doing it! He's not even trying to do her seatbelt!* He sneaked a look at Sandy and she was smiling and nodding. "Well done, Chapman," she said.

"Thank you Sandy," Leona said reaching up and taking her things. "Please tell Julie, Carla and the rest thank you too. I'm sure sorry I was so cranky those first days."

"No worries. I'll tell them for you. You take care now," she said as she pushed the wheelchair back towards the big doors.

Jack watched in amazement as Chapman simply walked around to get behind the wheel. "Would you please shut my door, Jack," Leona asked, almost primly as she tried to reach her seatbelt. Jack jumped forward and pulled it out for her to reach. "I'm following you to the farm," he said, his hand on the door.

Leona smiled. "I'm real glad," she said simply, as he pushed the big door shut with a solid thump.

Jack imagined he was like the mama cat about her kittens as he followed behind the old tank of a Buick. Chapman drove with competence, not too fast or too slow, still he worried. He was pleased to see Leona's brake lights and blinkers were working. When they were nearly to the farm, he noticed her tags were indeed expired. It made him think about Leona's problems and he sighed deeply, his buoyant mood dissolving. *Chapman pays her back taxes for use of The Lord's Bit, that's all fine and dandy, but what about the future? What then? What about next year and the year after that? It costs too damned much money to get old when you've got no family around to help you out.*

Suddenly, Jack stopped himself. *There I go again, Lord...thinkin' I know your plan. Thinkin' I got a crystal ball or a direct connect to the divine. Well I don't, and I'm finally glad about it.* He made a mental note to call Pastor Mike.

Chapter Thirty
Will

Will hung up the kitchen phone and looked at his still sleepy wife. "You were right," he said. "That was Chapman. He and Dad are on their way to get Leona's car. She's already been released and is waiting. They want you to bring Pansy when you come, but you don't have to be there for the hospital equipment people. Aunt Leona was released so early that they'll be there in plenty of time."

Millie nodded and lifted her cup. "Works for me," she said, sounding a little more alert. "I hope it works okay for Leona."

Will saw a twinkle come into her eyes. "You should have seen those two planning things out last night. I think Dad was tickled that Chapman needed him...after he got over his shock."

Will leaned back against the counter and folded his arms. "Big day for Leona. How Chapman got both those old people turned around so fast is a head scratcher, isn't it?"

Millie yawned, stretched and glanced over her shoulder at the Betty Boop clock. She nodded. "Awful nice thing you did, too; taking her out to visit with Pansy."

They heard thunder on the stairs. "Who was on the phone, Dad?" Abby asked, shrugging into her backpack and automatically reaching out a hand to help Matt get into his.

316

"Chapman."

"Did he tell you if he wanted riding lessons?"

"No, he told me Aunt Leona gets to come home from the hospital today for sure. But he did meet Bill yesterday, and he said he planned to call you."

"Well that's a good sign. If he doesn't call me, could I call him and ask him tonight?" she asked as she went to give Millie a good bye kiss.

"Sure. I can't see why not."

Millie said, "Remember, guys, you are going to your grandpa's after school. Matt, where's your glove?"

Matt grinned. "In my backpack, and you don't have to tell me to go straight to Grandpa Jack's after practice. I already know, Mom."

"Good boy!" said Will. "You guys want to help push the cows on over the other side of the butte this weekend? Weather might not be too good."

"Sure, Dad," said Matt, putting his arms around Will's waist and giving him a squeeze before heading towards Millie. "It's one of my favorite things."

"I'd like it better if I didn't feel so bad making those old horses work so hard," Abby said, directing her comment to his chest as she gave him a hug. "But I'll come, rain or no rain."

Will and Millie exchanged bemused looks as the kids headed out the door. Millie shook her head. "Those poor old horses! It's such hard work having to pack those monster big kids."

Will grabbed the coffee pot and refilled Millie's cup and then his own. He kicked a chair around until he was straddling it and facing Millie. "Tough night?" he asked softly.

"We were slammed on a Monday, if you can believe that! She yawned again. "Thanks for letting me sleep in as long as you could."

"Busy day?"

"Well, I promised Chapman that I'd pick up a memory foam mattress topper for him when I was doing my grocery shopping at Freddie's…thought I'd pick up a few things for Leona and Chapman to eat, too."

"And Chapman needs a mattress topper because…?"

"Remember he's going to stay in the boys' room and help take care of Leona."

Will nodded, "I remember. I also remember that those mattresses are like rocks."

Millie sat straight up. "Oops! I forgot to tell you, I volunteered you to come and help me move that big pecan dining room table over to the side so the hospital bed can go in there."

"Not a problem. I'll come on over after I go see Mom. I'll throw Pansy in the truck so you don't have to put her in the van. You got a timeframe?"

"Well, the equipment is to arrive between ten and noon. That's NORCO's window. I'll try to be there about ten just in case by some miracle they are on the early end. Remember to take your cell phone, so I can call you if I need you."

Will got up and started loading the dishwasher. "I will. I've decided to get a holder that goes on my belt. I'll just leave it there. Otherwise, it's always somewhere I'm not."

Millie said, "Leave the dishes, Will. Go get ready to go. I'm going to have another cup of coffee and make my grocery list; then I'll slick things up."

Will grabbed a note pad and pen from beside the phone and took it to the table. He leaned down, kissing her lightly on the cheek. "Thanks, Mil. I'm on my way."

As always, Will had to steel himself mentally. He had always convinced himself that the dislike he felt for the nursing home was due to the odor. Now he was admitting to himself that he wasn't so sure.

His mother was sleeping; her hand was curled into a fist by her mouth. *It almost looks like she's sucking her thumb...which wouldn't seem too far off the mark what with her diapers and drooling, I guess.*

He sank into the chair and let his sad eyes wander. The only place they had been allowed to hang things was on a wall mounted cork board. Millie and the kids had every inch of it filled with photos and hand-made cards. Abby had even hung one of the blue ribbons she'd gotten at the fair, looping the ribbon's string over one corner of the board, giving it a cheerful look. *Does it matter? Does she still have moments of clarity?*

Will remembered how fear had come to her face when they had all trooped into the day room where she was sitting on the day of his dad's party. The aides had gotten her up, her hair combed and into a nice robe. *I guess we shouldn't have crowded around her like that. We were all strangers to her. She didn't even know the kids. Wonder if she would have if we'd just sent them up to her first?*

He rested his forearms on his knees and dropped his head. *It would be so easy to just get up and go...not wake her at all.* He closed his eyes, letting happier memories fill his mind, like spending the night with Aunt Leona, Uncle Peter and the boys so his parents could go to a square dance convention. It was one of the only times he could remember his parents going anywhere without him.

He remembered coming home from school and sitting down at the big kitchen table to do his homework, his mom still in her frilly apron from Anchors sitting across from him, her feet up on a chair, "just in case you need help," she'd say. But even then Will knew she was elevating her aching legs.

He felt a soft hand on his back and looked up. "Are you all right, Will?"

"Hi, Candy. Yep. Just thinking. I couldn't decide whether or not to wake Mom or just let her sleep, she looks so peaceful."

"She spent a restless night, but if I don't get her up and moving around, she's liable to spend another one. That's what I came in to do."

Will knew the drill. Candy would give her a sponge bath, change her diaper and night gown, check for bed sores and then wait for someone to come and help her into a chair. He always felt awkward and out of place, and he hated how the aides seemed to holler at his mother to wake her.

He smiled at Candy. "Let me wake her for you." He covered her fist with one of his calloused hands and gave a gentle squeeze. "Mom! Wake up now, Mom. It's Will."

He reached out with his other hand and started rubbing her back. "Time to get up Mom; it's burning daylight." He almost choked on the words. How many times had his parents shouted him out of bed from the foot of the stairs with those very words? He wondered how they translated in her mind at this stage of her dementia. He watched as her eyes fluttered. "Wake up now, Mom." He gave her a gentle shake. "It's me, Will."

"She's coming around, Will. It's the medication that makes waking so hard, but she can't do without it."

"I know, Candy," Will said sadly as his mother let out a low, animal sounding moan. *And why do we have to wake her up, Candy? Why can't she just go on sleeping until her body gives up?* a secret voice whispered in the darkest part of his mind. He watched her struggle awake to look at him without recognition and perhaps even a little fear.

Will walked out of the doors and noticed immediately that the wind had picked up. He drew the fresh, cold air into his lungs before walking towards his truck. When he got there, he opened the passenger door and let Pansy's joyful greeting soothe his sadness. He held her face in both his hands and looked in her eyes. "You know, I'm going to miss you, girl. Maybe Leona's going to have to let me borrow you from time to time. You could get to be a damned fine cow dog with a little more practice."

He managed a small smile, made a mental note to add horse shoes to the list he had to shop for at the Big R. He also wanted to remember to ask Chapman if Danny had ever called him back. *That was pretty neat how Chapman didn't bail him out. Made him see the difference between principle and interest and how much that stupid dealership loan was really costing him.* He wondered if Chapman really wanted a big V-8 like Danny's and then shrugged. *He's his own man. Even if he decides against it, Danny knows a lot more than he did before; Jake too, for that matter. These kids should be learning that stuff in high school.*

When Will and Pansy pulled into the gravel parking in front of Leona's house, they were the only one there. No Buick and no Millie. *She's probably still at Freddies.* He looked at his watch. *Almost 10:00.* He smiled to himself. *She's pushing things until the last minute as usual; trying to get everything done.*

Will parked well away from the gate so both the NORCO delivery truck and Leona's Buick had full access to it. As he shut off the key, he looked at Pansy. He could tell she knew exactly where she was. "Come on," he said as he stepped out of the truck, crowded by the dog. She jumped down and made a bee line for the gate. She was so full of life and expectation he felt the last of his gloom fade as he let her through and into the yard.

His phone rang. He found it in his shirt pocket. "Will here."

Hi, Will, it's Chapman. "We're running a bit later than we thought. Is Millie at Leona's?"

"Hi Chapman. Nope, but I am. Just got here and I expect Millie'll be along any second."

"Am I correct in assuming there isn't a delivery truck yet?"

"I haven't seen one, but it's just now ten."

"Yes, I know. But Leona and I are on our way and hope springs eternal."

322

Will grinned. Chapman was worrying a bit, he could tell by the tension in his voice. "Listen, Chapman," he said. "From here on out, it is all a piece of cake. Leona can walk just fine. We both saw that. Once we get her in the house, she's going to be so happy to be home she'll just sit on a kitchen chair and tell us all what to do. If she gets tired, we'll put her on the couch. Okay if I talk to her?"

"Absolutely! Here she is."

"Hello, Will."

"How you doing, Auntie?"

"We just turned onto Coon's Market Road! How do you think I'm doing?"

"You haven't been urging Chapman to break the speed limit, have you?"

"I have, but he has been successfully ignoring me."

Will could hear a bit of sauce in her voice and could only guess what she was feeling. "Listen," he said, "What I wanted to say is, when you get here, you've got to decide if you want to try to walk up the front steps with our help. If not, we'll wait for your wheelchair and I'll make a ramp out of those 2 X 12s in the shed."

"Shoot, Will, you boys worry…me, I'm not worrying about a thing. We're almost home!"

"Pansy and I are waiting for you and here comes Millie. See you in a few. Bye, Auntie."

Chapter Thirty-one
Leona

Leona noticed, first thing, that Millie and Will had parked off to the side. The second thing she noticed as Chapman pulled up beside the gate was Pansy running the yard fence barking her head off. She made her face stern so she wouldn't cry and then decided, *Oh the hell with it!* Tears forced themselves from rusty tear ducts and slid, unchecked down her wrinkled cheeks.

She felt Chapman's hand cover hers. "Ready?"

She nodded. "Let's get me out of here. I don't believe home ever looked quite this good."

Millie and Will burst through her front door. She heard Jack's Explorer's engine die and in seconds, all the people she loved most were standing around her open car door grinning like fools. Will stepped forward and offered his arm. "If you don't mind, Will, I'd like to let Chapman give this a try. We've got to see just how we're going to manage this thing."

Will smiled down at her and she could see the love in his eyes. "Makes sense. I'll go get a hold of Pansy," he said and stepped back.

Chapman came around the car looking a bit paler even than was normal, but not gray. He didn't say a word, just stepped forward, braced himself a little and offered an arm. "You are doing just fine," she whispered as she carefully put both feet on the ground and grasped his forearm, very aware of feeling bones and sinew instead of muscle. Slowly, she pulled herself upright. "I've got a medicated pain patch on in addition to a back support gizmo, so don't be looking so worried."

"Why, Leona," she heard Jack say as he opened the gate, "It looks to me like you are doing fine."

She nodded but her eyes were on Pansy who had been firmly collared by Will. "Hello, girl. Here I am. You wait until I get settled. Can't have you upsetting me at this stage."

Standing very erect, as the elastic support was designed to encourage her to do, she walked slowly through the gate, each step firm and sure. It seemed her eyes couldn't see everything fast enough. The lawn needed mowing but there, in the garden bed where she'd weeded, nodding against the growing wind were tulips, daffodils, narcissus and couldn't she see the royal purple of her Tom Thumb Irises? *And my lilacs! How old were the boys when they gave me that bush? Seven? Eight?*

Chapman stopped with her at the foot of the steps. "How do you want to approach this, Leona?"

"Why, simple as pie. I'm going to grab this rail with both hands and then I'm going to up sideways, like a crab. You watch!"

Carefully, she grabbed the railing and began sidestepping up the stairs. "Nothing wrong with my hips, so I figured this would work and it is!" she crowed and heard a collective sigh of relief from the watchers at the foot of the stairs.

"Now, somebody come and open these doors so I can sit down and pet my dog."

Everyone ends up in my kitchen. They always have, and I hope they always will. Pansy was between her knees, eyes shut, soaking in Leona's touch. Will was leaning against the counter with his arms crossed. Chapman and Jack were sitting at the table though Chapman was straddling his chair like she'd told him to do. Millie was making coffee. "There's snickerdoodles and oatmeal cookies in the freezer, Millie; though you might want to warm them a bit in the oven."

Will smiled and reached out to pull Millie's pony tail. "Coffee and cookies, my wife's favorite breakfast, huh, Mil?"

Millie smiled at him as she plugged in the percolator and then opened the freezer door. "You going to stand there talking all day; or are you going to go push the dining room table against the wall?"

"No, wait, Will. That won't take but a minute and I've got something to get off my chest," Leona said in a determined voice.

Will leaned back against the counter and re-folded his arms, and Leona looked down at the top of Pansy's head wondering where to start. With a deep sigh, she looked up.

"A body has all the time in the world to think things through lying in a hospital bed, and I did a lot. I didn't like myself, not one little bit by the time I was done." She looked at Will. "These past years, you been adding my work onto your own, and I don't ever remember thanking you properly.

326

I'm doing it now, Will. You are a fine man and you've made Jack and Betty proud."

Leona saw Millie put her hand over her mouth in silent surprise and it made her want to bawl. "And you, Millie…God bless your kindness and goodness. I've never been better than snappish with you."

She looked away quickly when she saw tears start to form in Millie's big blue eyes. They about undid her and she found she had to swallow a couple of times. *I've got to finish this;* she thought as she looked down and fondled Pansy's ears, *I've just got to!* She looked up. "Jack, I know there's words locked up in this thick skull of mine that could tell you what your friendship has meant to my whole family all these years. I don't think I've done more these past few years than piss and moan about something or another every single time you showed your face around here, and I want to say I'm sorry. I'm real sorry, Jack, and I ask your forgiveness."

She watched Jack's Adam's apple bobbing up and down like he was a drunk swallowing his first beer of the day. He was looking right at her with his beautiful green eyes and she saw the sheen of tears. His nod said volumes. Leona drew in a ragged breath and turned to Chapman. His bony fingers were folded over the chair back and she reached out and covered them with her gnarled hand. "And you," she said. "Just when I was lying there at my lowest, finally admitting to myself that most of my troubles were my own fault, finally letting myself own the fact that I'd tried to kill an innocent man, there you were…thanking me because you had met," she waved an arm, "these folks."

Leona looked at the ravaged man before her and it felt like she could actually feel her heart turn over there was such turmoil in her chest. His gaze, behind the tinted lenses he always wore, was steady on hers. He was so thin she could practically see through him, but still, he was as solid as steel. "Then to top it off, you brought me a picture of Pansy." She looked down and stroked the dog lovingly. When she looked up, she looked around at the faces dearest to her in the world.

Then Leona said, "I just got this one more thing to say." She shifted slightly on the chair, getting more comfortable. "We've all suffered losses, everyone in this room, not just me. But you all bounced back and as far as I can see." She looked at Jack. "Even you, Jack, seeing Betty the way she is, you manage real well. I'm the only one who didn't get myself back on track, and I want you to know, from now on I'm going to be trying real hard."

Leona looked around. Everyone had their eyes dropped except Chapman. He pulled his fingers from under her hand and took it into his own. A soft smile was on his patchwork face. "That was some speech," he said softly.

"I know it was. It was from my heart, Chapman. I've finally come to understand that even if Neil never shows up, and I think he probably won't; even if I eventually lose this place, I'll be okay as long as I got friends."

She looked around the circle of faces, around her worn kitchen and down at her dog. "And you," she said, gently shaking Pansy's head back and forth, "are what Pastor Mike talks about when he's telling us to be good Christians, aren't you? You never ever gave up on me."

She heard Jack clear his throat. "Well, Leona, like Chapman said, that was quite a speech," he croaked. "I'd like to add that I'm glad you said all that you just did and I think," he said, looking at Millie and Will, "I can speak for all us Andersons when I say we plan to stick by you. You want friends; you got 'em."

"Will you include me in your inner circle, please, Leona?" Chapman asked softly. "I very much like your taste in friends." He reached over and scrubbed Pansy's head. "And I very much like your dog...and your hens...and Iris and Rose."

Leona sighed. "Well, it was good to get that off my chest...and, Chapman, the truth is, I already got the feeling I can't do without you. You got a way about you that just settles my soul."

The only sound in the kitchen was the 'plip-pliping' of the percolator until Will said, pushing himself off the counter, "I'm proud of you, Aunt Leona." He leaned down and put his cheek next to hers. "Real proud." She reached up and stroked the side of his head. "Thank you, Will. Thank you for everything."

"My pleasure," he said and went to move the table, Chapman and Jack getting up without a word to follow him out.

Millie came to stand behind Leona's chair. She put her hands on Leona's shoulder and gently kneaded away the stiffness. "You're something else, Leona Larsen. I think things are going to go a lot better for you now that you aren't carrying such a heavy load inside."

"Could be you're right, Millie. I sure hope so. I expect I'll have plenty of set-backs but don't give up on me."

"We won't." Millie said, giving Leona's bony shoulders a final pat. She turned and put the snickerdoodles in the oven and got down five of Leona's white mugs. "That's one thing about us Andersons, we stick like glue."

Leona noticed that Millie had turned off the oven after putting in the cookies, just like she would have done; just heating them through, not double baking them.

"You know, Leona" Millie said, "We've got a plan for your garden."

"My garden? You do? I didn't think I'd be having a garden this year."

Millie smiled. "Well, Jake did the plowing and the harrowing on Saturday and I got you some seeds. We have a little girl who badly needs a job." Millie sighed and said, "Abby is sure she has to have a new, younger 4-H horse; one that needs training. Her daddy says she has to earn half."

"You thinking she's going to become my gardener?"

Millie nodded. "Ours, too. We plan on paying her a decent wage for her work, if she sticks to it."

Leona looked at her sadly. "You know I can't pay her enough to spit at, Millie. I wish I could, but I can't."

"We know that, Leona. Now is the time you take a deep breath and say, 'It's okay to let friends help me from time to time.' This is about much more than gardening."

Millie got up with a frown on her face and Leona knew she had more to say. She sat quietly while Millie poured them each a cup of coffee.

"Will and I are a bit concerned about how manipulative Abby has become...and lately she's been such an attention hog..." Millie frowned and pulled at her ponytail. "I suppose it's just a phase, but I don't like to think she's going to turn into one of those self-centered tweens talking clothes and boys way before their time."

Leona looked thoughtful. "I see where you're going with this. If she wants this young horse badly enough, she'll work her tail off to earn it, maybe change her mind a little about how the world works."

"Exactly! That's why we're letting her ride her bike over here by herself to do the work, with your permission, of course."

Leona took a sip of coffee, thinking. "It's a good plan. A real good plan."

"What's a good plan?" Jack asked as the men came back into the room.

Millie got up from the table. "We were talking about Abby becoming a summer gardener and riding her bike over here to work on Leona's garden." She waved her mug at Chapman. "You want a cup, Chapman?"

"Sure. Just a little, please. I already had some at Jack's, but I think having cookies and coffee around a kitchen table seems a very pleasant thing."

Millie took the cookies from the oven and put them on a plate. Will said, "So what do you think of the plan, Auntie?"

"Cracker Jack!" she said. "There's nothing like earning a good honest wage to make a child feel good about herself."

Will looked at his father. "Millie and I think she should have to earn half of that new horse she's so set on having," he said in way of an explanation.

Leona watched Chapman as he carefully dipped the snickerdoodle into his mug. He was giving the process his full attention and the look on his face made it clear what he thought of her cookies. "Good, aren't they? I put just a touch of nutmeg along with my cinnamon in the recipe."

"This," sighed Chapman, "tastes like manna from heaven!"

Millie laughed. "Like Will said, give me cookies and coffee for breakfast and I'm happy. It just doesn't get better than this."

Jack snorted. "You call this breakfast? It's pushing 11:00. I don't know how you do it, Millie."

Millie laughed again and reached for another cookie. "Leave me alone, Dad," she said playfully. Then she turned to Leona. "If you'd like, I can go up and get some things from your bedroom for you...maybe your nightie, robe and slippers...a few things from your bathroom, like your hairbrush and toothbrush?"

"Why, Millie, I hadn't even thought that far ahead. Thank you. I'll take you up on that. I don't want to spook Chapman off first thing."

Millie laughed and got up just as the doorbell rang. "That'll be NORCO. You guys let them in while I go get some things. I'm thinking Leona might be glad to lie down as soon as that bed is set up."

The house seemed very quiet after everyone had gone. Leona lay in the hospital bed, secretly glad to be lying down. Pansy lay on the rug Millie had brought down from the bedroom. Chapman had gone to have a nap at the inn. Afterwards, he would check out and return. She could hear the wind picking up and as she drifted off to sleep she heard the first splats of rain striking the windows. Rain had finally come to Central Oregon.

Chapter Thirty-two
Chapman

Chapman had programed the whole Anderson family and Leona into the speed dial of his smart phone. Leona was number one. Knowing that Jack was there to answer, he pushed the button.

"Larsen's, Jack Anderson speaking."

"Hello Jack, it's Chapman. I trust things are going well."

"Sure they are. Leona slept for a good long while. It gave me time to read a bunch of her cookbooks and make you a little something for dinner out of the stuff Millie brought. I would have repaired her back stair railing, but that damned rain got here too quick."

"Jack. I thought I just heard you say you made us dinner."

"You did. It isn't much, but it will do. Means maybe you won't have to go out again once you get here. It's about to start raining like a son of a bitch if I know anything about Central Oregon weather."

"Well, that was very kind of you. I was wondering a bit how I was going to manage that this first evening."

"Well, it helped keep me busy. Leona doesn't have cable television," he said a bit peevishly. "So I was getting a little bored. Where are you?"

"I've had my nap and just checked out of my room. I have one stop to make at Radio Shack and then I'm heading your way." Chapman flipped the switch for his windshield wipers. "You should be home well before Abby arrives," he said, feeling certain he knew why Jack had asked about his location.

"Course I will. The weather sure has turned. I don't know if Matt will have ball practice or not."

"Do you go pick them up from school when the weather is bad?"

"Sometimes. They got their ski parkas on today so they should be fine. I'll see what the weather is doing by three o'clock."

"Well, I'll be there in about 30 minutes. Thank you for staying, Jack."

"My pleasure. My pleasure. This here's going to be a family affair. Bye, Chapman."

After Chapman disconnected he thought to himself, *one of the things I need get is a cable package that will give me the internet and television. Perhaps I can bundle in her phone as well.* With satisfaction he thought, *I have yet another item for my list.*

Even as a child, he had been a list maker. These past two years it seemed that it had been a one item list: Stay alive. His whole focus had been on himself. *It feels exceptionally fine to think I might be able to do a bit for others again.* He clicked his wind shield wipers up another notch.

Now is when doubt should set in. Now is when I should start wondering how to back-peddle out of this arrangement; start worrying about all that I have bitten off;

taking on another person's troubles when I can barely manage my own. Instead, the knowledge that he was one step closer to moving rocks had him smiling to himself.

When I left the Inn on the Rimrock, there wasn't even one sign that I had been there. Hopefully, the same won't be said about The Lord's Bit.

A gust of wind shook the Z as Chapman turned onto Coon's Market Road. He suddenly wondered if the hens were smart enough to go into the hen house when the weather turned.

Looking west, the mountains were lost in a black shroud. The dirty gray clouds he'd seen banked behind them earlier in the day had finally roiled over, driven by winds from the coast. *All my rain gear is in Washington. I am poorly equipped for weather such as this…one more thing to put on my list. Perhaps when I return to the Big R I can look for clothing in addition to my wall building supplies.*

He pulled up beside Jack's Explorer, anchored his hat even more firmly on his head and wrapped his scarf tightly around his neck, zipping his wind breaker all the way up over it. His computer lay on the seat beside him and his suitcase was in the hatch along with a bag containing the robe and slippers he'd purchased at the inn. Then there was his cooler of Ensure and yogurt plus his eye drops and his Vitamin B vials. He looked at his leather loafers and sighed. *Wet is wet. I guess two trips aren't going to make a lot of difference when one walks the pace of a snail in the first place.*

Jack had evidently been watching from the living room window and met him at the screen door. "Here, hand me those things and put on this coat. How many more trips you got to make?"

"Just one more," said Chapman as he slipped into the ratty looking rubber rain coat.

"Get going then. I've always said this house needs a better front porch to shelter folks against weather such as this!"

By the time Chapman got back with his second load Jack was clucking like a hen. "I told Leona I was cranking up the thermostat, and I did it too. You're going to need different clothes for this climate, Chapman. Weather here is just unpredictable, and that's a fact."

Chapman saw that Jack had put his computer and suitcase on the couch and was now zipping himself into a natty western cut canvas coat with a leather collar. He dumped his cooler and bag beside his things and then, after a few steadying breaths, reached down to stroke Pansy who was already there giving everything the sniff test. "Hello, girl. Do you have things under control here?"

She looked at him with intelligent eyes, wagged her plume as if to say, "of course" and then continued her inspection.

He gently slapped Jack on the back as he walked past. "Thanks for your help, and you are absolutely correct. I do need different clothes. Let's go see Leona."

"She had a hard time supervising what was going on in the kitchen lying flat on her back so I cranked her bed up so we could visit." Jack grinned and said, lowering his voice, "translate that as 'give me advice the whole damned time'."

Chapman saw she was watching him closely as he came into the dining room, her faded blue eyes alert. A worn

Sunset magazine lay on her lap and she held reading glasses in one hand and fiddled with a corner of the magazine with the other. He walked right up to the bed, pulling off his fedora as he went. *What in the world is she thinking? It almost looks like she's holding her breath.*

He stood very still, smiling his thin, curve-lipped smile, in no hurry to talk, letting her look her fill in case it was his appearance that had again startled her. Finally, he said, "Hello, Leona. How's your pain level on a scale of one to ten."

"Not more than I can handle. I'd give it a three or a four at the most, and I didn't take that blue pill Jack tried to give me."

"That's good then, isn't it? I'll bet you are getting anxious to get out of bed and do some walking, aren't you?"

"Course I am. Jack offered, but I told him I'd wait for you."

"Chapman noticed she was still looking at him with a question in her eyes. "What?" he asked.

She sighed deeply. "I guess I'm waiting for you to say you thought things over and changed your mind."

Behind him, he heard Jack draw in a breath. He reached out one cold, thin hand and gently placed it on top of Leona's, capturing both hand and glasses. "Not a chance!" he said firmly.

They looked at each other, unspoken thoughts thickening the air. Finally, Leona broke the silence. "Well, that's good then. I have to say, you don't look quite so awful now that I'm coming to know you."

Chapman leaned down towards her left ear, "And you don't scare me nearly as much without a gun in your hands."

337

He whispered loud enough for Jack to hear and was rewarded by a short bark of laughter behind him. He noticed that Leona was smiling. He'd taken a risk in mentioning their first meeting and was incredibly relieved that they soon would be able to joke about it now that he'd broken the ice.

"Well, I reckon it's safe to leave the two of you now that you got that settled," Jack said.

Chapman turned, unbuttoning the rain coat. "Show me what to do in the kitchen and we'll let you get on your way," he said as he walked through the kitchen to the mud room and hung the coat on its peg like he'd done it a million times before.

After Jack left, Chapman carefully positioned the walker, pulled the blankets out of the way and helped Leona turn in the bed so her legs were dangling. He then braced himself and offered his arm. "How you do this is up to you, Leona. You just tell me what you need."

He was watching her face carefully, looking for a grimace or wincing and was relieved to see neither. What he saw instead was fierce concentration as her gnarled fingers wrapped around his forearm and she smoothly pulled herself upright until they were face to face. She looked up into his eyes and he could see her satisfaction. "Piece of cake," he said as she turned with one careful step and grasped the handles of the walker. Pansy was sitting by the foot of the bed, ears perked at this new development.

"Piece of cake indeed" Leona said, looking down at her as she took her first step. But you have to stay out of my way until I learn to drive this thing, Pansy."

Chapman imagined that Leona would want to visit the bathroom and wondered if she needed help getting up from the toilet seat. Just as he was phrasing subtle ways to ask her about it, she said, nodding to the pile on the couch, "You go on and get yourself settled. I'm going to walk myself out to the little bathroom off the mudroom. They sent me this handy dandy thing that fits over the toilet; makes it easy for me to get up and down." Then, amazingly, her eyes twinkled as she looked at him. "I haven't wet my pants for seventy years and I don't mean to start now." With that, she turned the walker and headed through the arch into the kitchen at a clip that told him she was serious.

"I'll take my things upstairs. Just call if you need me," he said to her retreating back.

Chapman looked around the generous dormered room with satisfaction. He saw that Millie, or perhaps Millie and Will, had thoughtfully put the new memory foam pad on the bed nearest the door. *I can't forget to pay her. I hope she kept the receipts.*

Above the headboard was a poster of a scantily clad blonde straight out of his teen years. He looked at her blonde mane and acre of white teeth. *Hello, Farrah. You were definitely my favorite of Charlie's Angels.* He smiled, remembering the television show of pistol-packing hot women. *Leona might be able to teach them a thing or two.*

After slipping on a navy cashmere sweater, he hung his few clothes on the hangers he found in the closet. There was an empty bureau for his use and he deposited several pairs of his underwear and socks in one of the drawers. Most of his things were at the laundry waiting to be picked up. It was one of the things on tomorrow's list.

He had bought the soft thick terry robe he'd worn at the Inn on the Rimrock. As he pulled it from its bag, he thought of Leona's ratty robe. *I'm not the only one who needs new clothes; however, all in due time. I mustn't push her or make her feel beholden.* He reached into the large bag and pulled out a plastic bag from Radio Shack. Inside were baby monitors. He plugged one into the wall by his night stand with its swivel armed reading light. The other he took with him as he headed back down the stairs.

He found Leona in the kitchen looking out the rain streaked window. She turned her head when she heard him. "I'm trying to see what you see when you look at that godforsaken chunk of worthless land."

He stood beside her, feeling his heart accelerate at the vast potential of the field. He grinned down at her. "For now, think instead how good it is going to feel not to have back taxes hanging like the Damocles sword."

They stood silently, watching the day get darker as the storm moved in. A spattering of hail rattled on the window. "Will the hens and the sheep be okay?" Chapman asked.

"Leona nodded. "The sheep have the barn, and chicken have enough sense to get in out of the rain. Baby turkeys sometimes don't. I've heard it said, they lift their beaks right up to the sky and drown when it rains."

Chapman looked at her incredulously. "You don't believe that, do you?"

"Don't now; did when I was a child though. Then one day it came to me that I'd never ever seen any kind of bird lifting their beaks skyward except to sing. Never saw a bunch of dead turkey chicks after a rainstorm either."

He laughed. "I'm going to do a search on my computer and see if a turkey chicks drowning in the rain would qualify as an urban legend. Which reminds me, when I stopped at Radio Shack, they told me to call a company called Bendbroadband if I wanted internet service here. It appears they are the only carrier in your area. I hope you don't mind if I have your home wired for my electronics and cable television."

Leona shook her head. "Reckon it won't kill me." She looked down at the small white box in his hand. "What's that in your hand?"

"It's actually a baby monitor, but we're going to use it so you can call me if you need me during the night. After I plug it in, I'll be able to hear you from upstairs where I have the other one plugged in by my bed."

He watched thoughts fleet across her face but the only thing she said was, "I guess I'd better get used to living in the modern world, hadn't I?"

They looked at each other. "One step at a time, Leona," he said.

She nodded solemnly. "I'm thinking that is going to be my motto for the rest of my life. Just getting to come home from the hospital is a big first step. I'm mighty grateful to you, Chapman."

"And I'm equally grateful to you, Leona," he said as he helped her turn her walker. "As I said, money is what I have…a new life is what I didn't really have…until now.

Chapter Thirty-three
Millie

Abby and Matt were bundled against the rain, hoods up, cinched tight around their faces and heading for the door when Millie called to their retreating backs, "Remember, this is Wednesday, dumplins'."

Abby turned at the front door and said with a hint of disgust, "Mom, school's almost out. We've got the schedule to go see Grandma drilled into our brains. We're not babies anymore!"

"Sorry. You have a good day now. See you this afternoon," she said mildly from where she sat at the kitchen table nursing her coffee."

She looked up at Will leaning against the counter and sighed. "You find a smidgen of time to go look at those horses? Our girl is starting to make the old Leona Larsen look positively charming."

Will nodded. "I did. Unfortunately, Danny's dad doesn't know that horses are cheap right now, especially the green ones. I'm going to look at another one today. This one's only four. I found him on Craig's List. It said, 'free to a good home.' I doubt it will come to much, but it's out near Terrebonne, and they have some good horses out there. I am also going to make some calls."

Millie smiled at him. "Dad going with you?"

"I might call him." He patted the cell phone holster at his hip. "Thanks again for getting this, Mil," he said as he went to get his down vest and rain coat. "First thing I got to do is shoe two horses. I'm not complaining though. At least I've got the barn to use. I could be out on a tractor finishing the fields."

Millie nodded and took a sip of coffee. "I keep thinking how well yesterday went. Your dad was positively giddy. He's going to talk my ear off when I go over there today."

"Yep, he probably will. I swear he's lookin' younger. The other day, out at the new field, I was looking at him and thinking how he'd aged. Do you suppose it was worrying about Leona weighing him down?"

Millie frowned, thinking. "Leona and Mom both, I'd say. He's still looking for magical cures on the internet, you know, foreign herbs, brain stimulating machines, secret doctor's formulas..." Millie's voice drifted off. She looked at Will. He was frowning, looking at his boots.

"Don't we wish!" he said softly as he straightened and shrugged into his vest. "She was really bad yesterday so I hope she's a little better today, especially for the kids."

Millie got up and put her arms around his waist, leaning her cheek into his shoulder. "However she is, we'll handle it. Shoe those horses and come back and have a cup of coffee with me. You'll have earned a piece of Dad's birthday cake by then."

"That sounds real good. It shouldn't take me more than an hour. I'm just doing the fronts."

"That's about perfect. I'll be showered and ready to go to Dad's. Right now, though, I'm calling Leona and

Chapman. I'm going to relax a whole lot if things went well."

Leona answered on the third ring. "This is Leona Larsen speaking."

"Hello, Leona. This is Millie. I thought I'd check in this morning. I hope it's not too early."

"It's not too early for me, Millie. I'm still on hospital time." Of course, I got this fellow sitting here at the kitchen table looking like he's been drug out of a snake's belly. Had to get him up to help me out of bed to go you know where."

It took Millie a moment, but then she knew exactly where. "How did he hear you if he was sleeping upstairs?" she asked.

"Well, he was either smart enough or stupid enough to get some of those baby monitors they have these days. I did just like he told me. I just shouted out his name."

Millie could hear Chapman say something in the background. She heard Leona chuckle. "He said to tell you only coffee and cookies are saving his life. After I was up he went off and did his breathing exercises while I made the percolator full."

Millie's eyebrow arched. "Wow, Leona. It sounds like you are doing great."

"Yes, I believe I am. After I make us some eggs, I'm going to have a real shower. I just have to wrap myself with Saran to keep the pain patch dry. I can't wait to wash my hair."

"Well," Millie said, "it sounds as though you two have things under control. I'll tell Dad when I go over to clean for him."

"Yes, you do that. Tell him Chapman has laid the law down with me and is taking me first to the DMV to renew my registration and then to Les Schwab's for new tires on the Buick. He said he refuses to drive on my bald tires in this rain. That'll make Jack happy. "

"Wow!" Millie said again. She heard Leona laugh.

"Of course, he's holding the high card in this hand. After he gets the tires done, we're going to go put some of his money in my checking account and go pay off my taxes."

"Oh, Leona! You've got to be on top of the world!" was all Millie could think to say. She knew she could only half imagine the relief Leona was feeling.

"Now, before you start telling me not to over tax myself, let me promise you I won't. Chapman and I already have figured everything out. I've promised to use the walker or the wheelchair when I need to, and when he goes down for his naps, I'll go down too."

Millie couldn't believe the change in Leona's voice. *Cheerful! She's cheerful. This is going to take some getting used to.* Aloud, she asked, "Is there anything at all I can do for you?"

"There isn't a thing, and you've done too much already. Did you know Jack made us a tuna casserole and a salad from the things you brought us yesterday? I'm going to call and thank him later."

"No, I didn't know. It sounds like him though." Millie heard more talking in the background.

"Millie, Chapman wants to know how much he owes you for the mattress pad. He said he slept like a baby."

"Remind him that I said it was going to be a present, sort of a house warming deal, and I meant it. Tell him he can

345

boss you around, but he can't boss me around." There was a smile in her voice when she said it.

She heard Leona give a cackle. "I will tell him. Thanks for the call, dear. Thanks for everything."

"Bye, Leona. You two have made my day."

Millie found what she said to be true. She was humming as she poured herself another cup of coffee and headed for her shower. If she hurried just a little, she was going to have time to redo her nails. She looked at her hands; they were her one vanity. Her fingers were long and slim, her nails shaped into perfect ovals and colored in hot pink. She grimaced. *Perfect, that is until I start gardening, that is.* She shrugged. There wasn't a gardening glove in the world that was able to prevent dirt from getting under her nails and even though she covered her hands with heavy cold cream, they still suffered during planting season. *But...* she thought suddenly, *this year, I have my very own weeder. How cool is that?* She reached for her polish remover. *I'm thinking this is a day for purple polish.*

By the time Will came back in the house, Millie's nail polish was dry, her hair clean, curled and held back from her face with a jeweled clip. She had a fresh pot of coffee made and two slices of cake waiting on the table.

"It's raining like a cow peeing on a flat rock out there," he called hanging his rain coat to drip over the big utility tub and walking into the kitchen. I sure hope it blows itself out by Saturday. Driving cows in this weather would be a bitch."

He walked up to Millie, put his cold hands to her cheeks and gave her a resounding kiss. "That cake looks good enough to eat, Hon, but you look even better." He leaned in again and nibbled on her lower lip. "Delicious," he whispered in her ear.

Despite herself, Millie could feel her insides start to melt, but she pushed her hands against his chest and then swatted at him. "You stop that, Will Andersen. You know I gotta be outta here in a few minutes. Besides, I got lots of good things to tell you."

He grinned down at her and turned to sit at the table. "I can't wait to hear," he said drolly as she went to pour their coffee.

Chapter Thirty-four
Jack

Jack had not turned on his computer, his radio or his television. He had, however, talked briefly with Will and made his coffee. He sat with it, in his recliner, going over and over in his mind how the day before had played out. Yet, no matter how many times he went over the sequence of events in his mind, they wouldn't settle. He looked at the clock on the wall. Eight forty-five. He was waiting until nine to call Pastor Mike.

He sighed and took another sip of coffee. That is when he remembered that he hadn't fed the cat. Wind was rattling his windows, or trying to. Rain was still sluicing down. *How in the hell am I supposed to feed a feral cat who won't come inside in this weather?* He got out of his recliner and walked into the mud room, peering through the window of the door. *I expect she might come into the car port. But maybe she's under the house and won't even come. Cats don't like rain much.*

Jack put on his old slicker and poured food into the dish. When he opened the door a tiger-striped streak tore past him. "What the hell…"

He looked behind him. There, on the rug in front of the utility sink was the mama cat. His jaw dropped. She looked at him steadily for a long second and then daintily lifted a front leg and began to groom it. "You sure as hell are a surprise a minute, Mama. You don't act like any feral cat I ever knew." He said softly.

She dropped her leg and reached back to lick the rain drops from her coat, starting with as high as she could reach on her shoulder, her pink tongue making healthy swipes as she went. He noticed that she wasn't actually wet, just a little damp. *Still,* he thought as he slowly set her bowl of food by his feet, *she's got her priorities straight, getting herself all cleaned up before coming to breakfast.*

"Well," he said, "reckon I'll just leave you here and see what happens next. He picked up his coffee mug and lifted it towards her. "I believe I'll make myself something to eat and then call the good pastor. Let me know if you need anything."

He walked slowly back into the kitchen, glancing over his shoulder. *I guess you could say I'm being thoroughly ignored. Ain't she just like a woman?* He grinned to himself. *Abby isn't going to believe me, that's for damned sure.*

By the time Jack had poached his eggs, had a second cup of coffee and had his kitchen ship-shape, it was well after nine. He dialed the church and got Billie Jo on the first ring. "Howdy, Billie Jo. This is Jack Andersen. Is the pastor in?"

"He is, Jack. But he's in a meeting. Can he call you back?"

Jack thought a minute. "Naw, he doesn't have to. Just tell him that Leona Larsen is out of the hospital and back home and that I truly am beginning to believe in miracles. So long, Billie Jo…and thanks."

"What? Whoa there! What are you saying, Jack Anderson? You can't just deliver a message like that and hang up the phone! What do you mean about a miracle? Is Leona healed?"

"I do believe she might be, Billie Jo...in more ways than one. Don't be too surprised if she shows up at church one of these days."

"Well...I never! That would be a wonderful thing, wouldn't it?"

"Yep. In fact, I'm going to ask her to come with me soon as her back can tolerate that much sitting and standing. Right now she needs some help getting up and down."

"Is there anything we can do for her in the meantime, Jack?"

"Go visit when you can find a spot of time. She's got a fellow helping her at home. He looks like twelve miles of bad road, but he's solid gold once you get used to him."

"Well, I never!" Billie Jo said again. "I will go visit. I believe if I didn't my curiosity would kill me anyway."

Jack laughed. "I believe it too. Listen, if the pastor does want to call me, I'm here for a while more...maybe two hours. My daughter-in-law is coming over and then after that, I'm going with Will to look at a horse for Abby."

He hung up the phone, and feeling energized, decided to check his emails. When he turned around, the cat was studying him from the doorway. He studied her back and noticed her gaze was shifting away from him to the entire kitchen. He could almost feel her curiosity mount. "You and Billie Jo! Curiosity getting to both of you, eh?"

Her ears twitched, but instead of looking at him, she craned her neck further, wanting to see from the mudroom into the living room. He stayed by the phone watching as she uncurled her tail, stood and slowly, but with determination, marched into the kitchen. "Listen here, Mama, you can look, but if you jump up on my counters or on the table, out into the rain you go. Get it?"

She ignored him, and after a cursory examination of the kitchen, moved on to the living room. He could see she was on high alert as she peered around couches, slunk behind the television set, rubbed the side of her face on the magazines in the rack by his recliner and generally examined the room with a fine-toothed comb.

The phone rang, causing him to jump. He walked back into the kitchen and grabbed it off its receiver.

"Hi, Dad. I'm on my way. Do you have your bed stripped?"

"Howdy, Millie. No, I don't. I been distracted by a cat that's decided it wants to go over my entire house like it's a crime scene of some sort."

There was a pause and then Jack heard her laugh. "Looks to me like she's moving in, Dad. Evidently she doesn't like the rain."

"That appears to be the case. Right now, she's just walked into my bedroom. If she thinks she and her kittens are moving in there, she's got another think coming!"

"Well, I'll leave that decision between the two of you. See you in a bit."

Jack could barely muster a pleasant good bye before hanging up the phone. "Now, where did she go?" he said to himself as he walked towards his open bedroom door. Besides under the bed, there weren't many places she could hide. *I sure ain't getting down on my knees to look for her.*

Jack started yanking sheets from the bed. He heard a soft meow and looked over his shoulder. She was sitting in the doorway to his bathroom, wiping a paw on her whiskers and then licking it clean. He squinted at her. "You been drinking out of my toilet?"

He tried to feel riled, but found instead he was feeling guilty. *Of course she is. I never thought to put water down for her after she ate that dry food.* He finished pulling the sheets and pillow cases and by the time he was done, the cat was gone. He grabbed his towels, threw them onto the pile of sheets and headed for the laundry. He had suddenly realized, with a sinking heart, that this cat probably belonged to someone in the neighborhood. *She's been somebody's pet. A cat that's an outside cat won't come in and start drinking out of a toilet like that.*

He put the laundry on top of the washer and stood in the mudroom, thinking. *I expect the right thing for me to do is to call the Humane Society and see if anyone has reported her missing.* He sighed. *I'll do it. It's the right thing...but what on earth am I going to tell Abby?*

He was still standing in the mudroom when Millie pulled into the driveway on two wheels. She jumped out, flipped up the hood of her raincoat and then reached back in and retrieved two cups. He went to the door and opened it for her as she dashed up the steps.

"Well, aren't you an angel?" she said as she stepped past him, going into the kitchen. "I decided on a day like this, we'd better fortify ourselves with a latte," she said over her shoulder. "Where's your cat?"

"She ain't my cat," Jack said glumly, as he followed her into the kitchen. "I been wrong about her from the start.

She ain't feral, her kittens weren't newborns, she's not even afraid of people…she was just being…a cat…somebody else's cat…that found a safe place to move her babies. Thanks for the java, by the way."

Millie set the cups on the kitchen table and started taking off her coat. "How do you know you were wrong about the cat?"

"Feral cats don't come into your house and drink from your toilet," he said shortly.

Jack saw her blue eyes widen. She put a hand to her mouth. "Oh dear," she said.

"You got new nail polish on," he said. "What's this color called?"

"Purple Dreams," she answered. "But don't try to change the subject," she said as she pulled the lid and handed him a coffee. "What are you going to do?"

"I'm going to call the Humane Society and ask if anyone has reported her missing, that's what."

Millie reached out a hand and covered his. "Gosh, I know you didn't really want a cat. We just got you those toys sorta as a joke and because we couldn't think of anything else…but you've gotten attached to her, haven't you?"

Jack sighed and rubbed his chin. "That's a fact, Millie. Now, let's talk about something else. I'll do what I got to do."

"Okey dokey," she said and then after a pause she smiled at him. "I do have some good news."

"Well, I could sure use some."

"Chapman and Leona are getting along fine. I called and guess what?"

Jack started shaking his head. "Millie, this whole deal has set me on my ear. I sat for a good long time this morning wondering how I could have been so wrong about what was going to happen next that I couldn't make a single guess if my life depended on it."

He saw the deep question in her eyes and watched her tamp it down. She said, "Then, I won't make you guess. Here's the news: As soon as they get the registration and tires squared away on the Buick, Leona and Chapman are going to the assessor's office and pay Leona's back taxes."

Jack felt his mouth drop open. "And she's letting him? Just like that?" He grabbed his cup and took a long swallow while he thought. Slowly, a smile spread over his face. He looked up at her. "Well, now that's real good news, real good news, Millie. The Lord does have his ways, doesn't he?

Millie smiled at him. "You mean the Lord or do you mean Chapman Lewis?"

He looked at her with a gentle smile. "I'm coming to believe they are one in the same."

Her eyes were sparkling. She didn't question what he had just said. "Don't you feel like you've started a very good book, and you can't wait to see what happens next but you don't want to peek at the ending and spoil it by knowing how it is really going to turn out? You just have to let it unfold itself."

This time Jack grinned at her, showing his horsey teeth. He shook his head. "No, can't say that would ever even occur to me, Millie. But now that you've said it, I can see what you mean."

He could see she was on a roll. She took a sip of her latte and sighed. "Don't you just love how they are together? It's like each knows what the other is thinking. They do this little eye catch and smile thing when she teases him."

Jack sat back in his chair. "That's a glimpse of the old Leona you're seeing. As a young woman she was a real looker and smart as a whip…independent for those days. Liked her martinis and cigarettes, she did. I guess we all did…in those days. The four of us cut quite a caper."

"Why Dad, I never in all these years knew that. You make the four of you sound like wild and crazy kids."

Jack drummed his fingers and then gave the table a thump. "Yep," he said, "I guess we were…what with the war and everything."

He squinted. "Those days you never knew which kiss or which drink or which dance or which cigarette was your last."

He looked at her sitting quietly, her big blue eyes on him, and smiled. "Yep, sweet girl, we were awful wild and crazy…until the babies started coming. When we had Will, and Peter and Leona had Giles, you've never seen two women change so fast. Hell, Betty wouldn't let a baby sitter come until Will was nearly three."

"No more hitting the high life, right Dad?"

"That's right." He thumped the table again and changed the subject. "Did Will tell you we're going to go look at a free horse for Abby?"

"Well, he said he was going to call you. I'm glad you're going." Millie got to her feet. "I've got to get moving. Where do you think the cat is, by the way? I'm going to vacuum in a bit and I don't want to terrify her."

Jack took his last swallow of coffee. "The cat can fend for herself. She wants out, one of us can open the door. As for where she is, I reckon we'll find out when you turn the vacuum on."

Millie looked at him doubtfully, but he waved a hand and turned away. "Before you start, I've got to call the Humane Society," he said.

Chapter Thirty-five
Will

Will shut Tuffy and Digger into the back yard and trotted towards his truck, his head ducked against the rain. *This is probably one wild goose chase,* he thought as he jumped into the cab, slammed the door and pulled out his cell phone. His father answered on the third ring.

"I'm on my way, Dad. Be there in about ten o'clock."

"Take your time. I'll be ready and waiting. You want to have lunch at the Sun Spot?"

"Sure. We haven't eaten one of their gut buster burgers in a long time. Let's look at this horse first. Millie fed me some of your birthday cake a while ago and it's still with me."

"Well, it was a good cake. Maybe it's not as good as Leona's if I had to be honest, but real good."

Will laughed. "I take it Millie isn't there to listen in on this conversation?"

"You got that straight. She left about twenty minutes ago; gave me some good advice before she did though."

"Well, that got my attention. What advice is Mil handing out these days?"

"Aw, I had to call the Humane Society on this cat that ain't feral and might not be a stray. Had to ask if someone was lookin' for her."

Will grinned as he reached an arm around to grab his seat belt. "You want to back up on this story a little Dad?"

"No, no I don't. The short of it is that the gal at the Humane Society figures I got me a cat whether I want one or not. She said when a cat makes up its mind to make a move to a new place there's generally no stopping it."

There was a peevish tone to his Dad's voice, but Will figured it was pure acting. "So, what'd Mil say?"

"Well, that was the clencher. She said, 'That mama thinks she's doing what's best for her babies. Seems like the Christian thing to do…help her out a little."

Will snorted. "You're going to be helping out with the next batch too if you don't figure out how to get her into the vet pronto."

"Well, I know that. 'Course I know that. I just got to get used to being a cat owner first."

When Jack lifted himself into the pickup, he said, "Now, tell me again what the ad said."

Will shrugged as he put the truck into gear. "Not much. See that white piece of paper under my gloves? I wrote directions on it. The ad is up top. The fellow I talked to on the phone said we turn right just before the Sun Spot so that's real handy."

He listened as Jack read, "Free to a good home, four year old quarter horse gelding, gentle. Call (541) 548-9101."

He heard his dad snort. "I notice they don't say gentle broke, just gentle."

"What else did you notice?"

"They ain't got an email address."

"What else?"

"He probably don't have papers."

Will nodded. "Probably not, but I don't care about that. I'm guessing it is someone's back yard baby and that gentle means spoiled rotten."

"Maybe. Maybe so. But we'll never know unless we check it out."

"That's right," said Will. I figure if he is sound and has good feet, I can have some professional time put in on him, at least get him a good start before turning him over to Abby, beings he's free."

They pulled out onto Highway 97 and headed north. Will glanced over at this dad.

"Millie tell you about what Aunt Leona and Chapman are doing today?"

Jack nodded. "Yep. Yep. She sure did. I don't believe we can begin to understand the load getting those taxes paid is taking off her mind."

"Well, it's taking a lot off my mind, and I would imagine it is taking some off of your mind too."

Jack sighed. "It is. It sure is. I just got off the phone with Pastor Mike before you called. I told him how she apologized to all of us yesterday, how she valued our friendship. He's going to try and drop by and visit them later on this afternoon if things work out."

Will looked over at his dad. "If what works out? What are you cooking up, Dad?"

"What? Who? Me?

Will watched his dad splutter and simply waited.

"Damn it, Will. I hate it when you do that. I haven't said one single thing to make you ask a question like that."

Will continued to wait while his father scrubbed at his chin and then slapped his knee. "Oh, hell! Truth is…when I was waiting for Chapman to come back from checking out of his motel, Leona and I were planning this deal to see if we couldn't put some real weight on him. We started going through her old recipe books looking for food that was soft and tasty and packed with calories.

"Besides mac and cheese, you mean."

"Yeah, besides mac and cheese. We got a list started, and I happened to mention it to Pastor Mike. Before I knew it, he took the bit in his teeth."

"He took the bit in his teeth? How'd he do that?"

"Well, he's just sure the ladies in the church would all like to try their hand at one of those recipes or ones just like them; all have a hand in cooking for both Leona and Chapman for a while."

"Wow!" Will said. "I kinda see what you mean. What'd you say?"

"I told him that he should go see Leona and talk her into it. That's what I said. I said that if it was okay with her, it was okay with me."

"You mean it?"

"How's that?"

"Is it really okay with you? It sounds like you and Leona had worked out something kinda fun and useful to do; something you could do together."

"Ah, hell, let's see how it goes. It could be just right…get Leona going back to church even. For these ladies, it's probably a one-time deal. I figure Leona and I could be working to get some meat on Chapman's bones for a long, long time. I don't believe, other than those pictures after World War II of the G.I.s coming out of those concentration camps, I ever saw anyone so skinny."

Will lifted his foot off the accelerator as they entered the outskirts of Terrebonne. Okay, Dad. There's 11th Street, right before the Sun Spot, just like the guy said. We turn right at the next street. Then what?"

"Just keep driving until you see the Smith Rocks State Park sign and take the next gravel drive to your right. There's a big blue mail box. Number is 28908."

The rain had let up, or else they had driven out from under it. The big blue mail box with the faded numbers was easy to spot. Will eased his truck down the potholed lane. He glanced at the fields on either side.

The grass looked like it was coming in pretty well. "These fields look leased for haying to me," he said to his dad.

"To me, too. Otherwise, somebody would be keeping their fences in better repair," his dad answered.

The house looked as faded as the mailbox. They could see smoke coming from the chimney. *They got a fire going,* Will thought, *Still, if a house could look cold, this one sure does.* He shut off the truck's engine and looked at his dad. "You ready?" he asked.

"Yep. Let's do 'er."

Will knocked on the door with authority. A dog started to bark, an old dog, by the sounds of things. He heard a woman's voice shushing it. The door opened and a middle aged woman stood there, her face serene. "You must be the man my brother said called about Fox." She extended her hand for him to shake. "I'm Catherine Maxwell. Let me take you on back to my dad."

Will snatched off his ball cap and shook her hand. It was surprisingly warm. "Will Andersen. And this is my father, Jack."

"Hello, Jack. Nice to meet you both. Don't worry about the dog. She's friendly."

Will looked down at the ancient cow dog sniffing the ranch smells off his Wranglers. He bent down and trailed his fingers down her back. There was the stale smell of sickness in the air.

Catherine ushered them through a dark, cluttered living room and down a hall to an even more cluttered bedroom. There were, however, two empty chairs; obviously visitor's chairs for the man lying in the bed hooked up to an oxygen tank.

"Dad, this is Will and his father, Jack. They've come about the ad we put on Craig's List for you," Catherine said in a cheerful tone.

Will moved forward and reached out his hand. "Will Anderson," he said simply.

"Don Beels. Damned lung cancer's got me," the shrunken man said matter-of-factly as he reached for Will's hand. "I got some affairs to get in order and little Fox is one of them."

By the time he had finished his few sentences, he was gasping for breath. He still held Will's hand but his eyes were shut. Will glanced at Catherine. "Please feel free to sit down, Jack," she said calmly. To Will, she said, "It's going to be better for Dad if we do the talking. His lungs are pretty shot so talking, even with oxygen, is hard for him."

Will nodded, understanding immediately. He decided to come straight to the point. "I came because I got a little girl named Abby who wants a horse to train for 4-H." As he spoke he looked down at Don Beels who had opened his eyes and was still holding his hand, looking at him steadily through pain clouded eyes. He continued, "She's only ten, but she's a decent hand, and she sure needs a project to take some of the big out of her britches."

"Will's got a ranch west of Redmond," Jack put in. "He's looking for something sound and gentle that can be trained into something worthwhile."

Don let go of Will's hand. "Fox...my...last horse. Show them, Cat."

Will glanced at his dad. He looked anchored to his chair.

"I believe I'll stay here with Don where it's warm, if you don't mind. You two go have a look," he said.

Will nodded and kept his mouth shut. He saw a glance carrying something unsaid pass between his dad and Catherine. "Let me get my coat and boots," she said, gratitude lacing her words.

She let them out the back door and the old dog followed. Pulling a wool watch cap low on her head, and zipping her coat, she said. "Do you have other horses?"

Will nodded. "Three of them; all are older geldings. They're broke to death. Abby is right when she says she can't teach them anything more."

"You're going to like Fox," she predicted as she unlatched a corral gate and let him through. "As Dad said, Fox was his last horse. He used to buy two-year olds or sometimes three-year olds that hadn't been messed with much. They were cheap that way. So, he'd buy low, start them right and sell them high.

"What happened with this one?"

Catherine smiled sadly up at him. Three things: Mom died, Dad got cancer and Fox forgot to grow."

Just as she finished speaking, a horse walked around the loafing shed in front of them. Will stopped in his tracks. In front of him, with ears pricked and eyes friendly, a small palomino came to greet them. Will judged him to be between 13 and 14 hands. It was hard to believe he was four.

"Hello Fox." Catherine said and held out the back of her hand for him to sniff. Will did the same. "See what I mean?" She asked.

Will nodded. "I'm sure sorry about your folks," he said, one hand reaching out to stroke the blonde neck under a white mane tangled with witch's knots.

She sighed. "I'm a hospice nurse by profession and you'd think I'd breeze through this grieving thing…turns out…" Her voice trailed away and she turned to run her hand along the gelding's top side before continuing. "Turns out when it happens to you, that professional distance you were trained to keep, deserts you entirely."

Will looked at her across Fox's back. "And there's not a damned thing you can do but bow your neck and pull your weight the best you can."

Catherine looked at him, the dark circles under her eyes showing clearly. She nodded slowly and then encircled the horse's neck with her arms and buried her face in his mane. "That's exactly right," Will heard her whisper.

"It is," he agreed. "It's a speech I give myself from time to time." He stepped away from Fox and began a slow, thorough evaluation of his confirmation, bringing his mind back from the sad place where his mother dwelled.

As he looked, he realized he liked every single thing he saw. The horse had nicely shaped hooves, a clean throatlatch, a deep chest and enough whither to hold a saddle. But, most of all, he liked the little guy's attitude. "You know, he's liable to grow a little more, don't you?"

Catherine nodded and said. "Yes, but it doesn't matter. He's got to go. It's been weighing on Dad's mind about finding a home for Fox."

"I'll bring out Abby after school. If she likes him, and I'm certain she will, he'll have a good home," he said simply.

She smiled a small smile. "Yes, Dad evidently knew that right away. Some folks that have been here aren't even invited to come out and have a look. It matters to him that Fox will belong to a little girl, I think."

Catherine and Will returned to the bedroom. Jack was sitting in the same chair, Don was dozing; his hands clasped around the school picture of Abby Jack carried in his wallet.

Catherine found the prepared bill of sale on the nightstand and showed it to Will. "He's already signed it," she whispered. "I'll try to be here, but if someone else is here when you come back, you know where it is. Just write in Abby's name and the date and have her countersign it."

"Evidently you liked the horse?" Jack asked softly.

Will nodded and made a motion to leave and watched as Jack rose stiffly to follow him out. Catherine trailed behind them to the front door. On the porch, Jack turned to her. "I tried to set his mind at ease about Abby being a good girl. He can keep that picture. Maybe it will remind him of the good deed he's done."

The old dog came around the corner of the house and almost automatically Catherine opened the door and nudged her inside with a foot.

"Speaking of good deeds," she said, "thank you for staying with Dad, Jack. How did you know I would be worried about leaving him long enough to show Fox?"

Will watched as his father reached out and took Catherine by the shoulders. He leaned forward and said softly in her ear, "Call it an old man's intuition. You need help, you call Jack or Will Anderson. We're in the phone book." He saw Catherine give him a hug. "Thank you. I will, Jack," she said.

Jack made a face at his first sip of the Sun Spot's coffee. "Well, I got to say it is hot and strong, but it ain't made from Arabica fair trade, shade grown beans."

Will grinned fondly at his dad and took a sip of his own cup. "Tastes good to me. Course, I didn't inherit your refined taste buds."

"Nope, you didn't, Matt got those." Jack looked at him, a pucker between his eye brows. "You know there's not one chance in a million Abby would turn down that horse; seems like you should have signed that paper on her behalf."

"Thought about it, that's for sure. But we're expecting Abby to take full responsibility for this horse. She got a big break, beings he's free, but still, she'll have plenty of other expenses. Mil's going to help her with her budget...what comes in from her wages; what goes out when she buys stuff...that sort of thing. So, our job here is to leave her in charge and that includes making all decisions...including signing her name to the bill of sale."

"Well, if Matt doesn't have ball practice, we're coming with you when you bring her. I wouldn't miss this first meeting between horse and girl for all the tea in China."

Will nodded. "Works for me." he said. "We got room for two more skinny butts in this cab."

Chapter Thirty-six
Leona

Leona stood at the kitchen sink, a small basket at her elbow. Pansy sat, ears pricked, looking up at her expectantly. "Just a minute, dear," she said as she wiped away some of the strawberry-banana smoothie she'd spilled down the side of Chapman's stainless steel water bottle. She tightened the lid, put the small bottle and a baggie of banana bread slices in the basket and handed it to Pansy.

As she opened the door to the back porch she said, "Go find Chapman!"

Her words were not at all necessary as Pansy had already ducked through and was on her way, down the steps, across the lawn and through the gate Chapman had made in the fence by the Juniper.

She stood for a minute, her hand on the porch rail, watching as Pansy, head held high, basket clamped firmly in her mouth, trotted towards Chapman who was leaning over a set of blueprints under the biggest juniper tree. He'd made a makeshift desk out of saw horses topped with two 2 X 12 boards. Two folding chairs and a recliner were stacked against the tree. A clip board hung from a nail pounded into the vast trunk.

It had become Pansy's late morning ritual, this bringing of a protein packed smoothie to Chapman. She also took him his lunch and sometimes, when Abby worked long in the garden, Leona sent her a snack and drink by what Abby called "Pansy Express". Leona wondered who enjoyed the activity the most; the dog, Chapman, Abby or herself. She shook her head. *Hard to say. I know for sure that it feels real good to me, seeing all of them with jobs to do…it almost feels as good as having my taxes paid.*

She looked down at her hand and again tested the solid feel of the rail going down her back steps. There had been a lot of changes in the three months since Chapman had come and the new railing was one of them. So was taking her eggs to sell at Farmer John's Country Store. She no longer sold them from her house and that was fine with her. She looked back out to where he worked and shook her head in wonder. *It's like that old piece of ground was just waiting for someone to come and set it free to be useful to the world.*

Scattered in growing piles around the rocky field were rocks. All had been sorted by size with the help of Chapman's helper, Danny. Chapman had told her at dinner the night before that he figured he'd personally moved more than a ton of rocks. And from the looks of it, he had. Already, there was the good start of a beautifully crafted wall paralleling the country road to show for his efforts. One day, he said, the wall would enclose the acreage, there would be stone pillars and an arch with double gates and a sign that said: "Welcome to The Lord's Bit." She believed it. The work seemed to be going much faster now.

She looked at her watch. Abby would be coming any minute, peddling over on her bicycle to work in the garden. Leona had to give her credit. The garden was coming right along; it was mostly weed free, the beans were staked and the carrots and beets thinned just right. Abby, with her dad's help, even had a compost pile laced with chicken manure started in the back far corner.

The day pulled at her. She walked carefully down the steps and towards the garden where she looked at everything, but especially her three tomatoes plants and decided they'd never looked better. Already she could see the fruit hanging among the dark green foliage with more yellow blossoms coming. *And this is only July. We probably got a good two months until the first frost. I might not be able to garden, but I can sure as heck do a lot of canning come fall.* She shook her head, pondering how quickly summer seemed to be going.

She put her hand to her back feeling the brace. The pain was mostly gone now, she was back upstairs in her own bed, but feeling the brace reminded her of the phone call she had to make.

She had done exactly what Doctor Brown had ordered, including all the physical therapy Medicare would pay for. That he'd given her permission to start driving herself to her sessions seemed short of a miracle to her. Still, she knew she was living on borrowed time. A slip on an icy sidewalk, a fall on the stairs and she would be back in horrible pain. She needed surgery but had put off the doctor when he mentioned it. "I'll think about it." "Maybe this fall after my canning is done." "Soon as my ship comes in," she'd said at various times, knowing he wasn't fooled even a little.

But now, looking at the ripening vegetables, she realized that "this fall" wasn't so far off and that really, her ship, her really big ship, HAD come in. Should her surgery cost thousands of dollars, and it would…come November, she'd just write a check.

"I guess it is time for me to make that call," she said resolutely to herself as she turned back towards the house, carefully watching each step.

Leona plucked the card from where it was tucked behind a corner of the wall phone and gave a sigh as she read it once again. **'Art and Antique Appraisals'**--Karin Marshall, Owner-Appraiser.

It was at Chapman's urging that she had called Karin Marshall, told her about the old Audubon watercolor in her bedroom and asked if she would be interested in seeing it. Karin had told her not to get her hopes too high, that Audubon prints were mostly a dime a dozen, but that she would come.

"It's not a print," Leona had said tartly. "I told you, it's been in my family since before I was born and I'm old."

"That's exactly why I'm coming," Karin had replied pleasantly.

"You don't have to sell it, Leona," Chapman had said. "No one could make you do that. But, if it's been in your family for three or four generations, it should be checked out and appraised so you can get it insured. Audubon did sell quite a few things before he died, he just didn't get much for them and left his widow dead broke."

When he'd seen her frown, he'd held up his hands, "Just think about it," he'd said mildly.

And she had thought about it. *What he didn't realize was that saying, 'He left his widow dead broke' made me think of myself; brought back all those awful memories.*

Well, Karin had come and under all the flash of big jewelry and fake nails, Leona knew she was dealing with a true professional. First she had oohed and awed over just about every danged thing in Leona's bedroom including her old coverlet. Told her she would be glad to put the bedstead and bureau up for auction any time Leona wanted. Then she finally turned and looked at the painting. Her bracelets jangled as she put her hand over her mouth and stared.

"Oh my!" she finally said.

Then she put a cloth over Leona's coverlet, hooked up a bright light, carefully lifted down the watercolor and went over it with a fine-tooth comb, taking photos, looking at each detail with a little magnifying glass she held to her eye, measuring and making comments into a little recording device, saying things like, "Black Billed Darter or Snake Bird, sealed from back, antique frame consistent with 1800's work. 1900's. 28 ½ by 22 ¼ inches, original hand-carved walnut frame, no mark visible."

During it all, Karin had asked her to remain in the room as witness to her handling of the artwork. So Leona sat in her rocker, thoroughly entertained. "I'm telling you, Leona, when you said you had an old Audubon watercolor, as you know, I suspected it was a museum reproduced print. That's what his widow did to survive, sold all his work to the New York Historical Society. Don't get your hopes up, but this is different from what I, personally, have seen."

Leona could hear the building excitement in Karin's voice. In her own body she was aware that her heart was pounding like a race horse on the home stretch. However, when the picture was back in its place she had merely asked Karin in a neutral voice, ""What's next?"

Karin had looked at her strangely. "Now, we go downstairs, sit at your kitchen table and you tell me every single thing you can remember hearing from your family about this piece. It's called the provenance of a piece."

Leona had nodded. "I know about that from watching the Antique Roadshow on the boob tube. Makes things more valuable they say."

Karin had laughed. "Absolutely! But, back to your question. After I take your testimony, I leave you and go start my research. I think this may take a while and definitely some collaboration, but then you will receive a written report as to the value of your art and a certificate of authenticity. If you place the piece with the auction house I represent, we will expect a commission based on the price we get. If you do not wish to place the piece, you will pay me for my work and we will be done."

Leona had turned then, letting her gaze rove over the exotic bird. "It will take some thinking," was all she said.

That same afternoon, Karin had telephoned, her voice squeaky with excitement. "Is it possible I might bring the expert I mentioned to see the Audubon tomorrow, Leona?"

When Leona allowed that it was possible, Karin said, "Wonderful! I will need to draw up a contract with you to remove the watercolor from your premises, if he concurs with my opinion. Authentication for this piece is extremely important."

After Karin hung up, Leona could feel a slow thunder of excitement growing in her veins. *But I'm still going to have to think about this. I won't be stampeded no matter what it is worth.*

In the end, it was determined that her Snakebird was an original, early Audubon watercolor, enhanced by colored chalk or pastel to soften the feathers. At auction it could be expected to be worth millions, how many millions would not be determined until the piece was actually bought.

Still, Leona had thought about letting it go long and hard. For at least three generations her family had hung that beautiful watercolor. As a child, she remembered it from her grandparent's Pennsylvania home. It had always been there as far as she was concerned and part of the musty smelling house. When she was very small, the bird frightened her just a little. Her sympathy was for the fish he was about to spear.

In the end, she finally realized the struggle in her mind was not about the watercolor, not really. The hard part was coming to accept the fact that she was the last of the line; she no longer had heirs. Her mind had accepted that fact in the hospital; her heart was another matter entirely. She shook her head. *Both those boys would say, 'Mom, are you crazy? Sell that damned thing and get that operation.'* She squeezed her eyes shut, released a pent up sigh and dialed Karin's number, knowing beforehand that she would more than likely get a recording and she did.

"Karin, this is Leona Larsen. I got your report by special delivery. I know you told me it was authentic, but seeing it all written down was really something. Made it real. Seems like I still can't quite take it all in. But, I figure I'll go ahead and let you sell it. Wish I'd known I was a rich woman before, when I thought I was losing the farm. It would've saved me buckets of worry. You just give me a call when you got time and we'll get this show on the road. I got an operation to schedule."

Leona set the receiver gently back on its hook. *Now, why'd I go and tell her all of that? She didn't need to know more than that I was willing to make the deal. I hope I'm not going queer in my old age.*

She stepped away from the phone and glanced out the window. Chapman was sitting, hunched over, in one of the folding chairs, Pansy flat on the ground, sound asleep beside him. She'd seen him in that same position many times. It was like he was looking at something in his lap. On a whim she walked to the back porch and pulled her old set of Bushnell's from the hook on the wall. These were her bird watching binoculars. Peter and the boys had given them to her many Christmases before.

She steadied herself against the kitchen counter and with the full awareness she was snooping, set her glasses on Chapman. She fiddled with the adjustments until he was razor sharp and seemed just under her nose. He was holding something, looking steadily at it…but it wasn't until she saw him lean forward, take the thing into his right hand and push it into his back pocket did things click. *He's got something in his wallet that he looks at. That's what he's doing.* With sudden conviction she knew it was a photograph. *What else could it be? A poem or proverb, perhaps?* She didn't think so. *Makes a body real curious to know just who he's looking at.* She moved from the sink and re-hung the binoculars on their hook, biting her lower lip. Already her conscience was pricking her.

Minutes later, a sharp bark told her Pansy was back with the basket. She opened the back door. In addition to Pansy, she saw Abby looping her helmet strap over the handlebars of her bicycle. She pulled a floppy sun hat from her pocket and was tying it on when Leona called, "Howdy, Abby. If you want, come on in for some banana bread before you start."

"Hi, Aunt Leona. I'd love some!" She trotted for the back steps, stooping to scratch Pansy behind the ears before bounding past Leona.

"I was just visiting the tomatoes earlier," Leona said. "I've never seen them look better. You evidently have a green thumb, child."

Abby beamed. She looked brown and healthy. Rivulets of sweat were running down the sides of her face under her sun hat and she was panting lightly. "I guess I do. Mom says her garden looks 'Gorgeous, simply gorgeous.'" Abby spread her hands under her chin and fluttered her eyelashes, mimicking her mother being silly.

Leona smiled. "You sure do take the cake, Abby," she said, shaking her head. "You want milk with those slices?"

"Yes, please," Abby said as she scooted onto a kitchen chair. "Bicycle riding makes me thirsty."

"Thinking about you riding a bicycle all that way makes me thirsty too," Leona said, pouring two glasses.

They sat companionably while Abby caught Leona up on her progress both with Fox and with Chapman's riding lessons on Bill. "It seems like Bill has a lot more personality now that Chapman has taken an interest in him," Abby said.

"Don't I know the feeling?" She replied drily and then laughed at Abby's puzzled face. "Never mind, honey, I was just thinking how many ways my life has changed since Chapman started taking an interest in me. If you'd have told me not to worry, that my life would sort itself out, I'd have handed you your head."

Abby looked up at her, brushing a crumb of banana bread from the corner of her mouth. "That's the way you used to do, Aunt Leona. Me and Matt were a little bit afraid of you then. You aren't like that now."

Leona nodded, "Now, that's a good thing." She smiled at Abby and got up to reseal the banana bread into its aluminum foil when the telephone rang.

"Howdy, Leona." Jack's voice came cheerfully down the line.

"Good morning, Jack."

"Say, I almost forgot that you were going with me to see Betty today. I'm running a little late, but I'll be there. I got a new dish concocted to try out on your boy."

"What country this time?"

"Moroccan!" Jack said without hesitation. "It's got prunes in it. I made enough for you too. I put extra butter in the rice. It should be real fattening."

Leona laughed. "The trouble is, Jack, these recipes are working on Chapman, but they're working even better on me."

"Well, old girl, I believe it is true that you ain't looking bony any longer. It's a nice change, you ask me."

Leona paused. "Thank you, Jack. That was nice of you to say."

"You're surely welcome. See you in about an hour. Abby there yet?"

"Yep, we've been sitting here gabbing, but she's about done with her banana bread and is heading for the garden."

"Tell her Trenton down at Anchors told me one of the customers was talking to him about her. Turns out he's her 4-H leader. He says she's got the makings of a real horsewoman and is doing a fine job with her project."

"You mean Fox, the Wonder Horse?" Leona said drily. "I swear, she'll be teaching him to fly next." Her eyes twinkled at Abby as she said it.

She heard Jack chuckle. "You just tell her what I said, Leona. Real compliments are good things. I'll be there quick as I can but I got a whole mess to clean up here first."

Leona hung up the phone and said, "That was your grandpa. He said to tell you that your 4-H leader says you got the makings of a real horsewoman and are doing a fine job. He said it to Trenton and Trenton told your Grandpa."

The next thing she knew, Leona had an armful of girl. "Oh, thank you, Aunt Leona. That's so super! When you get a compliment second hand it means it's real."

"Well," said Leona, "Well, I guess I never thought of it quite like that." She gave Abby a warm squeeze and a peck to the top of her sun hat. "Seems like you found a good horse," she said.

Abby drew back and looked up at Leona, frowning a little. "Dad is the one who found him on Craig's List..." She brightened and the frown disappeared. "But I was smart enough to say, 'I'll take him,' to Mr. Beels, you know."

"I do know. I also know you have brought both Fox and Chapman along nicely. It's a compliment well deserved. Chapman was saying just the other day how much he likes it when the two of you just take off through the back gate and onto BLM land, you putting miles on your colt and teaching him the finer points of riding."

"Did he? Well now, that just makes my day!"

She sounded so much like Millie that Leona had to hide her smile behind her hand and change the subject.

"Your mom called to tell me she had you pick her beans today. I suppose you'd better pick mine too. There's Mason jars down in the root cellar. You might as well bring a box of them up. I'll can the beans this afternoon after your grandpa and I come back from seeing your grandma. Then, if you don't mind, put in the rest of your time on the front flower bed. I never did finish it properly and Doctor Brown has laid me off for the entire summer."

"No worries, Aunt Leona. I've got you covered." Abby said over her shoulder as she left for the garden.

After Abby had gone, Leona touched her hair thinking of Jack's observation and went to look in the dining room mirror. The woman looking back at her was dressed in a crisp blue blouse that brought out the color of her eyes. Her silver hair was softly permed. *It's true, I don't look haggard anymore. And Chapman doesn't look like a skeleton either. It was a good plan that Jack and I hatched up.* She thought of her freezer, which at one time had been jammed with carefully packaged portions. Some were her recipes, some were Jack's and some were from church ladies. Chapman had eaten them all with relish. *In a way, they are what got me going back to church. Would have been unseemly to take their food and not their hospitality is the way I look at it. Besides, it sure made Jack happy.*

When Jack dropped Leona off after visiting Betty, she saw that Chapman and Pansy were walking towards the house. *I'll bet he's going to lay waste to Jack's new dish and go to bed early tonight. He's put in quite a day.*

She waved to him and smiled to herself as she carefully climbed the front steps, her cane over her arm. Both Chapman and Doctor Brown were going to be real surprised when she scheduled her back surgery. *I'll do it too, but not until I get on Medicare Part B this fall during open enrollment; might as well let Uncle Sam help pay for this one.*

Abby had left a full basket of beans and a box of jars on the kitchen counter. Leona nodded to herself. *I believe I'm going to let those go until tomorrow. I'm a little tired myself.*

She got a protein drink from the refrigerator and went to meet Chapman and Pansy at the back door. Since she had moved back into her bedroom, Leona had noticed he seldom used the upstairs bathroom, using the downstairs one instead and using the utility sink to brush his teeth.

"You gotta be tired, Chapman. You just drink this and get in the shower. I'll go up and get your duds."

Dust filmed his face and his shaved head. He looked at her gratefully. "I'd appreciate it, Leona. I'm going to have to learn to pace myself better. I mean it."

She smiled. "Don't expect any lectures from me. You just get under that hot water and relax for a bit. The way I see it, being able to go up and down those stairs like I'm doing, makes me think maybe learning to pace myself, even at my age, is still worth doing."

When Leona returned to set Chapman's clean clothes on the washer, she noticed his wallet lying there beside his watch and pocket change and felt an irresistible force grab hold of her. Before she could stop herself, she grabbed the wallet, flipped it open, looked at his Washington State driver's license, saw the picture of the woman and the little boy and whispered 'I just knew it!" For long seconds she just stared, her hand over her mouth. Then she moved faster than she had since before the accident, into the kitchen, grabbed her shopping list and wrote down his old street address.

Later that evening, Chapman safely asleep, Leona sat hunched over her writing tablet at the kitchen table, staring at the blank page in front of her. When she thought of what she'd done, she still couldn't quite believe it.

Now she was going to write a letter to Chapman's old address and she couldn't quite believe that either. She picked up her pen and began to write.

> ***Dear Mrs. Lewis (I think),***
>
> ***You don't know me but I know Chapman Lewis. I'm probably being an interfering old busy body...***

Leona threw down her pen in frustration. It's true. *I AM being a busy body, something I really cannot abide. What I did, snooping in Chapman's wallet like that, was just plain wrong. Someone did that to me, I have a stroke. Besides this whole thing is liable to bounce back and bite me right square in the butt.*

Leona squeezed her eyes tight, opened them and looked down at her tablet. *I got to stop thinking the devil is making me do this and start thinking maybe it's Chapman guardian angel, that's what I got to do. Immediately a*

381

feeling of quiet resolve settled over her and she picked up her pen without hesitation.

> **The thing is, I can't seem to help myself in this case as Chapman is very dear to me.**
>
> **I want you to know how often he studies the picture of you and the little boy he carries in his wallet when he thinks he's alone. I know this because I 'borrowed' his wallet and snooped when my curiosity got the best of me. That is how I got your address. It is still on his driver's license.**
>
> **I also want you to know that Chapman is regaining his health here on the farm and should you ever want to visit, you are welcome. I think he misses you both more than words can say.**
>
> **Please feel free to call anytime. Chapman lives here so, if I can't talk, you'll know why.**
>
> **Sincerely yours,**
> **Leona Larsen**
> **1 (541) 548-0607**

Without re-reading what she had written, Leona folded the page carefully and put it in an envelope and sealed it. Already she had addressed the envelope and had written her return address. She rose and went to find a stamp.

Chapter Thirty-seven
Chapman

Will hopped back into Chapman's new Ford F-150 club cab after closing the gate by the beam from the truck's headlights. The truck's silvery-gray color blended seamlessly with the coming dawn. Going through the gate had put them off ranch property and onto land owned by the Bureau of Land Management. "This used to be all private. You can still see some old wire fencing here and there," Will said.

Chapman nodded. "I've seen it when Abby brings me here. We have our lunch in a Ponderosa grove and then we look for a way down to the river." He eased his pickup gently over the rocks protruding out of the faint dirt track. He smiled. "Unfortunately for you, we found it."

Soon Will, lulled by the rocking of the pickup, was half dozing in the gray of the false dawn. He said groggily, "Remind me what we're doing out here when I could be home sleeping for another couple of hours before putting a full 10-hour day on a baler."

"It's entirely your fault," Chapman said lightly. "You're the one who told the kids about how you and the Larsen boys rode your horses down to the swimming hole about a dozen times just since I've known you. Isn't that why Abby was so determined to find the trail? Isn't that why we're out here...because Abby told you about the downed

Ponderosa? And then you told her maybe you'd clear the trail, and then everyone could come for an outing."

"Shit!" Will finally said, sounding more awake, "So I did. Must be this hot weather made a back-to- school picnic and a swim down there sound worth the effort. Good thing I got Jake, the Wonder Farmer, home from Corvallis these two weeks. I'm not as behind as I might be. Thanks for the offer of help to do this, by the way."

"It's going to mean a lot to your family, so I'm glad to do it."

As he said the words, another picture took hold of him, a snapshot of what it would be like to see Marcie and Jock along with the Andersons lounging around a swimming hole. He felt the familiar jolt of pain in his chest as he fought, once again, to block the image.

They rode in companionable silence, windows down, enjoying the coolness of the morning while they could, the day lightening as Chapman drove.

In the back of his truck was an old Husqvarna chainsaw with a 20" guide bar, an equally old Stihl chainsaw with a 14" guide bar, two shovels, a pry bar, a long, stout towing chain, a maul, splitting wedges and an ice chest packed with what Leona thought they needed, including Ensure for Chapman, homemade cookies, sandwiches and two gallons of water.

Will groaned. "Why don't we get this sort of stuff done when it's not 100 degrees in the shade?"

"That's why we're up so early, big guy," Chapman said mildly as he put the truck through what used to be a gate but was now just leaning, weather beaten posts and headed down a steep narrow ravine. Tall volcanic ledges flanked

384

either side of them and the land fell away steeply towards the Deschutes River. Chapman put the pickup into low four-wheel drive. "Are you planning to bring the stock trailer down here?

"Nope, we'll unload up at the old gate and ride down."

"That makes perfect sense. I believe I'll be glad I have four wheel-drive when I try pulling up out of here." He pulled to a stop in a small flat spot dotted by rabbit brush and sage. Beyond, a game trail curved around an outcropping of lava. "The tree is just up ahead, behind that outcropping," he said.

Will was looking around. He gestured to the flat land and said, "Believe it or not, this is where a cabin sat years ago. It was still mostly standing when I was a little kid, but BLM tore it down."

"Why would they do that?"

"Didn't want squatters starting a fire and burning the range, I guess." Will shrugged and changed the subject as he opened the door and stepped down.

"You bought the right truck. Danny glad you didn't buy his Dodge?"

Chapman smiled. "Not half as glad as I am. This one suits me better. Blue is my color."

"I don't know, Dude, black is basic and big is better." Will chuckled and then said, "Seriously, seems like that whole deal worked out just right."

Chapman nodded. "Danny's a good kid. He's been a tremendous help. I know he was very happy to keep the truck, and I'm equally happy to pay him a good wage because I needed help...especially at first."

Will nodded and said, "Follow me. Let's go see what we got to get done."

By the time the men had reached where the Ponderosa had fallen, it was light enough to see that it had evidently toppled during a winter storm. Its shallow root structure, still clutching an occasional rock, rose like a witch's claw into the silvering sky. The men stood silently, appraising.

Will said, "You'd think God would have the sense to build a deeper root system on a tree this big, wouldn't you?"

"Yes, indeed. One similar to that of the juniper would have done nicely," Chapman agreed.

Will snorted. "Those trees are water hogs. That root system they have is too efficient. They're drinking the springs dry up on the butte."

Chapman nodded and said nothing, instead looked around and noticed that there was not to be a beautiful sunrise, just a gradual lighting of the sky and the promise of another 90 plus degree day.

Will sighed in resignation, turning his attention back to the task at hand. "We don't even know if the swimming hole is still there. It used to be a real pretty eddy, willow trees overreaching the banks, a couple of big rocks you could swim out to and sun yourself…trouble is a river can change a lot with just one flood." But even then he was moving forward. He grabbed two branches and hoisted himself up onto the trunk to look over the edge.

Chapman waited quietly, conserving his strength for The task ahead. "Well, damn!" he heard Will mutter to himself, "I got to remember we don't need a winter's wood supply. We just got to cut up enough to get the horses through.

"Can you see any of the trail from where you are standing?" Chapman asked.

"Sure I can…but only towards the bottom, not the steep part. These dead needles and the branches are blocking the rest of the view. Be something if we work our asses off and then find the trail is washed away somewhere in the middle, won't it?"

"Be something if on Sunday you can surprise Millie and the kids with a trail ride and a swim after church." Chapman said gently, reminding Will of his original plan, feeling again the still living pain under his ribcage that never quite went away. *I suppose Marcie and Jock are my phantom limbs and I need to try harder to accept their loss,* he thought.

Will snorted and strode towards the back of the truck, pulling on heavy leather gloves and his safety glasses as he went. "I'm going to start cutting the limbs."

They'd talked on the way out how Chapman was to haul the bigger limbs a safe distance away from the trunk, clean each one of branches with the smaller and lighter Stihl and then cut them into stove-wood lengths.

As Will went past him with the Husquvarna he said, "Wait for me on the bigger stuff" and then went after the tree.

As the chainsaw roared to life, Chapman donned his safety glasses, buttoned the top button on his denim shirt against the dry needles, settled his new cowboy hat and pulled on his gloves while thinking, *this project wasn't even in the realm of possibilities I could have conceived when I arrived in Central Oregon.* He shrugged his shoulders and felt muscles ripple under his shirt. Then he drew a breath, not deep, not ever again would he be able to draw a deep breath...*but a satisfactory breath without pain is good enough.*

As he worked, he thought of the tons of rock Danny and he had moved in the last few months. The wall, to him, was a thing that grew like a living organism. Each day, as he fit the shapes and the colors together before cementing them in place, he considered how each piece caused the wall's character to change. He had finished the front wall and was well started on the pillars that would hold the gate.

He had given Leona a catalog of decorative gates saying, "If you don't see something in here that suits you, let's think about designing our own."

Chapman's thoughts jerked back to the present as he heard Will's chainsaw shriek to a stop in the particular way it has when it's been jammed. He heard Will swearing and headed for the truck to grab the maul and wedges, moving as quickly as his lungs would allow.

As he handed them up, Will said, "Guess it has to happen at least once. But we're making good progress."

"It's not even seven o'clock. So far, so good," Chapman responded as he watched Will jam the wedge beside the stuck saw and tap it smartly with the butt of the maul.

"Piece of cake," Will said as he freed the saw, handed the maul and wedges down to Chapman before powering the chainsaw back up with quick pulls to the starter cord.

Will called a break before tackling the trunk. The men sat on the tailgate, Chapman drinking an Ensure, both tucking into the water and baggie of oatmeal cookies Leona had packed.

After a bit Will said, "It was a real good thing you did...hiring our girl to teach you to ride. She says you and ol' Bill are doing good together."

Chapman nodded. "It seems we are," he said modestly. "Abby's a fine instructor and he's a wonderful horse. The first time he left the other horses in the field and came to meet me at the gate I felt as though I had been gifted with something very special."

Will said quietly, "It is. Means he likes what you are doing together. You been practicing with the roping dummy?"

"Not from Bill's back. No."

"Time you start then. In another couple of months we start branding. You and Bill should make a good team." Then he stood, as if Chapman joining the branding crew was a given. "Let's get her done. It's not going to get any cooler." He grabbed his water jug and upended it one more time. Chapman followed suit, drinking long but far more slowly, thinking about Will's words. *Why not? Why in the world not? Roping on Bill at a branding is actually something I would enjoy very much, I think.*

Will squinted at him. "When I get that trunk sawed in a couple of places, think your new truck has the muscle to pull the pieces out of the way?"

Chapman capped his jug and put both his and Will's back in the cooler.

"Might as well find out," he said, noting that he too was starting to drop pronouns and adjectives from his speech. "Salesmen don't ever lie, do they?"

Will laughed. Then Chapman said, "Will, won't you or Matt need to use Bill during branding?"

Casually, Will said, "Nope. Abby said we should probably just give you Bill and the rest of us agreed. So, you want him, he's yours. I got friends more than willing to let me use their horses, Danny's dad for one. You think about it. We know it's got its own complications, the owning of an animal."

He tipped his hat and walked away whistling, leaving Chapman speechless at the tailgate.

Chapman was still thinking about it long after the F-150 delivered the torque promised by the salesman and pulled the 10-foot trunk section Will had cut out of the way, using the chain Will had put in. He was thinking about it even as he put the chain and both chainsaws back in his truck and went to sit on a boulder to watch Will walk the trail with the shovel, making certain it was safe all the way to the bottom. *It's why I decided to learn to ride in the first place,* he thought. *Bill's lungs give me the freedom to do what my own lungs restrict me from doing.*

Will went out of sight around a bank. *He's checking out the swimming hole,* Chapman thought idly, his mind now on his own situation and the ramifications of owning a horse. He realized with a dull shock, that one day soon his time at Leona's would come to an end. He would have to move on, to find his own place. *As soon as her back has healed from surgery, she won't need help anymore. Actually, when the sale of the watercolor goes through, she becomes very wealthy. She really doesn't need me anymore. Even if there's rockwork left to do, I don't have to live there to finish it.*

In his mind's eye, he could picture the completed site. In the beginning, he'd done a simple line drawing of The Lord's Bit in its new guise. It showed the graceful metal arch over the gate held up by stone pillars. He drew a road winding through the property. It was well away from the juniper tree that held the hawk's nest and led to the high point of the bluff with its stunning backdrop of mountains. He and Leona had often looked at the sketch and when they did, he often had the nagging feeling that it looked incomplete.

Now, on the edge of the canyon, waiting for Will, he realized what was missing from the drawing. *What it needs is a house.* The thought came unbidden and stuck like a burr in his mind.

Chapman shifted on the boulder. He watched Will come back into view and make his way back up the trail, shovel over his shoulder. He stood up and put his hands on his hips. Where that thought left him, he wasn't certain. Maybe he'd talk more with the attorney about Proposition 49, to see if it was at all possible to split off the two acres...though there wasn't one reason in the world Leona needed to sell off any of her property now.

One thing he was entirely certain of, he wanted to remain a part of the lives of Leona and the Andersons. He wanted that even more than he wanted to own Bill and he wanted that a lot.

"Chapman, it's all good...man!" He heard Will call. "I've got...some machete work...to do, but the...swimming hole...is still there. It just like...I remembered...maybe better."

Will came puffing up to the top of the trail, his shirt sweat-soaked in circles under his arms from the growing heat. The chip toothed grin a mile wide. Chapman thrust his thoughts aside. "Is the trail safe enough for horses?"

"You bet!" Will stepped up to the boulder and sat heavily on it.

Will looked down at him. "That was a tremendous amount of exercise and you only have 10 hours to go," he said, poker faced.

Will grunted and glanced at his watch. "Nine o'clockish. Not bad. Let's get going. It doesn't get dark for another 10 hours.

Chapter Thirty-eight
Millie

Millie bit her lip, her hand gently holding Jack's, as they sat across the desk looking at a very tired, disheveled Dr. Brown.

"Thank you for coming in. I know it's past time for us to be having this talk about Betty. Frankly..." He pinched the bridge of his nose under his glasses for long seconds while they waited quietly, each thinking their own private thoughts.

The doctor sighed. "Ah, hell, I'm not going to tell you much you aren't already seeing when you go visit Betty. You know she's fast losing any ability to communicate and you've seen how much trouble it is for her to even sit up independently. But I'm wondering, because you visit so often, if you really are aware of just how quickly she's losing ground?"

Jack looked at Millie, his eyes imploring, and she could see it was going to be up to her to do the talking.

Past the lump in her throat she said. "We don't keep chart notes like you do, but I guess we do know. I guess we sort of put it down to her medications when we talk about it. But I've been noticing how cold her hands are when I hold them...and her feet when I give her a foot massage. That's real different. Mom used to be such a hot body. And I guess

393

she hasn't recognized any of us, at least the way we want her to, for more than a month, maybe two."

Dr. Brown nodded. "Yes, things are slowing down for her, including her circulation. That's why her extremities are cold and that's why you are here. I want to be clear that we are at another stage. This next one could involve pain and a total loss of connection with the real world."

Millie looked at Jack whose head was now bowed and soldiered on. "Are you saying it is time for hospice to be called in?"

Dr. Brown shook his head. "Don't I wish! What you might not know is that less than one percent of hospice patients have the primary diagnosis of dementia. That's because Medicare will not pay benefits to hospice unless the patient is within 6 months of dying."

Jack's head snapped up. "It's only been two years!"

"I know Jack. I know." He looked at Millie. "I don't know if you remember, but when I diagnosed Betty I told Jack that the life expectancy for dementia was thought to be 3-6 years."

Millie nodded, thinking. *More than two years, but less than three...Dad's mostly right.* "I remember," she said. "I also remember one time you talked with us about the stages. What I think you are trying to tell us is that if Mom had another diagnosis, say cancer, you could put her under hospice care and they would pay for it. BUT, since it's dementia and so it's hard to predict its course, you can't do it."

He looked at her with relief. "Yes, that is exactly right."

Millie could see thankfulness in his eyes because she understood. *This is a rotten job sometimes, and this is one of those times. He's trying to tell us the care Mom will get won't be as good as it would be if hospice were in charge.* Beside her, Jack's head was again bowed. She sighed and soldiered on.

"So this next stage not only involves medicine to calm her down, but pain medicine, too. Am I right?

"That's right, it will."

"Besides telling us what to expect next are you wondering if the Andersons can afford all the medicine since Medicare won't pay?"

"I'm not wondering, I'm simply trying to inform you," Dr. Brown said.

"How much we talking about, Larry?" Jack's voice sounded like it was being forced from a blocked wind pipe. "How much do I got to come up with?" He looked straight at the doctor. Millie could see his spine stiffening as he spoke and heaved an internal sigh of relief.

"I can't tell you exactly. I can tell you that it typically will be more than double what you are paying right now."

Millie heard Jack sigh. "It's okay, Larry. I been planning on this as best I could. You do what you need to do to keep her out of pain."

It was Millie's turn to bow her head and hunch her body against the pain in her heart. *Lord, you sure made a good man in Jack Anderson, that's the truth. Now, I'm needing more strength than I got here. You're going to have to lend a hand.*

The silence in the room was profound. She knew that Larry was giving them time to digest the plateful he had handed them. It surprised her when Jack was the first to speak.

"You keep a good eye on her, Doc. Medicare don't cover your visits, I will. This is a hard time. Has been and will be. But we'll do the best we can for our own with your help."

Mille turned and wrapped her arms around his slight frame. "I'm so proud of you, Dad," she choked out. "You said it just right."

She turned back and said. "I'm proud of you too, Larry Brown. You are a good man. By the time we settle enough to think things through; we're going to be thanking you for giving it to us straight. We know it wasn't easy to say."

"Millie," he said, "You have no idea."

She got to her feet. "No," she said, "no, I expect I really don't. No way to walk in another person's moccasins, is there?"

She felt Jack stand beside her and thought, *If I feel a hundred years old, what is he feeling?*

She heard Jack clear his throat and say, "One more thing I got to know, Larry. Does it make a difference for her now…that we come every day but Saturday, I mean?"

The doctor stood. "As her dementia progresses, Jack, visiting is more for you than it is for her. It is something you have to reconcile with yourself."

Jack waved his hand as though he were either saying goodbye or batting the words away. He turned and walked from the office.

Millie watched him go, turned back to the doctor. "Hard," she said and hurried after her father-in-law.

"Yes," she heard him say to her retreating back, "very hard."

When Millie got to the Explorer, Jack was already turning the key. She opened the door and put her hand on his arm. "Wait, Dad. I got something to say."

He turned and looked at her with a question in his eyes. "I'm real glad we were here together," she said simply. "That's all. That's what I wanted to say."

He took his hand away from the ignition and turned a little in his seat, nodding. "It felt real good to have you there, Girlie Girl, I can tell you that." He squinted. "I got to thinking about Leona, about how she wouldn't give up and let Larry tell hospice to come ahead and help Peter. Then I got to thinking about the difference they made for Peter when they did come. I want you to know, when Larry tells us it's time, I am going to sign the paperwork as fast as I can…not because of the money, I hope, but because it will give me some peace to know she's got the best pain managers in the world on her side."

They looked at each other for long minutes before Jack again reached to turn the key. "I'll tell you something else, Millie. I'm done looking for cures on the internet. I know she's dying and I believe I'm going to feel some relief when the Lord finally calls her home."

Millie felt a as though someone had loosened the fist clinching her whole rib cage. "Yes," she said. "I know I will, and I expect Will is just barely hanging on. Visiting is awful hard on him."

"Well, I'm going to tell him…tell the kids too…that going to see her is a matter of choice. I'll make that clear."

She nodded. "I know you will," she said as she firmly shut the door. "See you at the ball field."

Interesting, thought Millie, *how we can just go on and start doing other stuff, like going to Matt's tournament, after that. It's like we just corner it off somewhere in our bodies and ignore it for a while. I've seen people do it time and time again. Guess we'd all go crazy if we couldn't do that. Least, that's how I'm going to look at it.*

She pulled the minivan into the parking lot at the baseball field. Jack's Explorer was already there, parked beside Chapman's new blue truck. She jumped out and slid open the side door. Dairy Queen was having a 'buy one get one free' sale so lunch was taken care of at the drive in window. *Okay, it's all working out. Here's hoping Will remembered the drinks cooler.* She glanced at her watch, grabbed her purse and the bag of burgers and started off at a trot.

Lately, she and Will had been aware of how easy it was to overlook Matt. He was such an easy kid, happy to go along with whatever the program was, that they had gradually overlooked the fact that Abby was receiving most of their attention. As Will had said, "Shit, Mil, Dad is being more of a dad to him than I am. Dad's been to most of his games, and how many have I been to? Like three."

It was like getting hit over the head with a ball peen hammer, Millie thought as she climbed the bleacher stairs. *Luckily we don't have to be hit a second time.* She heard Abby call and lifted her head. *Well now, that's the kind of support system our son deserves.*

"Howdy, one and all," she said as she put the bag of burgers into Abby's reaching hands. "Somebody catch me up on what's happening."

"Bottom of the 3rd, we're up and we're ahead by 2. Matt's playing first base, same as usual. He got in a double play last inning." Jack said with evident pride in his voice.

"Has he been up to bat yet?" Millie scanned the field and answered her own question. She saw her son with his foot on second base, his eyes intent on the batter."

"Sit down, Mil," her husband said, "You're liable to be just in time to see him steal a base."

"Thank you for the hamburger, Millie," said Chapman from the far end of the row.

"You're sure welcome." Millie said, settling in beside Jack and giving her full attention to the field.

Chapter Thirty-nine
Jack

Jack was whistling under his breath as he turned onto Coon's Market Road. By the time he pulled his Explorer into the graveled parking space in front of Leona's house, he was humming *Sweet Georgia Brown* and finger tapping out the beat on his steering wheel. As he killed the engine and got out, he glanced at Chapman's wall. It was almost done. *You sure have to give the man credit,* he thought. *That's some wall. I like the way he's inserted the wrought iron pickets. It makes it look more like the fence is enclosing something special rather than keeping something out.*

He hustled up the front walk, still debating whether or not to tell Leona what the doc had said about Betty, but had mostly decided against it. *No sense raining on her parade.*

Leona had called. "Jack," she said, "my ship has come in. The check is in the bank. What I want to do is take you out to dinner tonight to celebrate, if you don't have other plans. And I don't mean Anchors Away!"

He heard high excitement in her voice. "Why, you couldn't keep me away with a stick, Leona Larson. That's fine news. What time and where?"

"Well, you're driving, but Abby tells me I'm not to say where. Make sure you got gas in your rig and put on your best bib and tucker. Show up here about four o'clock if you can. I got something I want to talk about and show you before we leave."

He gave the doorbell his traditional SOS ring, recalling how her voice had changed when she talked about the something to tell and show him. *It sure didn't sound quite right. Not altogether happy, as I remember. This celebration should be all about happy.* He looked again over the rock-free acreage. *As long as it isn't her health or Chapman's health, I believe she can weather just about anything because of that boy and that painting.* He straightened his tie and patted his inside jacket pocket, making sure the Deschutes County Fair Exhibitor's Guide was still there.

Leona opened the door, Pansy at her side. "Howdy Jack." She looked at him through the glass of the screen door. "You clean up pretty good, if I do say so myself. I've always liked that western cut sport jacket."

The woman smiling at him through the glass was wearing a soft rose cardigan over a white blouse with a lace collar. He couldn't see for sure, the screen door blocked his view, but he thought she might be wearing a skirt. He hoped so. He straightened his tie again and stepped back for her to open the screen door.

"Howdy, Leona. You're looking mighty fancy yourself," he said as he walked in. He had been right about the skirt. It was good to see her trim legs again. He thought about telling her so but decided against it.

"Well, come on out to the kitchen table. I got something big to share. Half of me is proud, half of me is scared to death and the other half of me is just plain excited.

If I don't share this with someone, I'm liable to just blow up, leaving nothing but tail feathers."

Jack decided not to correct her on the number of halves. He wasn't sure if she was that rattled or if she was making a joke. He chuckled and pulled the exhibitor's guide from his inner sport coat pocket. "Well, before we get started, I got Abby's schedule of events here. She's circled everything she's competing in."

"That sounds like our girl." She took it and led him through to the kitchen, where Pansy had settled on the braided rug in front of the sink.

"Thank you, Jack. Chapman and I are planning to do them all if we can." she said as she tucked the guide between her salt and pepper shakers.

Leona gave a small, rueful laugh. "If he's still speaking to me, that is."

"What? What do you mean, speaking to you?" Jack sat in his chair and squinted up at her, shaking his head slowly from side to side. "What're you saying, Leona? Have you done something to piss off that boy?"

She sat across from him, her crooked fingers splayed on the table cloth, her faded blue eyes unreadable, just as her voice had been on the phone. "I truly don't know," she said. "I'm sure praying not, but I did take the bull by the horns and write his wife a letter."

To Jack it seemed about five minutes before he could even blink, he was that surprised. It was only when he drew a deep wavering breath that he realized he had forgotten to breathe as well. He sighed. "You talking about a wife, you better start this story at the beginning, old woman."

"I will. I will, Jack. I been sitting on this for some time now, and truth to tell, I'm about to bust." She drew a deep breath. "But, before I start, I got to tell you I got ahold of a lawyer today. I plan on giving Chapman The Lord's Bit, no matter what else happens."

Jack rubbed his hand over his curls. "But I thought Chapman said it would take a lot of time and money to do that."

"I got time and I got money now. Besides, the man said when I described the two acres that it sounded like 'less productive resource land', whatever that mouthful means, and should be able to be approved for a boundary adjustment as well, because the piece is suitable for a non-farm dwelling."

There was a note pad and some paper on the table. Jack nodded to it. "That the pad you took notes on?"

She laughed. "Yep. Can't even read my own writing." She reached in the pocket of her cardigan for her spectacles and put them on. "A piece of the Oregon Revised Statute 215.700 has got words that say it will..." Leona found the line with her finger and read, "...provide opportunities for dwellings on less productive resource lands and be decided on a case by case basis."

Jack drummed his fingers on the table. "Ain't that something! Seems like you owning the land for so long should have special weight, too."

She nodded. "That's what the lawyer thought."

"Well, this sounds real good, Leona, real good. That boy has put his heart into that worthless chunk of ground. But I sure don't connect the dots to how it's liable to piss him off."

"Oh, well, the land is one thing. Something I needed to get set in motion before everything else blows up in my face from being a busy body...maybe." She smiled at him. *No,* he thought, *that ain't a smile, that is a full blown, ass kickin' grin.* The thing wasn't making sense. "You better keep talkin'," he said.

Leona set aside the note pad and smoothed the papers left on the table with her hands, looking at Jack. "You got to promise me you won't interrupt 'til I'm done."

He nodded vigorously. "Hell, I'm practically speechless already."

"Well, here's how it started...I noticed, when Chapman thought he was alone, he took out his wallet and stared at something inside...sad like...he'd just sit and look. I'd see him out the kitchen window when he was taking a break from lifting rocks. Other times too...sitting on the back porch after his shower, waiting for me in the car when we were running errands and such. I couldn't see what he was really doing until I got the Bushnells down one day. Then I saw for sure he was looking at a wallet and he was rubbing his thumb over something in it. Made me real curious."

Jack saw her look at him to see if she had his attention. *Attention, hell! I feel like a bird dog on point.* He made an impatient gesture for her to go on, not saying a word.

"I'll make this short and simple, Jack, and then you can talk. I just got to get this off my chest." She sighed. "I couldn't seem to help myself. When he came in that night, after I'd spied on him with the binoculars, I 'borrowed' his wallet and saw that he was looking at a pretty woman and a little boy…3-4 years old, I'd say by looking. I figured that I was looking at his family…from before the accident. While I had the chance, I quick-like wrote down the Washington address that was on his driver's license and put the wallet back on the washer. That's where he had left it. The whole time this is going on Chapman is in the shower. He has no idea what I'd done…and to tell you the truth, I didn't exactly know what I'd done, or why I'd done it either. It made me real mad at myself at first. You know how I can't abide snooping busybodies…take the varnish off this deal and that's just what I was.

"Leona…" Jack said.

She held up her hand. "Wait. Don't start. There's a little more, Jack. This is the part that scares me to death…I wrote that woman in the picture a letter. Told her how much I liked Chapman, what a good man he was and how his health had improved. I gave her my phone number, too."

Jack could feel his heart beat begin to accelerate. "She call?"

Leona didn't seem to mind his question, which was good. He had about a million of them, but his mind felt full. Now, he knew what Millie was talking about when she said hers was.

"Nope. She didn't call; not then. She sent me a letter. Said she couldn't call because talking to me would make her cry."

Jack reached out a boney finger and tapped Leona's knuckles. "You hiding that letter under your hands?"

Leona nodded and handed it to him. "This is what I wanted to show you. You can read it if you want, but since I got it practically memorized; I guess I can tell you just as well."

Jack jerked his chin for her to continue and saw her swallow. "Like I thought, she WAS Chapman's wife. Her name is Marcie and the little boy's name is Jock. After the doctors saved Chapman and started doing all that reconstruction stuff, he got real mad at everything and everybody. It was a real hard time for all of them. Chapman wasn't at all himself; bitter and angry and lashing out even at Jock."

Jack felt all hollowed inside as he tried to make sense of Leona's words. He put his elbows on the table, his head in his hands and closed his eyes. He couldn't reconcile the man he knew to the man Leona was describing. "That sure doesn't sound like the man we know, does it?" he said as he opened his eyes and folded his hands in front of him.

"No, it doesn't, and it isn't." She waved a hand. "That was back then. We're talking about now. Anyway, as I was saying, one day she was bawling on the phone to her mom about it and Chapman overheard. The next day he was gone. Had divorce papers served. Told his lawyer he wasn't to speak to her about him, ever. Took some of the money he got and set her up for life and disappeared."

Jack was shaking his head from side to side. "Just disappeared. Walked out…so she didn't know if he was even alive?"

"That is what she says." Leona leaned forward and covered Jack's hand with hers. "Here's the good part, Jack. She says she didn't want to be divorced. She hated his behavior but she still loved him."

Jack looked down at their hands and then up at her. What he saw in her eyes was the wish for a happy ending. He found more than anything that he wanted it, too. Then he had a gut churning thought. "You mean she loves him now, or she loved him back then?"

Leona sat up straight. "I'm clear on this Jack, because we've been talking on the phone, too. She still loves him and wants to come here to see him, if I think it's a good idea. I told her I'd talk it over with you and get back to her."

He felt himself start to grin. He pulled his folded hands out from under her hand and gently captured it. "Leona, you are one surprise after another. I got to think on this some, but right on the surface it seems to me you got it right. That boy is looking at his wallet like that all these years later; he's still missing his family something fierce." He frowned and fell silent.

Finally, he said, "The other piece that's true is that he left for a reason, and you don't know what it is. Don't have a clue…this reunion could cause him a lot of pain, dredge up stuff he's tryin' to forget."

They looked at each other with sad eyes. Leona sighed and pulled her hand free. "I know, Jack. I do know that. But, I'll tell you this: after I wrote that letter, I slept like a baby, got up the next morning and put it in the mail box when I got my paper." She leaned forward. "I was so sure, Jack. I was so damned sure I was being guided…" Her eyes grew suspiciously shiny.

"Then, don't go backing away from it now. You did your interfering for the right reasons." He slapped the table with his palm. "You love that boy. We all do. We want him to be happy. Hell, he IS better! You told his wife the truth.

You saw how he ate that hamburger at the ball game. He was careful, but he ate it and it went down fine. Now, he'll never be handsome again, but he's got some weight and some muscle back on. Besides, he's so damned nice you forget about his looks in about thirty seconds. If ever a man needed a chance to undo…"

Jack was stopped midsentence by the joyful look on Leona's face. She had leaned back in her chair and had lifted her hands to her cheeks.

"Oh, Jack," she said softly. "You just said what has been rolling around in my heart. "That boy has come so far. He been such a blessing…to all of us, not just to me. If doing what I did brings him even half the quality of life he has given me, well…I guess, with your support, I'm willing to take the risk."

They looked at each other, and Jack nodded his assent. He thought she'd never looked prettier with spots of color in her cheeks, dancing eyes and a soft smile curving her lips upward. When her phone rang, he jumped. They both did. As Leona rose to get it she said, "For some reason I feel like a kid caught with his hand in the cookie jar."

He smiled and stood from his chair, for a minute looking for his ball cap and then remembering that they were going out to celebrate. While he waited, he heard Leona say, "Why, hello Abby."

"Yes, he sure did. I have it right here.

"Yes, Chapman and I are going to be there watching you clean up on the competition."

"No I haven't told him yet. You think I should, or just give him directions until he figures it out for himself?"

"Well, let me think on it. I'll tell you tomorrow what I decided."

"Well, thank you sweetheart. I'll be sure to do just that."

When Leona hung up, she turned and said, "Your granddaughter just told me it was getting cold out and not to forget to take a coat."

Jack grinned. "She tell you to keep me guessing as to where we are eating?"

"Of course she did. Let me get my coat…we're going to Black Butte Ranch. I got us a table facing the lake." Over her shoulder she called, "I can't have that girl totally running my life, now can I?"

Chapter Forty
Will

It was all Will could do to stand beside Millie after the church service and listen with a smile on his face, while his dad and Leona told them the details of their dinner at Black Butte Ranch. It was good to see them both so tickled with themselves, but out of the corner of his eye, he could see Abby and Matt power-walking towards the minivan. He wanted to be right there beside them. Gritting his teeth behind his smile, he brought his attention back where it belonged.

It came to him that both old people seemed higher than kites. *I didn't know better, I'd swear they'd been smoking something. Wonder what's up?* He glanced at Millie and thought he saw a question in her eyes as well.

He turned his gaze back to his father and squinted his eyes in speculation. Then something totally unexpected happened. His dad caught his look, stopped talking mid-sentence, grabbed Leona by the elbow and said, "Well, we can't stand here gabbin' all day, Leona. We got to go see Betty and these kids got a picnic to go to." Without even saying a proper goodbye, he hustled her down the walk like his tail was on fire.

Will looked at Millie who was looking after their retreating backs. "Now, what in the hell was that all about?"

"I don't have the faintest. But I'll tell you one thing, whatever it is, it's something big. Did you see the look on Leona's face? She was right there with him, beating that fast retreat. Under other circumstances she would have handed him his head for being rude."

"Big? What do you mean big?" Will asked, the long-planned picnic temporarily forgotten until he heard Abby and Matt calling.

He grabbed Millie's hand and started towing her along the path. "Come on, we can talk in the van. We're wasting sunshine."

Millie laughed. "Who's more excited here, you or the kids?"

"I believe I am. Hard to say for sure. Nice of Chapman to let you use his horse."

"Yes it is. I wish he would have joined us though. Matt was willing to ride double behind you."

"I think the point he was making, is that we don't have to include him in every single family event. Since this is one thing Dad can't do anymore, Leona either, we get to concentrate just on each other."

She nodded as she opened her door. "Point well taken."

As Millie fastened her seatbelt, she half turned and said, "You kids got any idea what your grandpa and Leona are up to?"

Will looked into the rear view mirror just in time to see the kids shoot each other slant-eyed looks. A long silence ensured. It was long enough for Millie to turn back around, look over at him and say, "Oh, oh! The troops have been sworn to silence."

"Looks like it," said Will as he backed out of his parking spot and stomped on the gas. "I guess I'm not going to think about it, much less worry about it right now because we can torture it out of them once we get to the swimming hole."

When they got to the ranch, the first thing Will noticed was his truck and stock trailer were hooked up with all four horses standing, hip shot, saddled and tied to the shady side of it. "It's got to be Chapman's doing," Millie said.

"Yep, he's figured it was something he could do to get us on our way quicker." His chest felt tight. "You kids, soon as I get this thing parked, go get your clothes changed."

He glanced at his wife and saw her blue eyes were suspiciously bright. "Isn't that just like him," she said simply. But he knew what they were both thinking; they'd talked about it before. They knew the accident had probably taken away the likelihood that he'd ever get to marry and have a family of his own. *But he's helping out, making our lives a little easier and a little better in ways that he can. Making sure we got what he doesn't.*

As they got out and started towards the house, they saw Abby grab Matt's hand to detain him. Their heads bent briefly. They saw Matt nod and then give Abby a shove before barreling up the back steps.

"I've got everything we need ready to go into your saddle bags, Will," Millie said, "Just look in the fridge. You'll see the grocery bags."

While he did what she said, he heard her call up the stairs, "Matt and Abby, don't forget your swim suits. I've got the towels."

He heard Abby call down. "Okay. Don't forget the camera, Mom."

He grinned and headed down the hall to get his own clothes changed. *Sometimes, it's not so bad to have a take-charge kid.*

When they off-loaded the horses at the rim's edge and bridled up, Will noticed with pride how Matt, without comment, held Bill steady while Millie climbed up. He grabbed the camera from his shirt pocket and said, "Turn around Matt, I got the sun at my back, let's get a picture."

Then he turned and noticed Abby, already mounted, relaxed, smiling and running her fingers through Fox's white mane. It flitted through his mind that before, she would have been clamoring to be in the shot. On the heels of that thought came ones of how she had insisted on attending Don Beel's funeral, and the modesty she showed when she and Fox won the purple ribbon for showmanship at the fair. *Things have changed for our little girl,* he thought with satisfaction.

"Okay, Matt, swing on up and get Dandy over by your mother. You, too, Abby." The sun felt warm on his back as he waited. "This is going to be some day to remember," he said as he clicked away.

He grinned to himself as he moved Rowdy through the cut in the Ponderosa trunk and then on down and over the edge. Behind him, he heard Millie give a squeak as Bill's front feet dropped down onto the trail. She didn't ride often, didn't have the chance. *But, by God, she's game and she looks fine in her Wranglers,* he thought and then burst into a song he was sure the kids would know. It was the theme song from the old Roy Rogers Show. Their grandma had taught them, just as she had taught him.

"Happy trails to you, until we meet again.
Happy trails to you, keep smiling until then.
Who cares about the clouds when we're together?
Just sing a song and bring the sunny weather.
Happy trails to you, 'til we meet a-gain."

He could hear the kids join in and the volume build. He let Rowdy pick his way and turned in the saddle to look back over his shoulder at his family. Millie was beaming at him.

"Lordy, but that takes me back," she said. "Remember all those VHS Roy Rogers tapes she got for Jenny and Jake to watch?"

Will turned back, checking trail. "Then, all those years later, Abby and Matt watched them too," he said, raising his voice so she could hear him over the clicking of hooves over rocks. "They made a fine babysitter for Mom."

"Let's sing something else, Dad." He heard Matt call.

Will, hat tipped forward, shading his face, was leaning back against a sun warmed rock watching his family. The heat would soon be going from the canyon and he knew it was time to call everyone away from the river. He almost couldn't stand to do it. Matt was turning over rocks along the shore, looking for bugs, but Millie and Abby were still in up to their necks, their hands on each other's shoulders, face to face. He imagined Millie's feet were touching the river bottom. He wondered idly what they were talking about.

With a sigh he stood. "Okay kids, time to get your butts back into your Wranglers," he called. He tried to remember a time he had enjoyed more, but couldn't. It wasn't only the day on the river, he realized. It was also the morning phone call from the stock contractor who wanted to buy his entire crop of blue grass straw for his Corriente roping steers. *Takes a load off a man's mind, that's for sure.* He whistled as he changed back into his jeans, pulled on his boots and went to re-bridle horses and tighten cinches.

Millie came up behind him with his saddlebags and the remnants of their picnic. "Seemed like you and Abby were having quite a conversation out there in the river, Millie the Mom," he said.

"We were. She was asking if it was a sin to keep a secret. I told her no, as long as it was legal and no one was getting hurt from the keeping."

Will put down a stirrup and turned, a frown on his face. "Dad and Leona," he said grimly. "They should know better than to put kids in a loyalty bind."

"We don't know that, Will. Maybe she was just asking from something she heard at church today."

He shook his head. "Nope." Some of the contentment he had been feeling washed out of him, but he forced himself to smile at her. "Can't do a thing about it now. Let's get the little buggers mounted. It's going to be getting cool down here now that the sun has left."

After dinner, Will sent the kids to lock Tuffy and Digger in the yard and give them their food. Then he looked at Millie. "I believe I'm going to go over and have a little chat with Dad."

She looked at him, started to say something and then stopped and nodded. "Well, alrighty then. You might as well get along, cowboy. There aren't enough dishes to spit at, so I planned to give the kids the night off from clean up and put mom's old Roy Rogers tapes in for them to watch…sort of a last hurrah before it's back to school and homework."

He nodded and stood. "You do that. Seems like a just right end to this day." He reached down and kissed the top of her head. "Thanks for dinner, Babe."

She snorted. "Hamburger helper is a wonderful invention. See ya."

Will pulled his old Ranger into Jack's driveway on two wheels, jumped out and strode to the door. He knocked sharply, but didn't wait for Jack to answer, just strode on in, twenty pounds of resentment riding on his shoulders.

His dad was in his recliner. The cat jumped down in alarm and raced behind the couch as Will stomped into the living room. "Put your chair up and hit the clicker, Dad, we are about to have a little talk," he said, ice in his voice.

"Why, howdy, Son," Jack said, following Will's directions. "What brings you out this time of night?"

Will thought he looked guilty as hell. "You're going to tell me what you and Leona got up your sleeve. And what's got Abby asking her mom about secrets being sins, that's what."

Jack blinked and then looked trapped. "Aw," he said, scrubbing a hand over his wiry curls. "Aw, this is Leona's doin's, but since it's pretty much a done deal, I guess I'll tell you before you hit me."

Will grunted, crossed to the couch and sat down. "I guess you'd better," he said grimly.

"Well, it's like this: Leona has invited Chapman's wife and son for a visit."

"Chapman's wife and son? How'd she know Chapman has a wife and son?"

Jack waved a hand. "Never mind. Their names are Marcie and Jock and they are coming tomorrow if things go right."

"Tomorrow? Does Chapman know this?"

Jack shook his head. "He doesn't have a clue. That's the rub. Leona is real afraid she's meddled in something she shouldn't have...that Chapman is going to be real mad at her."

Will was still trying to get his mind around the fact that Chapman had a wife and son as part of the past he didn't talk about. "He hasn't a clue..." Will repeated his father's words, letting their meaning sink in. "You mean Leona's plan is to just spring them on him out of the blue?"

"Well, the woman, Marcie, had some strong feelings about that. She said she knows Chapman and that is the only way to do it."

Will sat back. "And you two didn't tell us this...because?"

"Because, if Chapman never speaks to us again, at least he's got you and Millie to turn to, that's why," Jack said defensively.

Will sat looking at his dad, the mad gone out of him. "How'd Abby get in on this?"

"Eavesdropping over at Leona's."

Will nodded. "Sounds right. You know she told Matt?"

"Nope, but I ain't surprised. It was kind of a big secret to keep." Jack laughed ruefully. "Leona and me ain't sleeping worth a damn!"

"Tomorrow. She's coming tomorrow?"

"Yep. Sometime in the afternoon."

Will sighed and stood. "Well, as soon as you know how this whole deal turns out, you'd better call me on my cell phone, one way or the other."

Chapter Forty-one
Leona

Leona turned the crockpot to low, picked up two glasses of lemonade and walked towards the back porch. "Millie called. They had a real good time swimming down in the canyon. Told me what you did to get them on their way. That was an awful nice thing to do, Chapman," she said as she held the screen door open with her elbow and slid through.

Chapman smiled up at her and accepted the glass. Pansy, curled up by his chair didn't even lift her head. "It felt good to be able to do something for them. If someone had told me back in May that by the end of August I would be familiar with grooming and tacking horses, I would have thought them demented."

He paused, "How was church?"

Leona looked at him. So far he had chosen not to come with her and that, she decided, was okay with her. If ever there was a Godly man, it was Chapman Lewis. "It was all right. The visit with Betty wasn't so good though."

Chapman, who had been sitting deep in the old over-stuffed rocker with his feet on the porch rail, looking out at the view, heard the tone of her voice. He put his feet down and gave her his full attention. "Tell me," he said quietly.

Leona sighed, and sat down in a straight-backed chair. "The doctor told Jack she's at another stage; a stage where she's in pain sometimes. Then, there's times when things we can't see, scare her and she's liable to holler and strike out. Other times, Jack said, it's like something is making her sad or anxious and she whimpers and moans..." She looked down at her lap, remembering. "...like she did today."

Chapman reached out and touched her shoulder. "I can't even imagine how hard it is to witness, Leona. How is Jack handling this new state of affairs?"

Leona fished in the pocket of her apron for her hankie and dabbed her eyes. "It's hard," she managed to get out before her throat closed.

"Yes. It's hard on all of you."

Leona knew he was thinking of Will and his family, too. She nodded and picked up her lemonade, waiting for the fierce emotion to pass. She'd long ago given up on the concept of fairness in favor of the belief that life was a crap shoot and whoever was rolling the dice played by rules she'd never understand.

They sat in silence, sipping their lemonade and looking out at the peaceful view. As the sun began its western descent, everything turned golden on the plateau. And then, later, when it actually began to disappear behind the mountains, the snow took on the faintest pink with hues of lavender. Leona heard Chapman let out a small breath. Like herself, he never seemed to tire of the moment. She looked at him, still dusty from his work; his feet back up on the rail, totally relaxed, his eyes at half mast, drinking in the beauty. She decided the time to tell him was now or never.

"Chapman, I'm changing the subject here. I've got some news for you, something I've done and I figure now's as good a time as any to spring it on you."

He chuckled. "Spring away, Leona. I'm in a pretty good mood since the wall is nearly done and I'm contentedly partaking of your delicious lemonade, thank you very much."

She took a deep breath. "Okay, here goes…I hired a lawyer who is doing a property line adjustment so I can deed over The Lord's Bit to you."

She turned in her chair just in time to see him sit bolt upright his feet hitting the porch boards with a thump loud enough to make Pansy jump to her feet. He looked at her in disbelief.

"What did you just say, Leona? Rather, what did you mean by what you just said?"

"I said it straight, Chapman. My mind's made up beyond changing. I'm giving you The Lord's Bit."

He sat back in the rocker and after a moment said, "That is exceedingly dear of you, Leona…but I don't believe it is possible."

"My lawyer says according to HB 3661 and Oregon Revised Statute 215.700, it is."

She watched him chewing on the information. Finally, he asked, "How is that possible when my attorney suggested it might only be a possibility after a lengthy tussle with the ODLCD?"

"I don't know, maybe you forgot to tell him The Lord's Bit was non-productive resource land."

He sat staring at her, emotions chasing across his scarred face. She could see doubt and hope warring in him.

"This is absolutely astonishing! Of course I can't allow you to do it, but I am incredibly touched by your amazingly generous offer."

Leona snorted. "You actually don't have a choice, Chapman. What are you going to do? Turn me down and break my heart? I know you too well. Besides I already sent him a check for half of what I owe."

She saw him open his mouth and then close it again and realized he was temporarily speechless. *I believe I'm beginning to enjoy this she thought.* She laughed. "Give an old woman a little money and she just goes crazy. Now, you just say, 'Thank you, Leona, I accept,' and make me real happy."

Instead of doing what she asked, he stood. His Adam's apple was going up and down and he looked a little pale, but she couldn't read his face. "Leona, would it be permissible to go to my bedroom in this clothing? I have something I would like to show you."

"Sure," she said, her voice puzzled. "Course it is."

She could hear the faint sound of him walking up the stairs at what was a fast pace for him, and frowned, totally at sea. Doubts began creeping in. *What on earth does he have to show me? What have I interfered with now? He's probably made other plans for himself and now, I've put him in a bind. I am an interfering old busy body and that's a plain fact. Wait until Marcie and Jock show up. Then the fat's really in the fire.*

After a few minutes, Chapman came back. "I'll need you at the kitchen table, please, Leona."

When she walked into the kitchen she saw Chapman flattening several large sheets of paper and anchoring them with her napkin holder, salt and pepper shakers and the small vase of daisies she had on the table.

"Leona," he said, his gravelly voice choked, "This is what I want you to see."

She walked to stand beside him and her hand flew over her mouth.

"I have been working on this for some time now, but only as an exercise, a plan of what could be for that site. I was simply entertaining myself…visualizing, if you will."

She knew immediately what she was seeing. *Why, it's his dream house, right there on The Lord's Bit. That's exactly what it is!* It wasn't just a simple sketch. She could see elevations, dimensions, landscaping, how the driveway would preserve the trees and how the windows looked out on the mountains. It was a simple house, not too different in architecture from her own.

"Why, Chapman," she said, "I don't quite know what to say. I had no idea…what's on those other pages?"

Reverently, Chapman moved his makeshift paper weights and lifted the first page, carefully re-rolling it and revealed the second. Leona moved quickly forward to help replace the salt and pepper shakers, using her own hands to hold down the bottom corners.

"It's the layout of the rooms," he said. "You'll notice I've replicated some of the detail from your house…only as you can also see, I've designed a verandah all the way around three sides."

Leona laughed. "Jack's been telling me I need a bigger front porch for years. You get done with your house; maybe you'll design one for me."

Chapman drew in a sharp breath and she stood up to look him in the eye, letting the blueprint curl. Before she could spit, as she would later tell Jack, "He put his arms right around me and gave me the biggest, strongest hug. Then he kissed me right on top of my head."

"My God, Leona, I can't quite believe this is happening. One minute I'm drinking lemonade and looking at the view, reconciled to the fact that the wall is nearly done, my health is as restored as it will ever be and I was over-due for a conversation with you about my next move…and the next minute you walk out with lemonade and hand me my dream."

"Well, then," Leona said, fishing for her hankie while tears rolled down her cheeks, "I guess that's settled and I can't think of anyone I'd rather have for a neighbor. You've made me real happy, Chapman."

Chapman was shaking his head. "I have heard that saying, 'Don't wake me if I'm dreaming,' and now, I absolutely know what it means." He had loosened his hug but still held Leona firmly by both arms. "You mean the world to me, Leona. I have been happier since I met you and the Andersons than I ever dreamed possible after the accident. There is simply no way to thank you."

Leona patted one of his hands where it held her arm. "I reckon I can say the same. You've made a real difference. Now, you've got to turn me loose, so I can blow my nose."

He laughed and then sobered. "Listen," he said, "if this deed transfer doesn't go through, just know you tried your best to something so incredibly generous that I still can't quite believe it. I'll always think the world of you, Leona, and nothing is going to change that."

Now...she thought to herself... *now's the time to tell him what you've done. Tell him about Marcie and Jock coming tomorrow.* But she couldn't bring herself to do it. The snap of joy in his golden eyes nearly sank her. "Well, no matter what, I hope you just keep thinking that way. I'm real fond of you too."

It was the best she could do. Inside, the words of love she felt were too tangled to be retrieved so easily. She patted him on the shoulder instead and said, "Yep, I don't know what I would do without you, Chapman Lewis." And then she sent up a prayer that she hadn't done something that was about to make her find out.

Long after Chapman had bid her goodnight and made his way up the stairs, Leona sat in her living room in the only chair safe for her back, Peter's mother's armless sewing chair. She was knitting by rote, her mind far away, assailed by doubts. It wasn't only what she'd done, interfering with Chapman's personal life, it was that she'd drug Jack into it...and then Abby had overheard them talking and she'd had to swear her to secret, too.

When she was a little girl and lied, her mother would say, "Oh what a tangled web we weave when first we practice to deceive." Usually her mother said it just before she got out the old wooden paddle. *That's about how I feel right now, like someone should tan my hide.*

Her knitting didn't feel right. Until she had her surgery she couldn't sit in her wooden rocker, the one she used to rock the boys to sleep. The angle was just wrong for her back now, but that is what she was used to...to rock in time with the clicking of her needles. She sighed. *I should be thankful I can still knit. I can't do fancy work very well, but I can still knit. I should be grateful, thanks to Chapman that I got enough money to buy yarn.* She closed her eyes in the silence, Pansy snoring lightly at her feet. *I got to get a hold of myself and see this thing through. Could be it will turn out all right. I got to remember how right it felt when I sent off that letter and how glad Marcie sounded that I had. I have to believe in Chapman. Even if he had decided he didn't want to be married to her anymore, who's to say he can't change his mind?*

Finally, she dropped her knitting, which was a winter scarf for Millie in a lovely shade of rose, in her lap. She removed her glasses and pinched the bridge of her nose and sighed again, sticking the tips of her needles into the ball of yarn and sticking everything into the knitting bag beside her chair. "Come on, Pansy, dear, wake up and let's go to bed. Tomorrow is liable to be one hell of a day."

Leona sagged against the kitchen counter, holding the phone receiver in both hands, looking out the window where Chapman worked on the wall. She was waiting for Jack to answer his phone, not caring if she interrupted his session with Rachel or Martha or some other fool cooking show. When she heard his cheery good morning, she screeched, "Jack, she just called. Marcie just called on her cell phone. She's on I-84 and heading towards Biggs Junction."

"Whoa! Easy there. Calm down, old woman. Breathe!"

To Leona, it sounded like Jack was talking to a scared horse. She took a deep breath. A part of her knew that is exactly what she felt like, but she said, "Don't talk to me like I'm some fool horse, Jack. You know how upset this whole thing has got me. I love that boy! If I've done something to cause him pain, I'll never forgive myself." A sob tore through her.

"Leona. You got to get a grip on this situation. There ain't a thing you can do at this point, but wait to see how it all turns out. Try to think on the good side."

"Jack," she said, "Jack, don't think I haven't been trying. I've got myself in a state, that's a fact."

"Well, now listen, Leona, I'm thinking we have got to think positive on this. We've got...what? I'd guess maybe two to maybe three hours until she and the boy get here. In the meantime, you are going to do what she asked and let her handle this."

At Jack's use of "we" Leona felt immeasurably comforted. She nodded into the receiver. "Yes, yes, you are right. I know you are." She drew a ragged breath. "But Jack, however am I going to stand the wait?"

She heard him chuckle. "That's better. That's my gal. I'm thinking what we're going to do is do what we do best. I'm going to come over and we're going to cook up a storm...who knows, we may be having a celebration party and we got to get prepared."

"Why, Jack, that's about the best idea I've ever heard. You got any ideas?

"Yep, I sure do. You get on your 'go-to-town' duds. I'm coming over to pick you up. We got shopping to do...and Leona..."

Leona heard Jack's voice strain. Her heart dropped. "What is it Jack?"

"You got to know my son stopped by last night and lit into me. I don't remember ever seeing him quite so pissed. I had to tell him what was up."

Without missing a beat, Leona said, "Course you did. What did he say?"

"You mean after he could talk again?"

Leona was holding her breath. "Tell me, Jack. Don't make me wait, I'm about to expire from all this mess I've made."

"He said I didn't call him the minute we knew how it was going to go, he'd string me up by my thumbs. Then he lectured me good about keeping secrets and how it was real hard on children to be put in a bind like that."

Leona was quiet for a moment. "It was me he should have been talking to."

"I suppose so. But you'll probably get in on it, too, so don't worry. But we are going to have to call him soon as we know how it turns out. This is a family deal."

"Thank you, Jack. I believe I got a handle on myself now. You get on over here and let's do our shopping. What's the new recipe, by the way?

"It ain't new, it's improved is all. It's macaroni and cheese; something I figure that little boy, Jock, would like well enough. You come up with the dessert and salad."

"Glad to. I got a gallon of Marion berries to do something with. See you soon. Bye, Jack."

Leona hung up the phone, spatula in hand. Jack, in the process of making yeast biscuits, his hands working the dough, drilled her with his eyes. "She's in Redmond and she's got my address in her GPS," Leona said, her hand over her heart.

Jack nodded calmly. "We got about 15 minutes to go, then."

Leona swallowed and walked to her kitchen window. Not 10 minutes ago she had sent Pansy off with Chapman's afternoon snack. Now, the dog was sprawled out under the Juniper tree, watching Chapman leveling the entrance where the gate was to go with a shovel. From the looks of things, he was nearly done. She felt Jack behind her, heard his big sigh. "I think you'd better make me some coffee, old woman. You got my nerves as bad as yours. That boy out there, working away, don't have any idea of what's about to hit him."

"I will. Glad to. Just let me put this last batch on the rack." Deftly she removed her secret recipe 'cowboy cookies' from the cookie sheet. "I sure hope that little boy gets to stay around long enough to taste these," she said; worry a tired thread in her voice.

After Leona had started the coffee and put the next batch of cookies in the oven, she gave up all pretense of doing anything other than watching out the window, tracking Chapman as he finished at the gate and walked back to the Juniper tree. He bent down to pet Pansy, sat in his chair and reached into the basket. It was at that moment Leona watched Pansy's head swing and her ears perk. The little Border Collie got to her feet, looking at something past the gate entrance. Leona leaned forward and craned her neck.

"Oh, oh! This is it." She cupped the smooth rim of the old sink with both hands as she felt Jack move in beside her. They watched as a woman came through the lovely arched entrance, her hand holding a little boy's. He was

429

lagging slightly behind her. They could see her grip was firm and her steps unfaltering. They saw Pansy start forward and Chapman look up to see where she was going. They saw him go perfectly still and then slowly stand. Marcie's steps never faltered. When Pansy greeted them with her tail wagging in welcome, the boy pulled free to pet her, but the woman kept walking in her steady way. "Jeezus!" whispered Jack.

Chapman took one step forward and then another until they were facing each other, just under the sheltering shade of the ancient tree. It looked as if words were being exchanged. They saw Marcie reach out a hand and take one of Chapman's in her own. He didn't pull away.

"So far, so good," Leona heard Jack whisper.

Marcie was gesturing with her free hand, back towards Jock. They saw Chapman nod and reach out and take her gesturing hand into his own. They stood, facing each other, appearing to be drinking each other in. At that moment, Leona felt a fierce singing in her heart. *I believe this whole deal is going to work out just fine.* Tears ran unchecked down her wrinkled cheeks. She was weak with relief, but she was unprepared for what happened next.

Later, she and Jack would both swear that their eyes never left the couple but that the move from holding hands to a tight embrace happened so quickly that neither of them actually saw it. Beside her, she heard Jack whoop and felt him grab her. She threw her arms around him and matched the hug that was going on under the tree. "Oh, Jack," she choked out, "I believe this is all going to work out."

"Yes," he said. "Yes, I do. I do believe it is."

Leona looked into his eyes and saw that they were as wet as her own. For a tiny second she dropped her head on his chest and then they turned back to the window, his arm around her shoulder, hers around his waist, watching as the two walked towards Jock and Pansy hand in hand.

"I believe I'd better get Will and Millie called." Jack said softly.